Henry William Little

Henry M. Stanley

His Life, Travels and Explorations

Henry William Little

Henry M. Stanley
His Life, Travels and Explorations

ISBN/EAN: 9783337207328

Printed in Europe, USA, Canada, Australia, Japan

Cover: Foto ©Raphael Reischuk / pixelio.de

More available books at **www.hansebooks.com**

HENRY M. STANLEY

HIS LIFE, TRAVELS

AND

EXPLORATIONS

BY THE

Rev. HENRY W. LITTLE

AUTHOR OF "MADAGASCAR: ITS HISTORY AND PEOPLE," "A HISTORY OF RUSSIA,"
ETC., ETC.

LONDON—CHAPMAN AND HALL, LIMITED

PHILADELPHIA—J. B. LIPPINCOTT, COMPANY

1890

LONDON:
PRINTED BY GILBERT AND RIVINGTON, LD.,
ST. JOHN'S HOUSE, CLERKENWELL ROAD, E.C.

Dedication.

TO THE "SONS AND DAUGHTERS OF THE EMPIRE,"

AND

TO THE YOUTH OF THE GREAT AMERICAN REPUBLIC,

THIS SIMPLE STORY OF A BRAVE LIFE

IS AFFECTIONATELY DEDICATED, BY THE AUTHOR.

London, 1890.

PREFACE.

THE great Anglo-Saxon and English-speaking nations of the old and new worlds have no continuous and convenient record of the travels and explorations of Mr. Henry Morton Stanley. This book it is hoped will supply the need.

The narrative is mainly based upon the graphic accounts, from the pen of the famous traveller himself, of his journeys and explorations, and upon copies of official despatches, reports, and original papers which have been placed at my disposal.

The helpful lessons of a career so strong in purpose, so direct in aim, and so prolific of results, are too valuable to be overlooked or lost.

The intrepid man who "found Livingstone" and discovered the Congo, has ceased to be regarded any longer as a "smart newspaper writer" or "an unreliable adventurer."

He has helped to make the history of the century, created a New State, and secured for himself a front place amongst the noblest pioneers of civilization and the truest friends of humanity of our time.

His life is therefore worthy of careful and attentive study. It conveys a message of encouragement to the man who governs, to the man who thinks, and to the man who acts. It also reveals to us an unique example of "one man" power—of the strength of an Individuality directed by lofty intention, and sustained by an abiding sense of duty.

With the pages of this Memoir open before us, we are constrained to acknowledge that the days of chivalry and heroic enterprise are not altogether past —that, now as ever, there are strenuous spirits, giants in the land, who are ready to "Do and Dare." There is a quaint fable which hints at the possibility of pigmies increasing in stature by habitual intercourse with giants. Carlyle teaches us that if we would be full of courage we must surround ourselves, by daily perusal of their doings, with the atmosphere which nourishes heroes.

The achievements of the brave explorer of the "Dark Continent" are incentives to all men, in an age of speculation and over-much theorizing, to have the "Courage of Doing." His African followers, the constant witnesses of his prowess, his conflicts, and his triumphs over every obstacle which faced him in his efforts to unravel the enigma of the ages, and to open up the great heart of Africa, proclaimed him "The Stone Breaker." In this cognomen his history and character are eloquently and tersely expressed.

Leon Gambetta, on a celebrated occasion, said of him, "Stanley has given an impulse to scientific and philanthropic enterprise. He has influenced Governments." Plutarch records an incident in the life of a king of Macedon, who, when severely pressed on one occasion by his enemy, retired from the scene of conflict for the pious purpose, as he gave out, of sacrificing to Hercules. Emilius, his opponent, at once rushed into the fight, with his naked weapon in his hand, and, calling upon the gods, won a brilliant victory. The exploits of Stanley remind us of the method of Emilius, for with him Doing is Thinking and Working is Praying.

Mr. Stanley has never been envious of the Missionary or the Trader. He has opened the way frankly and generously for both, along the tawny waters of his beloved river and its thousand affluents. He has disclosed to us, in most convincing words, the only solution of what is pre-eminently the African question—the Slave Trade. Free and unrestricted commerce he declares and proves to be the fatal enemy of the Arab man-stealer, the only cure (to use Dr. Livingstone's pathetic expression) for the " running sore of Africa." In revealing to us the true condition of Central Equatorial Africa, with its vast areas of prolific soil, peopled by " myriads of dusky nations," its magnificent water-ways for the transit of its produce, its busy markets, its rich stores of native wealth, and its superior capacity for civilization and legitimate trade, he has conferred a lasting benefaction upon the important artisan populations of England and America.

But a galaxy of illustrious names surround the origin and rise of the Congo Free State, with which region the fame of Henry M. Stanley will be for ever identified.

To his Majesty Leopold II., King of the Belgians, belongs the proud title of " The Generous Monarch," who so nobly conceived, ably conducted, and magnificently sustained the enterprise which has secured the recognition of the Great Powers of the World, and has ended in the establishment of the " Free State" (Stanley's Congo). To the marvellous perspicuity, the ceaseless ardour, and quenchless courage of Livingstone, who first directed the eye and mind of Stanley to the mysterious Luapula and its far-reaching tributaries, and who himself traced its north-ward course to the fork of Nyamge, we owe the earliest knowledge we possess of the mighty Congo " at the very source and fountain of its being." To the astute Chancellor of the German Empire, Prince Bismarck, the author of the political constitution of the infant State, must be awarded the credit of obtaining for the newly created Province perfect commercial freedom, and liberty to develop its marvellous resources without fear of being "let or hindered " by rival or more powerful communities.

We must not fail to remember (in this connection) that it was through the liberal patronage of the *New York Herald* and the *Daily Telegraph* newspapers that Mr. Stanley was able to undertake his eventful journey in 1876, through the entire continent from the sources to the mouth of the Congo, an adventure which, as an exhibition of sheer human courage and endurance, will never probably be surpassed.

To those humbler companions of the great explorer, the sons of the soil, who obeyed him because they had learned to trust his word, and to confide in his courage, who followed him " not knowing whither they went," and without whose aid Stanley would have been powerless to secure success, I gladly devote a word of admiration. " Unwept and unsung," they are scattered over the East, or have ceased to be. We must freely acknowledge, however, the important services which " these dark-skinned children of the land " rendered in faithfully sharing the toils and perils of their indomitable leader in the noble task which he set himself, of redeeming their continent from oppression and despair.

The Life and Labours of Mr. Stanley fill up the most fascinating, and at the same time most instructive page in the History of Modern Exploration.

With him, in brief, we learn that under all conditions of life, it is " Better far the silent tongue but the eloquent deed : despatch than discourse : and *Doing* the best answer of all."

H. W. L.

London, 1890.

CONTENTS.

CHAPTER VI.

CHAPTER VII.

CHAPTER VIII.

CHAPTER IX.

CHAPTER X.

CHAPTER XI.

CHAPTER XII.

CHAPTER XIII.

CHAPTER XIV.

CHAPTER XV.

PAGE

CHAPTER XVI.

CHAPTER XVII.

CHAPTER XVIII.

CHAPTER XXIII.

CHAPTER XXIV.

HENRY M. STANLEY.

CHAPTER I.

Early days—With the Army of the North—Visit to Europe and the Syrian Peninsula—In the Mediterranean—Captured by brigands —With Hancock's expedition—Indian warfare—A raft-voyage on the Platte River—*Herald* special correspondent to Europe and the East.

HENRY MORTON STANLEY was born at Denbigh in Wales in 1841. The town, which has an eventful history, reaching back to ancient British times, occupies a striking position upon the sides and at the base of a rugged mass of limestone rock, overlooking the rich pastoral scenery of the Vale of Clwyd. It is peaceful enough now, even to dulness. In past days, however, as a mountain stronghold of the native Welsh princes, it was the scene of many stirring and important incidents, and the magnificent ruins of its old castle bear everywhere upon their crumbling walls and broken towers, abundant marks of " sieges, struggles, battles and surprises." The locality abounds in romantic traditions of gallant deeds and feats of valour, performed by the ancient heroes of the Principality, and these legends are carefully treasured, and proudly handed down, from father to son, by the simple and warm-hearted peasantry of the district. The Denbigh of to-day is almost entirely

B

given up to trade. It has a thrifty population of six thousand inhabitants, who are chiefly employed in making shoes and gloves.

The cottage home of Stanley's parents (a humble but worthy couple) was situated within the precincts of the old 'fortress, which embraced a large portion of the southern slope of the hill. At an early age, owing to the death of his father, he was placed in the Free School at St. Asaph, where he remained for ten years. Those who knew him at this period describe him as industrious, and by no means wanting in ability. High-spirited, and fond of all physical exercises, he entered with eagerness into the attractive ventures and hazardous exploits of schoolboy life. At the same time he developed a special taste and capacity for mathematics and drawing, and to the future explorer of Africa a lesson in geography was always a welcome recreation, rather than a dry task. On a memorable occasion in the history of the school, the boys were invited to the Palace of the Bishop to receive their annual prizes for good conduct and proficiency in their studies, at the hands of the venerable Prelate. The bright looks and general demeanour of Stanley attracted the notice of the Bishop, who, touching him upon the shoulder, said, "This is a clever boy, and if he has his health, he will make his mark." The heart of the fatherless boy was cheered by the gift of a Bible, as a special mark of favour from the Bishop. This book was much valued by its possessor, through all the changing circumstances and varied fortunes of his youth, and it was taken with pride by him to the Palace some years after, when he returned from the American War in 1866. He had scarcely reached the age of sixteen when he left St. Asaph to assist a relative who was in charge of the parish school of Mold in Flintshire. At Mold, as formerly at St. Asaph, he appears to have gained the goodwill of his associates in the school, as well as the confidence and esteem of those whom he served. Although fitted by nature and inclination for a life of activity and bodily exertion, he was able at all times to appreciate and enjoy the companionship of clever books. He read everything that came in his way, and a friend who visited him at Mold on one occasion tells of his surprise at finding him intensely engaged, during the playhours, in the perusal of Dr. Johnson's instructive and charming story of "Rasselas." A sturdy frame, full round features, a stubborn will, a quick temper, an attractive venturesomeness, and "the air of an uncompromising and deep fellow," were the prominent characteristics of Stanley at this time. It is not surprising, therefore, to find that the quiet, plodding life of a parish school teacher was by no means congenial to his restless and sensitive nature. He suddenly left Mold, and turning northward, he took the shortest road to Liverpool, resolved to find, in some land beyond the seas, a home and fortune for himself. With this purpose in view he made his way through Birkenhead to the crowded, busy quays and docks on the banks of the Mersey. Driven by his destitute condition to accept any offer of work which might be made him, he accepted an engagement with the captain of a small vessel, of an inferior class, to act as ship's boy on the passage to New Orleans, where he arrived after a dreary voyage of eight weeks. The great and populous port of the Southern States was then at the height of its commercial prosperity. Ships of all nations crowded its harbour, and the evidences of commercial success were visible on all sides in the splendid buildings and spacious mansions which adorned this Venice of the New World. After some delay Stanley found a suitable post in one of the huge stores near the river, in which the shippers transacted their business. His diligence and energy soon commended him to his employer, who after a time, it is said, actually adopted him as his son. This was an eventful crisis in the career of the young Welshman, and as a practical specimen of his deep sense of the confidence thus shown in him, he determined to take the name of his patron—H. M. Stanley—in the place of his own, which had up to this time been John Rowlands. Life was now opening in real earnest for him with a fair pro-spect of speedy success in his new calling. He was regarded by friends and neighbours as a lucky youth, who would, without doubt, in good time, come to be the head of the house over which his foster-parent presided. His career as a merchant's clerk was, however, brought to a sudden and complete termination. On the death of his benefactor, the whole of the property was taken over by the relatives of the deceased trader, and Stanley was once more adrift upon the world. He now made his way to the State of Arkansas, where he remained for two years. On the outbreak of the Civil War in 1861 he enlisted in the Army of the South, "joining," as he said in a speech which he made seven years afterwards, "the ranks of the enemies of his country because at the time he knew no better." Having been taken prisoner in the battle of Pittsburg, on April 6th, 1862, he con-

trived to effect his escape, at the peril of his life, by
swimming the river, under the fire of the sentries, in
the dead of night. Some time after this he reappeared
at Bddelwyddan in North Wales, where his mother
had gone to reside. He made only a brief stay, however, in his native country, and after spending a few
months at Liverpool, he re-embarked for America.
The terrible conflict between North and South was
still raging, and every effort was made to secure
smart and eligible recruits for both services. Stanley
was induced to enter the Federal Navy, and was
promoted at the end of his first month of duty to the
clerkship of the vessel to which he had been drafted.
The satisfactory manner in which he discharged the
duties of his office soon secured for him the favourable notice of his superiors, and in less than a year
we find he had become secretary to the admiral of
the fleet on board the flag-ship *Ticonderoga*. The
young writer soon showed something of the spirit that
was in him.

During a terrific engagement, in which the flag-ship
was constantly under fire, he volunteered to swim off,
in the face of a scathing discharge of shell from the
enemy's batteries, over a distance of five hundred
yards, and attach a hawser to a rebel steamer. This
audacious feat was performed with complete success.
The prize was drawn out of the harbour, and secured
by the flag-ship, and the hero of the adventure was
rewarded by being made an ensign upon the quarter-
deck of the *Ticonderoga*. Stanley was frequently
engaged in important naval operations from this time,
and he took an active part in the final assault upon
Fort Fisher on January 13th, 1865, which virtually

decided the fate of the Confederacy. In 1866 the *Ticonderoga* was ordered to proceed upon a cruise in Southern Europe, and in the summer of that year, Stanley obtained leave of absence and left his ship at Constantinople, with a view to revisiting his Welsh home. His appearance amongst his old friends in the smart uniform of the United States Navy, and the accounts which had reached Denbigh and the neighbourhood, of his prosperous and distinguished career across the Atlantic, combined to make him now a person of some distinction and fame. He was heartily welcomed on all sides, and his reception at St. Asaph, when he visited his old school, was most enthusiastic. He addressed the boys who were assembled to greet him in a cheery, practical speech, full of useful exhortations to ready obedience at all times to the call of duty. The boys were entertained at Mr. Stanley's expense, and they were granted the usual holiday in honour of their friend and visitor. It was previous to this visit to the Principality that Stanley met with some thrilling experiences with armed outlaws in the heart of Syria. During the visit of the fleet to Constantinople, with two companions, he penetrated the country for about 100 miles east of Smyrna, when the party was attacked by brigands, who robbed them of everything they possessed and barely allowed them to escape with their lives. The unfortunate travellers returned to Constantinople, where their leader, with characteristic energy, at once wrote a graphic and telling account of their treatment to the *Levant Herald*, and complained in no measured terms of the deplorable condition of the Turkish provinces in Syria, and of the otiose and indifferent attitude of the authorities in

that province, where there seemed to be no real protection for either life or property. The letter was as
follows:—

"OUTRAGE ON AMERICAN TRAVELLERS.

"*To the Editor of the "Levant Herald.*"

"SIR,—When about seven hours from Afiuna-Kara-
Hissar, on the 18th September, *en route* for Tiflis and
Thibet *viâ* Erzeroum, from Smyrna, I and my two
companions, Mr. H. W. Cook of Illinois, and Master
Lewis Noe of New York, were attacked by a band of
robbers, hailing from the village of Chi-Hissar, headed
by a fellow named Achmet of Kara-Hissar, and robbed
of all our money, valuables and clothing, to the tune
of about 80,000 piastres. It would occupy too much
space were I to enter into minor details; suffice it
to state that after robbing us, they conveyed us as
prisoners in triumph to Chi-Hissar, accusing us of
being robbers, which brought down on our devoted
heads unparalleled abuse from the villagers: the
women pelted us with stones, the children spat at us,
the men belaboured us unmercifully with sticks, clubs,
and fire-tongs. Not comprehending in the least what
direction affairs had taken, I must say for myself
that I was plunged in a state of stupefaction not un-
mingled with rage, as to how and why we were thus
treated. We had instantly acquiesced in all their
demands, and were as docile as lambs in their hands,
and though when attacked we were armed with the
best Sharp's fliers and Colt's revolvers, we had offered
no resistance.

"When night arrived they bound us with cords,
drawn so tight round our necks that it nearly pro-

duced strangulation, in which suffering condition they allowed us to remain twelve hours. During the night three of our captors, Vely, Muet, and Mustapha, when all seemed buried in slumber, committed the diabolical —[it is not necessary to describe the outrage. Sufficient to say that it was of a very shameful character, and that the lad was coerced into silence by the robbers flourishing over his head a long knife, with a significant threat to cut his throat]. No explanations that they can render can gloss over the wanton cruelty and malignant treatment to which we have been subjected.

"Next day, two of them conveyed us, bound, with the most daring effrontery imaginable, to a small town called Rashi Kein, with the statement that we were robbers, when, of course, we were powerless to explain the mystery that hung over us. We were treated as prisoners, accompanied by the most cruel abuses; chains were hung round our necks, like garlands, for the night. From this place we were sent to Afiuna-Kara-Hissar, where we received the benefit of an interpreter, in the person of Mr. L. D. Peloso, agent of the Ottoman Bank at that place, who acquitted himself very creditably in that capacity; the fruits of which were that we were immediately freed from 'durance vile.' Nor did his generosity stay here; he lent us ample funds, procured us comfortable rooms at the Khan, and fed and clothed us, thus acting the part of a good Samaritan to three unfortunates. And again, through his energetic and repeated appeals to Raouf Bey, the sub-governor of that place, all the robbers were arrested. A strict search was made by soldiers in the village, and about forty piastres and two or three articles of clothing were recovered. The prisoners Achmet, Ibrahim, Hassar, Mustapha, Beker, Vely, Muet, and three others were sent under strong guard to Broussa, there to be detained till tried according to law. We arrived at Constantinople *viâ* Broussa yesterday, to lay our case before the American Minister, through whose influence I hope justice will be meted out to the unbaptized rogues. Hoping you will give this letter a small space in your valuable paper, I remain one of the victimized.

"HENRY STANLEY.

"Pera, October 11th."

Through the kindness of the Hon. Jay Morris, the American representative at the Sublime Porte, assistance was at once afforded to the sufferers, who presented themselves at the private residence of the minister in a most deplorable and destitute condition.

In 1867 an expedition, under the leadership of General Hancock, was organized for the suppression of the Sioux, Cheyenne, and Kivia tribes of Indians, who had for some time been making formidable and brutal raids upon the more exposed railways of the North-Western States. Stanley accompanied the troops in the capacity of correspondent for the *New York Tribune* and the *Missouri Democrat*, and distinguished himself not so much by the style as by the matter of his descriptive letters to the papers he represented at the scene of operations. He displayed a wonderful patience in obtaining facts and information, and often ran great personal risks in his desire to have the earliest and most reliable news of any fresh incident of the campaign. This was his second actual commis-

sion as a " War Special," a calling as perilous as it is
honourable in which he has since gained the highest
eminence. The qualifications requisite for an efficient
" Special Correspondent " are various in kind and
many in number. In the exercise of his vocation
he has indeed " to play many parts." A splendid
physique, a cool head under fire, a keen eye to take in
at a glance the physical features and peculiarities of a
district, an intimate knowledge of military strategy
and the tactics of war, an unflinching courage, great
prudence and sagacity in communicating his facts, a
smart style, a fluent pen under all circumstances of
climate or health, expert horsemanship, business tact,
and a capacity for enduring fatigue and privations—
these are only a few of the characteristics of a successful " War Special." The accounts of Hancock's
expedition, published in the *Tribune* and *Democrat*,
soon attracted public attention, and they were acknowledged by literary critics to have been written
by a man who knew his work. Efforts were at once
made by the leading journals of America to secure the
services of the graphic pen which had depicted so
powerfully the various phases of the latest conflict
between civilization and savagery in the Far West.
Meanwhile, the now famous " newspaper man " was
returning at his leisure, with a solitary companion,
upon a rude raft which he had constructed and
launched upon the Platte river, and upon which he
accomplished a journey of over seven hundred miles
without a mishap. He preferred this method of
travel, he said, to the dull and dreary monotony of the
coach-road. Leaving the river when he reached the
Missouri, he crossed overland to New York, where he

found the proprietor of the *Herald* ready to offer him the lucrative but responsible position of travelling correspondent to that journal. The offer was accepted (1868), and Stanley was ordered to proceed without delay to Europe, and attach himself to the British forces under Sir Robert Napier, who was about to invade Abyssinia, in order to crush the power of King Theodore, the inhuman monarch of that country, who had excited the indignation of all civilized nations by his barbarous treatment of a band of European missionaries and artisans, whom he had seized and imprisoned in his remote and well-nigh impregnable fortress of Magdala. The gallant officer who had charge of the expedition was already distinguished by a succession of brilliant military services in India and the Far East. He had been mentioned in despatches for the manner in which he had discharged the responsible duties of brigade-major in the arduous and exhausting Sutlej campaigns, in which he had received a severe wound, which, for a time, unfitted him for active employment. At the siege of Moultan he had directed the operations of the corps of Royal Engineers as acting chief, and been again severely wounded. As commander of the Engineers during the assault on Lucknow he had been awarded high honours for the ability and sagacity with which he had planned and carried out the complicated system of field and siege works, which eventually effected the overthrow of the city (1858). He was made a K.C.B. for this achievement and received the thanks of Parliament. In 1861 Napier had been ordered to China, to assist in the combined attack by both arms of the service, upon Pekin, a walled town of enormous strength, with a mixed population

of over a million Tartars and Chinese. The city,
which occupied a formidable position about one
hundred miles from the sea, near the Peiho river, soon
fell into the hands of the British, with all its treasures,
and the " skill, energy, and intrepidity" displayed by
Napier in the course of these extensive and difficult
operations again secured for him the thanks of
the Parliament, as well as the admiration of the
entire French and English forces engaged in the war.
The son of Major C. F. Napier, R.E., he was born at
Ceylon, during his father's term of duty in that
island. In due course he went to the military college
at Addiscombe, and entered the Bengal Engineers in
1826. He obtained captain's rank in 1841, and
rendered good service at this period to the Indian
army generally by the promotion of the Lawrence
Asylums for soldiers' orphans. His experience in the
frontier wars with the half-savage Husseinzai and
Afreedee tribes, and as commander of a flying column
which was sent out to hunt down the rebel commander
Tantia Topee, admirably qualified him for the special
work which lay before him amongst the hills of
Abyssinia. The march to Magdala was by no means
an undertaking to be lightly entered upon. The
region to be traversed by the invading force was to a
great extent a land of mystery. Reliable information
as to the physical features, population, and resources
of the territory had to be mainly gleaned from the
records of Bruce and Beke, the only travellers who
had actually made anything like a detailed examination of the region. Up to the time that Sir R. Napier
landed at Massowah, the only port of Abyssinia, the
country, although presenting every attraction to the

traveller and the man of science, was, strange to say,
almost a *terra incognita* even to our geographers and
explorers. The kingdom of the doomed monarch was
found to consist of a wedge-shaped area of highland,
rising in a series of plateaux to an average elevation
of six thousand feet, with a small coast-line bordering
on the Red Sea, and surrounded by the desert sands
and steppes of the Egyptian Soudan. Lofty serrated
mountain-ranges, with towering and rugged peaks
reaching in some cases to an altitude of sixteen
thousand feet, rise out of these tracts of table-land,
and the hill-ranges are intersected and broken in all
directions by deep and almost inaccessible ravines and
low-lying valleys. The Blue Nile, and the Atabora,
the sole tributary of the united Nile, have their
sources in the recesses of the Abyssinian mountains,
and these dark, turbid streams, heavily laden with the
rich, loamy soil, which is carried down by their headlong rush in the season of the tropical rains, go to
swell the majestic volume of the great Egyptian river,
which empties its waters into the Mediterranean, after
pursuing a direct course of over three thousand miles.
Owing to the peculiar position and conformation of
the country, the traveller in ascending from the
lowlands to the more elevated regions, passes
through three distinct zones of temperature. The
valleys and low-lying districts are tropical, the hill-
sides present more or less the conditions of life which
are found in a temperate climate, whilst in the highlands the temperature is identical with that of
Northern Europe. In the *Kollas* or tropical belt of
temperature, which ranges from 3000 to 4000 feet
above the sea-level, and which embraces the lower

edges of the plateaux, vegetation in all the glory of tropical luxuriance abounds. The cotton-tree, gum-yielding acacias, the ebony, the sugar-cane, bananas and dates are cultivated to the highest perfection, and in the forests are found the lion, the elephant, the zebra, the panther and the antelope.

The *Wonnia Degas* or temperate belt is the richest and most habitable. It has the climate of Spain and Italy, and produces European grasses, hard-shell fruits, the apricot, peach, citron and vine, and its verdant and prolific pastures sustain multitudes of domestic animals, among which all those familiar to Europeans are found, except the pig.

The *Degas* or highland belt, which takes in all the country between about 9000 and 14,000 feet, consists of the loftier plains and the slopes of the numberless Alpine ranges or cluster of hills which break the surface of the country in all directions. In this region there is little wood, the cultivation of the soil is neglected, snow and ice are prevalent in winter, and life is altogether harder and less attractive than in the lower districts of the country. This region is not without a sombre and awful beauty, however. The vast panorama of jagged peaks, the knots of sharp and lofty hills, inter-sected by deep narrow abysses and impassable chasms, re-echoing with the noise and tumults of the foaming torrents which sweep through them, and the tiny towns perched like birds'-nests high up upon some crag or peak of barren rock, and only to be reached by rope ladders, or slings rudely fashioned from a raw ox-hide—are some features of a picture which is impressive, if not altogether delightful. In June and September the country is flooded by an unremitting downpour of thunder-showers and tropical rains. Every brook becomes a stream, and every stream is swollen into a river, which rushes down the steep declivities of the plateaux and scours a way for itself with terrific force, till it reaches the plain and is lost in some affluent of the ancient and mighty Nile.

The area of Abyssinia was one hundred and fifty thousand square miles, with a sparse and scattered semi-barbarous population of three millions. It was divided up into a number of small states, out of which were formed the three important provinces of Tigre in the north, Shoa in the south, and the central state of Ambara. There are many interesting relics of an ancient and remote civilization, and from a study of these it is evident that the people as a nation have retrograded with the passage of the centuries, rather than progressed. The present inhabitants are a mixed race, but the Arab type predominates. Their colour varies from a rich bronze to deep black. Their religion is a peculiar form of very debased Christianity. There is an important Jewish element in the population, which claims unbroken descent from the Patriarchs, and is distinguished by a higher moral tone than that which prevails amongst their neighbours. These Falashes, as they are called, are the husbandmen and artisans of the country. Mohammedanism was planted in the uplands of Tigre as far back as A.D. 622, by the family of the great prophet of Islam, who fled to the security of these mountain fastnesses during that eventful crisis in the fortunes of Mohammed known as the Hegira, or the flight, when he himself had to seek refuge for a time in a desert cave, from the fury of his disappointed converts. The Portuguese attempted to settle in the northern province in the seventeenth century, but they did not remain. Some traces of their presence are still to be seen in the finished artistic productions of the native weavers and jewellers, and in the splendid castle of Gondar, which, although the capital, is now only a city of ruins.

CHAPTER II.

In November, 1867, the English army, a small but compact and carefully selected force, of about 14,000 rank and file, began to arrive at Annesley Bay. The point of debarkation was the best that could be found, after careful search, along the low narrow slip of Abyssinian coast-line. It was exposed to the full blaze of the African sun; the atmosphere, at times, was unbearable, and there was no water to be had for miles round the hastily-constructed pier of Zoulla. But the position afforded easy access to the table-lands of the interior, and at the same time afforded excellent and safe anchorage for the fleet of transport and steamers engaged in conveying war-material and stores to the invaders. It would be difficult to imagine any place more desolate, and wanting in natural attractiveness. For fifteen miles inland a dreary waste of sand, broken by rugged boulders, and covered by patches of stunted bush and coarse herbage, stretched away to the mouth of the enormous rift in the hills through which lay the only road to Magdala.

The district produced no sustenance for man or beast, and the natives even avoided it at certain seasons of the year, as quite unfitted for human habitation.

C

But the arrival of the " Feringhees " (as the foreigners
were called in the native tongue) suddenly threw life
and colour into the scene, and turned the desert into
a flourishing commercial settlement, and an important
naval and military *entrepôt*, which soon became the
centre of a busy traffic between the friendly natives
from the highlands and the Government agents, who
were instructed to buy up all the forage and rice which
was brought into market. For the first few weeks
confusion reigned supreme in the novel and over-
crowded station, and when Mr. Stanley landed, he
found everything in the " settling down " stage.

Myriads of human beings, of all nations and languages,
had been gathered together to assist in discharging
and housing the cargoes brought ashore from the
shipping in the Bay. Mules, camels, elephants, horses,
cows, coolies, natives, Parsees, sailors, soldiers, Arabs,
Greeks and Jews, were all mixed up in a motley crowd,
which presented at every turn some new feature of interest or amusement. A small railway had been constructed as far as Komayli, an encampment a few
miles up the country, along which heavily laden transport waggons were constantly passing, and the busy
and tumultuous scene was bounded by the deep waters
of the Bay, upon whose heaving and glittering surface
lay hundreds of vessels of all sizes, from the superb
British ironclad to the tiny and fleet-winged Arab
felucca. The sudden collapse of the commissariat de-
partment threatened to bring disaster upon the undertaking thus early in the history of the Expedition.
The report furnished by Colonel Merewether as to the
resources of the country had been much too sanguine,
and the officers and heads of departments looked in

vain, on their arrival, for the flowing streams, rich
pastures, prolific forests, and unlimited supplies of
game to be had for the hunting, which had been promised them. The mortality amongst the herds of
baggage animals, which were landed without drivers
or attendants to look after them, was fearful. Thousands died for want of water, and their putrid carcases
scattered about the shore in the tropical heat, added to
the unpleasantness and danger of the situation. Order
was at length evolved out of chaos, and when Sir R.
Napier arrived with his staff upon the scene of operations, he immediately decided to prepare for the
advance in force. The army at his disposal was constituted roughly as follows : officers, 250 ; European
troops, 4250 ; Native Indian troops, 9447. The camp
followers numbered 26,214 ; the civilian traders and
others, 433 ; and the women followers, 140, making a
grand total of 41,000 combatants and non-combatants.
The number of animals imported for the purposes of
the campaign were 46, 659,viz.: horses, 2538 ; elephants,
44 ; mules, 16,000 ; ponies, 1651 ; camels, 4735 ;
donkeys, 1759 ; bullocks, 7071 ; and sheep, 12,839.

Stanley at once found himself thrown upon his
own resources. He knew no one amongst the
many thousands of persons of all countries and degrees
who composed the population of Zoulla. He had no
tent, horses, or servants for the journey to the uplands,
and no suitable equipage for the arduous enterprise
upon which he was about to enter. But he was equal
to the situation. Being happily provided with a com-
mendatory letter to an officer in the English camp, he
sought him out and delivered the epistle. He found
the gallant captain who was destined to be " his friend

in need," occupying a handsome and delightfully appointed canvas-house, carefully separated from the
rest of the camp by a fence of baubool. Not seeing
any one about, the crafty " War Special " drew attention to his presence by pulling at the tent-cover. A
languid voice at once called upon the visitor to enter,
and he found the owner of the very pleasant abode,
reclining in the airiest of costumes upon a couch,
evidently overcome for the time by the enervating
effects of the tropical atmosphere. Stanley thus
describes the scene.

" I came to see Captain Z—— of the Commissariat,
sir ! " said I, surprised at his nonchalance in the
presence of a stranger. ' Are you the gentleman ? '
I asked.

' Yes, I am the gentleman,' he replied, slightly lifting
his eyebrows. 'Who are you, and what do you want?'

' I am the bearer of a letter of introduction to you
from Major S——,' said I, at the same time bending
forward to hand him the letter. ' Hum, ah ! to be
sure ; Major S——, aw ! let me see. Won't you sit
down ? Excuse my indolence ; this country is so hot
that it melts the marrow in a fellow's bones ! '

He had half-risen when he commenced to deliver
this apology, but directly relapsed into his former
attitude with a deep sigh of relief, turning an almost
helpless look upon me before he read his letter, which
told as well as volumes of the anguish he had suffered
in rising.

Soda-water and brandy having been called for by
my host, and served by a dark-featured native, to the
great relief of both of us, I asked if I could procure a
tent and rations.

'Oh, yes,' replied the Captain; 'easy enough. Make out your indent. No, let me see. First, you will have to go to Major X——, and get an order for your rations and a tent, after which you will be pretty comfortable.'

Major X——, he further told me, was Acting —— of the Force at Zoulla, 'a very nice gentleman, splendid fellow, first-rate chap; do anything in the world' for me! Wishing to see this paragon of an officer, and settle my business, I bade Captain Z—— 'a good morning,' telling him I should see him again before long.

I was about to depart when the Captain bawled out, 'I say, you; can you dine at our mess, and would you please consider yourself as an honorary member of ours while you are in camp? We have a fine set of chaps, all perfect gentlemen. There's A—— of the Commissariat, B——, an old sailor, now Bunder-master; then there is C—— of the 3rd Light Cavalry, D—— of the Elephant lines, and lastly, we have E—— of the Bombay. Do come, will you? Be sure now! dinner sharp 9 p.m. Ta-ta, old fellah!'

'Certainly, my dear Captain, with the greatest pleasure. *Au revoir.* Ta-ta, old fellah!' and out I departed to find the quarters of that 'splendid chap,' Major X——." [1]

Making his way with difficulty over the hot sand, the *Herald* correspondent at length reached the quarters of Major X——, who furnished him with the order for a tent, a mule with all accoutrements, rations for himself and followers, and other necessaries for the road. Determined to get to the front, without

[1] "Coomassie and Magdala" (H. M. Stanley).

loss of time, in order to secure, if possible, some tidings
of the movements and intentions of Theodore from the
advanced scouts and spies, he completed his outfit, and
decided upon his mode of travelling directly on landing,
and on the morning of his second day in Abyssinia he
started southward upon his memorable journey, in the
van of the steadily advancing columns. As he left the
sea-board, the country assumed a new and brighter
aspect. The scenery was in places almost terrible in
its massive and towering grandeur. The road which
had been roughly levelled along the beds of empty
watercourses and up the sides of the hills, by a party
of pioneers under Colonel Phayre, was a marvel of
engineering skill and patient toil. In parts it rose
suddenly from some yawning chasm, up the perpendicular cliffs of solid rock, only to descend again into
some gorge or hollow, deeper than ever, and the
pioneers had often to blast or break a path in the
granite slopes or slate-stone precipices for the passage
of the troops. Progress along this rudely extemporised way was not only tedious, but exhausting to
body and mind. Ten miles was the average length of
a day's journey. Arriving at the camp of Komayli,
Stanley for the first time found himself in contact
with the native races of the country. In the bazaar,
which occupied a site which a few months before was
the centre of a mere desert, he was surprised to see an
extensive trade going on, under temporary awnings
and tents of reed and straw—London, Paris, Delhi,
Cairo, Turkey, Greece—all were represented in the
goods displayed for the inspection of buyers, whilst
native produce of all kinds was on sale, and found ready
purchasers.

The tent which Major X—— had caused to be issued to Stanley, had been left on the coast with other impedimenta, as the *Herald* correspondent desired above all things to "travel as quickly as possible towards Magdala." A buffalo-robe was therefore the only protection he allowed himself at this time in his bivouacs upon the bare earth. The early morning saw him again in the saddle, climbing step by step some narrow defile, with huge walls of solid stone towering to a height of 800 feet on each side of the mountain-path, where the echo of the human voice rang like thunder through the pass, and the fall of a hoof upon the stones resembled a discharge of musketry. Many of these rents in the hills were gloomy, and full of weird sounds and shadows, and it was always a welcome change to emerge from their chill and melancholy depths into the fresh air and bright sunshine of the open country which lay beyond them. Viewed from these lofty tablelands, the surrounding prospect is one of striking magnificence on all sides, and it is from these altitudes that the eye is able for the first time to realize the majesty and rugged beauty of the irregular mountain systems which give a distinctive character to all Abyssinian scenery. No definite tidings of the enemy had yet reached the vanguard of pioneers, although every effort had been made to obtain news by means of the native scouts who overspread the entire kingdom of Theodore. Meanwhile, the avengers were cautiously but steadily advancing towards the stronghold of the tyrant. "Would he fight?" was the question eagerly asked by the soldiers of each other, as they tramped resolutely on. No one could tell. The native chiefs who came into

camp to barter produce, or to make treaties of amity
with the General, would give no definite opinion.
" Todoro " might, they thought, offer a stubborn resistance, or he might in a paroxysm of terror yield up
his prisoners, and capitulate to save his own life—this
was the substance of the native view of the situation.

The history of Theodore III., Emperor of Ethiopia by
the power of God, as he styled himself, was not without many points of romantic interest. He was of
obscure birth, but having heard somewhere of a certain
prophecy as to a Messiah who should be born in
Abyssinia, and deliver the Holy Land from the
dominion of the infidels, he assumed the character of
a prophet, and declared himself to be the person
whose coming had been so long predicted and looked
for. Brave in battle, strong in frame, and highly intelligent, he gradually increased his power and the
number of his adherents. Asserting that he was
ordained of God to extirpate all Mohammedan nations,
he attracted to himself vast multitudes of followers, and
in 1851 he assumed supreme dominion over the whole
region of Abyssinia. He was at this time thirty-five
years of age. He decided to evacuate Gondar, the
ancient capital of the land. " I will have no capital,"
said this Napoleon of Africa ; "my head shall be the
empire, and my tent the capital." He encouraged
European artisans to settle in his dominions, and for
some years his reign promised to be a time of blessing
and prosperity to his people. Missionaries were
courteously received by the young Emperor, schools
were opened, and educational schemes for the regular
instruction of his subjects were discussed and adopted
by Theodore.

Suddenly, however, upon the death of his favourite wife, he gave way to intemperate habits, and to fearful fits of brutality and violence. Horrible punishments were inflicted upon innocent victims. Crucifixion and the torture were his favourite methods of punishment. Upon the arrival of Mr. Consul Cameron, Theodore addressed an official letter to the English Government, which reached Earl Russell at the Foreign Office, in February, 1863. Some unfortunate mistake in the policy of the Government with reference to affairs in Egypt, the ancient enemy of Abyssinia, and the neglect of Theodore's communication, roused the sensitive monarch to a state of ungovernable fury. Cameron, then on a visit to the court, was cast into prison (July, 1863). Stern, a missionary, was beaten because he covered his mouth to prevent a shout of anguish when he saw his wretched servants scourged to death before his eyes. Theodore, suspecting that Stern was using some sign of vengeance, at once had him thrown upon the ground, and in accents of raving passion yelled out, " Beat that man ! beat him as you would a dog; beat him, I say ! " One by one the Europeans in the country were deprived of their liberty, loaded with chains, and cast into noisome dungeons, whence they were taken at times to be tortured and degraded with indignities, and then sent back with the threat that they would soon be executed. This awful condition of suspense and misery lasted for four years. All means were tried by the English Foreign Office to secure the release of the captives. Messengers, letters, presents—all proved of no avail. The Consul was taken from the wretched hut in which he was fastened by a chain to the wall, and horribly treated.

"Twenty Abyssinians," he said, "tugged lustily on
ropes tied to each limb until I fainted. My shoulder-
blades were made to meet each other. I was doubled
up until my head appeared under my thighs, and while
in this painful posture, I was beaten with a whip of
hippopotamus-hide on my bare back, until I was
covered with weals, and while the blood dripped from
my reeking back, I was rolled in the sand."

In 1866, after offering a heavy money ransom for the
liberation of the miserable, and by this time despairing
prisoners, which was indignantly and peremptorily refused by the mad monarch, it was determined to deliver
the unhappy people by force of arms. The idea of an
Expedition into the heart of Abyssinia was at first
severely criticized in the English press. Untold dangers,
it was declared, awaited the troops, from reptiles, fevers,
wild beasts, impassable roads, inaccessible heights
tempests, the well-known treachery of the people,
poisoned wells, and a most fatal form of dysentery
which prevailed in the hot season in all the provinces.
But the decree had gone forth, and Theodore was a
doomed man. Indian troops were to be employed in
the enterprise, and only the necessary equipments and
baggage animals were to be drawn from Europe. The
force was not to exceed 12,000 men; 2000 to protect
the pier and settlement at Zoulla, and afford a garrison
for the highland post of Senafe, 2000 for Antalo, a
point about half-way on the road to Magdala from
Annesley Bay, 2000 to protect the convoys and secure
free communication with the base of operations, and
6000 for the march into the interior in search of the
implacable tyrant, who was known to be somewhere
amongst the mountain fastnesses of the South. The

distance to be covered was something under 400
miles, and with interpreters, guides, an abundant
medical staff, and Captain Speedy, a former favourite
officer of Theodore, a man of gigantic frame, and great
sagacity and ability, as the Political Agent to negotiate
with the princes of the native provinces, the valiant
little force set forth to vindicate once more the honour
and humanity of old England.

Great care was taken to secure the friendship and
goodwill of the various tribes along the route the troops
had to traverse. This important duty was entrusted
to Major James Grant, C.B., who had already become
known through his connection with the Nile Exploration, and it is pleasant to be able to state that no
trouble of any kind was experienced by the Expedition
from a breach of these temporary treaties of good-
will by the Ethiopian chiefs.

Travelling in the Abyssinian highlands without a
good escort is by no means unattended by danger.
Hordes of hill-robbers, the dreaded Gallas, occupy the
darker and more intricate paths, and suddenly fall
upon the incautious or unarmed horseman, and after
divesting him of his possessions, including his horse
and clothing, disappear as mysteriously as they came.
These brigands live in curiously placed villages built
high up on the slopes or peaks of the remotest
mountain ridges, whence the cry of the alert watchman can be constantly heard signalling the approach
of enemies, or the possibility of securing fresh plunder
as the case may be. The woods resound with the cries
of the butcher-bird, and the clock-bird, and troops of
monkeys may be seen occupying in noisy state the
wide-spreading branches of the sycamore-trees. An

Abyssinian village might well be described as a miserable hamlet of low mud hovels, about which the children scramble in a disgusting state of greasy filth, and without any clothing whatever. The adults, who affect some decency of attire, like to bask in the sun, or idle away the time between meals, lying in the shade, and discussing the tidings of the day with the last new-comer.

The colour of the people, as has been before remarked, varies in shade. Some of the highland tribes are nearly white; other sections of the population, especially those with Negro blood in their veins, are black as Nubians. The hair is plaited by both sexes in long tails, which are usually coiled up at the top of the head. Their houses, churches and palaces all showed deplorable signs of a vulgar and degraded taste in personal and domestic matters.

The arrival of Stanley at Shoho, an important native market in the vicinity of one of the British camps, created, he tells us, great and undisguised astonishment. The whole population turned out into the street to gaze upon him. One detachment after another scanned the Feringhee, and every motion of eye, hand, or lip was most carefully noted. The colour of the eyes, skin, hair, the shape of the limbs, the tone of voice—all these matters were evidently subjects of mysterious bewilderment to the sable or brown-skinned spectators, who said nothing, but simply gazed with a wondering stare at the phenomenon in their midst, with feelings quite too deep for words. The houses are rudely constructed of red clay, with a thatch of straw or reed and a top-cover of mud to keep the whole secure and solid. An Abyssinian funeral pre-

sents an odd mixture of Christian forms with the ritual
observances of a barbarous and benighted superstition.
All the people of a neighbourhood are expected to attend the burial of the dead. The corpse is wrapped in
the every-day attire of the deceased, and is carried by
the elders of the village or family, with hideous howls
and gesticulations to the grave. Crowds of men, women, and children follow the body, and keep up a
frightful din all along the route of the procession till
the cemetery is reached. Everything is done in a
most slovenly and irreverent manner. The priests are
ignorant and needy, and seem only anxious about their
tithes, which the people appear to pay with readiness.
During the progress of the funeral ceremonies the
clergy strive to outdo the laity in the extravagance and
violence of their outward manifestations of sorrow.
They first shout out from rude and antiquated missals
the requiem for the departed in jerks and snatches,
and then by way of variety they attack their own
headgear, ripping into shreds the long folds of linen
and silk which form their turbans, concluding the
absurd and heathenish performance by plucking out
their hair by the roots and casting it upon the ground.
The churches are dark, gaudy, and unclean as a rule,
even to foulness, and their whole system of religious
observance is painfully marred and degraded by a
coarseness and want of spirituality, which reveals the
sad depth to which the once famous and venerated
church of Ethiopia has fallen.[2]

At Antalo, the half-way station on the road to Magdala, Stanley came up with the Pioneer detachment
under Colonel Phayre, and found the place in a state

[2] See "Coomassie and Magdala" (H. M. Stanley), p. 209.

of intense excitement, and busily preparing for the reception, with due honours, of the Commander-in-chief
and the main body of the forces. Up to this point the
energetic and alert representative of American journal-
ism had pursued his way, with one or two companions,
without attaching himself to the main body of the
army. It was necessary now, however, that he should
present his credentials to the Chief of the Expedition
without further delay, and on the morning after the
arrival of Sir R. Napier at Antalo he went to headquarters and asked for an interview with the General,
who received him with courtesy, and after inquiring as
to his needs, promised him every assistance, and assured him that he should have the same privileges as
to special items of intelligence which were enjoyed by
the other gentlemen of the Press who accompanied the
staff. At the General's table in the evening, Stanley
was introduced to the officers, and also had the opportunity of becoming acquainted with the various correspondents of the English papers—viz.: Dr. Charles
Austin, D.C.L., *Times;* George A. Henty, Esq.,
Standard; W. Owen Whiteside, Esq., *Morning Post;*
Alexander Shepherd, Esq., *Daily News;* Mr. Adare,
Daily Telegraph. The Press Tent was a perfect abode
of harmony, and true fellowship, and the most " social
lovable, and good-tempered mess in the Army."

Affairs now began to assume a more business-like
aspect as the serious work of the campaign might open
at any moment. Orders were issued for the curtail-
ment of baggage, kits were not to exceed seventy-five
pounds in weight, and only two horses were allowed
to each officer, whilst twelve soldiers were to occupy
one tent, and two officers were directed to share the

same accommodation for the future between them.
Forward went the Pioneers once more, and everybody,
from General to bugler, felt that something was about
to happen. Many weary leagues of mountain and ravine had yet to be covered, however, before the blow
could be struck which would for ever destroy the dominion of Theodore, and set free the unhappy victims
of his impotent fury. The spies came in day by day
with fresh but painfully conflicting scraps of information as to the movements of the King. One by one
the tribes which had professed allegiance to him, in
his days of triumph, were rising against him. His
army was crumbling to pieces, and he was powerless
to prevent the wholesale desertions from his standard.
His revolting cruelty, in his hours of drunken delirium,
only exasperated those whom he sought to restrain by
fear. The foreign prisoners in his camp he treated
with increased severity. 30,000 of his own subjects
were reputed to have been slaughtered by him in less
than three months. The rulers of provinces, and the
tribal leaders turned in terror from the service of
the " Lion of Ethiopia," to the assistance of the brave
man, who with calm singleness of purpose was making
his way into the heart of the land, in spite of all obstacles, to seek out and chastise the inhuman oppressor of
his people. On March 14th, the head of the column
left Antalo. Theodore was known to be withdrawing
with a force of 30,000 men to the shelter of his fortress
of Magdala. The Prince of Tigre, the King of Shoa, the
Prince of Samea, and notabilities of less degree had taken
active steps to aid the General by hanging on the flanks
of Theodore's dwindling hosts, or by taking measures to
cut off his retreat in the event of a battle. Nature,

for the time, however, appeared to have arrayed herself upon the side of the tyrant. The difficulties of the
road increased as the end drew near. The skill of
the engineers, and the fortitude of the men were tried
to the uttermost.

Still onward lay the narrow path over those
" sky-wrapt walls of granite," along which the
road twisted and turned " like the windings to the
summit of a cathedral spire." Elephants, camels,
horses, and mules, as well as men, staggered
along footsore and weary up the precipices and down
the almost perpendicular sides of those terrible
ravines, till human endurance could sometimes bear
the strain no longer; and strong men fell out and
fainted by the way. Again and again it was seen that
Theodore had overlooked splendid opportunities which
his country afforded everywhere for the total destruction
of the little band of valiant men who were slowly tracking him to his mountain lair. A barrel of gunpowder,
judiciously placed, would have brought down the rocks
which overhung many a pass, and put a stop at once
and for ever to the progress of his enemies. But fate
had ordained it otherwise. That Theodore was by no
means ignorant of the art of making or destroying roads
was amply proved by the causeway he had constructed
a few weeks before through the solid basalt, and which
was now utilized by the English General. Traces of
iron implements were perceived on all sides of the
ravine, and the man who could construct a road could
also " kill " it. Other matters of even greater importance, however, doubtless occupied the brain of the dismayed monarch in the few lucid intervals which followed his periods of intoxication and debauchery.

Another source of anxiety now weighed upon the leaders of the enterprise. There was a scarcity of food and forage, and the army waggons, with limited supplies in hand, failed to keep up with the troops. Crushed and worn by the terrible ascent, soaked by the rain and chilled by the cold blasts which swept over the plateau which they had at last reached, the weary soldiers cast themselves down where they stood, and tried to forget the misery of their surroundings in sleep. On the morning of April 8th, however, the prospects of the invaders suddenly and permanently brightened. Abundance of provisions had been secured from the surrounding district, and through the exertions of Captain Speedy, assisted by Stanley, a large supply of flour, grain, horses, mules, and other necessaries were collected from the adjacent villages and brought into camp. For this service at a crisis in the affairs of the contingent, Stanley complains jocosely that he never received the thanks of the British Government or even a medal, an oversight which he thinks deserving of the most severe reproof.

At ten o'clock on the morning of the eventful 8th, Napier had his first view of Magdala. Expressions of satisfaction were heard on all sides and in all ranks. The camp resounded with bursts of merriment and mutual congratulation. The army of Theodore had been seen encamped at the foot of his citadel, and there were unmistakable signs of the presence of the King himself behind the guns which peered down from the crest of his rocky stronghold. Secret messages had come out from the captives in Magdala, to the effect that Theodore was on the alert, and meditated a night attack upon his pursuers, and that they were in momen-

D

tary terror lest he should order them all to instant death. Every precaution was therefore taken to give the besieged garrison a warm reception should they attempt a sortie, but the night of the 9th passed without any event of importance.

CHAPTER III.

On the morning of Good Friday, April 10th, 1868, the signal was given to advance upon Magdala. The camp had been struck some time before dawn, and at the peremptory but welcome call of the bugle, which announced the onward march of the British infantry, the men stepped out with all the energy and cheerfulness of a battalion about to take part in a holiday parade. One by one the regiments defiled before their Commander, and proceeded to take up the positions marked out for them in the place of attack.

The following is a description of the formidable fortress of Magdala from the able pen of Sir Robert Napier himself :—

"The fortress of Magdala is about twelve miles from the right bank of the Bechilo, but the great altitude and the purity of the atmosphere exhibited the whole outline distinctly. The centre of the position is the rock of Selasse, elevated more than 9000 feet above the sea, and standing on a plateau called Islamgee, which is divided into several extensive terraces, with perpendicular scarps of basalt; a saddle connects these terraces with the hill called Fahla. Fahla is a gigantic natural bastion, level on the top, entirely open, and commanded by Islamgee. It domineers completely, at an elevation of 1200 feet, over all approaches to Islamgee; the sides appeared precipitous, and the summit, surrounded by a natural scarp of rock, accessible only in a few places, and from eighteen to twenty feet in height. Nearly concealed from view by Selasse and Fahla, the top of Magdala was partially visible. The road to Magdala winds up the steep sides of Fahla, subject to its fire, and to the descent of rocks and stones. One part of the road is so steep that few horses, except those bred in the country, could carry their riders up or down it. The whole road is flanked by the end of Selasse and the broadside scarp of Islamgee. Altogether, without taking into account Magdala itself, the formidable character of its outworks exceeded anything which we could possibly have anticipated from the faint description of the position which had reached us. The refugee chief, Beitwudden Hailo, was very anxious that I should try the south side, at the Kaffurbar (gate), from the opposite range called Lanta, saying, " If you want to take Selasse, go from hence ; but if you want Magdala you must go from Lanta." This, however, would have been impossible. I had not force enough to divide, and I could not place this vast combination of natural fortresses between me and my direct line of communication. I also perceived that the real point to be taken was not Magdala, but Islamgee, where Theodore had taken post with all his guns, and that Fahla was the key to the whole."

Theodore was himself a spectator of the scene from the summit of his citadel. Stanley attached himself to the Armstrong Battery, which was soon to do terrible execution amongst the disordered masses of Theodore's fanatical followers. Suddenly the advance of the British troops was momentarily checked and a discharge of chain-shot came crashing down through the silence over the heads of the intrepid besiegers. Almost at the same moment 3500 Abyssinians poured down the mountain side, and made a dash at the artillery. Theodore would fight then, after all. With hideous cries and gesticulations, his rude levies bore down upon the ranks and columns of the invaders, but their ranks were speedily broken by the deadly fire of the rocket battery of the Naval Brigade. Shot after shot swept through the swaying mass of savage warriors, and dazed and confounded they fell back, although urged by their leaders to continue the fearful struggle. The missiles of the avengers pursued them, and they fell in groups to the earth unable to escape the terrible fire of the English rifles. The remnant of the force rallied bravely in the very face of the bayonets of the Sikhs. The Indian infantry swept down the valley to assist their comrades, and the slaughter of the flower of Theodore's army was terrible. Shells hurtled through the air from the native batteries above the scene of conflict, but they passed harmlessly over the heads of the advancing force. Night put an end to the carnage, and fatigue parties were sent out to bring in the wounded, friends and foes alike, and to bury the dead. Ravenous beasts had already gathered upon the scene of suffering and death, and some of the more seriously injured with difficulty defended themselves from the persistent ravages of the hyænas or jackals which scoured the battle-field in search of prey.

Overtures were again made by the General to Theodore with a view to stop further hostilities, but they were rejected with scorn. The British casualties so far had been one officer—Captain Roberts—and thirty privates wounded, the officer and eight privates severely. Happily no life had been sacrificed, although the strife had at times and in places been severe and at close quarters. Of the enemy 560 were found dead, and seventy-five wounded were admitted to the hospital. During the night various reports floated about as to the tactics to be pursued on the morrow. Two of the captives suddenly appeared in camp, bringing a message from Magdala. Theodore was fast sinking into despair. He had attempted his own life more than once, since the English force had invested his last retreat, which he had fondly hoped they would never venture to attack, and he had even ordered the massacre of his anxious and terrified captives, whom he charged in bitter terms with bringing destruction upon him. Rassam was brought out of durance, and consulted by the King as to the course he must pursue to save himself and his city from destruction by the troops encamped outside the walls. He was advised instantly to release and send down to the British General all the prisoners with their belongings, Rassam promising, on his own authority, that the invaders should at once leave the country if this were done. The King assented. The prisoners were immediately led forth to the Thak-futban Gate, where Theodore was waiting to bid them "Farewell." At seven o'clock in the morning the news spread through the British lines that the captives were free, and that they were even then arriving in the camp. The wretched group, when assembled before the quarters of their deliverers, numbered sixty-one, and included women and even children, all more or less bearing traces of their past confinement, and exhibiting every sign of the inexpressible joy which possessed them at being once more free !

About noon of the same day one thousand bullocks and five hundred sheep were sent down from the King for the use of the troops, but the present was refused, with the haughty message from Sir Robert that he could take no gift from the enemy of his country and his Queen. Final preparations were now made for the assault upon the fortress. Guns were placed in position to cover the scaling-parties, ladders were constructed, and all the necessary appliances got ready for blowing up the gates, or forcing a breach in the wall of the Abyssinian bastile. A last offer was made to the infatuated prince, who was watching every movement of his pursuers, with tiger-like vigilance. The generous message remained unanswered. 50,000 dollars were offered for Theodore, alive or dead, and the 33rd regiment was ordered up once more to lead the way. With relentless and consummate strategy the English army environed the heights upon which Theodore, the Emperor of Ethiopia, was about to make his last stand for liberty and life. Riding in the front of a troop of his horsemen, the fated monarch could be seen, clothed in long flowing garments, waving his sword overhead, and crying out, " Come on ! are ye women that ye hesitate

to attack a few warriors." At length the heavy guns
were brought into action, and under an uncertain fire
of musketry from the walls overhead the Engineers
advanced towards the massive gates of the citadel.
The thunder rolled amongst the hills and the lightning
flashed over the scene, whilst a heavy fall of rain
added to the discomfort of the English regiments
as they toiled up the slope towards the entrance to
the fortress. The huge postern had been carefully
strengthened inside by tons of rock. The position
of the little band of brave men who sought to gain
an entrance, was, for a brief space, critical in the
extreme, for the bullets of the Abyssinians fell thick
at first amongst them. There was a cry for the powder-
bags. "Hasten up with the powder!" cried the
officer in charge of the party. "Hasten up with the
powder! hasten up with the powder!" was re-echoed
all down the line. But where was the powder? and
where were the implements needed in this moment of
extremity to break down the towering ramparts, and
secure an entrance to the long-talked of Magdala?
The question was never answered. Meanwhile two
soldiers of the 33rd had entered the city, and
stumbled over the quivering frame of Theodore, who
was lying prone upon the earth, with a fearful wound
in his head inflicted in the extremity of despair by his
own hand with the revolver which lay beside him.
They took up the weapon and found upon it the
inscription : " Presented by Victoria, Queen of Great
Britain and Ireland, to Theodorus, Emperor of
Abyssinia, as a slight token of her gratitude for his
kindness to her servant Plowden, 1854." Soon the
interior of the fortress was crowded with the English

troops, elated with victory and ready to fly upon the spoil. Wild shouts of triumph rose from the rugged heights, and the dying monarch lived long enough to see the flag of his conquerors waving from the battlements of Magdala, and to hear the rapturous greeting with which Sir R. Napier was welcomed by his soldiers as he rode through the streets of the vanquished fortress.

Every one was anxious to see Magdala, and all day long a stream of soldiers, camp-followers, and idlers of all sorts and conditions kept steadily pouring into the dismantled and dishonoured city. Theodore was buried with decency, if not with honour. His wife and his only son, an interesting boy of ten years, were placed in charge of their old friend Captain Speedy till the home authorities should decide as to their final destination. Everything of value had been secured, and four days after the place fell into British hands it was evacuated, and fired by the departing and exultant forces. 30,000 Abyssinians migrated from the district to the far off lowlands, and soon Magdala, the renowned seat of the ablest, perhaps, as well as the most brutal of African tyrants, was left to silence and decay. On April 18th, 1868, the expeditionary force started on its homeward journey. Cheer after cheer went up and echoed through the ravines, and along the rocky slopes, and among the mountain peaks of Magdala.

The return journey to the coast partook at times of the character of an old Roman Triumph. The natives came out to shower congratulations upon the conquerors of Theodorus; and the clergy in solemn state bestowed their benedictions upon the victors as they

passed along. One officer only died during the
campaign. At Antalo fresh honours were awaiting the
returning column. The following gracious message
had been flashed from Windsor to the highlands of
Tigre : " The Queen sends hearty congratulations and
thanks to Sir Robert Napier and his gallant force on
their brilliant success." The following General
Order was also posted up :—

"Camp Antalo, May 12th, 1868.
" The Commander-in-Chief has much satisfaction in
publishing to the troops under his command the fol-
lowing messages received by telegraph from his Royal
Highness the Field Marshal Commanding-in-Chief,
and from the Right Honourable, the Secretary of
State for India, respectively :—
" We all rejoice in your great success, and in that
of your gallant and enduring army."
" ' I congratulate your Excellency with all my heart.
You have taught once more what is meant by *an army
that can go anywhere and do anything. From first to
last all has been done well.*' "
The native Abyssinian allies of the British were
well rewarded for their loyalty in the hour of peril.
Nothing was overlooked, and no duty was left undis-
charged by the man who had attracted to himself the
notice of the world, by the masterly manner in which
he had led his brave troops to Magdala and back,
without the loss of a single soldier at the hand of the
enemy.
Stanley, however, did not reach the coast without
one serious adventure. He was in deadly peril at one
point of the journey from the floods (which, in the wet

season, absolutely drown the country in a few hours),
and could only secure his safety by casting as a prey
to the waters a valuable carpet of Theodore's, which he
had secured for 50 rupees, as well as tents, curios,
camp equipage, and even his own clothing.

The return from the highlands was only effected
just in time to escape the rainy season. In fact the
troops had barely sighted the white sails of the fleet,
waiting upon the blue waters of Annesley Bay, to
receive them and bear them away to home and kindred,
when the first real deluge descended upon the land,
flooding the valleys, and converting the ravines and
passes into rushing and deadly torrents of boiling,
seething, eddying flood-water, which swept down from
level to level till it reached the lowland lakes or rivers,
bearing upon its turbid bosom houses, cattle, crops,
and human corpses. The rush of water was so sudden
that parties of travellers were sometimes caught in the
middle of a huge gorge or cañon by the hissing stream,
which flowed on to a depth of ten feet, overturning
rocks and cutting out huge seams in the walls which
confined it on each side, and rushing forward with
an impetuosity which no living power could withstand.
The "Yankee Sahib," as Stanley was called, was
pushing his way, with his attendants, at the head of
the troops to get down to the landing-place, a few
miles off, in time to catch the mail which left in a few
hours for Suez. The adventurous Special was warned
by experienced officers of the danger he would run
in entering a certain narrow ravine which offered
special facilities, as he thought, for a rapid and easy
descent to the coast. After travelling for a short
time, the cries of his servants caused him to look

round. It had been raining heavily for some hours past, and now, coming down behind them with terrific force, was a hideous flood of considerable depth, dashing and roaring and reaching out towards them like some frightful monster bent upon devouring them. Stanley at once saw the frightful nature of the peril which threatened him and his party. They climbed in terror to the top of a great rock of granite which stood in the centre of the ravine, and watched with breathless interest the rush of the water on both sides of their place of refuge. The scene was appalling and depressing in the extreme. Broken wreckage, tents, habitations, harness, gun-carriages, forage, and corpses, drifted past them, swirling and tossing in the foam of the angry waters. The Arab servants invoked the protection of Allah after their manner, and Stanley looked upon the rising waves, and the weeping skies, with grave and anxious countenance. The water had risen to the feet of the animals upon the rock, the fate of all upon the tiny sanctuary in the midst of the billowy flood appeared to be sealed, and at least one disaster, of magnitude, would have, it appeared, to be recorded in the annals of the return from Magdala. But at the moment when all seemed to be lost, a rift showed in the clouds above, the downpour ceased, the sun shone out, and in a brief space the waters in the pass subsided, and the imprisoned travellers were once more safe and free. They had been given up for lost by their comrades, and when late at night they reached the camp drenched and destitute, their appearance was regarded almost as a resurrection from the grave.

At length, however, the " Yankee Sahib " arrived in

safety at Zoulla, and the despatch of the correspondent
of the *New York Herald*, conveying the news of the
Fall of Magdala, reached America exactly a day before
the event was known in London.   On his return to
England, Stanley spent some time at Denbigh, where
he recounted to the friends of his boyhood and the
members of his family the marvellous story of Napier's
famous march to Magdala, and exhibited with no small
pride, the various trophies and specimens of native
workmanship and skill which he had secured during
his sojourn in the land of Theodore.

CHAPTER IV.

AFTER a brief period of rest and retirement in the midst of the familiar scenery and invigorating breezes of Denbigh and its neighbourhood, Mr. Stanley spent some months of 1868 in travelling on the continent. He visited the capitals of Western and Southern Europe during this tour, in which he happily combined duty with recreation, communicating his impressions of "men and places" to his countrymen across the Atlantic in a series of delightful letters to the *Herald*, which journal he continued to represent. The life and splendour, as well as the artistic and social attractions of the cities and localities, with which he now became acquainted for the first time, made a deep impression upon him, and he found congenial employment in describing and commenting upon the historical, political, and commercial associations of the various places of importance, at which he made a temporary sojourn from time to time. The rumours of serious internal disturbances and complications in Spain, however, soon drew his attention to the condition of the Peninsula, and he at once crossed the Pyrenees to find the army in a state of excitement bordering upon revolution. Political matters move quickly in Spain, and the

Herald representative only arrived in Madrid just in time to see Queen Isabella deposed, and a Regency declared under Marshal Serrano. During this stirring period, the various phases and developments of Spanish political intrigue were accurately noted, and carefully reported to New York, by the indefatigable *Herald* correspondent, who found himself once more in the midst of active military operations, and face to face with the indescribable misery and horror of civil war, and who was well qualified, by his past service in America and Africa, to follow with intelligence the military movements, demonstrations, and tactics which resulted eventually in placing Amadeus of Savoy upon the vacant throne. In the following year (1869) Stanley was summoned to Paris to consult with Mr. Gordon Bennett, the proprietor of the *Herald*, as to his future labours. At this time great uneasiness was felt throughout Europe at the absence of any reliable tidings concerning Dr. Livingstone, the illustrious explorer of Africa, who had disappeared into the interior of the Dark Continent, and had been unheard of for some years. His friends in England and elsewhere had become terribly anxious as to his safety, especially as reports had reached Europe from Zanzibar to the effect that the great explorer had perished at the hands of one of the tribes in the Equatorial regions. Stanley was therefore requested to go at once to Suez, and there await any information which might reach the Red Sea by way of the Soudan or the East Coast, concerning the lost traveller, and he was furnished with a large sum of ready money, for the purpose of telegraphing to the *Herald*, without delay, the earliest news he could get of Livingstone, alive or dead. He heard nothing, however, of the missing explorer, and finding the time pass slowly at Suez, he decided upon making a trip to Bombay, by way of Persia. Mr. Bennett had requested him to report upon the Suez Canal; Upper Egypt and Baker's Expedition; Underground Jerusalem; Politics in Syria; Turkish Politics in Stamboul; Archæological Explorations in Caucasian Russia; Trans-Caspian affairs; Persian politics, geography, and present condition, and Indian matters generally—a sufficiently varied programme, and one calculated to test the ability and physical powers of the smartest and most vigorous of special correspondents. But Stanley accomplished the task committed to him "without," as he says, "a break-down," and "to the complete satisfaction of his employers."

Central Asia, which Stanley crossed at this time, is the designation applied to the entire region situated between Russia and our Empire of India. The term is not an accurate one, as the district does not occupy the middle of the continent, but lies considerably to the south-west. This territory was the old Khanate of Tartary, but with the Eastward advance of Russia the name came into common use, and has since become a recognized geographical expression. It is, however, sometimes applied to those portions of the district which have not as yet come under the dominion of the Czar. Thus the deserts of the Kirghiz, then Khokand, then Bokhara and Khiva, and lastly the territory of the Turcomans ceased to form a portion of Central Asia; and Afghanistan and Persia, as independent provinces, were never rightly included in the area so named, and Kashgaria, since its re-conquest by China, has also been shut out from it.

Entering Syria by Constantinople, Stanley had much satisfaction in finding his former friend and bene-factor, the Hon. J. Morris, still in the position of American Minister to the Government of the Sublime Porte. Stanley was cordially received and hospitably entertained at the Legation, where he was always a welcome guest during his stay in the Turkish capital. The Minister furnished him with useful introductions to Russian officials and governors, and placed at his disposal all the information he could obtain from official sources concerning the lands which Stanley was about to traverse. The venture was a serious one, and likely to be attended with considerable danger, and Mr. Morris, while commending his hardi-hood, presented him with a practical mark of good-will in the shape of a Henry repeating-rifle of the newest pattern, which he had just received from America. Mr. Morris was so much impressed by the improved physique and manly bearing of the young traveller (he was now about twenty-eight years of age) that when he heard of him again as the man who had " Found Livingstone," he was not at all surprised, he said, at the success of his first African expedition.

But the journey through Russo-Asian territory and Persia to India, was in the estimation of the American Minister a greater feat of endurance and courage even than the direction of the expedition in search of Livingstone. Nothing was heard of Stanley for some months after leaving Constantinople, till *The Times of India*, of September 16th, 1870, announced his safe arrival at Bombay, and published four elaborate letters from him, full of statistics, facts, and wonder-fully executed word-sketches of his adventures and impressions by the way. Stanley's concise and bold remarks upon the famine in Ispahan, the Russians in Western Turkestan, the Shah in the Telegraph Office, and General Stoletoff upon the Central Asian Question, were not allowed to pass without some adverse but good-natured criticism. The letters, however, attracted much attention throughout the East at the time, and added considerably to the reputation of the author as a man gifted with keen powers of observation, and an attractive and humorous style of narrative.

Of the Shah, he says in his Persian letter:—

"The Shah of Persia visited the Telegraph Office in person, and—cunning fellow!—after examining the modes of operating, professed to be delighted with everything he saw. He regarded the apparatus of telegraphy intently, and then begged Mr. Pruce to explain how he manipulated the little round knobs which flashed the mysteries. Mr. Pruce did so very readily, and as he speaks eloquently, no doubt the Shah was much enlightened. For during the exposition of telegraphy, the Shah laughed heartily, and delivered many a fervid 'Masha-allah!' Then the Shah wanted to telegraph; he tried a long time, but as the words would not march, he gave it up as a difficult job. His fingers, he said apologetically, were dumb; they would not talk. Then he summoned one of his own employées from the Persian office, and bade him telegraph as follows :—

"*Telegram No.* 1 *to Koum, from the Shah in person.*

"' How much money hast thou for the Shah, Khan?' (to the Governor.)

"*Answer.*—(After a pause of about three minutes, the

rascally governor evidently considering, for all along
the line the governors had been forewarned.) 'When
the asylum of the Universe commands less than the
least of his slaves, he will give all he is worth.'

" *Telegram 2 to Koum.*
" 'How much is that?'
" *A.*—'10,000 tomans (£4000.)'

" *Telegram 3 to Koum.*
" 'Send the money, the Shah commands, he is well
pleased.'

" *Telegram 4 to Kashan.*
" 'Oh! Khan, the Shah wants money, how much hast
thou to give him?'
" *A.*—'Whatever the light of the world commands is
at his service. I have 5000 tomans (£2000.)'

" *Telegram 5 to Kashan.*
" 'Too little. Send me 20,000 tomans (£8000), the
Shah has said it.'

" *Telegram 6 to Ispahan.*
" 'Khan, thou knowest thy position is a treasure.
What wilt thou give the Shah to keep it? A man has
offered me 50,000 tomans (£20,000), for thy place.
Speak quickly. It is the Shah that waits.'
" *A.*—'Oh! King of kings, thou knowest my faithful-
ness, and hast but to speak. I have 60,000 tomans
ready.'

" *Telegram 7 to Ispahan.*
" 'It is good. Thou art a wise Khan. Send the
money.'

" *Telegram 8 to Shiraz.*
" 'Shah-zadeh, speak for thy place. There are evil-

minded men who desire thy position. Art thou wise,
and is thy hand open ? '

" *A.*—' The throne is the place of wisdom. When
the Shah speaks, the world trembles, the ears of his
governors are open. I have 30,000 tomans on hand."

" *Telegram* 9 *to Shiraz.*

" The Ameen-ed-Dowleh offers me 45,000 tomans.
Oh ! little man, thou art mad.'

" *A.*—' The Shah has spoken truly. I will send
50,000 tomans.'

" From his telegram to Bushire, he received answer
that 10,000 tomans would be sent immediately, which
was accepted.

" Thus in one morning the Shah netted the handsome sum of 160,000 tomans, or £64,000 sterling,
from the governors' privy purses."

The following is Mr. Stanley's account of the relative positions of the English and Russian ambassadors
at Teheran. He says : " . . . The esthesis of politics
has been studied to advantage by the respective ambassadors. I always thought politics a very dry
subject of study before I came to Teheran. I have at
last seen its esthetic side. The two ambassadors are
like two bazaar merchants. Mr. Beger exhibits with
a certain amount of taste, his stock in trade, consisting of friendly alliance, loving letters from the Czar
of all the Russias, Russian power, mutual aggrandise-
ment, and deadly hellebore. Mr. Allison has a varied
assortment of British notions, consisting of traditions
of John Company, old friendships, English wealth and
power, rich presents, Borasjoon memories, ubiquity,
Argus eyes, Abyssinian glory, and English ironclads.

" The Russian ambassador has a fine palace, much finer than Mr. Allison's, and Cossack guards. The British Government is building a palace which shall cost £50,000, and utterly eclipse the Russian. Ostentation aids diplomacy in Persia, and supremacy is rotative. Bravo, Mr. Beger! bravissimo, Mr. Charles Allison!" In another letter he says that General Stoletoff assured him that the designs of Russia upon Central Asia are " purely commercial." The General said:—" If Russia had merchants as enterprising as the English are, it had been done long ago ; but unfortunately, she has not. The Government has to take the initiative in everything, so that every movement made by it incurs suspicions, which, I can assure you, are perfectly groundless. I will give you an instance of Russian apathy. About five miles from here (Bakou), at Soukhanch, are naphtha wells productive of immense wealth, yet Russian merchants, cognizant of this important fact, were for a long time indisposed to work them upon speculation, until the Government moved in the matter, then they came down from St. Petersburg by the dozen, and have now very large establishments for the refining and distilling of the petroleum. In the same way is it with Central Asian trade. Our merchants, being so timid and unspeculative, will not venture to Khiva and Bokhara, because one or two of their number have been hardly treated, until the Government has cleared the way, and established colonies and fortlets for their protection."

In the last letter, which appeared on the 23rd September, 1870, Stanley comments on the famine in Persia, which filled the people of this country with such horror and sympathy at the time. He says:

"In times of drought the governors lay in a good stock of corn, and keep their granaries full, while the peasants—placid fatalists!—eat on without stint or care. The water is all spent, the snows of winter are all thawed, the beads of dew are not sufficient, without water the ryots cannot irrigate their land, so the crops assume a premature brownness, then fade before the parching drought. Their store of last year has been consumed, the religion with which they are saturated, will not feed their stomachs, they must eat material corn to live, but where will they get it? They cry out in despair. No charitable souls step forward to their relief, for there is not an atom of charity in the soul of a Persian. They turn to their governors, and the governors respond with a denial, for the famine prices are not high enough yet. Then the ryots besiege their bakers' doors, and after mortgaging their property, and finding themselves still in want, prompted by esurient hunger, they break out into open-mouthed, and tumultuous mobs. Then the governors open their granary doors, and issue driblets of corn and flour at extraordinary prices, to be paid (if the ryots have no money), with next year's harvest."

Having completed his journey through Southern Asia, Stanley now decided to proceed without further delay to the East African coast, with a view, if possible, to obtain some authentic tidings of Dr. Livingstone, and of his recent travels and discoveries in the inner central regions of the great continent.

CHAPTER V.

CROSSING the Indian Ocean, by way of the beautiful islands of the Seychelles, which rest calmly upon the heaving waters, like " emeralds set in a silver sea," Stanley reached the busy East African port of Zanzibar on January 6th, 1871. The last, but most important duty, which Mr. Gordon Bennett had entrusted to him was now to be entered upon. He was to FIND LIVINGSTONE. That illustrious man had started upon his third and (as it proved) final journey of exploration on March 28th, 1866, taking with him a small band of thirty-eight men. With these followers and a company of baggage-bearers, he had struck right into the heart of Africa, thirty miles north of the estuary of the Rovuma. Scraps of news about him and uncertain tidings of his progress, continued to reach the coast from time to time, but at last what appeared to be a circumstantial account of his murder by the lawless Ma-zitu on the shores of the Nyassa, startled his friends both in Africa and Europe. As the minds of those who knew him best grew calm, however, the terrible fears which this report had raised began to give way to strong feelings of doubt as to its truthfulness. Sir R. Murchison (President of the Royal Geographical Society), and other eminent scientists and explorers refused to accept the story, and an expedition was sent out, under Mr. W. E. Young, on June 11th, 1867, to verify or disprove the alarming narrative. Mr. Young's party entered the continent by way of the Zambesi, and after several months, spent in the region of the Nyassa, they succeeded in disproving every detail of the supposed massacre. It was found that Livingstone was alive and well, and that he had passed on long before, far beyond the spot at which he was declared to have been killed. Livingstone's primary object in undertaking this journey was to clear up, once for all, the mystery which had so long surrounded the great river systems, in the territory lying beyond Lake Tanganika. He had set his heart upon tracing these waters and exploring in detail the lakes, which he knew to exist in this vast and unexplored region.

"The correlation of the structure and economy of the waters of these great lakes, Bangweolo, Moero, Kambolondo, Lake Lincoln and another, and the lacustrine rivers is," he said in a letter to Sir R. Murchison, "the theme of my prize."

In 1868 communications reached England from him announcing the partial completion of the first portion of his task. They were dated February, 1867, and expressed the satisfaction he felt at having solved the problem of the sources and flow of the Chambezi. Time passed, and Livingstone was again reported by the caravans of Arab slave-traders and others which arrived at Zanzibar, to be dying, if not actually dead, of a sickness brought on by privation and the want of clothing, medicines, and food. His followers had deserted him, the chiefs through whose territories he sought to pass, had delayed his party, and robbed his stores, and the hardships and anxieties of this his last African journey, had, it was said, prostrated him in mind and body, and at length brought about his death in a native village somewhere in the equatorial regions. The last letter from his pen up to the arrival of Stanley on the coast, was received from Ujiji, May 30th, 1869. Thus, for nearly two years, no word or message had broken the perfect silence which enveloped the doings and fate of the heroic man who was still wandering on, or perhaps buried in the heart of the Dark Continent. Was Livingstone still alive, and if alive could he be found, or if found would he return or even allow Stanley to see him? These were some of the questions which the dauntless leader of the *Herald* search expedition often put to himself in the midst of his preparations for the advance into Africa. No time was wasted in unnecessary delay. There was no anxiety whatever as to the expense of this humane and noble enterprise. "Spare no cost to make the expedition a success," were the exact words of Mr. Gordon Bennett to Stanley during their memorable interview at Paris. "Draw a thousand pounds now, and when you have gone through that, draw another thousand, and when that is spent draw another thousand, and when you have finished that draw another thousand, and so on, but FIND LIVINGSTONE."

Zanzibar has a natural beauty and attractiveness which at once excites the admiration, and arouses the interest of the visitor. Seen from the deck as the steamer enters the crowded harbour, the island presents a bright and verdant surface of hill and valley, covered with a dense growth of luxuriant vegetation. Along the low sandy coast-line, groups and belts of lofty feathery cocoanut palms, and shapely cinnamon and mango trees, add grace and variety to a truly oriental picture, which is rendered complete by the long line of the white square consular buildings on shore, the gay flags of the war-ships and trading-vessels in the bay, the lofty palace of the Sultan, and the substantial Anglican Mission House in the distance. A closer acquaintance with the streets and homes of the Zanzibaris themselves is not, however, quite so agreeable. The squalor, filth, nakedness, and undeveloped sanitary arrangements of the native quarter, give an air of indescribable and repulsive wretchedness to the town, which is by no means creditable to the government of his Highness Prince Seyd Burghash, Sultan of Zanzibar and Pemba, and absolute monarch of the entire East African coast from Somali Land to the Mozambique. Zanzibar is the great trade mart and emporium of commerce of Eastern Africa, and it increases in wealth and importance year by year. It is the open gate through which the outer world communicates at all times with the whole of the Eastern and Central provinces of the vast and productive continent to which it belongs. Here goods are landed in enormous quantities, from the European steamers and American ships, for the up-country markets, which are regularly supplied by the numberless caravans which constantly leave Zanzibar laden with stores of all descriptions for purposes of trade and barter in the interior. The ivory, gum-copal, or chilla-weed, india-rubber, cloves, wax, oil-seeds, and cocoanut oil, and

other native produce, gathered up in the remote but
productive regions of the Zambesi, the Shire, and
Ujiji, find here a ready sale and easy shipment to the
markets of Asia, Europe, and America, and the slave
mart of Zanzibar is daily crowded with the spoils of
tribal wars on the mainland, and the fruits of Arab
raids upon the defenceless villages and unprotected
native settlements along the sea-board of the Mozambique, or the more distant shores of Nyassa or Tanganika. From this centre, which has an import trade
of £800,000 per year, and an annual export trade of
£900,000, there extends at the present time a powerful and ever-widening circle of commercial activity
and enterprise. The Zanzibar trader goes as far
south as Natal, and penetrates northward and westward to the desert fastnesses of the Soudan, and the
main waters of the Congo. Every East African
potentate of any rank has his agent or man of
business located upon the island. The great and
rising Central African monarchy of Karonge, which
cannot be crossed in a steady march of fifty days, has
or had its representative at Zanzibar, in the person of
a well-known Arab, with whom I came into personal
contact some years ago in the Indian Seas, and who
was declared to me, on the authority of Her Britannic
Majesty's Consul at Madagascar, to be "the greatest
rascal unhung." This man has had an exceptional
career, even for an African man-stealer. He told me
himself that as a boy he always accompanied his father
and brothers on their murderous raids up the country
in search of slaves. Their plan of operations was
very simple. They attacked the villages in the night,
and if the startled and outraged inhabitants resisted

or gave trouble they simply set fire to the huts, leaving
the aged and sick to perish in the flames. They only
carried off the youthful and commercially valuable
portion of the community they ravaged, leaving the
rest to perish by fire, famine, or exposure. The
utter depravity of this fellow was as remarkable as it
was disgusting. His heartlessness was thoroughly
exhibited on the occasion of his own capture, red-
handed, by the cutter of one of H.M.'s cruisers on the
East India station, when his dhow was found packed
to the gunwales with wretched Africans of all ages and
conditions. Many of the miserable creatures were
lifted out of the hold dead, and the captain of the
man-of-war decreed, to the intense satisfaction of the
English seamen, that the Arab should be hung at the
yard-arm of the ship on the following day at sunrise.
The prisoner spent the intervening space of time in
devotional exercises, varied by frantic appeals to
Azrael, the dreaded angel of Mortality of the Moslem
Creed, not to approach him with the chill touch of
death. A few hours before his execution he sent for
an officer, and asked to be allowed to make a statement to the Admiral or superior authority in the fleet.
This was allowed, and in the coolest manner the Arab
announced that his parent and brothers were about that
time likely to be engaged in a slave expedition off the
coast of Johanna, and expressed his readiness, on
condition that his life was spared, to lead the boats of
the cruisers to the very spot. The proposal was
accepted, as this band of desperadoes was notorious
for its atrocities, and for the terror with which it was
regarded by the tribes all along the coast. A few
days after, the boats of the English squadron were

sent to the south under the guidance of the cowering
wretch, who sat in the stern of the leading cutter,
covered by the revolver of the commander of the
flotilla. The whole of the band were captured, with
the exception of one brother, who is now believed to
be none other than the renowned Tippo Tibb, the
invincible monarch of the sub-tropical empire of
Karonge. The betrayer of his kin was allowed to
depart with his life, but he was obliged for many years
to hide himself from the vengeance of his tribe, as well as
from the too close attention of the British authorities.
When I saw him, however, he was at his old trade again,
and he had amassed a large fortune by his traffic in
human merchandise in the district where he resided,
and where he occupied a small but profitable territory
of his own. But for all this he was an arrant coward.
Steeped to the lips in the most diabolical and revolting
cruelty, he feared the sound of " a falling leaf." His
cheek would blanch, and his whole frame appear as
if convulsed with terror, when in peril of death in a
leaky canoe, or when the possibility of ending his days
after all at the yard-arm of a British man-of-man was
hinted to him. His family had set a price upon his
head, and he feared the wrath of his own clan probably more than he dreaded his re-capture by the
English fleet. In person he was handsome, with fine
features, and a striking carriage, though somewhat
short of stature. He was soft and sedate in his manners (after the manner of his kind), a clever talker, and
could converse fluently in English, French, and Arabic.
In fact he was a fine gentleman in appearance, attire,
and conversation. The loss of an eye gave him an
unpleasant look, which he cleverly disguised by the

use of a pair of handsome gold eye-glasses. So far he has saved his neck, and he is typical of a large and influential class of men who have extensive commercial relations, secret and open, with Zanzibar, and who will have to be reckoned with, once for all, if Africa is ever to be enlightened and free.

Twenty-eight days after landing at Zanzibar, Mr. Stanley had made all necessary preparations for his march into Africa. The work of hiring suitable men, purchasing bales of cloth, and sacks of beads, securing transport animals, and enlisting an armed escort for the party, was all new to him. Information as to the kind and quantity of stores best suited to his purpose, was difficult to obtain, and he found the toil of getting his expedition into anything like order, for the serious duties which lay before it, most exhausting to mind and body. He met with kind friends, however, at Zanzibar, who gave him what assistance they could, but from whom he carefully concealed the exact purpose of his mission, for reasons which will be given hereafter. At the American Consulate he was received with the most unrestrained hospitality by Captain Francis R. Webb, U.S. Consul, and his family, who placed their delightful residence at his disposal during the restless and anxious months which he spent in getting ready for the passage of the caravan across the straits to Bayamoyo.

How much money shall I require ?

How many pajazis (carriers) ?

How much cloth ?

How many beads ?

How much wire ?

These questions were constantly passing through

his mind as he lay meditating upon the undertaking in the sleepless watches of the night. But day by day the labour of preparation and careful provision for any possible emergency in the future (when far away from all sources of supply) went on without any cessation. He was fortunate enough to secure some recruits for his escort from amongst former followers of Speke and Grant, and he gladly availed himself of offers of service from two British seamen named Shaw and Farquhar, who appeared at the time to be a couple of smart, ready hands, and likely to be useful on the road, in a variety of ways. Arms, ammunition and uniforms were supplied to the " soldiers " of the Search Party, and they were placed under the charge of " Bombay," a favourite servant of Speke's, who ranked as Captain of the detachment. Two canvas boats were rigged and fitted by the sailors, with which to navigate the blue waters of the Tanganika Lake, should the Arabs of the district prove boorish, or disinclined to assist the expedition on its arrival in their vicinity. A cart of special design, and supposed to be just the thing to meet the peculiar exigencies of African travel, was also constructed and taken some miles on the road, when it had to be abandoned by the wayside, as a useless and troublesome piece of lumber. Guns, powder, ball, tents, medicines, coils of rope, saddles, cooking utensils, piles of boxes, flour, preserved meats, bales of cloth for barter, and for satisfying the extortionate demands of the native chiefs (who exacted a heavy tribute in kind from every caravan passing through their territories); beads, blue, white, long, round, and egg-shaped to gratify the capricious tastes of the dusky beauties of the interior, and to purchase food and shelter on the road; horses, donkeys, soldiers, and bearers—all at last were safely stowed away on board the tiny fleet of dhows, which spread its canvas to the breeze at noon on February 5th, 1871, and sailed out of port, heading straight for the mainland amid the hearty "Farewells" of a multitude of friends, who had gathered at the water-side to shake hands with Stanley and wish "Good Luck" to him and his hazardous enterprise.

The passage of the Straits, a distance of twenty-five miles, was made in ten hours, and on the day after leaving Zanzibar, the debarkation of the entire party was effected without mishap, upon the beach at Bagamoyo, the starting-point of the road into the interior. Stanley rejoiced to find himself once more on African soil. He longed now to press forward with all possible speed upon his errand of mercy. He feared that Livingstone, if alive, might hear of his arrival and deliberately keep out of his way. He had been told that the Doctor was no longer the tender-hearted, cheery missionary of former days. He had become soured by disappointment; he was morose, it was said, and taciturn, and not at all agreeable to strangers. He liked to go his own way, and he was impatient of control or even of companionship. Misled by these reports, which all turned out in the end to be unfair and untrue, Stanley felt that the obstinate old man might resent being "found" by him, and the chances were that he might not get even a glimpse of him after all, unless the real purpose of the expedition was kept a close secret till it actually arrived at Ujiji. The dreaded season of the Masika, or tropical rains, was also approaching, and this meant nothing less than a persistent downpour for something like fifty days, during which movement in any direction would be simply impossible. It was therefore necessary to get away from the coast districts as soon as a start could be effected, but two months were passed within sight of the Indian Ocean before everything and everybody could be pronounced "ship shape" and in thorough travelling trim. The stores were all repacked in one-man loads, and secured with care, and in due course the six tons of goods, which had to be conveyed inland for the use of the party, were distributed amongst the carriers, who were divided into sections of one hundred men each, and sent forward in advance of the main body. Four of these pioneer caravans, with reserve stores, were despatched after considerable difficulty and delay, and on March 21st, the *Herald* Search Expedition itself, led by Stanley, turned directly westward on the road to Ujiji. For the first few weeks, owing to the novelty of the whole undertaking, notwithstanding his natural smartness, Stanley had been very much at the mercy of the Arab middle-men and others, who helped him to engage the host of pagazis, or bearers, necessary for the transport work of the expedition ; but he soon sounded the depths of their cunning and rascality, and long before he left the coast these unprincipled sons of Ishmael found that the *Herald* Special Commissioner was more than able to hold his own with them in any scheme of plunder or fraud which they devised against him. Full of solid health, fearless of danger, impervious to despair, and deeply sensible of the importance of the mission which had been entrusted to him, Stanley did not hesitate to assume from the outset of the undertaking a tone of authority and dignified

F

responsibility towards those who were under his orders, and the result of this exhibition of spirit was soon visible in the readiness with which men offered themselves for the caravans (in spite of the uncertain nature of the services upon which they were to be employed) and in the effectual removal, one by one, of difficulties which appeared at times to threaten the success, if not the very existence, of the expedition.

The men were all in high spirits at finding themselves on the road at last, after weary months of waiting and loitering about the bunda at Bagamoyo. The streets were filled with excited crowds assembled to witness the departure of their friends and relatives for the western road. The stars and stripes led the way as the long line of men and baggage animals filed slowly out of the town and took the caravan track for Ujiji. Behind the flag marched the armed escort, with rifle and bayonet, then followed the pagazis with their loads, whilst the rear-guard was officered by the two English seamen, who had charge of the ammunition and the more valuable stores. The column was closed by " Bana Mkuba " (the big master), Stanley himself, mounted upon a superb bay horse which had been presented to him by a friendly Zanzibari. The joyous excitement of the rank and file as they wended their way out of Bagamoyo, was soon communicated to their leader, who gave himself up freely to the enthusiasm and exhilarating influences of the hour, and thoroughly sympathized with his followers in their feeling of exultation that " now they were really off." He decided to follow the course of the sun, and make directly westward by the nearest road through Ugogo and the great Arab settlement of Tabora, in the pro-

vince of Unyanyembe, for Ujiji and the shores of Lake
Tanganika, about the region of which he felt sure of
obtaining some tidings of the lost explorer. The
distance to be traversed was over 900 miles. For the
first few weeks the expedition made slow progress.
The men were unused to the painful strain and
labour which the incessant marching entailed upon
them, and the discomforts of the road in the wet season
were especially disheartening at the outset to the
Europeans amongst the party. Leaving the maritime
and unhealthy lowlands of Mrima, the favourite hunting-ground of the slave-dealers, the direct course of
the advancing column lay through the country of the
Ukweve and the Ukami, and close to the strongly
fortified citadel of Simbanwenni, the City of the Lion,
in the country of the powerful tribe of the Usequhha.
The troubles annoyances and disturbing incidents
inseparable from a journey through inner Africa, soon
began to interfere with the steady advance and to dis-
turb the discipline of the party, and it required all the
skill and courage of the resolute man who rode now at
the head, now on the flanks, and now at the rear of his
little army, encouraging, coercing, and guiding it, to
prevent, at times, a retreat of the entire body, Shaw
and Farquhar included, back to the coast. Abundant
supplies of grain and flesh food were generally obtain-
able on either side of the route, from the natives who
flocked round the camp as soon as it was pitched, for
purposes of barter and friendly intercourse, and
to hear the latest news from down country Game
abounded in the plains, and herds of red antelopes,
zebras, elephants, deer, and hippopotami were seen in
the forest glades and low marshy lands about the

river banks. The soil was found in places to be productive of vast crops of maize, cotton, sugar-cane, indigo, the orchilla-weed, melons, and grain, and for days and weeks at times the country on all sides of the advancing expedition presented exactly the appearance of a well-kept and finely timbered English park. Often, however, the surroundings were sadly and purely African. The natives were treacherous or insolently aggressive, incipient mutiny delayed the onward march and threatened the very continuance of the enterprise, and famine and fever worked frightful havoc upon the members of the expedition, without respect to race or rank. Considerable difficulty was experienced in keeping the constantly straggling divisions of the column in touch with each other, and frequent halts had to be made to trace deserters and to hunt down runaways, who would decamp coast-wise without hesitation on the first opportunity, after receiving a substantial roll of cloth as wages in advance. The horses which had been brought from Zanzibar broke down at an early stage of the journey, and Stanley reached Msuwa on foot and driving before him the ten donkeys which had escaped the perils of the forest, and attended only by one faithful follower, Mabrak the Little. The entire expedition had succumbed for the time to the hardships and difficulties of the way, and tired out with repeated halts by the road-side, and jaded beyond endurance by the desultory efforts of his followers to press on to the next halting-place, Stanley determined to advance alone! The stage had been only a short one of ten miles, but the narrow footpaths had wound and twisted for hours through a dense miasmatic undergrowth of creepers and thorny shrubs, the decayed leaves of which gave out a peculiar and powerful odour, which had the effect of a poisonous narcotic upon the men, who came one by one under its influence as they plunged into the pestiferous and reeking swamp. The straightness of the way, enclosed by walls of sharp thorny plants, armed with hooked talons three inches long, which tore the flesh open to the bone, and caught at the baggage as it was dragged along, continually necessitated the unpacking and reloading of the bales and stores, and the fatigue of this operation again and again repeated, in the fetid atmosphere of the dense jungle, at length so disheartened the carriers, as well as the escort, that they one and all absolutely refused to go on till strongly remonstrated with by their determined but well-nigh exhausted commander. Thefts of baggage, more fever, and the prospect of having to fight a way through the Ugogo country, added to the anxiety of the leader of the column, which had now become considerably weakened by desertions, discharges, and surreptitious leave-takings.

At Simbamwanni, the Lion City and capital of the Usequhha, a well-built and flourishing town of 30,000 inhabitants, and defended by substantial stone towers, walls, and gateways, a halt was decided upon. Considerable anxiety was manifested by the Simbamwannis to have a good view of the "Great Musungu" Stanley, whose fame had already preceded him, and they turned out in multitudes in their gayest attire to greet the strange foreigner who was passing through their land, and who did not buy ivory, deal in slaves, or take any interest in commercial matters, beyond seeking food and shelter at a fair price for himself and his companions in travel. The trying experiences of the past few months now began to tell even upon the robust frame of the leader of the search party, and alarming symptoms of the debilitating " mukunguro," the malarious fever of the district, rapidly manifested themselves by pains in the limbs, incapacity for exertion, and distaste for food. For the time, however, the malady succumbed to " a quantum of fifteen grains of quinine, taken in three doses of five grains each, every other hour, from seven to meridian," a somewhat sharp remedy even for a man of his extraordinary stamina, and full muscular power. One hundred and nineteen miles of the way had now been traversed in fourteen marches, which had extended over twenty-nine days, allowing a stage of a little over four and a half miles per day. The blame for this painfully slow and tedious rate of progress, lay entirely with the indolent and half-hearted Wanyamwezi porters, those masters of the art of " how not to do it," who were for ever dawdling in the rear, under the pretence of illness or bodily inaptitude for the most ordinary exertions required of them.

New sources of danger and difficulty now began to confront and threaten the caravan, and soon after leaving the pleasant and hospitable precincts of the Lion City, flooded rivers and loathsome swamps of slush and reeking morasses of black mud (filled to overflowing by the incessant rains) had to be forded, or waded through. In some places rude bridges were thrown over the foaming torrents, which had to be crossed by leaping from the bank to the submerged branches of a trunk of a tree, and then springing off the quivering foothold to the

opposite bank; but notwithstanding the 70 lbs. of
baggage which each pagazi had upon his shoulders, the
stores were generally carried over in safety and without
damage or loss. "Bombay," the trusted captain of
the escort, began at this point of the advance to develop
unfortunate signs of an unhappy tendency to lying and
dishonesty. Valuable property, entrusted to his special
care, was neglected or left behind, stores were broken
into and rifled of their contents, or secretly disposed
of to the horde of camp-followers who brought in supplies from the country round for sale to the great
"musungu." The live-stock was neglected, the fellow
had grown altogether inert and spiritless, he had
allowed whole bales of cloth to get wet and rot, he had
lost axes, powder, and arms, and, in fact, the cup of his
iniquities was full to overflowing. There was nothing
for it but to degrade the peccant captain of the escort
to an inferior rank, and to give his command to
another and more worthy soldier. Shaw, who had
been failing in health for some time, now fell sick of
fever, and could afford no real assistance as pioneer of
the band, and Stanley himself was compelled, in the
beating rain, to lead his column of disheartened and
staggering porters through swamps and lakes of
filthy mire, in which the pack-animals sank and
floundered and fell about in a hapless, helpless way,
and through which the weary pagazis struggled with
many a groan and exclamation of disgust. The foul
slush of these marshes clung to the limbs and clothing
of the disconsolate travellers as they plodded on, hour
after hour, drenched to the skin and suffering agonies
of hunger and physical distress. Where the weary
strife with the leagues of mud and unwholesome

jungle ended, the struggle with the turbid, savage torrents began. Donkeys had to be unpacked, and dragged by sheer force through the rushing streams, which filled the nullahs and turned the rivers into huge broad, boiling, wave-crested floods, and then reloaded, while the bearers with their loads lifted above their heads at arm's length, plunged into the chill waters, and made the best of their way to the further bank, half dead with fright and paralyzed with cold. Small-pox, that most terrible of African scourges, laid hold upon the soldiers of the escort, and at times it was almost impossible to get the home-sick and naturally lazy sons of the Wanyamwezi to shoulder their burdens, and once more face the long miles of water and mud which lay with an average depth of a foot or more between themselves and the next halting-place. Stanley himself fell before an attack of dysentery, brought on by the miserable plight to which these constant swamp journeys had brought him, and at one time he confesses that he despaired of living to accomplish the work which he had promised Mr. Gordon Bennett he would perform, if his life was preserved to him.

But Africa is a land of climatical as well as physical and ethnological surprises and contrasts, and the experiences of the road to Ujiji were not unfrequently pleasant enough, and even enjoyable. Blue skies overhead, and bright sparkling sunshine all about, and fertile fields teeming with tropical produce, and broad expanses of rich pastural country rising terrace above terrace, dotted over with villages, and abounding with every kind of feathered and furred game, besides wild fruits and wholesome food in endless variety, soon re-

stored the tone of the men, and sent them on their way
for the time with renewed energies and revived hopes.
The third portion of the caravan, which was sent off
from the coast in charge of Farquhar, with instructions
to get it on ahead as fast as possible, was overtaken at
Kiora, a filthy and insignificant village, where the
sailor was found incapacitated by disease, and quite
unfit to render any further service to the expedition.
In three months he was dead. The scattered sections
of the column now drew together. Laggards were
allowed to come up with the main body, and the march
was continued under the eye of Stanley himself, who
kept his depleted ranks and dispirited followers from
despair by oft-repeated promises of ample rest and
abundance of food when Ugogo, the land of plenty,
"rich with milk and honey, rich in flour, beans, and every
eatable thing, should be reached." On May 22nd the
Chungo was in sight, and the search expedition joined
the caravans of two friendly Arab traders, for mutual
strength and greater security. The whole company
made up a formidable host of about 400 well armed
men, and it was placed under the temporary generalship
of Sheik Tamid an alert and widely travelled Arab trader,
who was thoroughly acquainted with the nature of the
district to be crossed, and the rapacity and tyranny
of the native chiefs who were the "lords of the land."
A waterless tract of wilderness, thirty miles broad, had
to be traversed, and for long weary hours the vast
troop of men, soldiers and slaves, Arabs and whitemen,
with aching heads and trembling limbs, moved over
the arid plain, to the intense astonishment of magnificent herds of elands, zebras, giraffes and antelopes,
which swept over the ground at terrific speed when

disturbed by the novel spectacle of the slowly and painfully advancing caravan.

Ugogo at last! with its broad green sloping pastures, its limpid streams, and its waving, laughing fields of grain. There in the sunlight lay the long-looked-for land of plenty, gladdening the eyes and hearts of the woe-begone and famished wanderers with its richness and fertility. Huge baobabs, the elephant of the vegetable world, and resembling nothing so much as a fat stone bottle with a few twigs placed in its neck, gave evidence of the fruitfulness of the soil, and the wearied and exhausted travellers entered the streets of the town, which gives its name to the surrounding country, with exclamations of joy, and followed by a mob all ages and sexes, who fought for place in the front line of the spectators to see the white men pass along. Food to suit every taste was soon brought into the camp, bales were opened, and milk, honey, melons, pears, and ghee-nuts were eagerly offered in return for dotis of menkana cloth and strings of Sousi-Sousi beads.

The question of the due amount of the tribute to be paid to the native chiefs is always in Africa a vexed and trying one. For intolerable impudence and insatiable greed in this matter of tribute, the great men of Ugogo were, and are still unhappily, notorious, but the smart *Herald* correspondent soon learned by experience how to conduct business with these gentlemen. He was fair in his offers, and courteous in his demeanour to " the magnates of the soil;" but he was also firm in his resolution not to be over-reached by them. " Bombay " was usually employed as a sort of middle-man in the delicate and protracted negotiations which always preceded the handing over of the bales of cloth, or coils of telegraph wire, or beads which constituted the whiteman's offering, and he managed, by the skill by which he met cunning by cunning, and falsehood by mendacity, to defend the interests of his master against the combined and separate attacks of the entire nobility and royalty of Ugogo land. Under these now continually recurring demands for tribute, the tons of supplies which had been brought up the country began to be woefully lessened, and it was a serious question whether they would hold out till the reserve stores sent on to Unyanyembe could be utilized. The population on the line of march increased day by day, as the country became more fruitful, and enormous villages and broad stretches of cultivated ground gave variety and motion and life to the landscape on all sides. Game was once more plentiful everywhere, but water was scarce, and the heat of the sun intolerable, and at Mizanza Stanley was once more laid prostrate by a violent attack of fever, and the whole party had to wait for some time till he was in a condition to take to the road again. Open conflict with the covetous potentates of Ugogo was with great difficulty avoided, and at times there seemed to be no way out of the difficulty except by forcing a path to Unyanyembe, sword and rifle in hand. The expedition was now hurried on at the rate of over eleven miles a day, and at length, after endless troubles and annoyances, and much suffering, on June 23rd 1871, Tabora, the most influential and famous Arab settlement in Central Africa, and the long looked-for halting-place in the central plain of Unyanyembe, came in sight. The change which passed over the entire line of men as they caught a first view of the Arab town, with its comfortable houses and cheerful surroundings, was marvellous. Burdens were tossed from shoulder to shoulder, as if they were merely of feather weight, and the pagazis, adorned with garments of glowing hues, which they had brought up from the coast, and the escort in their well-appointed uniforms and brand new turbans of many colours, made after all a brave and imposing array, as with flags unfurled and signal guns fired in the air, they were met by a group of venerable patriarchs and headmen of the settlement who had come out to welcome them to the capital of Unyanyembe Land.

CHAPTER VI.

WITH the arrival of the search party at hospitable Unyanyembe, the first and longest stage of the journey to Ujiji was happily completed. A comfortable house was set apart for the use of Mr. Stanley, and he was soon visited by the Sultan and other notabilities, who had pleasant remembrances of Speke and Grant and Livingstone, to whom they had often been of service when they visited or passed through the district. The reserved stores, which had been kept for the road to the Lakes, were unpacked and examined; the old coast pagizis were paid off, and sent home rejoicing with gratuities of money, and extra wages in cloth and food for the way; and a new body of bearers was hired for the onward march through the Ukonongo and Uvinza country to Tanganika. But the peace of Stanley's brief rest at Unyanyembe was soon broken by rumours of war between the Arabs of the place and the tribes to the west. The road to Ujiji had been "killed" by the native chiefs, who refused permission to the caravans to travel through their territories except upon payment of an extortionate and ruinous

tribute. The enemy was reputed to be advancing
upon Tabora, thousands strong, and led by a redoubtable chief named Mirambo. Having laid waste vast
regions of country in every direction, he sent word
that he was about to fall upon the Arab settlement.

Stanley had barely recovered from the effects of a
strong attack of fever, during which he lost count of
the days as they passed, and lay in a state of total
unconsciousness for some weeks, when the whole
settlement was called out to march upon the fortified
village of the dreaded and arrogant Mirambo. Stanley determined to proceed with the Arab warriors,
and on the 29th of July, the men were mustered with
their burdens for the march to Ujiji. The Arab
troops numbered, with the soldiers of the " *Herald*
Expedition," a round total of 2255 men. The Arabs
were armed with spears, long knives, guns—flint-lock
muskets and Enfields—and they had an abundant
supply of ammunition, the *Herald* men having
sixty rounds each served out to them. The goods of
the expedition were stored in the fort of Mfuto till
after the impending battle, as the leader of the expedition had decided to press forward without further
delay as soon as the road had been opened again by
the defeat of Mirambo. The fighting-men daubed
themselves with a life-preserving unguent, made for
them by their diviners, consisting of flour and the juice
of plants. Every one was certain of a speedy victory
over the " insolent foe ;" and the public orator of the
Wanyamwezi thus addressed the panting heroes, burning for the fray: " Words ! Words !! Words !!!
Listen, sons of Mkasiwa, children of Unyamwezi !
The journey is before you, the thieves of the forest

are waiting; yes, they are thieves, they cut up your caravans, they steal your ivory, they murder your women. Behold, the Arabs are with you, El Wali of the Arab Sultan, and the white man are with you. Go, the son of Mkasiwa is with you; fight, kill, take slaves, take cloth, take cattle, kill, eat, and fill yourselves! Go!"

The assault on Zimbizo, the stronghold of Mirambo, was successful, and the victors rushed forward, howling, dancing, and shouting, in pursuit of the flying natives. But soon the tide of war was turned against Stanley and his allies. Mirambo, by a skilful piece of strategy, worthy of a European general, succeeded in driving back and overpowering the Arab forces, and a hasty and disgraceful stampede back to Tabora was inevitable; and Stanley, again prostrate with illness, narrowly escaped being abandoned by Shaw and his Arab friends, in their anxiety to save their own heads. He had gone to the help of these men from a sense of duty and in return for the kindness they had shown him, but he now felt that he had done all that could be expected of him, and he determined to pursue his own way, irrespective of the movements of the Arab levies. He decided to avoid the dominions of Mirambo altogether, and follow another road to the south, by which course he hoped to succeed in reaching Ujiji without further molestation. On August 12th, a report was brought to him that Livingstone had been met on the road to Lake Tanganika, at the exact time that he was said to have been killed on the shores of the Nyassa. The doctor was described as wearing the well-known, faded uniform cap, with the band of tarnished gold braid, and a dress made of common calico shooting. He had lost his stores in one of the smaller lagoons, and his followers had fallen away from him one by one. He was walking in company with some Arabs, and was carrying his own arms and ammunition.

Before the expedition had time to take the road, Mirambo had seized upon Tabora, slain the Sultan and chief nobles, and fired the town, to the horror and astonishment of Stanley, who was a spectator of the catastrophe from his camp at Kwihara, a few miles distant from the scene of action. Without loss of time, the refugees from the burning and ravaged settlement poured into the tembes at Kwihara, and the *Herald* Expedition was, in a few hours, ensconced behind loop-holed walls, prepared to fight to the last for bare life. Stanley had 150 men at his disposal. These he carefully posted about the compound. The ground about the enclosure was honeycombed with rifle-pits in a few hours, and, with his Winchester breech-loading repeater in his hand, the leader and his little band of watchers awaited the army of the "African Bonaparte." All obstacles which stood in the line of fire were removed; the house was provisioned for fourteen days; and there was an abundant supply of ammunition at hand. But Mirambo never came. On September 20th, the word went forth that the expedition, now completely re-organized, was to advance once more upon the road to the west. Stanley was wearied out by delay and sickness, and at length a feeling akin to desperation had come over him. He brooded in silence over the past, and depressing thoughts haunted him as to the future. The solitariness of his lot, and the wretched forecasts of the

Arabs, who assured him that in moving forward at
that time he was going to his death, the fears that
after all he had come so far on a fruitless errand, the
lassitude of body and feebleness of mind, developed
by repeated attacks of sickness, dysentery, and fever
—all these pressed upon him, till at last he cried out
to himself in the stillness of the night, "I shall not
die! I will not die! I cannot die!—and something
tells me I shall find him! FIND HIM! FIND HIM!"
He would wait no longer. Eighty-nine precious days
had been consumed at Unyanyembe. He had lingered
too long already. He defied Mirambo to do his worst.
He shook off the friendly but craven-hearted Arabs,
who offered him their counsel, and warned him of the
unknown peril he was deliberately going out to face.
Forward! was the word. The drums beat, once
more the star-spangled banner courted the breeze;
farewell volleys rang over the heads of the wondering
spectators; and the search for Livingstone recommenced. The Englishman, Shaw, who had long ago
ceased to be efficient, at length fell by the way, and
was sent back with an escort to Unyanyembe. Again
vast extents of forest were traversed, and herds of
buffalo, zebra, and antelope furnished supplies of refreshing food to the men, who found diversion and pleasure in hunting the spring-bok, or stalking the herds
of giraffe which cropped the rich herbage of the vast
alluvial plains which lay in the line of march. Some
of the wooded scenery was very beautiful. Shady
nooks, sloping down to the water's edge, resonant
with the cries of the honey-bird and other feathered
denizens of tropical glades, and adorned with graceful
creepers, the beautiful and fragrant mimosa, and the

broad lotus lily floating lazily upon the bosom of the placid stream, were frequently found along the course of the Gombe, an important tributary of the Malagarazi. On Saturday, October 7th, a serious attempt at mutiny was made by the pagazis and some of the soldiers, under the leadership of "Bombay," who had already been deposed from his rank of captain of the escort for negligence and disobedience. The loads were sullenly lifted from the ground when the signal was given for moving forward, and after a mile of the road had been covered by the murmuring throng, the whole caravan came to a standstill, and the stores were dropped upon the pathway. Stanley, ever on the alert, at once took his rifle and some buckshot cartridges from the bearer, and preparing for action by hastily looking to his revolvers, he advanced towards the turbulent crowd. The fellows at once grasped their weapons, as if to fire upon their leader. Two barrels were levelled at him as he approached. In a moment his rifle was brought to the shoulder, and he called out that the two rascals who had aimed their guns at him were dead men unless they dropped their arms. The guns were thrown down at the feet of Stanley, who saw that a crisis had been reached in the history of the expedition. The cowardly crowd of malcontents were thoroughly scared and overcome by the dauntless bearing and cool determination of their commander, and they were soon crawling about his feet, after the fashion of the East, in abject and complete submission. A free pardon was granted on the spot to all but Bombay and Ambari, the ringleaders of the rebellion. On the termination of this awkward incident, the column resumed its progress through the forest-lands of Ukonongo to Mrera, where Stanley employed his brief halt in repairing the damage done to his clothing and boots by the thorns and curved fingers of the prickly vegetation through which, for some time, the party had been pushing its way. Mrera was left behind on October 17th. Peace reigned in the ranks. Bombay and his companions in insurrection had been completely crushed. The men trusted their leader, and Stanley had once more confidence in his men. Besides, every day was now bringing them near the end of their pilgrimage. "We can smell the fish of Tanganika," they repeated to one another as they trudged hopefully and cheerily along. Behind, in the far-off waste, were Mirambo and his mighty men, and the weak-voiced and lying prophets of Tabora. The loads felt less heavy, and the way more smooth as time passed on. For was not the road to be traversed growing shorter day by day? Care had to be taken now to guard the camp by night, for the land of the lion and the leopard had been reached, and the home of the wild boar, whose savage attack was almost certain death.

Stanley now decided to make direct for Tanganika, by compass route, and then push upward to Ujiji by way of the shore. The dread that Livingstone might wilfully disappear still possessed him, and therefore he thought it best not to follow a beaten track. The stores began to fail, and food was scarce in the surrounding country, but nothing was allowed to keep back the men one moment longer than was absolutely necessary for rest and refreshment. The broad stream of the Malagarazi was crossed in safety, but one of the donkeys fell a victim to the crocodiles as it was being dragged through the stream. On November 3rd, a party of Waguhha, a trans-Tanganika tribe, suddenly met the Search Party with the latest news from Ujiji. A white man, they said, had just reached there! "A white man?" said the excited and eager chief of the *Herald* Expedition. "Yes, a white man," was the reply. "How is he dressed?" "Like the Master," they said, pointing to Stanley.

"Is he young or old?"

"He is old. He has white hair on his face, and is sick."

"Whence came he?"

"From a very far country away beyond Uguhha, called Manyuema."

"Indeed, and is he stopping at Ujiji now?"

"Yes; we saw him about eight days ago."

"Do you think he will stop there until we see him?"

"*Sigue*" (Don't know).

"Was he ever at Ujiji before?"

"Yes; he went away a long time ago."

Could there be any doubt? It was Livingstone! A forced march was decided upon, and the men readily assented to the extra labour and exertion on being promised double wages. But more "lords of the soil" had to be reckoned with, and many doti of tribute paid on that (to Stanley) terribly tedious journey of eight days to Ujiji. As soon as the voracity of one magnate was satisfied, another chief more greedy and more insolent appeared, till it again seemed to be simply a question of cleaving a way for the expedition by sheer force of arms. Bale after bale of cloth, and one sack after another of beads disappeared in the shape of tribute, and still the cry was for more, till robbed, cheated, and baffled by the cunning of the kings and princes of Uvinza and Uhha and their satellites, Stanley declared that he would be deceived no more. But there were five other chiefs still, more rapacious by far than their sable majesties of Uvinza or Uhha, still between the expedition and Ujiji. These men, if they insisted in their demands, would beggar the caravan, and consume their last remaining bales, and they would enter Ujiji in a state of complete destitution. But Stanley faced the situation. " I lit my pipe, put on my cap of consideration," he said, " and began to think. Within half an hour I had made a plan, which was to be put into execution that very night." The dreaded Wahha chiefs, who were supposed to be ready to enact, at the expense of the *Herald* Expedition, an African version of " The Spider and the Fly," were to be circumvented. At midnight the bearers and soldiers were suddenly called together, and a route was taken which carried the whole body right away out of the danger, and far from those five grasping chiefs of the Wahha. On November 10th the expedition had reached its 236th day of travel from the sea-coast, and the fifty-first of its journey from Unyanyembe and the tyrannies of Mirambo, and had now approached within six hours of Ujiji ! The spirits of these men were fresh, and their hearts light, and they all appeared to have gained new vigour of mind and body as they stepped out in the cool, bracing air with elastic tread and rapid strides over the green hills and down into the thickly-populated valleys and fruitful fields of the delightful Ukaranga country. On the top of a steep hill they saw the glistening waters of Tanganika! In the distance they could trace the swelling sides and splendid altitudes of Ugoma and Ukaramba, its guardian mountains. They stood and gazed upon the scene, where Speke and Burton had stood and gazed upon the same marvellous picture of mountain and lake and sunshine, till at length they gave vent to their feelings of awe and delight by hearty and repeated cheers. A rapid descent of the hill, a sharp movement through the Linche valley, and another climb to the summit of a narrow height, which trended westward to the lake, and at their feet lay Ujiji. Flags were flung to the wind, and the guns loaded for the signal of triumph. Hearts beat high with the intense excitement of the moment, eyes flashed, and lips quivered, as a deafening report from the expedition announced its approach to the startled village below. The people soon filled the streets, and rushed out to meet the caravan, which came proudly along, headed by the flag of America, and followed by the red ensign of Zanzibar.

" Good morning, sir," said a voice to Stanley, as with scarcely restrained emotion the leader of the expedition walked proudly along at the head of his men. He turned and saw a man dressed in Zanzibari fashion, and asked him his name. The African declared himself to be Susi, the body-servant of Dr. Livingstone. " What! " said Stanley, " is Dr. Livingstone here? "

" Yes, sir! "

" In this village? "

" Yes, sir! "

"Then go!" said Stanley, "and tell the doctor I am coming." In the excitement of the moment the *Herald* correspondent had given no name. "I see the doctor, sir," said the standard-bearer. "Oh, what an old man! He has got a white beard." Stanley made his way through the throng which crowded about him, and came to the group of Arabs, in advance of whom "stood the man with the white beard." He was tired-looking, and appeared pinched by want. He was poorly but neatly dressed, and was wearing the official cap with the gold band. The two men met at last. Stanley, not knowing what to do at the supreme moment, removed his helmet and said,—

"Dr. Livingstone, I presume?" "Yes," said the heroic old man, as he raised his hand to his cap. "I thank God, Doctor, that I have been permitted to see you," said the new comer. Livingstone replied, "I feel thankful that I am here to welcome you." [3]

The two travellers had much to say to each other. The intercourse between them was cordial and unrestrained from their first meeting in the square of Ujiji. Stanley, with commendable tact and patience, allowed the doctor to tell the story of his wanderings for the past six years in his own way. The venerable explorer was in a destitute condition, and his health had given way under the privations and difficulties which he had undergone, before he had been driven back at last upon Ujiji to obtain the necessaries of life and rest of mind and body. He stooped considerably, and he walked with the heavy tread of a tired man. Livingstone was much cheered by the letters and

[3] "How I Found Livingstone" (H. M. Stanley).

papers which the expedition had brought up for him from Zanzibar, and by the stores which were handed over to him by Stanley on behalf of his friends in England and America. But he positively refused to leave Africa, even for a brief season of refreshment and relaxation. He said he longed at times to see his motherless children—their letters made him yearn to embrace them—but he must defer the joys and pleasures of home till he had cleared up the mystery of the Tanganika watershed. The companionship of an educated and warm-hearted friend, fresh from the scenes and surroundings of European civilization, acted like a charm upon the frame and mind of the doctor. Good food, a thorough change of ideas, and the social intercourse between the two men, as well as the freedom from anxiety as to "ways and means," which he now experienced for the first time for many weary months, soon made a visible change in Livingstone's appearance, and in a few weeks he looked younger by some years than when first Stanley saw him in the midst of his Arab friends.

The doctor appears to have been the victim of adverse circumstances from the very outset of this, his last journey of exploration. He started from the coast by way of the Rovuma in March, 1866, and his troubles at once began. His men stirred up the natives against him, and refused to follow him into the interior, declaring that they were only marching to certain death at the hands of the Mazitu, a roving tribe of plunderers, much dreaded in the Nyassa region. The doctor determined to continue his journey at any cost, and to fight the Mazitu if no other alternative offered. His pagazis thereupon fled back to the coast, and invented the circumstantial report of the murder of their master, which at once startled and dismayed the whole civilized world. Livingstone, in the face of enormous difficulties, was able to explore the interesting and densely-populated kingdoms of Babisa, Bobemba, Barungu, and Lunda, of which latter territory, his friend, the renowned and gifted Cazembe, was king. By patient and thorough research, sometimes retracing his steps hundreds of miles to be quite sure of his figures, or to be perfectly accurate in the compilation of his maps, he succeeded in gradually bringing to light the wonderful physical phenomena of the great lake region westward of Tanganika and Nyassa, which had never before been explored or visited by any European geographer. Following the course of that comparatively insignificant stream, the Chambezi, which he at first was disposed to identify with his own Zambesi to the southward, Livingstone found not only that it was a distinct stream from the latter, but that it flowed westward into Lake Bangweolo, and then northward as the Luapula through the Lake Moero (named by the doctor, Webb's river), and soon after passing through Lake Kamolondo, resumed its northerly course, which the indefatigable and enthusiastic traveller was unable to trace further on account of the brutal treatment which he met with from the Arabs of the district, and the base conduct of his own bearers, who first robbed him, and then taking advantage of his enfeebled condition from chronic dysentery, deserted him, and left him to find his solitary way back, forsaken, suffering, and without stores, medicine, or means of any kind. Two months would have sufficed to enable the diligent old man to solve the problem as to whether the streams he had been following were after all the head-waters of the mighty Nile, as he fondly believed, or the sources and fountains of the Congo, as they eventually proved to be.

The weeks glided rapidly by at Ujiji, and still the wonderful story of those six years of honest toil in the heart of the Dark Continent was only half told. Stanley was anxious to see something of the great Tanganika and its magnificent surroundings, and, accordingly, the two travellers arranged to proceed to its northern end to clear up any doubt as to the course and flow of the Rusizi River, which was by some eminent geographers supposed to connect the Albert Nyanza with the broad waters of Tanganika, thus making the latter lake the *southernmost reservoir of the Nile !* The question of the Rusizi stream was therefore one of some interest to the world at large, and it was with evident pleasure, not unmixed with excitement, that the two friends set out for a canoe voyage to the mouth of the river, which emptied itself into the lake at the north-eastern corner. The passage was not without danger and loss from the thieving propensities of the boatmen and bearers, who seemed to think the doctor might be fleeced with impunity as "he did not beat them," they said, "like his white brother," of whose plan of prompt retaliation for any acts of neglect or dishonesty they had begun to entertain a wholesome dread. An inspection of the river soon settled for ever the doubt as to its character and the part it occupied in the great water system of

the region.   It was merely a sluggish and unimportant
influent of the Tanganika, and had no connection
whatever with the Albert Nyanza or the ancient and
historic Nile.   Satisfied upon this point, Livingstone
was persuaded before attempting to retrace his steps
to the banks of the Lualaba, in order to complete his
observations of that mysterious waterway, to return
with his companion to Unyanyembe, with a view to
secure fresh supplies of stores, and a band of efficient
pagazis for the prosecution of his researches through
the newly-discovered provinces in comfort and
security.

On December 27th, 1871, the search expedition said
"farewell" to Ujiji, its friendly Arabs, and its
beautiful lake, and turned eastward for Zanzibar, and
home.   The two white men travelled together; but
Stanley was responsible for the line of march, and the
conduct of the caravan.   The redoubtable Mirambo
was still a terror to the whole region between the
Nyassa and the Victoria Nyanza, and the wearisome
and irritating question of tribute would have to be
faced and dealt with once more all along the road.
But the little column was now homeward bound.
The great object for which it had been sent forth
had been fully accomplished.   Livingstone had not
only been found, but relieved, comforted, and refreshed
in mind and body, through the instrumentality of the
brave and exultant leader of the enterprise.   The
caravan was divided into two portions, one party
following the path along the shore, and the other
proceeding by canoe southward over the blue waters
of the lake.   The songs of the men rang over the
rippling surface of the great inland sea, and sounded

far away amongst the crags and woods of the surrounding hills. The boats shot swiftly forward, impelled by the strong arms of the willing and light-hearted pagazis, who chanted extemporized odes as they floated along, in which they extolled the valour and prowess of their chief, and the delights of home.

Shaw, poor fellow, had died of fever at Unyanyembe, some time after returning there. This and other news of a disquieting nature met the returning party, and damped their spirits or checked their expressions of joy for the moment. But onward and eastward was the order of the day. Some capital sport—giraffe, zebra, antelope and other game falling to the rifle of Stanley—enlivened the journey. Letters and papers sent on from Zanzibar were eagerly opened and read. On February 18th, 1872, Stanley and Livingstone reached Unyanyembe, after travelling 750 miles in company, and here it was agreed—to the sorrow of both—that duty compelled them to part.

One hundred and thirty-one eventful days had passed since the search expedition had set out from Kwihara, determined in spite of every obstacle to force the road to Ujiji, and it had marched during that period a distance of considerably over 1200 miles. Livingstone was made comfortable for the first time for some years in the house set apart for his use, with ample leisure to write up his journals, arrange his notes, and overhaul the bales of cloth and number-less packages of all sorts and sizes which he found awaiting him. Letters of grateful thanks were written by him to Mr. Gordon Bennett, Jun., and more formal despatches were prepared for the Foreign Office, and the President of the Royal Geographical

Society. In these the aged explorer expressed himself as having been much helped and cheered by the presence and kindly attention of Mr. Stanley, and gave an outline of his work in the past, and his plans for the future. With these documents in his charge, and a package of private notes and diaries for the doctor's own relatives, Mr. Stanley took what proved to be a last farewell "of his illustrious companion." On the evening of March 13th they sat together, face to face, in the doctor's quarters. "To-morrow night, Doctor," said Stanley, "you will be alone!" "Yes," was the reply, "the house will look as though a death had taken place."

At daylight on March 14th, the caravan mustered in line, and the signal for the march was given. "Doctor," said Stanley, "now we must part—there is no help for it. Good-bye!" "O! I am coming with you a little way," said the lonely old man. And still the two wandered on in company.

"Then am I to understand, Doctor, that you do not return home till you have satisfied yourself as to the 'Sources of the Nile,'" said the departing traveller. "When you have satisfied yourself, you will come home and satisfy others. Is it not so?"

"That is it exactly," said Livingstone.

"How long do you think the work will take you?"

"A year and a half at the furthest," was the reply. And then the parting came.

"Good-bye, and God guide you safe home and bless you, my friend," said Livingstone.

"May God bring you safe back to us all, my dear friend. Farewell!" said Stanley; and the two most adventurous African explorers of our time thus parted in the heart of the great continent, never to greet each other again in the flesh.[4] Stanley confessed that the pathos of the hour overcame him. He could with difficulty restrain his emotion. His heart went out after the old man he was leaving behind. He turned and looked after the bowed figure. He waved his handkerchief, Livingstone responded by lifting the gold-braided cap, and a swell of the ground hid him at once from view. The party were soon once more well within the territory of the rapacious lords of Ugogo, and careful watch was kept on the road through the forests and almost impenetrable jungle, which afforded ample opportunities for the secretion of ambuscades, or the execution of foul deeds of treachery. No event of importance marked the course of the expedition, however, through Ugogo land. There were the usual attempts at extortion, under the guise of asking for the customary tribute, but these attempts were habitually and triumphantly foiled. Threats of enforcement of the kingly dues were met by prompt preparations for the defence of the bales and baggage of the stranger. Stanley by this time had mastered the secret of dealing with this vexed question of "taxes." As the caravan approached the coast, it was more than once in considerable peril from the Masika, with its angry floods, surging nullahs, and ceaseless downpour. The whole district of the Mukondokwa River, along which lay the road to the sea, was sounding with the noise of the rushing waters, and the men fled before the inundating tide, as from a hungry and overwhelming flood. These "perils by

[4] "How I Found Livingstone" (H. M. Stanley).

water" nearly proved fatal to the most precious treasure which Stanley's men conveyed. The tin box in which Livingstone's journals of his researches in the trans-Tanganika land were preserved, and his letters for home, was being conveyed across a hideous raging torrent upon the head of Rojab, a stalwart young negro. In the centre of the river, the bearer, unable longer to resist the force of the current, which foamed and eddied about him, fell headlong into the seething waters. He staggered to his feet, however, still retaining his hold upon the priceless casket. "Look out," shouted Stanley, from the shore, "drop that box, and I'll shoot you." The men stood gazing with intense interest upon the scene. Rojab gave one manful leap forward and safely reached the bank with the contents of the box intact and uninjured. Onward again through rain and mud, and swamps, to the "Lion City" of the Useguhha. It was found that the wall of the town had been swept down and at least 100 of the inhabitants drowned by the sudden swelling of the river, which flowed past the citadel. Signs of ruin and devastation—the work of the floods—were visible on all sides. Entire towns were washed away with all their cattle, crops, and people in some districts; and it was computed that over 100 villages had been destroyed by the waters in one valley alone near the Ungerengeri River. The people had retired to rest as usual, when they were suddenly startled by the crashing of what they (at first) thought to be thunder. When fully aroused and able to take in the facts, they were appalled to see a solid wall of water sweeping down upon them, and carrying trees, houses, and everything before it.

More jungle and swamps reeking with nauseous odours, and foul with the poisonous exhalations from the thick black mud and rotting vegetation. Malaria in the atmosphere, "hot-water ants" in the dust, boas above, venomous snakes and scorpions gliding about the feet—these were some of the minor annoyances of this portion of the homeward way. But is not that Bagamoyo? and are not those the houses of the tiny port from which the weary wanderers are to take passage over sea to Zanzibar and home? The signal blast, which tells of the return of the party, brings out a crowd to welcome back the gallant expedition which enters Bagamoyo, conscious of success, and waving in triumph the tattered banner which had headed the column to Ujiji and back. On the evening of the 7th of May, 1872, the people of Zanzibar went forth to greet the man who had "found Livingstone." The news of his success had already passed, with lightning speed, all along the coast. Worn and wasted by the trials and worries he had undergone, he was for the moment unrecognized by his most familiar friends in Zanzibar. "How are you, Captain Fraser?" said the returned traveller to an old acquaintance he met in the street, immediately after his arrival. "You have the advantage of me, sir," the gentleman replied, and jokingly added when Stanley gave him his name, "that he believed it was another Tichborne affair." Yet he had been absent only about thirteen months.

Abundant supplies of goods, and fresh recruits for Livingstone's party were sent off without delay to Unyanyembe. Wages were paid, and rewards bestowed upon the men who through the strange vicissitudes of the past had been faithful to their leader. Breaches of discipline and outbreaks of temper were forgotten or forgiven. The serious, and, at times, disastrous failings of " Bombay " even, were no longer remembered against him, and the *Herald* Search Expedition ceased to exist. On May 29th, Mr. Stanley left Zanzibar for England by the steamship *Africa*, which landed him with other passengers at Mahé, the chief port of the Seychelles. He missed the mail to Aden by twelve hours, and was detained in consequence for a month till the next vessel touched at the islands. At Aden he took passage in the *Mei-Kong* to Marseilles, where he was met by the correspondent of the *Daily Telegraph* and other friends, who told him " what they said in England " as to his latest and most successful exploit. On August 1st the official documents entrusted to Mr. Stanley by Livingstone were duly handed in at the Foreign Office, and the papers and journals, so long and so jealously guarded, were forwarded to the relatives of the Doctor, who expressed in the warmest terms their appreciation of the splendid services which the *Herald* search party had rendered to their illustrious relative. The Gold Medal of the Royal Geographical Society was conferred upon Mr. Stanley, who was entertained at a complimentary banquet by that learned body, and on August 27th, Earl Granville in the name of the Queen conveyed to him " Her Majesty's high appreciation of the prudence and zeal which he had shown in reaching Dr. Livingstone, and relieving her Majesty from the anxiety which, in common with her subjects, she had felt with regard to the fate of that distinguished traveller." The thanks

of the Queen were also expressed for the service he
had rendered, and her Majesty congratulated him upon
the success of the mission which he had so fearlessly
undertaken. A magnificent gold snuff-box, with the
Royal monogram in brilliants, accompanied the letter,
as a memorial of the great and arduous enterprise
which he had so ably conducted with the most gratifying results.

CHAPTER VII.

In the summer of 1873 the people of England were
startled by the news from Western Africa that the
forces of King Coffee, the potent monarch of the
Ashantees, had crossed the Prah. This river forms
a natural line of division between the territory protected by the British, and the region governed by
independent sovereigns or chiefs. The invaders
had suddenly burst upon the Protectorate, which
was inhabited by the Fantees, the Accru, the Crepee,
Aquamoo, Assin, Agoona and Ahanta tribes, who
were dwelling in unity with the authorities of
the British Government, and had without warning
cried "havoc, and let slip the dogs of war,"
amongst the craven-hearted allies of England,
who fled before their implacable foes, without even
attempting to make a stand in defence of their
lives or property. Goaded beyond endurance by the
despicable treatment, which the young and ambitious
Ashantee prince declared he had received at the
hands of the English officials at Cape Coast Castle,
and annoyed at the sale of the important fort and
town of Elmina to the British by the Dutch in 1872,

he had secretly summoned to his aid an army of rude and untrained levies, 40,000 strong, and having taken an oath in the most solemn Ashantee form to drive the white men into the sea, his generals with admirable strategy fell upon the " protected friendlies " at three distinct points at the same moment. Nine months elapsed before any adequate force could be brought to bear upon the marauders, and they were with difficulty kept from advancing into the immediate vicinity of the fortress and guns at Cape Coast, by the activity and courage of Lieut.-Col. Festing, R.M.A., the officer in charge of the military operations, pending the arrival of the Commander-in-Chief, who was daily expected from England. Festing had come off victorious in more than one sharp brush with the " insolent foe," on the banks of the Prah and in the bush about Elmina, and had effectually kept in check the adventurous troops of the sable monarch of Coomassie, and in some instances had driven them back with heavy losses across the river into their own territory. The scattered battalions re-formed, however, and armed with rude old-fashioned muskets, loaded with shells, stones, iron slugs or other primitive missiles thrown into the barrels of the weapons, and fired without wadding or ramming, they created terrible consternation amongst the feeble Fantees and their neighbours of the Protectorate. Villages were burnt, cattle and grain and property of all kinds carried off, and the people slaughtered without mercy by the Ashantee hordes who sought to retake Elmina, and reduce the " friendly " natives from their allegiance to the British crown by an overwhelming display of military power. For the safety of the great commercial centres upon the Coast, as well as for the preservation of the peace of the Protectorate, it was necessary that a British Army should, with as little delay as possible, take the field, and reduce King Coffee and his legions to submission. Sir Garnet Joseph Wolseley was chosen by the Home Government as the chief of the expeditionary force, and it was decided that Cape Coast Castle, the most accessible port on the Gold Coast, should be the base of the military operations which might be necessary to bring the aggressive monarch to take a right view of his position. A spasm of something like dread passed through the army of Great Britain, when it was seen that war with the Ashantees was imminent, not from any fear of the enemy, for that the British soldier has never known —but a sense of terror at the gruesome horrors of the generally unhealthy and pestilent locality, which was to be the scene of action. The West Coast was known with too much reason as "the white man's grave," and, probably, in no part of the habitable globe has malaria done its deadly work upon the European so rapidly and so effectually, as upon the surf-beaten shores of the West African sea-board.

The Gold Coast Colony extends along the Gulf of Guinea, from 2° 40′ W. to 1° 10′ E. of Greenwich, reaching inland only for about 50 miles, and embracing an area of about 16,620 square miles, with a polyglot and semi-barbarous population of something like 520,000. The whole region was once a province of the Dutch, who still held some stations on the coast up to April 6th, 1872, when, by virtue of a private agreement on April 6th, 1872, the entire tract of coast-line became the property of the British crown. As far back as 1672 a number of factories had been established at various spots throughout the country, notably at Secondee, Accra, Winnebut, and Anamaboe, by the famous Royal African Company, which was succeeded in 1750 by the African Company, which received the sanction of Parliament to establish commercial relations with all the native tribes of Western Africa residing within the territory bounded by 20° N., and 20° S. lat. In 1821, the colony of Sierra Leone was empowered to take over these settlements, which had become crown property, and in 1874 the new colony of the Gold Coast, including the island of Lagos, was established with independent jurisdiction over the whole of the country bordering on the Gulf of Guinea. Gold is the chief export of the region, the productions of which are almost entirely absorbed by the English markets, and consist of ivory, gum copal, monkey-skins, palm-kernels, and oil extracted from a species of palm which flourishes abundantly on this coast.

The gold is found in the form of dust in the sand of the numerous streams, or in the beds of the mountain torrents, mixed with red mud and gravel, and is carefully extracted by the natives by a tedious process of washing by hand. The principal settlements of the colony are Cape Coast Castle, the seat of the Government, Elmina, desired by King Coffee, as a place where "his ancestors had from ancient times eaten and drank at their pleasure," Accra, the actual capital, Axim, and Dixcove. The public revenue reaches 198,817*l.* Its total exports to the

United Kingdom are of the yearly value of 400,000*l.* The island and port of Lagos, which is an appendage of the colony, is a territory of some importance in the Bight of Benin. It comprises the north coast of the Gulf of Guinea from 2° 50′ to 4° 30′ E. long., and has a population (chiefly coloured) of 75,000 people, who are actively engaged in the export of lead ore, indigo, and camwood, all salable native products, and valued at about 500,000*l.* per annum. The climate of the entire maritime district between the Atlantic and the mountains of the Kong is most enervating and deleterious to European constitutions. The malarious exhalations from the densely-wooded swamps and river-courses, and the presence of vast areas of stagnant and fetid marsh-land, from which the subtle fever poison is incessantly being distilled or thrown off into the warm damp atmosphere, contribute to make the colonies of Western Africa without exception the most insalubrious foreign possessions held by Europeans in any part of the globe. The season of danger is from May to November, when epidemics of fever and dysentery prevail with more or less virulence. The vegetation of the region is prolific and distinctly tropical. Dense, impenetrable forests—every variety of the great palm family, the sugar-cane, india-rubber tree, the ginger plant, the mangrove—all these are found to give character and charm to the prospect, as the traveller wends his way over the umbrageous and immeasurable wilds and tracts of bush and woodland between the coast and the distant heights of the Kong range. The chief imports are articles useful for barter with the natives, and consist of old uniforms, muskets, gaudy calicoes and prints, crockery of vivid hues, cutlery, glass-ware, beads, boots, odds and ends of European costume and adornment, tobacco, kerosine, gunpowder and shot, hats, flour, spirits and wine. Gin and rum are greedily demanded by the whole of the population, and the demoralization brought about by the wholesale distribution of alcohol in these forms amongst the Fantees is becoming a grave public scandal, for the native races are being decimated by the fiery poison. The stuff (i.e. the damaged or badly manufactured spirit) is brought to "The Coast" to be bartered for native produce. The story is a simple one. The native villages soon become scenes of frightful havoc and misery, crime in its most revolting forms is fearfully increased, the worst passions of the savage are aroused by the stimulant, and like a hideous epidemic, far more terrible than the malaria in its effects, both physical and moral, the drink craze sweeps over the land till it invades the remotest corners of Inner Africa. A passion for intoxicants is spreading with terrible rapidity over the continent, and in cases where the native authorities, keenly alive to the fate which awaits them, have protested against the importation of the "slayer of men," their pathetic appeals have been unheeded by the most humane and Christian nation in the world. From the north to the south a flood of spirit is poured into the territories of the native chiefs, and in Fantee-land alone whole villages may be found in a state of blind intoxication—chiefs, people, women and children, all in a state of indescribable filth, and hideous frenzy—born of the fire-water of the white man. In one district more than 10,000 barrels

of rum were distributed amongst half-a-million of
people in one year!

On November 1st, 1873, Mr. Stanley, as special
correspondent of the *New York Herald*, landed at
Cape Coast Castle, and at once attached himself to
the press contingent, which included Mr. Henty of the
Standard, and Mr. Melton Prior of the *Illustrated
London News*, and which was prepared to start for
the interior with the General and his staff at an hour's
notice. But the order to advance was delayed again
and again, and weary weeks were spent upon the
coast and in sight of the Atlantic before everything
was ready for the start upon Coomassie. Sir Garnet
Wolseley, the youngest General on the roll of the
British army, and the Commander-in-Chief of the
forces on the Gold Coast, had already achieved high
distinction in his profession, and he looked every inch
a soldier. Trim and quick, rather short of stature and
spare of habit, cool and reticent, but at the same time
courteous and agreeable in manner—he seemed to be a
General "to go anywhere and do anything." Mr.
Stanley was very much disposed to act the part of
candid friend to the general throughout this enterprise.
The brilliant soldier had provoked to bitterness the
restless and eager " newspaper man " by his harsh
remarks upon special correspondents in his " Soldier's
Pocket Book," a manual written for military men of
every rank, and a work which is acknowledged on all
sides to be by far the best of its kind. Sir
Garnet had not hesitated to write down the " war
specials " as the " curse of modern armies," " drones,"
and "a source of constant trouble and annoyance" to the
responsible authorities in the field. Stanley, however,

was generous in his wrath, and from the first day of the campaign freely bestowed upon the general the commendation which was due to him for the splendid and careful manner in which he handled his troops, and led them through a difficult and unknown country to final and complete success. Mr. Gordon Bennett had supplied the representative of the *Herald* with a small but powerful steam-launch for use upon the shallow rivers of the coast, or for the ascent of the Prah, in the event of the river route being decided upon as involving less fatigue to the troops. *The Dauntless*, as Stanley called his yacht, was soon brought into requisition, and proved of good service in a trip which the "war specials" made in company to the River Volta, the scene of the operations of Commissioner J. H. Glover, who was preparing to invade Ashantee simultaneously with Sir Garnet, along the course of the Volta, a stream of considerable volume, reaching right up into the territory of King Coffee, and offering magnificent facilities for the passage of troops. The commissioner received the press men with marked cordiality, was frank and open as to his movements and intentions, and gladly offered them the hospitality of his camp, which was located at Addah Fort, a cool, shady spot, environed by groups and clusters of palms, and surrounded by an undulating tract of country, covered with low bush and jungle, redolent with the perfume of the orchid and the African lotus flower, and offering even at mid-day a leafy and pleasant retreat from the fiery blaze of the tropical sun. It had been decided to enlist from amongst the Houssas, an active negro and Mohammedan tribe, a regiment of men to march into Ashantee, by the Volta route, and Glover, who had a remarkable reputation amongst the natives of the coast, was engaged in organizing the force. Glover's movements were all marked by that decision and completeness which pertain to the man of capacity. Everybody appeared to be busy getting up men and stores to the first halting-place on the river, which, for the deadly mephitic atmosphere and miasmatic surroundings of its estuary cannot be equalled in Africa. A great deal of sickness prevailed, but the preparations for the ascent of the Volta by the gallant little Houssa force were pushed bravely on, and in spite of the fact that Glover had only about ten officers at his disposal for a force of some 23,000 men, he was up and away long before the general commanding had reached his first camp on the road to the Prah. The dashing leader of the Houssa and Accra levies was a naval officer, and had already served his country with courage and high distinction. In 1863 he was selected by the Home Government for the responsible post of Administrator at Lagos, where he succeeded in elevating a miserable, profitless territory of swamp, peopled by a spiritless and unenterprising race, into one of the most remunerative and energetic British colonies on the coast. For his distinguished services in this capacity he was rewarded by the thanks of the heads of the Colonial and War Departments, and in 1873 he was appointed special Commissioner to the friendly native chiefs in the eastern districts of the protected territory of the Gold Coast. He engaged and defeated the Aboonah tribes, in December, 1873, and he will always be lovingly remembered by the natives in West Africa, who, in the words of one of their number thus expressed their high estimation of his character and ability: "English officers very good, sir, but they no Capitain Golibar,"—the native pronunciation of Glover. The force assembled at the mouth of the Volta consisted of representatives of various "friendly tribes," who, through the personal influence of Glover and his subordinates had been induced to send their best fighting-men to aid their English allies in the subjugation of the haughty and ill-advised Ashantee king.

The English troops were in due course landed upon the coast, and they presented a magnificent appearance as they filed up from the shore to the martial strains of the "British Grenadier" and "The Campbells are Coming." First in order marched the renowned 42nd Highlanders—known to fame as the Black Watch—and distinguished by the sombre hue of their tartan, then followed the 23rd Fusiliers, and the smart-looking business-like brigade of Royal Rifles, with a small but compact and highly disciplined naval force under the command of one of the most popular officers in the service, Captain Hewett, V.C., brought up the rear. On January 6th, 1874, the baggage was packed and sent off upon the lusty shoulders of gangs of Fantee bearers, and soon the column was advancing northward, along the broad path which the pioneers had cleared to the front for the passage of the expedition. The journey to Coomassie, a distance of 140 miles, was to be broken by frequent halts, and every precaution was taken to keep the men well provisioned and to provide them with ample and comfortable quarters on the road. The field-telegraph followed the line of march, and to the inspiriting music of the

military bands, the little army, full of confidence and
"eager for the fray," struck into the low thick bush
which clothed the country on all sides with its deep
green umbrageous and impenetrable thickets as far
as the eye could reach. The stations were about
nine miles apart, and at each halt the soldiers found
carefully-prepared sleeping-huts, a good supply of
water, stores, and abundant rations awaiting them as
they tramped in weary with the tropical heat, and
unrefreshing atmosphere of the narrow, airless path,
arched by the tree-tops, which they had traversed
during the day. As the expedition penetrated more
deeply into the interior of Fantee-land, the forest
changed from a solid mass of underwood and bush to
nobler proportions, and palms, tamarinds, cotton-
woods, and wide-spreading teaks, shot up towards the
sky in rich profusion, affording an agreeable variety
to the somewhat depressing uniformity of the
vegetation in the neighbourhood of the coast. So far
the line of march had been unbroken by any formidable difficulties in the physical conformation of the
region which had been crossed. Broad stretches of
country, thickly covered everywhere with patches of
jungle, and groves of rank tropical vegetation, which
never rose to any considerable height, and rivulets
which in the dry season were easily fordable, were the
chief natural characteristics of the way. Stanley's appearance at the camp at Barraccoy, the seventh station
on the way to the Prah, as he rode up, mounted upon a
solemn-looking mule, was, he says, a matter of great
amusement to Jack-a-shore, and his ship-mates, the
marines of the fleet. "Why?" asks the *Herald*
correspondent, "do sailors always find the sight of a

mule provocative of mirth?" The solution of the problem no doubt lies in the odd contrast between the never-relaxing gravity of the animal, and the overflowing tide of good spirits and boisterous fun with which the genuine son of the sea appears to be endowed. The Naval Brigade was the life and soul of the entire column. The portion of the camp occupied by the sailors rang constantly with the loudest laughter, and their camp-fire meetings were the liveliest and most pleasurable of all the social gatherings which brightened and cheered the way to Coomassie. Immeasurable tracts, covered by valuable woods and extensive areas of rich, productive soil well suited to the growth of heavy crops of cotton, maize and sugar, gave unmistakable evidence of the capacity of the territory to become in good hands a wealthy and remunerative province. In the hands of the Fantees and the other tribes who occupy the Protectorate the land is little better than a desert. Here and there a village was seen, with its tiny patch of badly cultivated ground near; but, for utter worthlessness and want of any redeeming quality, the lazy, rum-loving, superstitious and degraded Fantee seems to excel any other tribe on the West African Coast. Foul and coarse of person, darkened in mind, unpleasant in habit, and given over to the lowest form of grovelling fetich-worship, the Fantee of to-day, in spite of his long intercourse with the white man, is a sorry spectacle. The medicine-man is all-powerful, and carries on his horrid mummery over the sick-beds of the natives of Cape Coast Castle, with the same assurance as did his ancestors two hundred years ago, when the English power first established itself upon this coast. So much for the march of civilization in North-Western Africa and Fantee-land! The work of bridging the broad swelling waters of the Prah was at once undertaken by Major Home and his active bands of pioneers, and in a few days a broad, substantial road was carried across the stream which divided the Protectorate from the enemy's country. On the 2nd of January the commander-in-chief arrived to lead his troops into the hostile territory. The real work of the column was now about to commence in downright earnest. No one could tell what complications an hour might bring forth, and officers and men were on the alert for more tidings of the Ashantees, who were known to be in considerable force not many miles off. At daybreak on the 2nd, a stir was noticed in the bush on the Ashantee bank, and some natives were seen to emerge from the thicket, making overtures of peace. They were brought across the river, and proved to be a party of ambassadors, led by the town-crier of Coomassie, who was amply distinguished by a broad metal plate suspended from his bare shoulders. The messengers had been sent by King Coffee to ask particulars of the outrages which, he maintained, his people had recently met with at the hands of the Europeans of the coast. He professed the most amicable intentions towards the English, and asked for detailed information as to the purpose of this visit in force of Sir Garnet and his army! Was this Ashantee prince a mere simpleton or a finished statesman of the first rank? Sir Garnet was fairly puzzled by this royal and studiously inoffensive missive. Meanwhile councils were held at which the document was discussed with due gravity and caution. The reply was, however, brief and to the point. The invasion of Fantee-land had been regarded by the British Government as a breach of its treaty with the Ashantee monarch, and as a declaration of hostilities on the part of the king, who also kept Europeans in a state of miserable captivity at his royal town of Coomassie. Sir Garnet demanded the release of the prisoners, an ample indemnity for the injury and outrage done to the "friendlies" of the Protectorate, and the formal ratification of a new treaty which would give security for the future good conduct of the Ashantee people. At the same time the commander of the British troops gave his Majesty of Ashantee to understand that unless hostages were sent into the camp, with a definite understanding to accede to the terms proposed, the expedition would press forward and invest Coomassie without delay. The Rev. W. Kuhne, of the German Mission, who had passed a wretched existence of over five years in the capital of King Coffee, as a prisoner of state, suddenly reached the station on the Prah, in a deplorable condition of health on January 14th, bringing the latest news from the head-quarters of the enemy. He described the young monarch as not without capacity, but utterly in the hands of his chiefs and ministers, who deceived and cajoled him by the basest and most contemptible servility and obsequiousness. "Mighty! King of Kings! Great All-Powerful! Chief of the great men of the earth! Who is like unto the King of the Ashantees?" were the epithets by which he was addressed in public as well as in private by his sycophantic followers, and the final voice of the people being for war to the death

with the invaders of the sacred soil guarded by
the blue waters of the Prah, to the great delight
and intense relief of every man, officer or private,
in the advancing column, the ultimate decision of
the infatuated king was given for an active and
immediate resistance to be offered to any further
progress of the British through his territory.

So far the progress of the avenging host had been
without any incident of importance. The Fantee
porters had distinguished themselves, on more than
one occasion, by flinging down their loads and vanish-
ing into the remotest thickets of the forests which
bordered the road, at the slightest hint or whisper of
the approach of the enemy.

The Press tent had been the scene of many enjoyable gatherings, and the camp on the southern bank
of the Prah had been considerably enlivened by
the arrival of the 2nd West Indian Regiment, one of
the finest coloured body of troops in her Majesty's
service. The dress of the corps is a smart Zouave
uniform, a gay turban, with long tassel and white
gaiters. The men looked a fine, well-formed set of
fellows, and they soon won the admiration of everybody in camp by their cheery loyalty and light-hearted-
ness. With the disposition of the various sections
of the expedition, as well as with the details of the
transport and commissariat services, Mr. Stanley
took occasion frequently in his letters to complain.
He did not hesitate to give his own view of these
matters, and his criticisms of the General were as
severe, at times, as they were able. But Sir Garnet
appeared to be impervious to provocation, and a perfect master of the art of keeping his own counsel.

I

His reticence as to his intentions from day to day was always a source of great annoyance to the "gentlemen of the Press," and his sphinx-like silence as to the Plan of Campaign sometimes inspired some very sharp sentences in the letters of the *Herald* correspondent and his fellow-campaigners to the home journals. The possible intentions of the Ashantee king were often the subject of anxious discussion by the camp-fires on the banks of the Prah. The fear was that, after all, he might show the white feather, and send back a conciliatory reply to the stern ultimatum of the General. In that case peace would follow, and the order to tramp back to the coast would be given at once, so as to avoid the approaching wet season, if possible. The prospect of a peaceable solution of the quarrel with King Coffee distressed the expedition, as all were now anxious for a fight and a march upon the Ashantee capital. Speculation ran high as to the amount of loot which would be found in the royal palaces and secret treasure villages, and visions of houses stored with ivory, bags heavy with gold dust, or the precious metal in nugget form, and abundance of treasure of all kinds—silks, jewels, and precious stones of rare size and beauty—floated before the eyes of the troops as they prepared for their departure from the banks of the Prah. Some of the stories recounted for the amusement of the men in their hours of relaxation, after the heavy duties of the day were over, were amusing enough. Now and then a nervous soldier on his solitary "sentry-go" in the still watches of the night, would be startled by sounds and sights which, in the broad daylight, would appear to be harmless and even commonplace, and many a hearty laugh was raised at the expense of one of the youthful and inexperienced recruits of the Rifles, who had been placed on duty in rather a lonely and secluded spot in the forest. All went well through the still hours of midnight, till suddenly there issued from the underwood a cry of the most blood-curdling and startling nature. It died away and revived in the strangest manner, and the bewildered soldier, with trembling knees and blanched cheek, was almost beside himself with terror. To fire into the wood and arouse the whole of the sleeping regiments around him was too serious a step to take without further inquiry, and the only alternative was to stand at the ready with fixed bayonet, and receive the mysterious foe, be he man or beast, at the charge. On the officer visiting the point to relieve guard, the valiant son of Mars was discovered with his bayonet unsheathed, and in a state of considerable excitement, which he thus explained: "If you plaze, zur, there's some snake of a wild baste a-constantly screaming close by here. Divil a bit has he stopped since oi have been standing here, and oi'm thinking the crathur can't be far off. Sure, the divil must be in him. So oi just fixed my sword for him to give him some cold steel." The cause of the poor fellow's terror was discovered to be a lemur, a tiny, harmless creature, something less in size than a rabbit, and the joke of the man who stood at the charge to receive the attack of a lemur was long remembered. The story of the sergeant who was nearly frightened out of his wits, after an evening spent in conviviality in the blaze of the hospitable camp-fire, is worth repeating as showing the peculiar effect of the odd sounds and sights which prevail at night in an African forest expedition, upon the highly-strung nerves of the excited soldiers. The time was, of course, the middle watch of the night. The place, a lonely spot overshadowed by wood, and dark as a wolf's throat. The chief actor in the scene, a brave non-commissioned officer of the sharpshooters. "Caution, my boy," said the soldier to himself, as he cocked his pistol, "who can tell what may happen to a fellow in such an unchristian land?" Crash, bang, a rush and a tumble, and then all was silence again. He peered into the gloom with dilated eyes, and thought he saw steadily advancing towards him a monstrous animal of strange and startling aspect. He could not alarm the camp, he feared to retreat, and nothing remained for him but to proceed with his weapon in his palsied hand, pointed straight at the head of the terrible brute, which now appeared to be making a dead set at the horror-stricken soldier. He had heard gruesome accounts from his comrades of the hideous beasts to be met with in the solitudes of the jungle, and he felt that in a few moments he would probably be engaged in the death-grapple with the ravenous man-slayer silently stealing upon him. At length the strain upon the nervous system was too much for the agonized man, and he screamed in accents of terror, "I say, Bill, Dick, Tom, for God's sake hurry up and show a light here, for some awful brute is on my track! Quick, for mercy's sake! the thing is about to attack me!" Rushing out to the succour of their comrade, whom they expected to find face to face with a tiger, or a jackal at least, they found him confronting a mule!

As a diplomatist King Coffee was a failure. He

had met his match in the youthful but sagacious leader
of the English forces, who lost no time in throwing
his tiny legion of brave men across the Prah, and
marching direct upon Coomassie. Seventy-four miles
of road had been covered from the coast to the camp
upon the river side, the health of the troops had been
fairly good, in the face of the most trying climate in
the world, the entire force was animated by a glowing
enthusiasm and an increasing desire to be brought
face to face with the Ashantee levies, and the rank
and file to a man entertained a feeling of admiration
for their General, who, despite his years, had shown
himself to be the possessor of all the varied qualities
which combine to make a successful leader in such an
enterprise as that in which they were engaged. Reinforcements were ordered up to the front, a careful
disposition of the regiments at his disposal was made
by Sir Garnet, and, headed by Major Baker Russell,
of the 13th Hussars, and his native contingent, the
advance into the enemy's country began.

CHAPTER VIII.

THE road to the capital of Ashantee-land lay almost
directly north of the river. It was decided to make
nine halts on the route of 78½ miles to the royal city.
The country in advance was carefully examined by a
party of scouts under Lord Gifford, whose valour and
discretion in this campaign secured for him the
gratitude of his sovereign and the unstinted admiration of his companions-in-arms.

On the 19th of January, 1874, the Press party
left the Prah, and they were quickly followed by the
commander-in-chief, who was escorted by the seamen
of the fleet and the Rifle Brigade. For days the
march was continued through the dense jungle of the
Trans-Prah-land. On all sides the eye was met by
the thick, heavy, unlovely foliage, which exhibited no
variety of colour to lend even a momentary interest
to the scene.

The presence of a hostile force was now looked for
day by day. The advanced post of one division of
the Ashantee army had been reached by the
indefatigable Gifford and his plucky band of scouts;

but Foumannah, the chief town of the tributary
kingdom of the Adansi, was occupied without a
struggle. Here, for the first time, the members of
the expedition were able to gain some knowledge of
the manners and customs of the natives of the
country. The houses appeared to be well built, with
stout mud walls, ingeniously covered over with
delicate patterns, wrought upon a pure white material
resembling the choicest marble. The contrast
between the neat and cleanly-kept domiciles of the
Ashantees and the miserable rude huts of Fantee-
land and the Protectorate was most striking. In the
former, rooms were set apart for the uses of the
various divisions of the family, and food, utensils, and
other household articles were usually kept in a
separate apartment. The dwelling-rooms were lofty
and well ventilated by recesses in the walls opening
to the air and light, and a dado of rich red covered
the walls for a distance of several feet from the
floor, which was usually painted to correspond in
colour with the dado. The wood-carving, iron-work,
and cleverly designed patterns worked out upon the
walls of the residences of the great men of Adansi,
clearly proved that the people were by no means without taste and skill, and that, like many of the African
tribes, they are gifted with great powers of imitation,
and able to produce marvels of mechanical art with
the rudest and simplest tools.

A surprise was in store for Sir Garnet at Foumannah
which threatened at one time to cause a rearrangement
of his plans. The intelligence reached him, as he was
preparing to leave the place, that the king had thought
fit, in a moment of generosity and remorse, or in a

paroxysm of fear, to release the European prisoners, who had been in his power for years, and that the captives, Mr. and Mrs. Ramseyer, with two children, and M. Bonat, a Frenchman, had reached the vanguard of the advancing column under Major Russell. The released party brought a letter from the king to Sir Garnet, in which he undertook to pay the indemnity of 500,000*l.*, demanded by the general, and to make a treaty of amity with the British Government if the troops remained where they were, and did not attack him or attempt to take possession of his capital.

To halt now was impossible. The die had been cast, and the king and his advisers heard with dismay Sir Garnet's reply that he could and would only make terms of peace within the walls of the royal city. On January 31st, the first serious struggle with the enemy took place at the village of Adubiasse, where Gifford, ever on the alert, had discovered a large Ashantee force under the Prince of Adansi. Russell, with his company of native troops, suddenly advanced upon the place, and the abruptness and spirit of the attack at once disheartened the enemy, who yielded up the village after firing only a few harmless volleys over the heads of the leaders of the assault.

The report of Lord Gifford as to the condition of the country in front of the invading column increased in interest hour by hour. On the 28th he discovered a strong post of Ashantees at Borborassi, and very nearly ran a risk of being captured and beheaded in his reckless zeal to gain accurate information of the numbers and disposition of the hostile forces. The British under Colonel McLeod,

after a weary tramp through the cheerless bush,
came upon the village, which stood in a wide opening which had been made by clearing the forest for
some distance all round it, and at once carried the
place by surprise. The Ashantees fled to the wood,
and opened fire from the undergrowth of the jungles
into which they crawled, and where they lay hidden
most effectually by the thick screen of tangled
creepers and vegetation from the observation of the
white troops. From behind the leafy cover they
poured a desultory but harassing discharge into the
British ranks, and men and officers began to fall before
their rude missiles. A few well-directed volleys from
the Sniders of the Naval Brigade, however, quickly
cleared the woods on either side, but not before a valuable officer, Captain Nicol, had lost his life, and several
brave fellows had been more or less severely wounded.
But it was at Amoaful that the Ashantee army in
force was expected to make a stand, with a view to
check, if possible, the threatened destruction of
Coomassie and the palaces of the king. The invaluable information gleaned by Lord Gifford of the
tactics and position of the enemy was carefully considered by the General, who was satisfied now that the
proposals of the king for an armistice were insincere,
and only intended to gain time to collect his own
levies for a final and, as he hoped, triumphant engagement with the invaders of his territory. On January
31st, at 7 a.m., the English force was on the march
to find the foe. Blithely and hopefully the " Black
Watch" strode on in the place of honour. The
Fantee porters, half-dead with fear, followed the
Highlanders, and then came the native artillery, with

their two seven-pounders. Next in order, with their steady swing and reckless air marched the sailors, "blue-mouldy for a fight," and enlivening the way with snatches of song and chorus, which must have considerably astonished any lurking Ashantee, who might be watching the passage of the troops from the recesses of the jungle. At the rear of the right wing Sir Garnet himself was carried by his Fantee bearers upon a bamboo palanquin, and the Rifles formed the rearguard of the centre column of nearly 3000 men. Gifford had gone forward "to stir up the enemy," which he did effectually, and ever and anon the sharp rattle of the Snider, or the dull boom of the oldfashioned and badly loaded muskets of the Ashantees fell upon the ears of the eager and resolute little army which was so soon to try conclusions with the largest force King Coffee had ever sent into the field. Gifford had secured the outpost of Egginassie, and the tide of battle rolled on towards Amoaful. But the forest in front and on all sides had to be cleared of the ambushed enemy, who poured destruction into the ranks of the 42nd, from the bosky depths on either flank of the advancing troops. The contest was stubborn and protracted. Still the British line pressed on, whilst men fell with fearful rapidity on all sides from the fire of the enemy, which swept round the front and along the sides of the attacking force, and it was only after a sternly fought combat of some hours that the Ashantees fled before the steady fire of the European regiments, and left an open road so far to Coomassie.

"Ah, Sandy, my lad, it was a brave fight," said a lusty Highlander to a comrade. "What a pity we didn't have our kilts and bonnets; how they (the Ashantees) would have cleared, and no mistake!" remarked another Scotchman of the gallant 42nd. "By jingo, but they cut a gangway through my beard anyhow. I say, Bill, what will they say at home when they hear how these fellows have spoiled my beauty?" said a bluff sailor of the fleet whose beard had actually had a clear passage shaved through it by an Ashantee bullet. The enemy's loss was put down roughly at 1000 killed and the same number wounded, out of a force of something like 12,000 which the king sent into the field. On the side of the British the list of wounded and killed at Amoaful amounted to about 250 all told.

On February 1st a section of the column was detailed for special operations against the village of Becquah, a place somewhat out of the line of march, but likely to prove troublesome as a harbour of refuge and rallying-place for the fugitives from Amoaful. It was decided to clear the town, and the task was committed to the 23rd Fusiliers and a portion of the "Black Watch," under the command of Brigadier-General Sir Archibald Alison. The work was speedily and effectually accomplished, and Becquah, after being cleared of its inhabitants and defenders, was committed to the flames.

Light marching was now the order of the day, and the General, keenly alive to the necessity of pressing forward his troops as rapidly as possible, insisted that all heavy stores and regimental impedimenta should be left behind at Amoaful. Evidences of the utter discomfiture and disorderly flight of the Ashantees were to be seen scattered over the road in all directions in the shape of packages of food, clothing, arms, and household treasures, which had been cast on the wayside or into the forest by the panic-stricken natives in their haste to escape from the terrible fire of the English rifles. A desperate attempt was made to check the progress of the vanguard of the column by a body of the enemy posted upon the spot which had been fixed upon for crossing one of the smaller streams in the line of march. A sharp struggle for the passage soon resulted, however, in the complete rout of the dusky foe, and the main body of the expedition passed onward to the banks of the Ordah, occasionally disconcerted for the moment by the discovery of bands of the enemy lying concealed behind the foliage on each side of the path, who fired out savagely upon the victors as they filed along the narrow way. Here and there along the road, the corpses of those who had been mortally wounded in the fight for the river passage were discovered neglected and unburied, although the Ashantees had hitherto been careful, as far as possible, to get their dead or disabled warriors off the field and out of sight of the white men with marvellous alacrity. Every village had its human fetich stretched out headless, with its feet pointing north-ward to Coomassie—a ghastly charm which the natives believed would effectually dishearten their implacable enemies, and in some way despoil them of their courage and power. The livid corpse appeared to say to the proud leader of these invincible foreigners, " Regard this face, white man, ye whose feet are hurrying on to our capital, and learn the fate awaiting you."

On the night of February 3rd, Sir Garnet rested his wearied and harassed but enthusiastic brigades upon

the banks of the Ordah, where they passed the long
hours till the dawn in utter misery, as, without
coverings or tents, they were exposed to the ceaseless
pelting of the tropical rain, from which the brave
fellows had no shelter or defence of any kind. But
at length the shadows disappeared, the leaden clouds
overhead dispersed, and February 4th broke upon the
already busy and excited groups of men, who felt that
the most eventful stage of the campaign in Ashantee-
land was about to be entered upon.

Away slightly to the north-west in a hollow of the
distant hills lay the capital of King Coffee. The
Engineers succeeded, in an incredibly brief space of
time, in throwing a temporary bridge, fifty yards long,
across the Ordah, the only remaining river between
the invaders and the royal city. The Rifles led the
way over the stream, piloted by the keen-sighted and
stout-hearted young Gifford and his faithful followers.
At 7.40 a.m. hostilities commenced. Casting themselves upon the bare earth, the British regiments sent
a perfect storm of bullets into the masses of the
enemy, which swept down upon them in vast crowds
maddened by despair. The strife was fast and furious.
The din and roar of the musketry rose and fell upon
the air, as the sturdy little phalanx of Sir Garnet's
men cleared a way for itself through the serried
ranks of natives. The baggage was ordered up at
this juncture, and a possible stampede of the Fantee
bearers effectually provided against, by placing them
in position directly in the centre of the column and
closing up the rear with the Naval Brigade and the
native regiments. At noon the 42nd were moved to
the front line, and Colonel McLeod was instructed by

the General to open the way for the column ahead, and to stop at nothing till he had taken Coomassie! Terribly weakened by the fearful onslaught of the infuriated Ashantees in the early part of the day, the Highlanders responded to the call of their leader, and with the order, " The 42nd will fire volleys by companies according to order. Forward ! " the actual advance upon the famous city of King Coffee commenced. Stanley's favourite style of action, " fire fast and advance fast," was adopted, and as the Scotch faced the short but stubbornly contested forest path which led to the capital, with bag-pipes braying, and cheers ringing out above the crash of the firing and the hissing of the shot from the seven-pounders of Rait's battery, the scene was one of lurid but grand impressiveness. Shoulder to shoulder, and back to back, the regiment fought on, now delivering a deadly fusillade into the jungle on the right, now clearing in like manner the woods on the left, till Coomassie came in view. Ambassadors from the king were passed on the road, but the 42nd were not to halt till they piled their rifles before the royal palaces which rose before them in the distance, across the marshy lagoon which surrounded the doomed city.

Onward, too, marched the 23rd, closely followed by the native regiments and Hewitt's naval heroes. Sir Garnet grasped with pardonable pride the slip of paper which reached him from the Brigadier at the front with these words written across it, " We have taken all the villages but the last before entering Coomassie. The enemy is flying panic-stricken before us. Support me with half the Rifles, and I enter Coomassie to-night." The king had fled to a country-house at a distance, but he had sent messengers with authority to negotiate with Sir Garnet for the preservation of the town and its treasures.

Once across the foul unhealthy morass, the British force was in possession of Coomassie. The capital of Ashantee-land was found to be a town of considerable size, with broad open thoroughfares, and well-built houses, and full of objects and features of interest to the army which was now encamped within its walls. The startled inhabitants could scarcely realize at first that all was over, and that the soldiers of the "High and Mighty King of all the Ashantees" had been defeated and scattered like the dust, by the handful of white men, who now were quietly enjoying the cool shade of the palaces and colonnades of the city, and rejoicing that the end had come at last, and that in a few days they would be marching back to the coast.

The town was built upon two broad flat rocks of iron-stone, having a slight declivity between them, and extended for a distance of nearly two miles. It was impossible to estimate the extent of its population, but it is supposed that the average number would be probably about 13,000. It was environed on all sides by a malarious marsh and stagnant pools, and seemed to occupy the worst position possible from a sanitary point of view. Some of the streets were fine and imposing. They were all named or distinguished in some way, and the arrangements for the order and government of the capital reflected some credit upon the wily monarch who had hastily abandoned his city, and fled before the victorious advance of the British

General. During the first night of the British occupation the natives managed to carry off, under cover of the darkness, a considerable portion of the more valuable treasures from the palaces and houses of the chief nobles, as well as a large supply of rifles, muskets, and ammunition, to the dismay of the General, who found, when it was too late, that he had made a mistake in not placing the whole town at once on his arrival under martial law, and surrounded it with picquets.

The royal residences stood midway between the hills upon which Coomassie was built. They were enclosed in a stockade, and extended over a space of some 500 square feet. They simply consisted, however, of a number of native dwellings grouped together, and a substantial stone house of two stories in the corner of the compound for the special use of the king. The style of architecture and ornament exactly resembled that of the houses at Foumannah already described. The same recesses in the walls, the dado of red, the creamy-white of the ceilings, the rufous floor, and the beautifully delicate carvings of the cornices, beams, and columns which supported the roofs, all betrayed the refined taste in domestic decoration and finished execution in detail for which the Ashantees are distinguished amongst the degraded and unartistic races of West Africa. The state apartments presented a disordered and dismal aspect as the conquerors strode from room to room in search of loot, or for the purpose of examining the curious collection of articles of all ages, countries, and descriptions, which had gradually accumulated in the palace during the reigns of King Coffee and his

ancestors. English engravings, a sword of honour
from Queen Victoria, porcelain and chinaware, large
glass goblets, silver dinner-services, English cutlery,
ivory war-horns decorated with human jaw-bones,
umbrellas of silk, woollen, satin, or crimson damask,
copies of European newspapers, golden toys, piles of
faded Kidderminster carpets—all these were found
dispersed through the rooms of the king's house, and
the best of them were taken with the more valuable
treasure to Cape Coast and sold, the proceeds being
distributed amongst the troops.   The Sammonpone or
Spirit-House of Coomassie had become a place of evil
notoriety all along the West Coast, and horrible stories
of the inhuman atrocities of which it was the scene
had long excited the disgust and indignation of
civilized nations.   Day after day, according to report,
human victims were flung into its foul recesses to
appease the gods who presided over the fortunes of
Ashantee, and the track to its reeking portals was
stained and marked at every step with the blood of
120,000 victims, slain in sacrifice to propitiate
the sanguinary deities of the country.   The Spirit-
House was situated in a small strip of forest which
reached into the centre of the town.   Following
a path through the trees, a fearful sight presented
itself to the spectators.   Heaps of bodies in every
stage of decay, skulls lying about in all directions,
human limbs reeking with effluvia, and appalling in
their ghastly corruption—the horrors of the place
were too abominable and too suggestive, and the white
men rushed speechless and with a spirit of loathing
from the hateful locality.   The release of the Fantee
captives by the king added considerably to the lawless

K

bands of pillagers who took every opportunity to sack the houses or set fire to the native huts, with a view to securing the plunder during the confusion created by the frequent conflagrations. Armed parties of Ashantees also hung about the outskirts of the place, and the messengers of King Coffee were found treacherously removing arms and ammunition and gold-dust from the houses. The defeated monarch refused to treat with the Commander-in-Chief on the spot, and so save his capital from ruin ; and as Sir Garnet was anxious to get his troops back to the coast before the regular fall of the tropical rains, he decided to fire the capital and march at once for Cape Coast Castle and home.

The return was only decided upon just in time to escape serious disaster to the troops, from the deluge of rain which had now commenced to fall and flood the rivers throughout the country through which the expedition had to march back to the coast. Having evacuated the city, therefore, on the 7th of February, it was delivered over to the Royal Engineers, who, after placing mines beneath the palaces and chief buildings, proceeded to fire the thatch of the native houses, and as the gallant soldiers of Sir Garnet's expedition turned southward for the bridge of the Ordah on their journey homeward, the proud city of the Ashantees became a mass of blackened, shapeless ruins. On the 9th a fresh attempt was made by the king to open negotiations with the General, who demanded 5000 ounces of gold-dust, "as an earnest of their king's sincerity, and as a first instalment of the indemnity," and waived the question of hostages as no longer necessary. King Coffee was directed to send a representative into the British camp of sufficient authority to treat for terms of peace, and a promise was sent that the expedition would await the arrival of the royal reply at Foumannah.   In due course the king's ambassadors returned to the camp, but only bringing 1000 ounces of gold, declaring that this was all the king could possibly raise in the time allowed him.   Sir Garnet then discussed the terms of a treaty of peace and friendship between the sovereign of Great Britain and the monarch of the Ashantees. By the terms of this document, King Coffee was to pay a war indemnity of 50,000 ounces of gold-dust in such proportions and at such times as her Majesty's Government might decide.   The Adansi people were to be declared free from the Ashantee power, and a free road was to be kept always open to the coast by the king for the safe passage of traders and merchandise.   The treaty was to be sent to Cape Coast Castle within a fortnight, with the signature of the Ashantee ruler, or the terms would be less favourable to himself and his people.

By the end of February, 1874, the whole of the troops had again reached the coast, where they were embarked on board the transports awaiting them, and at once conveyed from the coast and its enervating and malarious atmosphere to the fresh breezes and sunny heights of Gibraltar and England. The Houssa force, under the able and dauntless Glover, reached the capital of the Ashantees by way of the Volta some days after its destruction by the main body of the expedition.   Twenty miles from Coomassie, the news reached the leader of the Houssas that the royal city of King Coffee had fallen into the hands of Sir

Garnet. He, however, pressed forward a small detachment of men under Captain Sartorius to open up communication, if possible, with the main column. They found the blackened ruins of Coomassie still smoking, and the spot deserted and silent, and hurrying on came up, at Foumannah, with the General, who spoke most flatteringly of the help which both Glover and Sartorius had rendered during the recent operations and advance into the country.

Just five days after the last British soldier had turned his back upon the burning city, Glover arrived before the shattered walls with a force of nearly 5000 native troops. But the time for deeds of heroism was past. There was nothing now left to do but to carry through the prosaic work of disbanding the special levies, and returning them to their respective localities with well-merited gratuities and rewards. Glover was Stanley's ideal officer. His visit to the camp on the Volta impressed him in a remarkable way with a sense of the soldierly qualities and splendid capacities for organization exhibited by the Special Commissioner, and again and again the *Herald* correspondent returns to Glover and his work with words of the warmest commendation. For Sir Garnet, on the contrary, the letters of Stanley betray no particular affection—they speak in the highest terms of the caution, bravery, and keen perception of the "youngest General in the British Army;" but the expedition just missed the point of perfect success, according to the views of Stanley, by the fire in Coomassie on the night of its capture, (which could have been prevented had martial law been proclaimed at once), the neglect of Sir Garnet to protect the place from marauding bands of thieves, and the hurried evacuation of the capital before a stringent treaty had been exacted from the disheartened king. But the English people were satisfied with the results of the campaign, and a magnificent reception was accorded to the victorious regiments when they once more landed upon their native shores. Glover was publicly thanked for his services by the Houses of Parliament, Sir Garnet was made a knight Grand Cross of St. Michael and St. George, and upon the gallant young Gifford was bestowed the proud and rare distinction of the Victoria Cross, for his valour in the face of the enemy, when directing his scouts on the fatal fields of Borborassi, Amoaful and Ordahsa.

Mr. Stanley was the second of the band of "War Specials" to reach the coast, where he arrived in safety on February 12th, on his way back to England, having made the journey from Coomassie in a little more than a week. The work of the expedition had been completed. Coomassie had been destroyed, the power of the ruthless king of the Ashantees had been broken, and a treaty had been signed which secured peace to the native allies of the British power, and opened out a large and populous region of Western Africa to the pioneers of commerce and Christian civilization.

CHAPTER IX.

ON his way home from the Gold Coast, the news reached Stanley of the death of Dr. Livingstone, who had at length fallen a victim to the trials and privations of African travel, upon the shores of Lake Bemba. The arrival of the body of the illustrious explorer in England, and its solemn interment at Westminster Abbey, made a deep impression upon the man who had spent so many happy months with the departed hero at Ujiji, comparing notes of past experiences, and discussing fresh plans of exploration. Livingstone, although sadly weakened by sickness, and suffering from the effects of his terrible journey to the eastern shores of Tanganika, after being deserted by his followers, and despoiled of his stores and necessaries by the Arabs to the north of the lake, was full of hope for the future. He had determined to follow up his discoveries in the great central lake region, by tracing the course of the newly-found Lualaba to its estuary, and to solve for ever the mystery which surrounded the stream and its affluents. After Stanley's departure from Unyanyembe for home, the ardent old

man had retraced his way back to the country west
of the Nyassa, where an acute attack of dysentery
abruptly closed his brilliant and honourable career.
The fond hope of his heart, the great dream of his life
—the exploration of the great river and its tributaries—had not been realized, and he had perished
whilst still upon the confines of the vast lacustrine
area of Inner Equatorial Africa, which, with all his
old resolution, he had set himself to investigate.

Stanley resolved to take upon himself the unfinished
task, and to follow up the thread of Livingstone's
researches. He secured and studied every available
book upon Africa, its people, products, climate, and
physical conformation. For weeks, night and day, he
devoted himself to mastering the one absorbing
subject of Africa, as presented to him in his special
collection of over 130 works.

The proprietors of the *Daily Telegraph* and the
New York Herald combined to supply him with a
splendidly-equipped expedition for his journey through
the Dark Continent, and on August the 15th, 1874, he
left London, accompanied by three young Englishmen
of excellent character, Francis John and Edward
Pocock and Frederick Barker, for Zanzibar, *en route*
for the great African lakes. No outlet of the bright
waters of Tanganika had so far been traced, little
was known of the wide-reaching Victoria Lake, and
the top waters of the mighty Nile were still unknown,
and the whole western half of the Central Equatorial
region was a mere blank space upon the map. Stanley had undertaken, before leaving home, to devote
himself, body and mind, to the satisfactory solution of
these various geographical puzzles.

"Do you think you can settle all this, if we commission you?" asked the promoters of the enterprise.

"While I live," replied Stanley, "there will be something done. If I survive the time required to perform all the work, all shall be done."

"The purpose of this undertaking," said the editor of the *Daily Telegraph*, in a leading article, "is to complete the work left unfinished by the lamented death of Dr. Livingstone; to solve, if possible, the remaining problems of the geography of Central Africa; and to investigate and report upon the haunts of the slave-traders. . . . He (Mr. Stanley) will represent the two nations whose common interest in the regeneration of Africa was so well illustrated when the lost explorer was re-discovered by the energetic American correspondent. In that memorable journey, Mr. Stanley displayed the best qualities of an African traveller; and with no inconsiderable resources at his disposal to reinforce his own complete acquaintance with the conditions of African travel, it may be hoped that very important results will accrue from this undertaking, to the advantage of science, humanity, and civilization."

Just twenty-eight months had elapsed since Stanley left Zanzibar for Aden, on his return to Europe after having found Livingstone at Ujiji. On September 21st, 1874, he reached the island once more, and proceeded to make the necessary preparations for his new venture. From the Wangwana, or native freemen of the island, he selected a band of trusty followers, who were to be his comrades in the journey across Africa, and upon whose fidelity and goodwill the final success of the undertaking would largely depend. The vicious, the feeble, and the idle were at once rejected. None "but good men and true" were to be allowed to enter the ranks of the expedition, and, as the reputation of the commander-in-chief had by this time become thoroughly established throughout the entire dominions of his Highness Séyid Barghash, no difficulty was experienced in obtaining suitable recruits. But a matter of such importance could not be finally adjusted without the usual formal palaver. Stanley, now an experienced African traveller, was not surprised, therefore, when it was announced that the native members of his party of exploration desired to have a formal interview with him on the subject of the proposed enterprise.

The men were satisfied with the explanations of their leader, and by 5 p.m. on the 12th of November, 224 most eligible recruits had been enrolled, and five native vessels were in readiness, laden with the *impedimenta* of the expedition, to make the trip across the narrow straits to the mainland of the continent. At Bagamoyo, some trouble was experienced in getting the crowd of soldiers, porters, and hangers-on of the party, into order for the march inland.

On the 17th of November, however, everything was in readiness for the start, and the expedition, numbering 356 souls, took the road to the lakes. Four chiefs marched in front; then came twelve guides clothed in scarlet; these were followed by a party of 270 porters, bearing head-loads of beads, wire, cloth, and provisions of all kinds for the way; next came the *Lady Alice*, a specially-built canoe of cedar, carried by the men in five sections of eight feet each; a number of women and children followed; then came the riding-asses, the Europeans and gun-bearers, and sixteen stalwart chiefs brought up the rear. A route considerably north of the usual road to Unyanyembe and the west was chosen, and the natural beauties of the district soon began to unfold themselves as the highlands and open country were reached. On the 16th of December, Ugogo, the inhospitable, with its broad, bleak, desolate plains and barren rocky hills was reached. The heat in the lowlands of the maritime region had caused great suffering to those members of the party who had never before experienced the penetrating power of the sun in the tropics, but the whole company pressed bravely forward, undeterred by the hardships which must of necessity be encountered in a journey through Equatorial Africa under the most favourable circumstances. The people on the road had shown a friendly disposition towards the caravan, and had freely brought their produce into the camps for sale. At times, however, provisions were obtained with difficulty, and a famine threatened the whole party on Christmas Day, 1874, when detained by ceaseless rainstorms in the impoverished territory of Ugogo. " I myself," wrote Stanley at this time, " have only boiled rice, tea and coffee, and soon I shall be reduced to eating native porridge, like my own people. I weighed 180 lbs. when I left Zanzibar, but under this diet I have been reduced to 134 lbs. within thirty-eight days. The young Englishmen are in the same condition of body, and unless we reach some more flourishing country than this we shall soon become skeletons."

True to their innate spirit of greed, the chiefs of Ugogo were found to be as insatiable as ever with regard to the question of tribute, and weary hours were wasted in trying to bring their demands down to something like reasonable limits. On January 1st, the direct path for Unyanyembe was forsaken, and the expedition turned due north through the fruitful and populous country of the Wahumba, a pastoral people, who possessed fine herds of cattle, flocks of sheep, and asses and dogs, and who were much interested in the white man, with whom they showed a wish to be on the most friendly terms. A trifling attention on the part of Stanley to a young chief of the tribe, induced the youth, as a special mark of good-nature, to "tell the fortune" of his white friend. Twisting and tossing his sandals in a curious fashion, he divined with much gravity the future of the stranger who had made him supremely happy by the present of a gilt bracelet with a green crystal set in it, a smart wooden pipe, and a cloth robe. The decree of the oracle, thus strangely invoked, was propitious, and all good things would follow the white visitor wherever he went. As the party advanced, however, the supply of food became more and more reduced every day, and the whole expedition by degrees was brought to a state of semi-starvation. The condition of affairs in the camp was most serious, and a special party was sent out to scour the country round, and purchase food at any cost for the famished multitude. Men, women, and children, natives and Europeans, all were exhausted for want of sustenance, and Stanley was at his wits' end to devise some method of warding off the horrors of famine till succour should arrive. The ground was examined by the fainting people for nuts or berries, or edible roots, with which to stay the gnawing pangs of the terrible hunger which was upon them, and Stanley, rifle in hand, searched the district for game with which to feed his perishing column, without finding a single head. A bag of oatmeal was luckily discovered among the stores, and a sheet-iron dress-trunk having been cleared of its contents and filled with water, the oatmeal was thrown in with a quantity of Revalenta Arabica, and the whole boiled up into a supply of thin gruel, sufficient to allow to every person in camp two cupsful of the mixture. Eager crowds surrounded the extemporised boiler, and great was the gratitude of the miserable creatures, as they received their limited portions of the steaming liquid. Relief came, however, at length, and the weary caravan moved on to the fruitful land and pleasant, well-stocked fields of the Suna region. Clusters of small towns and farm-like settlements were scattered over the plains, and flocks and herds roamed over the uplands, testifying to the general prosperity and productiveness of the country. But the meagre diet and long marches through heavy floods of rain had begun to tell upon the health of the expedition, and on the afternoon of the day that the camp was pitched at Suna (January 12th, 1875) thirty men were on the sick-list with fever, dysentery, lung disease, and chest complaints. Edward Pocock had fallen a victim to the climate and the privations of the roads ; and, to add to the anxiety of the commander, the natives of the district evinced signs of unmistakable hostility and mistrust of the white men and their armed followers. Pocock had to be placed in a hammock, and carried with the other incapacitated members of the expedition in the centre of the column,

which was followed and hemmed in by hundreds of
heavily-armed natives, who kept up with the feeble
and disheartened band on each side of the road.
At Chiwyn, 400 miles from the Indian Ocean,
the poor English lad passed away. In the blazing
sun, covered as a temporary shelter by one of the
hollow sections of the boat, the noble fellow breathed
his last, whilst Stanley was pressing forward with all
speed the erection of a cool hut of grass for the use
of the sick. A grave was dug at the foot of a wide
spreading acacia, and with the simple pathetic accents
of the burial service, the body of Edward Pocock was
laid to rest, in " sure and certain hope of the resurrection to come." " When the last solemn prayer had
been read," says Stanley, " we returned to our tents,
to brood in sorrow and silence over our irreparable
loss."

This district which the expedition had traversed
between Suna and Chiwyn, is the veritable birthplace
and nursery of the mighty Nile. A tiny rivulet flowing to the north-east, and uniting with other slender
rills and streams, winds on its sinuous course now westward and now northward again till, as the Leewumbu,
then as the Monongah, and finally as the Shimeeyn,
it pours its swollen volume of waters into the Victoria
Nyanza on the south-eastern extremity of Speke Gulf.

At Vinyata a temporary halt was made, to enable a
search party to find Kaif Halleck, a trusted member of
the expedition, for whom Stanley had considerable
regard. Loads were rearranged, and it was decided
to leave behind everything which was not absolutely
required, as the question of transport was daily
becoming more serious. Many of the bearers were

sick, numbers were incapacitated, twenty had died, and eighty-nine had abandoned the service without leave and returned to the coast. Great grief was caused in the camp by the report of the search party, who had discovered the corpse of the faithful Kaif Halleck cast aside into the forest, some distance from Vinyata, and terribly mutilated from head to foot. The people of the district evidently entertained no very amicable feelings towards the strange body of men whom the white chief was leading through their country without their leave, and without attempting to secure their consent by any offer of tribute. It was found necessary to stockade the camp, and this had barely been done, when crowds of armed men marched into the clearing, 200 yards wide, which had been made all round the temporary citadel. Stanley decided now to strike the first blow, as a policy of patience only encouraged the natives to fresh deeds of violence, and he ordered out the armed escort of Zanzibaris to scour the bush in detachments and drive off the enemy. The day's loss was twenty-one soldiers and one messenger killed, and three seriously hurt. Disheartened by the resolute attitude of the beleaguered garrison, the Wanyaturu, who had suffered considerably from the fire of the Zanzibaris, after another ineffectual attempt to dislodge the expedition from their stronghold, retreated, and on the 26th of January the column filed out of the stockade, on its way to the southern shores of the Victoria Nyanza.

At the village of Mgogo Tembo the startling intelligence was received that the terrible Mirambo, the scourge of Inner Africa from the Victoria Nyanza to the northern shores of Nyassa, had again " taken the field," slaying and enslaving the panic-stricken population, and carrying death and desolation into the remotest corners of the entire Central Equatorial region east of Tanganika. The " terror of the land " seemed to be everywhere. To-day on this side, to-morrow on that—who could escape from his far-reaching arm? The name of Mirambo was now heard on all sides. The scouts of the various tribes were crouching in the forests, or perched in clefts of the hills, eagerly scanning the horizon or watching the various paths for signs of the first approach of the tyrant. Across the broad green pastures, and down the deep valleys clothed in verdure, and dotted over with kine, and goats, and sheep, the signal was repeated from one district to another, that the rapacious tyrant was on the move. " Mirambo ! Mirambo ! " was heard echoing from village to village, till north and north-east and west nothing else was thought of but the advent of the invincible destroyer. The first stage of the journey was now nearly completed, and on the 27th of February the waters of the Victoria Lake were only nineteen miles off.

After marching for some hours through a pleasant pastoral country, broken up into broad and well-tilled fields, and abundantly watered by small rivulets, the vast silvery expanse of the Victoria Nyanza came into view. The men cheered heartily as they sighted the great waters spreading away into the distance, and the Wanyamwenzi bearers burst into rude songs of delight, as they descended the heights towards the village of Kaduma, the friendly chief of the Kagehyi. The populace had been startled at first by the outburst of cheering from the caravan, and had seized their weapons and come forth in battle array to meet the new comers, whom they had mistaken for the marauding levies of Mirambo; but confidence was soon restored, and a hearty welcome extended to the weary and decimated column. The survey of the lake had not been completed by Speke, who was the first European traveller to gaze upon its gleaming waters, and Stanley was anxious, if possible, to circumnavigate the enormous area, and clear up, once for all, the mystery which surrounded it. The expedition had advanced 740 miles from its starting-point on the coast, and 103 days had been spent in reaching Kagehyi, from which place Stanley prepared to embark upon the lake on his journey of exploration. The *Lady Alice* was soon afloat, and a crew of twelve men having been chosen, who were supposed to have shown special capacity for boat work, the sail of the canoe was shaken out to the winds on March the 8th, and the tiny vessel started upon her eventful voyage. The men by no means liked the prospect which their friends on shore had sketched out for them. The islands and banks of the great inland sea, upon whose treacherous surface they were venturing, were said to be inhabited by strange races of savage monsters, who lived on human flesh and trained frightful beasts to tear their enemies in battle. So vast was the area of the Nyanza, that a lifetime would not suffice to traverse its sinuous margin.

With heavy hearts and unwilling arms the cowed and terrified oarsmen bent to their work, and for leagues the little craft with its listless burden, skimmed over the rippling wavelets, without a word of cheer, or a look of animation, from the craven-hearted crew. An eastward course was taken, and soon the stern grandeur of the region began to arouse the attention of Stanley, who found on inquiry from the natives that fifteen days' journey from the lake the lofty heights which bounded the horizon sank down to "low hills which discharge smoke and sometimes fire from their tops." The progress of the party was, at times, seriously threatened by hostile demonstrations from the numerous tribes on the shore, who warned off the strangers with gestures of contempt, or threats of violence. At one point of the passage, the *Lady Alice* was in imminent peril from a band of ferocious and drink-maddened Ugamba men who dashed up to the side of the boat, and began to lay violent hands upon her gunwale, with a view to terrifying the white man into surrendering himself and party into their hands. Stones were viciously hurled at Stanley, who calmly surveyed the proceedings of the pirates without betraying the least sign of fear. The insolent and aggressive demeanour of the freebooters became at length, however, so pronounced that he felt the time for action had come. Seizing his revolver he fired it sharply into the lake. The scene changed instantly, when the report rang over the waters, and as the balls hissed and splashed around the astonished savages; they threw themselves headlong into the waves, and swam at their utmost speed for the shore. "Come back, friends, come back. Why this fear?" said the strangers. "We simply wished to show you that we had weapons as well as yourselves. Come, take your canoe; see, we push it away for you to seize it." The good-nature of the crew of the *Lady Alice* soon induced the return of the fugitives,

who gave vent to their unbounded appreciation of the
weapon of the white man in loud cries of delight and
rough imitations of the " boom, boom, boom " of the
revolver. A tuft of banana-fruit was presented to
Stanley as a peace-offering, and the whole party
became the best of friends.

The various inlets and thick groves of forest which
reached to the water's edge were narrowly watched
by the exploring party, as these were points of danger,
and the lurking-places of the natives when bent on mischief. The lake tribes were found to be very numerous,
and scattered all along the banks, so that as soon as
one locality had been passed in safety, preparations
had to be made for encountering fresh foes and new difficulties. On the southern shore of the Uvuma district
Stanley very nearly fell a victim to the cowardly treachery of the people, a small and inoffensive-looking
party of whom emerged from the woods, as the boat
came in view, and made signs for the crew to land. As
soon as the *Lady Alice* drew near the bank by order
of her commander, who had no suspicion of the fate
which threatened himself and his companions, the fragile
craft was battered by huge masses of rock, which were
hurled down upon it from the shore. The Wavuma,
who are adepts in the use of the sling, then rushed out
from their leafy ambuscade in an immense crowd, and
began to pour in a shower of sharp stones upon the
unfortunate strangers, who by a strong effort pushed
off, and succeeded in getting out of range of the
missiles with only one man seriously wounded. On
rounding a small point some distance farther north, the
explorers suddenly found themselves in the midst of a
fleet of thirteen canoes, which, under pretence of a

desire to trade, had completely hemmed in the *Lady Alice* on all sides. The canoes were crowded with a ruffianly horde of armed Wavuma, who seized the oars, and held on to the boat to prevent her from moving in any direction. The commander of the captive vessel at once seized his weapon, and called upon his small but well-disciplined crew to prepare for action. With hideous yells and excited gestures the savages whirled their spears overhead and derided the defiant attitude of the white man, whom they regarded as already in their power. In a moment, at a signal from Stanley, the boat shot forward to force a passage through the ring of canoes which environed her, whilst he fired shot after shot overhead to daunt the lawless ruffians, and, if possible, induce them to desist from their attempt to coerce him. The Wavuma replied to the harmless fire of the guns with a shower of spears which fell upon the boat from all directions, but happily without any fatal effects. It was now necessary to adopt prompt and stern measures to check the assaults of the Wavuma, and the big rifle had to be brought into action. Directing his fire at the water-line of the advancing canoes, Stanley succeeded in piercing their frail sides with the heavy balls, and his enemies had to make strenuous efforts to save their shattered craft, and to get back at once to shore, leaving him to pursue his way in peace. Some days were spent in examining the deep waters of Napoleon Gulf as far as the Ripon Falls, upon the fine stream which connects the top head-waters of the ancient Nile with the Albert Nyanza to the north-west. Numbers of densely-peopled bays and points of land were passed, as the boat followed a course due

west along the thickly-wooded shores of Usoga-land,
for the kingdom of Uganda, the dominion of the
greatest man in Equatorial Africa.

The name and doughty deeds of Mtesa, monarch of
the vast empire which Stanley was now approaching,
had long been famous throughout the inner regions
of the Dark Continent, and it was with no small
pleasure that Stanley at length found himself in the
vicinity of the illustrious monarch and his court.
The influence of the civilized policy, and enlightened
ideas of the king, was manifest on the remotest
borders of his far-reaching territory, and the white
stranger was at once treated with profound respect
and cordial hospitality directly he crossed the borders
of the Empire of Uganda. Savagery and suspicion
now gave place to politeness and liberality, and
whilst a messenger was sent off to the royal city to
announce the arrival of a European visitor, an
abundant supply of choice delicacies was set before
the wayfarers for their refreshment, and every care
was taken to secure their comfort. With complete
rest, and the feeling that the party had no longer to
watch day and night against peril to property and
life, brighter hopes and happier thoughts possessed
the little band, and Stanley himself confesses that he
began once more to feel that African life was not
so despicable after all. "My admiration for the land
and the people steadily increased," he says, "for I
experienced with each hour some pleasing civility.
The land was in fit accord with the people, and few
more interesting prospects could Africa furnish than
that which lovingly embraces the Bay of Buka."

The *Lady Alice* was met, in a few days, by six

handsomely formed canoes conveying a state messenger from Mtesa to Stanley. A very agreeable
interview took place between the well-decorated
emissary of royalty, and the chief of the party of
exploration, who had donned his best garments in
honour of the important occasion, and of the august
presence into which he was in due course with all
formality to be introduced. A young chief of rank
was appointed to attend to the needs and wishes of
the new arrivals, and bullocks, sheep, honey, and
milk were sent to their quarters in overflowing abundance, testifying to the regal hospitality with which
the guests of the king were greeted in imperial
Uganda. The king was at his hunting-village of
Usavara, on the northern shore of Murchison Bay
where he was enjoying the pleasures of the chase,
surrounded by a large retinue of nobles and officers,
and an imposing military escort of well-drilled and
well-dressed soldiers. The hour at length arrived
for the introduction of Stanley to the illustrious
potentate whose powerful influence was acknowledged
from the Equator to the shores of the Albert Nyanza,
and through whose extraordinary ability and superior intellectual capacity a sovereignty had been set
up in the heart of Africa, which was as unlike the
barbarous and pagan communities upon its borders, as
the England of to-day differs from the Britain of
prehistoric times.

As the visitors drew near the shores of Usavara,
they were astonished to see the ground occupied by
thousands of people standing in order upon the
sloping banks in two long closely-packed rows. As
Stanley, attended by his smart-looking crew, armed

with Sniders, walked up the vast avenue formed by the dense throngs, which pressed forward to catch a glimpse of the new-comer, he was saluted with volleys of welcome, the crash of martial drums, and loud cries of pleasure from the surging ranks of the excited populace on either side. A party of well-dressed nobles stepped forward, and shaking hands with Stanley, welcomed him heartily to Uganda. Everywhere neatness, seemliness of costume, cleanliness of person, and elegance of apparel was the rule, and a stately but fitting ceremonial marked each step of the way to the royal presence. Two of the state pages appeared to lead the strangers to the courtyard of the sovereign's residence, where Mtesa was awaiting his guests, seated, and attended by his great officers, ministers of state, guards, executioners, &c. A roll of the drums signalled the approach of the strangers, and the emperor rose with calm dignity, and a kindly expression upon his lank and somewhat dreamy features, to greet them. He was tall, thin, and nervous-looking, with large eyes, lean cheeks carefully shorn, and an impressive manner. The two men regarded each other for some moments in silence. Mtesa thought Stanley looked younger than his old friend Speke, and shorter of stature, but more carefully dressed. What Stanley thought of Mtesa is carefully noted by himself in his journals. As he gazed upon the Prince of Uganda in his simple black robe, belted with gold, he felt that he was in the presence of a man of remarkable powers, who was destined to become the regenerator of Central Equatorial Africa, the pioneer of civilization, and the august patron of all well-considered efforts for

the amelioration of the benighted condition of the
" vast myriads of dusky nations " by which his empire
was encircled. From the territory of this monarch,
under the Divine blessing, a light may eventually
stream forth which will brighten the darkest spots
in this broad and densely-populated lake region, and
inaugurate a new era for Inner Africa of righteousness, prosperity, and peace.

Stanley had, day by day, during his stay in the
country, abundant evidences of the extraordinary
power and extensive influence of his royal host. The
emissaries of mighty chiefs in far-off regions were
glad to form alliances with him, and to lay costly
tributes at the foot of his throne ; and in his presence,
the ambassadors of Mirambo—the Bonaparte of the
south—and Mankonongo, the petulant monarch of the
Usai, were prostrate and servile. Three thousand
soldiers guarded the person of the emperor, and carried
out his behests, and a group of chiefs as dignified, and
as richly clad as the merchant princes of Zanzibar or
Unyanyembi, attended him wherever he went. The
enthusiasm and lofty ambition of the commander of the
expedition were excited by the daily contact with this
marvellous man, who had completely won his confidence
and affection. He became the teacher and friend of the
amiable monarch, and hour after hour the two men sat
in solemn audience, whilst Stanley unfolded to Mtesa
those divine mysteries of the Christian faith, which
he was convinced would make the frank and generous
king, if he accepted them, a mighty power for good
throughout the whole of Central Africa. The king
showed great attention to his guest, and when he returned to his hill-residence of Rubaga, he pressed

Stanley to accompany him. Before leaving the coast
of the lake, Mtesa held a grand display of his naval
forces, at which a body of 1200 well-disciplined men,
in about forty canoes of superior construction and
perfect finish, carried out a series of well-executed
war exercises in the presence of the court, the Royal
Council, and the assembled thousands of Uganda.

The elevated site of the royal palace was delightfully chosen. On all sides the country lay spread out
and well-wooded, or highly cultivated plains intersected by sparkling streams, and broken by gently
rising and verdant hills, or terraces of fruitful soil,
which supported thick groves of palms and dense
masses of many-hued tropical vegetation. The spot
was environed with the beauties of nature, in her most
fascinating combinations of hill and water and forest
scenery, and there was an entire absence of that abject and loathsome filthiness, and repulsive wretchedness, which native African settlements continually
present.

On April 11th, a fresh excitement was created
at the Uganda capital, by the arrival of one of
Gordon's white chiefs of the Soudan, Colonel
Linant de Bellefonds.

The intercourse between the white men was very
agreeable, and Stanley found in Colonel Linant an
ardent helper in his laudable enterprise of converting
the king from the errors of Mohammed to the pure
faith of Christ. The two men laboured together at this
self-imposed task, and they met with their reward.
The method adopted for the religious education of the
royal pupil was a very simple one. The great facts
of the history of the human race were set before him,

with an outline of the Bible facts to the dawn of the
Christian era. The characters and lives of Christ and
Mohammed and other teachers were contrasted, and
the auditor was left to draw his own conclusions as to
which system was most worthy of his allegiance. The
words of the Ten Commandments were written out in
Swahili by one of the boat's crew, a former pupil of
the Universities' Mission at Zanzibar, and morality and
religion for the time absorbed the entire attention of
Mtesa and his zealous instructors.

The time had come for the return voyage to Kagehyi,
where the main body of the expedition had been
located in camp, and Stanley took leave of the generous and kind-hearted Mtesa, after having received a
promise of a supply of men and canoes sufficient to
convey the entire force to the shores of Uganda.
Colonel Linant had accompanied his white companion
to the banks of the lake, and there the travellers took
an affectionate leave of each other. The scene is thus
described by the former :—

" At 5 a.m. drums are beaten; the boats going with
Stanley are collecting together.

" Mr. Stanley and myself are soon ready. The *Lady
Alice* is unmoored ; luggage, sheep, goats, and poultry,
are already stowed away in their places. There is
nothing to be done except to hoist the American flag.
and head the boat southwards. I accompany Stanley
to his boat ; we shake hands and commend each other
to the care of God.

" Stanley takes the helm : the *Lady Alice* immediately
swerves like a spirited horse, and bounds forward, lash-
ing the water of the Nyanza into foam. The starry
flag is hoisted, and floats proudly in the breeze ; I im-

mediately raise a loud hurrah with such hearty good-will as perhaps never before greeted the traveller's ears.

"The *Lady Alice* is already far away. We wave our handkerchiefs as a last farewell; my heart is full—I have just lost a brother. I had grown used to seeing Stanley, the open-hearted sympathetic man and friend, and admirable traveller. With him I forget my fatigue; this meeting had been like a return to my own country. His engaging, instructive conversation made the hours pass like minutes. I hope I may see him again, and have the happiness of spending several days with him." [4]

The course lay along the western side of the lake to the large island of Sessi, where it was hoped that the canoes for the transport of the expedition would be obtained in compliance with an order of the king. After some delay the promised assistance not being forthcoming, the *Lady Alice* proceeded upon her way southward till the Makongo was reached. At the sight of the boat the natives seemed to be terror-stricken, and lined the banks of the locality fully armed, and drawn up in order of battle to oppose any attempt at a landing upon their shores. Drawing off into deep water the party held on its way, anxious, if possible, to avoid any further conflicts with the savage tribes, whose worst passions were aroused to a pitch of frenzy at the sight of the white man who was silently traversing their borders, with such audacious complacency. In the midst of a heavy and persistent storm of rain, which drenched the voyagers to the skin, they made for the islands of Bumbireh, where they

were anxious to obtain a fresh supply of food, and a
temporary camp was formed upon the northern point
of the group. The largest island of the cluster was
eleven miles long by two miles broad, and consisted of
a backbone of highland with verdant slopes falling
away to the level of the lake. It had a considerable
population, and the general aspect of the place was
one of fruitful prosperity. An attempt was to be
made at barter with the natives; but before a trade
palaver could be opened, hordes of lusty warriors
rushed furiously down the hill on all sides, and seizing
the *Lady Alice*, lifted her bodily out of the water, and
drew her some distance over the beach. The position
now became most alarming. The boat, in which Stanley was still seated, was surrounded on all sides by
painted, dark-skinned demons, who fought with each
other in order to get near the stranger, who had dared
to approach their islands, so that they might pour out
upon him volumes of native abuse, which they accompanied with signs of hatred and contempt, of a nature
too terribly real to be misunderstood by the cool but
anxious occupant of the disabled craft. Every means
was tried to pacify the wild fears of the natives, but
with no satisfactory results, and at last it became a
matter of fighting or death. A momentary with-
drawal of the crowd left open a way of retreat. Turning to his men, the leader of the little band upon the
beach said, " Are you ready, your guns and revolvers
loaded, and your ears open ? "

" We are," was the resolute reply.

" Don't be afraid; be quite cool."

" Push, my boys; push for your lives," shouted
Stanley, and the *Lady Alice* was in a moment hurried

over the stones, and into deep water again. The crew sprang in after their leader, and as Safeni, the last of the Zanzibari, sprang over the thwarts, the crowd of disappointed natives reached the edge of the water, their faces daubed with black and white pigment, the dread signs of irreconcilable hate. The oars of the vessel had been stolen by the miscreants, and Stanley ordered his men to pull up the planks from the bottom of the craft and use them as paddles. Spears fell thick and fast upon the little *Lady Alice* as she shot out into the flood, and flights of poisoned arrows flew overhead as the fugitives bent to their work. Canoes were now launched in all haste, and cruel shouts of defiance and vengeance rang over the smooth grey waters. The fire from the rifle of Stanley soon checked the further progress of the pursuers, who fell back in disorderly retreat, with the hoarse cry , " Go and die in the Nyanza." Stanley and his party were saved, but not before terrible execution had been done upon the natives by the deadly elephant-rifle, without which the crew and their leader would have been completely at the mercy of their fiendish enemies.

After safely passing through a storm of awful violence, during which the *Lady Alice* drifted before the wind, or fell into the trough of the huge waves, which threatened at times to engulf the tempest-beaten craft, or dash her with irresistible force upon the surf-beaten rocks, the tents of the camp of the expedition on Speke Gulf were seen, and amidst the joyous congratulations of his followers of all ranks, Stanley found himself with intense and grateful satisfaction again amongst his own people.

CHAPTER X.

THE camp was a scene of intense excitement as the
Lady Alice drew up to the shore, and Stanley and the
brave fellows who had shared with him the perils of
his cruise of 1000 miles over the waters of Speke's
Nyanza, rejoined his anxious followers, who had been
startled and perplexed again and again by sinister
accounts of the massacre of the entire party by the
lake tribes. Death had been busy in the ranks of
the expedition during the absence of its commander,
and another European, Frederick Barker, had died
and been buried just twelve days before the *Lady
Alice* hove in sight. Mabruki—the trusted servant of
Burton, Speke, and Grant—and Jabiri, one of the boat
porters, and others had also passed away, and trouble
of various kinds hung over the little settlement for some
weeks. A rebellion and a return to Zanzibar had been
discussed, and a serious calamity had only been averted
by the timely arrival of the commander-in-chief upon
the spot. There had also been threatenings from without, and a force of hostile natives had been assembled
to attack the camp. Stanley was anxious to leave the

district at once, and reach the friendly shores of Uganda, but the canoes for the transport of the expedition, which Mtesa had undertaken to supply, had not arrived, and the way northward by land had been "killed" by the unfriendly tribes. In his dilemma, Stanley sent a request for aid to Lukongeh, King of Ukerewé, a prince in whom he had confidence, and a few days after a fleet of twenty-three canoes, with a sufficient number of boatmen, was awaiting the commands of the white chief upon the shore at Kagehyi.

The flotilla, piloted by the *Lady Alice*, and laden with 150 people, 100 loads of cloth, 88 sacks of grain, and 30 cases of ammunition, left Speke's Gulf on June the 20th, and was soon heading westward on its course to the territory of Mtesa. The native craft speedily developed their utter incapacity for breasting the rough waves and beating up against the strong currents of the lake, and after several mishaps, which resulted in the loss of a quantity of arms and grain, and the total collapse of five of the canoes, a thorough overhauling of the fleet was decided upon. Fresh canoes were ordered up from Kagehyi, and a camp was formed on one of the islands for the purpose of allowing time for the crazy craft to be put into perfect sea-going order. The expedition having re-embarked, a course was shaped for the Bumbireh group, and every precaution was taken to secure the safe passage of the canoes through the waters which bordered this region, in which Stanley had already experienced something of the terrible power of the island population, whose parting execration, "Go and die in the Nyanza," still rang in his ears. As the flotilla neared the dreaded locality, the shores of Bumbireh became alive once more with crowds of natives, and canoes began to shoot over the waters to scrutinize the resources and observe the motions of the strangers. It was soon found that progress was impossible without a struggle, and the commander of the expedition decided to open up the water-way to Uganda, after harassing delays and futile negotiation, by an attack in force upon the savage warriors of Bumbireh, who had, amongst other outrages, massacred a number of Stanley's men, after cajoling them into landing upon their banks by false professions of peace and amity. The enemy had been considerably strengthened by the arrival of armed hosts of allies from neighbouring tribes, and it was not without great reluctance that Stanley ordered the men of the expedition to be supplied with twenty rounds of ammunition, and to be prepared for a stern and decisive conflict with the pitiless islanders. His force consisted of 250 men armed with spears or native weapons, and fifty men carrying rifles, and he decided to land his fighting-party upon the shores of Bumbireh in eighteen canoes. "My friends and Wangwana," he said to his men before leading them to the fray, "we must have the way clear. Whatever mischief these people meditated must be found out by us, and must be prevented. I am about to go and punish them for the treacherous murder of our friends. I shall not destroy them, therefore none of you are to land unless we find their canoes, which we must break up. We must fight till they or we give in, for it can only be decided in this manner. While in the fight, you will do exactly as I tell you, for I shall be able to judge whether we shall have to fight or land." [5]

At 2 p.m., of August 4th, the canoes of the expedition headed for the island. By a skilful trick of navigation the whole strength of the enemy was revealed to the leader of the advancing force, who steered for the open water, and then suddenly dropped anchor. To the challenge of his interpreter the men of Bumbireh replied with scorn that they did not want peace, but war. " Come on ! " cried the multitude, shaking their spears in savage fury, " we are ready." A withering fire from the rifles of the expedition threw the masses of the enemy into wild confusion for a moment. But they stubbornly held the shore, and hundreds of them plunged boldly into the flood to grapple with their foes at close quarters. Another volley and another from the canoes, however, began to shake their resolution, and soon the panic-stricken islanders were in full retreat across the hills into the interior of Bumbireh. The passage was now clear, and the order was given for an immediate advance northward to Uganda-land. As the victorious flotilla sheered off from the banks of the beaten and disheartened Bumbireh, a few of the headmen came towards the lake.

" Shall we begin the fight again," cried the victors.

" Nangu, nangu." (" No, no.")

" The trouble is over, then ? "

" There are no more words between us."

" If we go away quietly, will you interfere with us any more ? "

" Nangu, nangu."

⁵ " Through the Dark Continent " (H. M. Stanley).

" You will leave strangers alone in future ? "

" Yes, yes."

" You will not murder people who come to buy food again ? "

" Naugu, nangu."

After a few words of wholesome advice to the vanquished and penitent foe, the fleet sailed on its way, and reached Dumo, the first halting-place in the territory of Mtesa, on August 12th.

The great king of Uganda was at war with the powerful tribe of the Wavuma, and had already entered Usoga, and fought his first battle. The *Lady Alice*, with Stanley on board, at once proceeded to the Bay of Buka, where her commander disembarked in order to make his way without delay to the royal camp. He wished to reach the Albert Nyanza to the north-west without delay, and he hoped that the amiable monarch of Uganda would furnish him with guides for the journey to the lesser lake. On nearing the precincts of the encampment, Stanley was greeted by kindly messages from his princely pupil, who also forwarded to his visitor the royal walking-stick as a sign that the words which were brought to him were actually from his own regal lips. The news that the Uganda people were engaged in a campaign in Usoga-land somewhat disconcerted the energetic traveller. He was anxious to press forward upon his great task of minutely examining the Central Lake Region, and then to pass along the course of the Lualaba to the Atlantic. African tribal wars he knew by bitter experience to be long-drawn-out affairs, with no definite end to them when once blood has been shed, short of the extermination of one or other of the belligerents. He was by no means disposed to linger on in attendance upon Mtesa until he had "eaten up" the Usoga people, and as there was no possibility of the Usoga tribes "eating up" the invincible Mtesa, the outlook for the expedition was by no means inspiriting.

The hosts of Uganda were found occupying a splendid position near the Ripon Falls, the only outlet of the Victoria Nyanza, and the meeting between the prince and his white friend and preceptor was most cordial and flattering to the latter, who felt that there was something more than mere imperial courtesy in the hearty greeting with which he was welcomed again to the royal presence. The Uvuma had resisted the claims of the King of Uganda to a yearly tribute from them, and had enslaved his subjects, and sold them to other tribes for "a few bunches of bananas." They had descended upon the shores of Chagwe, burning and plundering the villages, and defying the royal authority, and Mtesa had determined to chastise them effectually for their insolence, and reduce them to a proper spirit of meekness and submission. In reply to the request for guides to pilot the expedition on its way to the Albert Lake, the king begged that the advance might be delayed till the conflict with the Uvuma was over. It was not the custom of the country, he said, to allow travellers to go through the land in time of war, and besides, a large force would be necessary to reach the shores of the Nyanza in safety. Patiently abiding the issue of events, Stanley decided to follow the fortunes of the army of Uganda, as Mtesa had given his royal word that when hostilities ceased, he would immediately

send his friend overland with an armed escort, and an
influential chief to guide him to the great waters
which he wished to explore.   The fighting force of the
Uganda monarch numbered about 150,000 men, and the
entire number of people of all ages and ranks following the royal army must have reached 250,000 !   Such
was the enormous host which was advancing into the
region of Usoga under the leadership of the all-powerful Mtesa, who marched on foot, surrounded by his
body-guard, bare-headed, and dressed in dark blue,
with a broad leather belt round his waist, and his face
painted a bright red, in order to strike terror into the
hearts of his enemies.   At Nakaranga, four days'
march from the Falls, a camp was formed, consisting
of 30,000 dome-shaped native huts, above which
towered the sharp conical residences of the officers of
the legions.   " Stamlee" was carefully provided for,
in the midst of the hurry and confusion attending
the housing and provisioning of such an immense
army as Mtesa had collected together, and cosy
quarters were set apart for his crew and himself near
the royal pavilions.   The fleet of Uganda consisted of
325 canoes, carrying a force of 5000 men, and it was
drawn up near the beach to be ready at a moment's
notice to operate upon the flank of the enemy.   The
valour of the Uavuma was by no means to be despised.
Alert and dashing on water, as well as on land, they
had in days past enjoyed the reputation of being the
stoutest warriors on the north-eastern borders of the
lake, but the martial glory of the rising empire of
Mtesa had gradually over-shadowed them.

A few days after the arrival of the army at the vast
camp at Nakaranga, the order was given for the

Mtesa addressed his friend "Stamlee," with the request that he would proceed with his most improving discourse. They all knew that the white men possessed a universal knowledge. They were renowned for their wisdom and subtlety. Many white men had visited Uganda, and had astonished the people of the land by their learning and goodness. Therefore the king knew that to gain knowledge you must have intercourse with the white man. "Now, Stamlee," said his royal host, "tell me and my chiefs what you know of the angels." Step by step the education of the king progressed, and great was the satisfaction of his white preceptor, when he found that Mtesa had, after a long and serious course of instruction, decided to forsake the creed of Mohammed, and become a follower of the faith of Jesus of Nazareth. Calling together his ministers of state and chief officers, the king reminded them of the fact that many of the tenets of the religion of Mohammed were foolish and contrary to reason : e.g. that men could enjoy earthly pleasures in Paradise, or walk along a pathway no wider than a hair. Besides, the Arabs who followed the book of the prophet of Mecca did evil, bought slaves, and were not always true, or pure, or kind. But the white men, Speke and Grant, and Abdul Aziz Bey (M. Linant de Bellefonds) and "Stamlee," who followed the book of Christ, had not bought slaves ; they had been men of honour, and had lived without reproach among them. Therefore the white man's book was better than the book of the Arabs. "We will then take the white man's book," cried the assembly, to the intense satisfaction of their monarch, and thus a way was opened for the spread of the

Christian faith in the great empire of Uganda. The new convert was supplied with a copy of portions of the Bible, written out in his own tongue, and a complete transcript of the Gospel of St. Luke, which is the fullest evangelistic narrative of the Sacred Life ; and Dallington, the young boatman who had been educated at the Universities Mission, was, at his own request, released from further service with the expedition, that he might devote himself entirely to the king, as reader and instructor, until a missionary should reach the court, and formally instruct and baptize the royal proselyte. " Stamlee," said Mtesa, as the two men looked upon each other for the last time, " say to the white people when you write to them, that I am like a man sitting in darkness, or born blind, and that all I ask is that I may be taught how to see, and I shall continue a Christian while I live." [7]

Meanwhile the war with the rebel chiefs of Uvuma was carried on with relentless vigour by Mtesa and his army, and battles were fought from day to day, without any decisive results. The island home of the insurgents was defended at all points with heroic fortitude, and the attacks of the Uganda flotilla were repeatedly repelled with success, to the great discomfiture of the king. At length his Majesty decided to take counsel with his white friend once more as to the tactics to be pursued to bring the conflict to a satisfactory conclusion. Mtesa had given way to most unchristianlike fits of rage at the defeat of his soldiers, and having secured one of the offending chiefs, he had given orders in a paroxysm of fury, that the prisoner should be burnt alive. The faggots and the stake were prepared for the dread

[7] " Through the Dark Continent " (H. M. Stanley).

act of vengeance, and the unhappy victim was about to
be led to his death, when Stanley appeared upon the
scene. The king was in a state of intense excitement,
and evinced unmistakable signs of his diabolical glee
at the prospect of seeing one of his hated enemies
undergoing the frightful agonies of the flaming pile.
" Now, Stamlee," he said, " you shall see how a chief
of Uvuma dies. He is about to be burnt. The Wavuma
will tremble when they hear the manner of his death."
The indignation of the teacher was aroused at this
evidence of pitiless ferocity in his new convert. He
reminded the barbarous prince of the solemn profession
he had just made of his disposition to accept the
humane precepts of Christianity, and pointed out the
right course for him to adopt with reference to the poor
wretch who stood by anxiously awaiting the conclusion
of this strange controversy. Regardless of Stanley's
expostulations, the infuriated despot, with gleaming
eyes, and features distorted by passion, decreed that
the sentence should be carried out. " I will burn this
man to ashes, Stamlee. I will burn every soul I catch.
I will have blood! blood! the blood of all in Uvuma,"
he cried in loud tones, and turning to the executioners,
he commanded them to seize the old chief, and bind
him to the stake. Once more Stanley intervened.
Overcome with horror and disgust, he advanced to the
king, and told him plainly that he would leave the
camp, and never look upon the country again, if the
execution was carried out. He would, he said, inform
every white man, north and south, and east and west,
of the frightful and atrocious deed. He would say of
Mtesa that he was unworthy of the friendship of good
men, and that his land was stained with outrage and

the blood of the helpless and the aged.   The spirits of his fathers would look down with repugnance upon the crime he was about to commit, and he dare no longer stay as the guest of a man who was no better than a ravenous beast of the forest.   The king was touched by the reference of his friend to the founders of his dynasty, and he hastily retired from the spot to the privacy of his own tent.   Shortly afterwards a page was sent to call the teacher to the royal presence. Mtesa was subdued and penitent.   "I have forgiven the Mavuma chief, and will not hurt him," he said, "Stamlee will not say Mtesa is bad now ; will Stamlee say that Mtesa is good ?"   "Mtesa is very good," was the reply.[5]

Stanley now set about a novel scheme for assisting the prince to settle matters with his stubborn and inaccessible foes.   Having secured three of the largest canoes of the fleet, he lashed them together, and with the help of Mtesa's men, he erected upon the platform thus provided a temporary fort, some yards in height, of stout poles and branches interwoven and bound together by thongs of bark.   Sixty men were placed inside the floating battery to propel the structure, and 150 soldiers armed with muskets were embarked for its defence in case of assault.   Long streamers of blue and white and red floated from the top of a tall mast in the centre of the craft, and as it moved silently over the water with its human freight carefully screened from view, the wondering islanders gathered upon the shore to gaze upon the approaching phenomenon.   A message was shouted across the strait that the strange object now crossing from Mtesa's camp contained within

[5] "Through the Dark Continent" (H. M. Stanley).

itself power to destroy the whole population of the island, and that it bore upon the waters the invincible and terrible fetish of the Uganda people. The superstitious and awe-stricken crowds of islanders were admonished to make terms of peace at once with the emperor, or submit to the fate which would over-whelm them directly the keel of the mysterious craft touched their shores. Drums beat, and the war-horns were sounded, until the fortlet had arrived within fifty yards of the banks, when a voice of appalling volume cried out to the crowd of trembling Mavuma. "Speak! what will you do? will you make peace, and submit to Mtesa, or shall we blow up the island? Be quick and answer." "Enough," said a chief from the bank, "let Mtesa be satisfied. Return, O spirit; the war is ended!" A few hours later, a canoe arrived from the rebels containing an ample tribute, and bringing pro-fessions of submission from the islanders, who had been completely vanquished by the odd device of Stanley. The old chief, who had been condemned to the stake, was sent back to his friends, and peace was proclaimed amidst the joyful cries of both camps. Preparations had been made for vacating the territory of the Mavuma, and Stanley and his party were about to follow the retinue of the king to the place of embark-ation, when he suddenly found himself and followers environed by a wall of fire. The dry, grass-covered huts had by some means become ignited, and with fearful rapidity the flames rolled over the site of the encampment, devouring everything which lay before them. The sick and aged and those who were unable to escape from the savage fury of the conflagration, perished in fearful agony, and it was only by great exertion that Stanley was able to lead his little band in safety through the sheets of fire and clouds of smoke which surrounded them on every side. On October 29th, 1875, Mtesa and his vast following were once more in Uganda. The victors were received with loud demonstrations of joy by the populace of the royal city of Uganda, and peace and contentment once more prevailed throughout the empire.

The kingdom of Uganda has been described as crescent-shaped. It is 300 miles long, and 60 miles broad, and covers an area of 30,000 square miles. The entire population is said to be about 2,775,000, and the soil is capable of raising enormous and valuable supplies of native produce, e.g. coffee, gums, resins, myrrh, sugar, bananas, cereals, &c. Herds of cattle and flocks of sheep roam over its fertile plains, and splendid timber and rich stores of ivory are found within its borders. The forest scenery is strikingly grand. Immense sycamores, far-reaching mvulé, and wide-spreading gums intermingle with delicate creepers and feathering palms, the tamarisk and the acacia, and afford a delicious shade from the vertical rays of the sun overhead. Broad plains, and terraces of grass and brushwood, and hills and valleys, covered with green, and wrapped in a soft, filmy haze, make up a landscape which, for simple grace and attractiveness, is unsurpassed throughout the Central Equatorial region.

The natives, as a rule, are tall and graceful in figure. They are cleanly, modest, and courteous in demeanour, and naturally predisposed to hospitality and the customs of civilization. They dress in clothes which are much superior in finish to the habiliments of other

African tribes; their houses are more suitable for
human habitation, more substantially constructed, and
more completely furnished; and their weapons of war
and their canoes are perfect in the symmetry of their
design and careful workmanship. Mtesa and his
courtiers could read and write Arabic with fluency,
and the king was accustomed to record in brief notes
the chief points of the discussions which he held, from
time to time, with his white visitors. These tablets
of smooth cotton-wood, upon which he wrote, were
called his "book of wisdom," and were highly valued
by their royal author.

At length Stanley ventured to remind the king of
his promise to aid him with an efficient escort and a
supply of bearers and canoes for his journey through
the country west of the lake, and for the return voyage
to the southern shore. Mtesa at once ordered a body
of soldiers to be selected for the expedition, and after
an affectionate "Farewell," the *Lady Alice*, attended
by her consorts, set sail from the shores of Uganda,
and made for the western borders of the great inland
sea. The entire force, including the men supplied by
Mtesa, numbered 2800 souls, and with this magnificent
following Stanley pressed forward to the region of
Muta Nzigé, one of the smaller lakes due west of the
Victoria Nyanza. The sudden appearance of this
enormous host of armed men, headed by their white
leader, created some consternation amongst the population on the line of march, but no resistance was
offered to their progress, and on January 1st, 1876,
the force had reached Kawanga, the frontier town of
the kingdom of Uganda, without any molestation or
casualties of any kind. Fears were entertained by the

chief of the Uganda men that trouble might be expected in the territory of the Unyoro. He professed to see in the total desertion of the district, and in the absence of any sign of life, unpleasant portents of coming strife. The Wanyoro were supposed to be gathered in some hidden valley or secret spot, for the purpose of assailing the strangers in force, and overwhelming them by sudden attack or ambuscade, and scouts were sent out ahead of the main column to give warning of approaching danger. These fears were happily not realized, and on January 8th a camp was formed on the Mpangu river, a tributary of the Muta Nzigé, which rises at the foot of Mount Gordon Bennett, and rushes with angry impetuosity down a series of cascades and rapids into the lake at its north-eastern corner. The entire region, with its towering mountain-summits wrapped in wreaths of white clouds, its rushing streams foaming down the hill-side and through the fissures of the torn and disordered rocks, and its rugged peaks breaking the sky-line in all directions, had a distinctly Alpine aspect, and was aptly named by Stanley, the Switzerland of Africa. On January 11th the lake was reached, and a temporary settlement formed upon its banks at an altitude of 4724 feet above the sea-level. A hostile message soon reached the camp from the chiefs of the surrounding territory, which necessitated a prompt defence of the position. A band of Uzimba, 300 strong, had been sent to the commander of the expedition, with the intimation that war would be made upon the white man, whose words were fair, but whose purpose, they were sure, was none the less evil. On hearing this communication the whole force was thrown into a state of wild dismay. Stanley at once proposed to descend to the waters of the lake, and erect a strong camp upon one of the islands at some distance from the shore, where they might hold out till some terms of peace were arranged with the Uzimba, or till succour could arrive from Uganda. But a spirit of fear had taken possession of the entire expedition. The levies of Mtesa resolved to return immediately to Uganda, and Stanley's own men absolutely refused to remain to be massacred by these dreaded warriors of the Uzimba hills. A retreat was decided upon, and the project for the exploration of the Nyanza had to be reluctantly abandoned. The decision of their leader was received on all sides with delight, and on January 27th the soldiers of Mtesa detached themselves from Stanley, and returned to the capital, where they met with a cold reception from their king, who had heard from his friend of their despicable cowardice on the cliffs of Muta Nzigé, and of the complete failure of the expedition in consequence of their craven conduct in the hour of danger. The king was, for the time, frantic with passion at the disgrace which had been brought upon the fair fame of his empire, and punishment was speedily dealt out to the delinquents with no sparing hand. "By the grave of Suna (a strong oath in Uganda), my father, will I teach you that you cannot mock Kabaka! Stamlee went to this lake for my good as well as for his own; but you see how I am thwarted by a base slave like Sambuzi (the chief malcontent), who undertakes to be more than I myself before my guest. When was it I dared to be so uncivil to my guest as this fellow has been to Stamlee? You, Saruti," said the enraged monarch to

the chief of his body-guard, " take warriors, and eat
up Sambuzi's country clean, and bring him chained to
me." A kindly message of sympathy was sent to the
disappointed traveller from his royal friend, and an
offer of a fresh body of men was made, with a view to
a return to the forsaken Nyanza ; but Stanley decided
to proceed on his way for the future free and unfettered
by " any other man's caprice, power, or favour ! " [9]

Crossing the dull waters of the Alexandra Nile, after
a peaceful march through the broad basin of the
noble stream and its thousand affluents, the expedition
entered Kaffurro, the semi-civilized Arab colony of
Karagwé. The travellers met with a cordial reception
from the wealthy Arab traders of the settlement, and
an interview was arranged with Rumanika, King of
Karagwé, at which Stanley, as a friend of Mtesa, was
welcomed with great warmth by the amiable and
gentle prince, for whom the great Lord of Uganda
entertained a special regard. Leave was frankly
given to his white visitor to explore his country in
any direction he might wish to examine it. " It was a
land," he said, " which white men ought to know. It
possessed many lakes and rivers and mountains and
hot springs, and many things which no other country
could boast of." Rumanika was anxious to hear from
his guest which country he preferred, Uganda or
Karagwé. To this somewhat pointed question Stanley
replied that Karagwé was lordly, and had pleasant
valleys, mighty rivers, and much cattle. But Uganda
was prolific, and full of wealth ; its people were well-
nourished, and Mtesa was good—so was Father
Rumanika. " Do you not hear him, Arabs ? Does he

[9] " Through the Dark Continent " (H. M. Stanley).

not speak well?" said the gratified monarch. "Yes, Karagwé is beautiful."

Pleasant, peaceful, happy days were those at Kaffurro. Lake Windermere (so named by Speke), the largest of a cluster of tiny Nyanzas in the enjoyable country of King Rumanika, was carefully explored. Its length was found to be eight miles, and its greatest breadth about two and a half miles. Its position was directly north and south, in the midst of a green and mountainous land, with rugged heights rising to 1500 feet above its sparkling waters. A boat-race was held upon the lake, to the intense delight of the enormous crowds which had assembled to witness the contest, who cheered the boatmen of Rumanika, whilst the white chief urged on his faithful Wangwana to the peaceful conflict. The old king came down to the shore to witness the exciting spectacle, clad in a robe of state, with heavy anklets of copper upon his legs, and large bracelets of the same metal upon his brown and sinewy arms. He was arrayed in crimson to do honour to his guest, and he carried a sceptre seven feet in length. He had an enormous stride in walking (a yard long), and he was attended by minstrels, spearmen, relatives, Arabs and Wanga-Ruanda. Four canoes entered for the race with the crew of the *Lady Alice*, commanded by Frank Pocock. The old king was in raptures of delight. He entered thoroughly into the fun of the thing, and the crowd of natives on the banks were pleased to witness the gratification of their sovereign. The course was 800 yards in length, in the direction of the point of Kankorogo, and the struggle resulted in a tie, neither craft distancing the other to any appreciable extent.

Much had been heard about the famous hot springs of Mtagata, and Stanley determined to visit them, and test the efficacy of their healing waters. The king furnished him with guides for the road, and the steaming fountains, six in number, were found occupying the base of a wooded gorge about thirty-five miles directly north of the Arab town. A cloud of damp warm mist lay over the spot, which was crowded with sufferers from various complaints, who had come long distances to drink the sulphurous waters, which had a high reputation in the surrounding region for their health-giving properties. Stanley's opinion of their virtues was by no means favourable, and he always attributed a violent attack of fever, from which he suffered after staying some days at the wells, to the malarious atmosphere of the much-vaunted health-resort of his friend Rumanika.

During the months spent at Kaffurro, much useful and interesting exploring work was carried out, and the noble stream of the Kagera, or Alexandra Nile, carefully examined along a great portion of its course. From this point Stanley determined to strike across the country in the direction of the Lualaba, and the great Arab entrepôt of Nyangwé, the highest, point reached by Livingstone in his examination of that obscure river. An affectionate leave was taken of open-hearted old Rumanika, his lovely lakes, and his gentle, courteous people. On March 30th the expedition entered Western Usui, only to find its further progress effectually arrested by the rapacity of the king, Kiborogo, and his subordinate chiefs. A distressing famine had impoverished the land through-

N

out its entire length, and the people were reduced to
a condition of abject misery. Making the most of their
deplorable state, Kiborogo raised the amount of
tribute to such an extent that the bales of the
expedition began to show lamentable signs of
depletion. It therefore became a serious question
with Stanley whether he should proceed further west,
or return to the coast and replenish his stores. Before
him lay the broad plains and valleys of the Uhha
country, whose princes were known throughout
Central Africa for their avarice and greed. Twenty
days' sojourn in Uhha would suffice to consume all that
was left of the tons of goods—cloth, wire, beads, &c.—
which had been brought over from Zanzibar in 1874. To
lead an expedition through the lands of the voracious
Mkamas or their grasping neighbours without cloth or
beads would be to court disaster and the utter destruction of the entire party; and beyond lay the impassable
district of Urundi and Ruanda, the people of which were
strongly adverse to the presence of strangers on their
borders, even when laden with supplies, and willing to
pay any tax demanded of them. On April 7th the order
was given, with great unwillingness, to take a southward course along the fruitful vale of Myagoma, the
quiet birth-place of the swift-flowing Malgarizi, which
rushes southward to the great waters of Tanganika,
and the rapid Lohugate, which, gathering strength as
it meanders through the rich loamy plains of Mzinza
Land, discharges itself into the Victoria Nyanza just
below the island of Bumbirch. Thus in the same
valley these two splendid rivers have their sources,
within a distance of 2000 yards of each other. But
issuing forth in opposite directions, the two streams

go out into the world apart, and remain " strangers throughout their lives."

The Expedition had been making good progress on its way back to Ujiji, and no difficulties of a serious nature had arisen to damp the ardour or quench the courage of the column. " Bull," the last of Stanley's canine friends, had died on the way from Nyambeni to Gambawagao. The animal was a splendid specimen of the pure-bred English bull-dog, and he had followed in the track of his master overland for above 1500 miles. The poor brute was full of " courage " to the last moment, and dragged himself wearily over the rough forest path in the wake of the bearers, but at length with piteous cries and moans he laid himself down on the ground and died, to the intense regret of his owner and the entire company. The chiefs of the districts through which the caravan was passing were content with a moderate tribute, and they showed themselves in many ways well disposed towards the strangers. But Uranga had scarcely been reached, before the terrible tidings flew through the country that Mirambo was coming! He was near, only twenty miles (two camps) off, accompanied by an enormous following of Ruga-Ruga (brigands)! The terror was universal. The town was at once put into a state of defence, " marksmen's nests " were set up, and heavy stockades of logs and beams of thick timber hastily constructed. Arms and ammunition were dealt out to the panic-stricken people, and the king, in long flowing garments of calico, ran frantically from place to place, directing the operations, and animating the workers by his regal presence. He said to Stanley, " You will stop to fight Mirambo, will you not?"

"Not I, my friend," was the reply, "I have no quarrel with Mirambo, and we cannot help every native to fight his neighbour. If Mirambo attacks the village while I am in it, and will not go away when I am here, we will fight, but we cannot stop here to wait for him." [1]

Early the following day the exploring party filed out of the roughly fortified town with scouts in advance to " feel " the country, and give due notice of the presence of any danger from Mirambo or his lawless hordes. Serombo, one of the chief towns of the Unyamwenzi, was reached without encountering " the terror of Africa," and it was found that the progress of the dreaded chief was one of peace, as he had come to terms with his old enemies, the Arabs, and was for the time intent only upon cultivating friendly relations with his neighbours and fellow-chieftains. The king of Serombo, a lad of sixteen, was connected with Mirambo, and he was expecting a visit from the famous warrior when the Expedition reached his capital. The next day the whole population was astir to receive the great man in a manner befitting his proud position as the most powerful prince east and south of the Tanganika. Volleys of welcome announced his approach, and the air rang with the crash of war-drums and the clamour of thousands of tongues, as Mirambo made his state entry into the town, attended by his body-guard of Ruga-Ruga splendidly attired in coats of red and blue, white shirts, and handsome turbans. The chief himself was " a nice man," said Mabruki, the head of the tent-boys, who had gone to see the procession enter

---

[1] " Through the Dark Continent " (H. M. Stanley).

the capital, and who described to Stanley in glowing
terms the brave clothing and arms carried by the
notable visitor.   In reply to a request from Mirambo
that the commander-in-chief of the Expedition would
send " words of peace " to him, a wish was expressed
by Stanley to shake hands with one who had made so
great a name for himself.   He had, he said, made
treaties of friendship with Mtesa of Uganda, Rumanika
of Karagwé, and other powerful princes from Uganda
to Unyamwenzi, and he should be pleased to be on
good terms with Mirambo also.   Stanley was much
astonished, when the notorious tyrant appeared at
the camp, with only twenty of his guard, to see before
him, not a "terrible bandit," but, "a thorough
African gentleman."   Well-formed, mild in demeanour,
soft of speech, with a striking face and masterful eyes,
there was nothing of the sanguinary savage about the
man, nor any marks of special genius to distinguish
this Napoleon of the Central regions from any ordinary
calm and inoffensive-looking chief of dignified bearing
who might be met with in the course of the march
through the Lake Country.

In the course of a deeply interesting conversation
between the two leaders, Mirambo, who was dressed
in an Arab fez, coat, turban, and slippers, explained
the constitution of his formidable army of invincible
warriors, by means of which he had carried terror and
destruction into the Arab settlements and doubled the
price of ivory throughout Central Africa.   He selected
boys or youths for his battalions (in curious accord
with Lord Wolseley's well-known predilection in
favour of young soldiers), as they had no domestic
ties, and were ready to march at a moment's notice.

Their lithe limbs and supple frames enabled them to cover the ground with the ease of deer, and they had the spirit of the lion when roused by valorous words. "Give me youths for ever in the field, and men for the stockaded village," said the proud victor in many a sternly contested fight. "The Arabs," he said, "got the big head" (proud), and there was no talking with them. But the war is now over—the Arabs know what Mirambo can do. Any Arab or white man who would like to pass through my country is welcome. I will give him meat, and drink, and a house, and no man shall harm him." Presents were exchanged between the prince and the white man, and an abiding compact of amity and good-will was sealed by the ceremony of blood-brotherhood, which was performed with all due solemnity in accordance with the rites and forms observed on such occasions. The warrior chief moreover furnished his white brother with guides on the way to the south, and on the 4th of May he accompanied the Expedition to the outskirts of Serembo, with expressions of great regret at the departure of his friend. Cows, calves, bullocks, and a valuable ass (afterward named Mirambo by Stanley), a bar of Castile soap, a bag of pepper, and some saffron were presented to Stanley by Mirambo and his companions as parting gifts; and the march was recommenced in a direction bearing south-south-west, along the borders of the Watuta, a people with a bad reputation for their churlish conduct to travellers or passing caravans. Ugaga, on the banks of the rapid Malgarazi, was reached on May 18th, and arrangements were made for ferrying the whole party across the stream, which was at this point about sixty yards

in width. The transport of the entire body having
been effected in safety, the desert beyond Uvinza was
traversed without mishap, and at mid-day on May
27th the weary, travel-worn band once more beheld
the gleaming waves and snowy surf beating upon the
rocky shores of Lake Tanganika. Before night the
Expedition was comfortably housed, and at rest in Ujiji.

The entire waters of the Victoria Lake had been
traversed, and its shores, inlets, and tributary streams
expored. The southern sources of the great river
of Egypt had been searched out, and followed through
all their devious windings to the shores of the
mighty Nyanza, into which they emptied their
tributary waters. Muta Nzigé and its inhospitable
regions had been visited, and the Expedition had
travelled the course of the Alexandra Nile, the chief
affluent of the Victoria Lake, for more than half its
length. New and valuable facts had been collected
concerning the wide morasses and prolific slopes
whence the slender rivulets and countless streams well
forth to supply the silvery flood which rolls with
majestic force over the Ripon Falls to feed the far-
reaching Nile. The work of Speke and Grant had
been completed. The Victoria Nyanza and its
surroundings had been for ever cleared from the
mystery which had hitherto surrounded them, and the
great watery expanse had been proved to form, not
five distinct lakes, as Livingstone, Burton, and other
eminent travellers had so long supposed, but one
vast inland sea, with an area far exceeding that of
any other lake upon the African continent.

CHAPTER XI.

The mystery of the Lualaba—Livingstone's legacy—Afloat on the Tanganika—Sad memories—A "south-wester"—The "Soko" (gorilla) country—On the track of Cameron—Friendly overtures declined—No letters—Mutiny and death—Strong measures—Native statuary—In the Manyema country—Traces of Livingstone—Heathen testimony to the virtues of the "old white man"—The children loved him—On the banks of the Lualaba—Tippo Tib and the Arabs of Nyangwé—Forward to the ocean !—A terrible jungle—The expedition in peril—Perpetual strife—Tippo Tib deserts Stanley—The cataracts—Encamped at the Stanley Falls.

STANLEY was by no means disposed to allow the attractions and comforts of Ujiji to divert him for any length of time from his fixed purpose, which was to strike the Lualaba of Livingstone at the great Arab settlement of Nyangwé, and follow it along its entire course, either westward to the sea, or eastward to the Great Nyanzas of the lake region. The question of the final flow of the stream had been invested with supreme interest by the tragic death of the veteran traveller, who was the first European to gaze upon its grey waters, and who had turned disconsolately back from Nyangwé, unable to trace the newly found waters beyond the confines of the Arab district, on account of the wholesale desertions of his men, who were terrified at the ghastly stories told of the man-eating tribes in the great forest-lands to the north, through which Livingstone proposed to lead them. But before finally taking the westward road, the

leader of the expedition was anxious to clear up some
problems of minor importance connected with the
great Tanganika, upon whose borders he was resting,
and he decided to coast along the eastern side of the
lake, carefully examining the shore throughout its
entire length, and then to return to Ujiji by way of
the western banks. On June 11th, 1876, the taut
and newly decorated *Lady Alice* was afloat for the
first time upon the deep blue waters of Tanganika.
Her history had been so far by no means uneventful.
She had successfully traced the sinuous shores of the
vast Victoria Nyanza, from Speke's Bay to Uganda
and back. She had travelled in safety on the
shoulders of her bearers over hundreds of miles of
swamp, and grassy plain, and bosky jungle; she had
forced her way through the reedy sedge of the
Alexandra Nile; she had taken part in a friendly
contest upon the smooth bosom of Lake Windermere,
in the presence of native royalty; and now, with a
crew of smart and able boatmen, she once more felt
the ripple of the waters about her bows, as she sailed
out of the port of Ujiji, attended by the *Morfo*, a
substantial but by no means rapid craft of native
make. With many hand-shakings and mutual felici-
tations, the exploring party set forth, doomed,
according to the Arabs and their followers, to certain
destruction. "Take care of yourselves," was the
admonition of the crowd of people upon the banks,
who had assembled to see "the last," as they said, of
the adventurous Stanley. All who saw the *Lady
Alice* had serious doubts as to her seaworthiness or
capacity to beat up against the heavy waves of the
lake, and the drowning of the entire party was looked

upon as a certain event by the desponding population of Ujiji. Memories of Livingstone were revived, as spot after spot was passed, which had been rendered for ever notable as the scene of some incident in the journey, which the two travellers had taken in company from the lake to Unyanyembe.

At Urimba, Stanley recognized the exact spot upon which they had pitched their little tent in 1872, and which now to him " was hallowed by associations of an intercourse which will never, never be repeated."

The district of the Ruga Ruga, the pirates of these waters, was passed without difficulty but not without danger, for the camp was on one occasion rudely invaded by these dreaded freebooters, who have literally swept the land of its inhabitants from the Malgariza River as far south as the Rungwa, and, like Ishmael of old, every man's hand is against them. With bated breath, but none the less sincerely, they are cursed alike by Arab, Wajii, and Wanyamwezi, and all have an account to settle with them some day. Towering above the lake to the south of Bonga Island are the interesting peaks of Kungwe, the rocky recesses of which afford a refuge for the few remaining families of the original inhabitants of the locality. The heights rise to an altitude of about 3000 feet above the water, and the dwellings of the last of the Karwendi are built in the clefts of the mountain, and are defended from hostile attack by huge boulders of rock, which are in a position to be detached at any moment by the people, upon the heads of their assailants. The country about Karema and the Mpembwé Cape was found to be well stocked with

game, and the crews of the boats were made glad
with an abundance of fresh meat, which was easily
obtained by the sportsmen of the party from the fine
herds of buffalo and red antelope which ranged over
the broad undulating prairie-like region. The rock
scenery of the shore at this point was very striking.
Huge masses of granite of gigantic size rose up
from the deep waters, imparting to the locality an
impression of rude grandeur. The titanic blocks
were scored and seamed with the effects of the mighty
waves, which had at some time or other swept with
irresistible force over and around them, scouring
every particle of soil from their rugged faces and
most inaccessible fissures, till by some terrible and
sudden collapse of the earth's crust, the basin of the
lake fell, and these grey pillars and castellated masses
of stone were left a hundred feet above the surface of
the water. Immense blocks and crags of granite
lined the edge of the lake, and rose up peak above
peak, presenting an extraordinary and weird scene of
disarray, ruin, and confusion. On all sides there
were abundant proofs of the gradual rising of the
lake. Villages which a few years before were
standing high and dry at some distance from the
shores, were found either completely covered by the
waters, or in imminent danger of the flood; and the
natives were alive to the certain change which was
taking place in the surface level of the Tanganika.

"Can you see?" said they. "Another rain, and we
shall have to break away from here, and build anew."

"Where does the water of the lake go to?"

"It goes north, then it seems to come back upon
us stronger than ever."

"But is there no river about here that goes towards the west?"

"We never heard of any."

The rugged heights of the western coast are highly venerated by the population, who speak of them as the abodes of the spirits of the mighty dead, of whom they stand in great awe. The natural towers of Mtombwa, which rise to a height of 1200 feet above the shore, are regarded by the superstitious natives with special dread, as they are supposed to shelter the ruling powers of the winds and waves, and to control the tempests which sweep down with terrible violence at times upon the waters of the Tanganika. The exploring party had some experiences of the power of a lake storm or Ma'ander "south-wester," soon after leaving the mouth of the Rufuva River. The guides declared that this was the very worst Ma'ander they had ever passed through. The *Meofu* was hopelessly disabled, her rudder was carried away, and she was only saved from complete destruction by being allowed to drift helplessly on to the beach. The *Lady Alice* flew, like a sea-bird, before the blasts, and topped the waves like a thing of life. The waves rushed along before the tempest with wild noises and foam-crested tops, threatening each moment to engulf the gallant little craft; but she passed safely through the peril, and succeeded at length in finding a secure anchorage in a small creek, behind the grey headland of Kasawa, out of the reach of any further danger from the ruthless hurricane. Mount Murambi, 2000 feet in height, is an impressive feature in the landscape, along the wooded coast of Marunga, and the gorges at its base are the favourite haunts of the "soko" or gorilla, whose voices when heard at a distance resemble, according to Stanley, the noise which is made by a number of villagers when engaged in some wordy quarrel or disputation. The leader of the expedition was anxious to decide the much-disputed question of the flow of the Lukuga, and after examining the mouths of the southern streams, he sailed up the east coast of the lake to the estuary of that river, which had already been partially explored by Cameron in 1874. "The entrance to the Lukuga," says this traveller in Vol. I. of his "Across Africa" was more than a mile across, but closed by a *grass-grown sandbank* with the exception of a channel 300 or 400 yards wide, and across the channel there is a sill where the surf breaks heavily at times, although there is more than a fathom of water at its most shallow part." These facts at once appeared to Stanley to prove that the river was inflowing, and his subsequent investigations, which were conducted with the greatest patience and perseverance, showed that he was correct in this opinion, and the fact was established that Tanganika, although a fresh-water lake, has no affluent or out-flowing river great or small. The tribes along the western banks were kindly disposed towards the visitors, and readily imparted to them any information as to the physical features of the country which they possessed. At a village west of the Kasansayara River, however, a somewhat peculiar reception awaited the boats, and as they drew near the edge of the water to enter into an amicable palaver with the dark-skinned groups upon the shore, the crews were greeted with hoarse cries and furious gestures, which were understood to mean that if they landed they would be attacked and slain. The excited villagers smote the earth and the water with their weapons, and sprang about in fits of passion, hurling huge stones and pieces of sharp rock into the boats, and otherwise conducting themselves in a distinctly uncivil manner.

The white man and his followers gazed calmly upon the scene, and never, by word or look, showed any sign of anger or pleasure, until, worn out by their unnecessary exertions, the excited natives became calm and sober in their demeanour. Para, the interpreter and guide of the party, then explained to them that their conduct had been so outrageously absurd, that the white man declined to have any communication whatever with them. The boats then turned away in silence, and tried to land at the town of Mabonga, where they again met with a far from flattering welcome. The people of Mabonga, in reply to the salutations of the voyagers, rudely derided them, and, when asked to supply them with food, cried out that they were not the slaves of the white man and his companions, and that they did not plant their fields with grain to sell to such as them.

On the 31st of July the *Lady Alice* was once more anchored off Ujiji, after an absence of fifty-one days, during which she had sailed, without disaster, a distance of over 810 miles.

The leader of the Expedition was cordially welcomed back to his old quarters by the Arabs and the main body of the force, which had been left behind during the cruise to the south, under the charge of young Pocock, who had suffered terribly from fever during the absence of his chief. Small-pox had also attacked

the town, and several of the native bearers had been
stricken down by the foul complaint, which, amongst
the natives of Africa, who are unprotected by vacci-
nation, takes a most virulent and loathsome form.
Villages are depopulated by the scourge, the healthy
flee from the epidemic in terror, and the sick and
suffering are left, untended and unsolaced, to die or
recover as chance may decide.   Something like a panic
had seized upon the place, every house was afflicted
with mourning and woe ; the Arabs were paralyzed by
fear of the pest ; and thirty-eight men of the Expedition had deserted and fled to the coast.   No letters
had reached Stanley for over nineteen months, and he
was naturally anxious to receive some news from home
before entering once more upon his wanderings through
the trans-Tanganika country, but he felt that if he
were to get away at all, he must decide to leave Ujiji
at once, before his native force was entirely decimated
by disease or desertion.

On August 25, therefore, the bugle sounded for the
advance to the canoes, to which those members of the
Expedition who were ready to take flight at the
earliest opportunity were conducted as prisoners by an
escort of the " faithful."   The entire force now numbered 132 men, but only thirty of these were trusted
with guns.   On the second day three more Wangwana
decamped, and finally young Kalulu, the lad who had
been adopted by Stanley, and partially educated in
Europe, decamped, and could nowhere be found.
Strong measures had to be taken to save the enterprise from complete failure ; and trusted parties were
sent out in all directions to scour the country in search
of the fugitives.   Six of the runaways were brought

back, and Kalulu was also obliged to return to his allegiance, after having been traced to the Arab colony on Kasengé Island. The labours of Livingstone had been more than once brought to an untimely end, for the time, by the cowardly flight of his followers, who preferred the indolent life of the Arab settlements to the terrors and privations of a march through unknown lands, and it was only after a display of stern determination on the part of Stanley that he was able to transport his people across to the western shores of the lake without further loss, and thus avoid the total collapse of the enterprise which he had taken in hand. Foolish and exaggerated reports had been industriously circulated amongst his men as to the fiery meteors, hobgoblins, terrible spirits, and man-eating tribes to be met with in the regions which their leader was about to traverse, and it required all the tact and courage of their commander to successfully combat the adverse influences which were at work to scatter his forces and destroy his hopes. Landing at Mtowa, the party found themselves in the territory of a peaceable and amiable people, who readily brought their produce into the camp, and evinced a mixed feeling of respect and fear for the white man, about whom they had their own ideas. "How can the white men be good, when they do not come for trade?" they asked, "whose feet one never sees, who always go covered from head to foot with clothes! Do not tell us they are good or friendly. There is something very mysterious about them; perhaps wicked. Probably they are magicians; at any rate, it is better to leave them alone, and to keep close until they are gone." In some of the villages of the Waguha and Wabinjwé, some interesting specimens of native skill in the arts of stone and wood carving were noticed. Figures in wood adorned the houses, and some of the men were ornamented with wooden medals, upon which a rough resemblance to a human face was portrayed. The route of the Expedition now lay for some distance through the country of the Uhombo people, a district remarkable for its fruitfulness, and abounding in delightful scenery. The people were busily employed in their fields of sugar-cane, millet, maize, and sweet potatoes, and kept the travellers well supplied with good food and delicious fruit of various kinds. In personal appearance they were by no means attractive, and, in fact, they presented the most repulsive and degraded type of humanity in Central Africa. Their features were forbidding and ugly, and their habits and dress were alike disagreeable and offensive; but in spite of their outward seeming, they proved to be a generous and tender-hearted race.

On the 5th of October the frontier-town of the Mangema people was reached, and Stanley was much interested by the native stories which he heard of Livingstone and his doings in this far-off land.

They showed Stanley the house which the doctor occupied during his sojourn amongst them, and Livingstone's various acts of kindness and his gentle manners were recounted and dwelt upon in sorrowful and affectionate accents by these uncivilized sons of the wilderness.

On the 11th of October the Luama river was crossed, and after passing unmolested through the dreaded region of the man-eating Manyema, the Expedition halted upon the banks of the long-sought and stately

Lualaba. The course from Ujiji to the banks of the
Lualaba had been one of unusual peace and compara-
tive comfort. The native chiefs had received the
travellers with hospitality, and sent them on their way
with cordial expressions of good-will, and often with
large gifts of provisions, or offers of guides for the
road. The little force had, happily, been free from
sickness, and the old dread of the strange nations of
the interior had almost died out. With wild shouts of
delight the tired bearers put down their loads for the
moment, and gazed with their gratified leader upon
the broad waters which they had journeyed so far to
behold.

At Mwana Mamba the Expedition came up with a
large body of Arabs, who were returning from a raid
into the Manyema country, which they had invaded to
avenge the murder of one of their own people, a trader
of some distinction. From these men Stanley was
able to obtain much useful information as to the causes
which had deterred both Livingstone and Cameron
from pursuing their investigations along the course of
the Lualaba. Tippo-Tib, a wealthy and powerful Arab,
who had accompanied the latter in some of his explorations, at once described to Stanley the difficulties
which lay before him, should he determine, at all
hazards, to follow up the course of the river.

The obstacles which had baffled and turned back
the two valiant men, who had already attempted to
solve the greatest problem of African geography, were
formidable, and apparently inconceivable. No canoes
could be had ; and the reported hostility to the white
man of the savage hordes who lined the banks of the
stream had so effectually scared the followers of Living-

stone and Cameron, that they resolutely refused to
accompany their leaders upon a river which led no one
knew whither. After considerable delay, however, a
small fleet of canoes was obtained by Stanley, and the
interest of Tippo-Tib having been secured by an offer
of liberal remuneration for his services, and a promise
of full compensation for any loss which he might sustain
in the course of the passage, the Arab agreed to accompany the Expedition with a force of 300 men for, at
least, a distance of sixty camps. The conditions of
the contract were :—

1. That the journey should commence from Nyangwé, in any direction the leader of the exploring party
might choose, and on any day fixed by him.

2. That the journey should not occupy more time
than three months from the first day it was commenced.

3. That the rate of travel should be two marches to
one halt.

4. That the Arab's force, after accompanying the
party for sixty marches—each march of four hours'
duration—should return to Nyangwé with the exploring party, for mutual protection and support, unless
they fell in with traders from the west coast, in which
case Stanley might proceed to the western sea, provided he allowed two-thirds of his people to return
with Tippo-Tib to Nyangwé.

5. That, exclusive of the 5000 dollars agreed upon
as the price of the Arab's support, the leader of the
exploring party was to provision 140 of Tippo's men
till the whole body returned to Nyangwé.

6. That if, after experience of the countries and the
natives, it was found impracticable to continue the

journey, and it was decided to return before the sixty marches were completed, Tippo was not to be held responsible, but he was to be paid the 5000 dollars in full, without any deduction.

On the 2nd of November, 1876, the combined forces were assembled at Nyangwé for the start down the stream to the great Atlantic. The men of the Expedition, 146 in number, were supplied with rifles, and a supply of ammunition was served out to them. Encouraged by the formidable array of Tippo's contingent, they renewed their promise of fealty to their commander; and the eventful journey, which was "to flash a torch of light across the western half of the Dark Continent," was begun.

On Christmas Day, 1876, the expedition had reached Vinya-Njaia, after a toilsome and perilous journey by land from Nyangwé. The people had suffered terribly all along the route, and they had well-nigh become disheartened when Stanley ordered a halt to be made, and a strong camp formed, in order to give the exhausted men a short rest from the toils of the road. The passage through the dense jungle, along the western banks of the river, where at times a way had to be cut step by step with axes, to allow the boat sections and bales of goods to be carried forward, had sadly tried the endurance and patience of the little army, and the Arabs were so much distressed by these fearful days and weeks spent in the foul atmosphere and slush and reek of the "pagan's forest," that they decided to break their contract and return to the south. The progress through the hateful woods was painfully slow. The marching column was utterly disorganized, and every man did the best he could for himself, as he plunged knee-deep in the slough, or fought his way through the tangle of creepers and convolvuli, which were as thick as cables, or scrambled along, his toes holding on to the path whilst his hands grasped the load upon his head, and his elbows pushed aside the sapling or the brush-wood which obstructed his path. The fetid and confined air of this doleful wilderness of woods soon began to tell upon the men, and the slopping moisture, the dreary monotony, the reeking malarious atmosphere, the horrible odours, and the constant necessity to crawl, and creep, and burrow a way like wild animals through the interlaced and closely matted vegetation, so thoroughly exhausted their energies, and crushed their spirits that a mutiny appeared once more to be inevitable. Forty-one miles north of the Nyangwé Stanley had decided to cross the Lualaba (henceforth to be known as the *Livingstone*) and pursue his course by water. The land-marches had proved disastrous to the health of the force, and small-pox had broken out in the ranks. The natives had ceased to be friendly, and day after day they had mustered in thousands on the banks, and upon the water, to oppose the advance of the white men. In vain Stanley explained to these ferocious savages that his purpose in travelling along their waters was one of peace, and that he had not come to ravage their lands or destroy their villages. The camps of the party were attacked, stragglers were cut off, and the road had for leagues to be forced in the face of hordes of enraged and frantic natives, armed with heavy spears and sheafs of poisoned arrows, which they cast down upon the boats with furious energy, as they drifted northward with the flood. At times every man of the expedition felt that he must fight or accept the only other alternative, a terrible and dishonoured death. The natives in vast numbers would assail the camps, and fling themselves against the hastily raised stockades with a determination and rude valour which severely tried the resources of the little garrisons which were thus brought to bay. The muzzles of the rifles of the besieged expedition at times touched the bodies of their dark-skinned foes as they pressed up to the barricades, and for hours the desperate conflict raged before the natives, terrified at the prowess of the white men, sullenly retired into the gloomy depths of the jungle, and allowed the strangers to proceed on their way in peace. On one occasion a clear passage was only secured for the expedition by an exploit which reveals something of that audacity and readiness of resource which are so characteristic of Stanley.

A tribe remarkable for the fierceness with which it repeatedly attacked the voyagers, had drawn up its canoes in force at a favourable point on the river to check the advance of the party. A desperate struggle for the passage took glace, but the enemy's blockade remained unbroken. In the darkness of the night, however, Stanley put off from his camp, in the midst of a storm of rain and wind, with muffled oars, accompanied by Pocock, to cut adrift the entire fleet of the enemy's canoes, and so effectually disable them from all further opposition to his advance. The adventure was carried through with spirit, and was crowned with success, and the result was that the chiefs of the offending tribe sued for terms of peace, and entered into blood-brotherhood with the daring and ubiquitous strangers. But Tippo Tib and his contingent requested to be released from their engagement. They wished to go back to Nyangwé. The terrible condition of the force, the number of deaths which occurred daily from disease, and the constant fighting for a free passage northward, had so discouraged them that Stanley saw it was useless to attempt to keep them with him any longer. But nothing could damp the ardour or quench the calm but strong enthusiasm of Stanley. His progress had been one continued struggle with difficulties and adversity. He had fought his way so far with invincible courage, and already his force had been painfully thinned by the ravages of disease and the assaults of his implacable foes. But still he did not hesitate for a moment as to the course which he would pursue. He agreed to cancel the agreement with his Arab allies, and decided to press onward, relying altogether upon his own resources. Addressing his men at this crisis in the history of the expedition, he told them that he would never turn back till he had accomplished the work which he had been sent to do, viz. to explore the Livingstone from its source to its mouth. "Therefore," said he, "my children, make up your minds as I have made up mine, that as we are now in the very middle of this continent, and it would be just as bad to return as to go on, we shall continue our journey, and toil on and on by this river, till we reach the great salt sea." The men once more declared their confidence in their leader, and active preparations were made for voyaging down the river. The fleet was mustered on the morning of Christmas Day, and it was found to number twenty-three canoes, to each of which a distinguishing number or name was attached. After taking a kindly farewell of the Arabs, the expedition, mustering 149 souls in all, was embarked; and the flotilla soon spread itself over the broad bosom of the Livingstone, and headed for the Equator. The morning of New Year's Day, 1877, found the party advancing peacefully and hopefully through a magnificent growth of tropical forest, the delightful stillness of which was most grateful to the harassed men, who were slowly drifting over the mighty stream which pierced its dreamy solitudes. From the Kankoré people, who received the expedition with hospitality, Stanley learnt that the district which he had just traversed was the territory of the Amu-Nyam, the most persistent cannibals on the river, whose war-song on sighting the boats of the strangers had been, " We shall eat Wajiwa (people of the sun), to-day! Oho, we shall eat Wajiwa meat, to-day ! " To Kalimbo, the interpreter, one of their chiefs had replied, on seeing the strings of shells and beads and the copper ornaments which were offered for barter, " Do you think we shall be disappointed of so much meat (pointing to the crews in the boats) by the present of a few shells and beads and a little copper ? "

From January 6th to the 28th, a weary period of twenty days, the members of the expedition were fighting their way, step by step, from the first to the seventh cataract of the Stanley Falls. The canoes had repeatedly to be hauled out of the stream and dragged over miles of rugged forest-road, and then launched again upon the wild and turbulent waters, in the midst of violent onslaughts from the cannibal tribes of the region, who hung about the locality, and kept up a perpetual strife with the heroic little band led by the white stranger. The scene at the seventh and last cataract of the series was one of great magnificence. To within a mile of this spot the Livingstone preserves a broad flow of 1300 yards in width; it then suddenly narrows, the current increases, and with a crash like thunder the huge volume of water is flung over the rocky precipice, which is only 500 yards across. The work of passing the rapids had been full of peril, and scarcely a day had passed without a struggle for life with the man-eating warriors of the renowned Bakumi, or the pitiless savages who inhabited the islands surrounded by the seething waters of these falls.

CHAPTER XII.

THE canoes of the expedition were once more afloat upon the grey-brown waters of the Livingstone. The surging, deafening torrents of the falls were left far behind, and aided by the swift current the expedition sailed gaily on its course, cheered by the rude songs of the boatmen, and thankfully feeling that at last the cannibal regions about the mighty cataracts had been safely passed. The health of the men had considerably improved since they had reached the purer atmosphere of the falls, and the absence of any active opposition to their progress after leaving the rapids, and the restful sensation which the entire party experienced, as the crowded flotilla drifted undisturbed over the broad bosom of the tranquil stream, contributed to render this portion of the journey not only pleasant but even enjoyable. Populous villages were seen at intervals along the fertile banks, and occasionally the people gathered in groups on the landing-places and exchanged friendly greetings with the voyagers as they sailed along. The river gradually widened, and in some places it presented a broad glistening expanse quite 4000 yards in breadth. Islands clothed with dense green foliage rose above the level of the waters, and imparted a refreshing tone of colour to the scene, and tall, wooded ridges, and brown, grey and red cliffs, crowned with luxuriant clumps of tropical vegetation, enclosed the silent but rapid stream on both sides. The travellers had grown weary of constant strife, and they sought by every means in their power to avoid conflict with the people along the shores. The woods swarmed with baboons and tiny, long-tailed monkeys. The long, low islands of alluvial soil were alive with flocks of spur-winged geese, kingfishers and flamingoes, and the narrow channels afforded shelter to the hippopotamus, crocodile, and the monitor. But the truce between the dusky sons of the soil and the force of the white man was soon destined to be rudely broken, and once more the sound of the war-drums rolled over the waters, and warned the expedition that danger was near. On approaching the villages of the Bangala, Stanley was startled to find the river blockaded by a crowd of sixty-three canoes, filled with natives who were all armed with guns or rifles, and were evidently bent upon disputing the passage of his men. A sharp conflict took place for the right of way; but after some hours of stubborn resistance, the Bangala drew off, and left the expedition to proceed on its course.

On March 12th the canoes entered a broad lake-like expanse of the river, which was at once named

"Stanley Pool" by the brave fellows who were the first to look upon its glistening waters, and who thus desired to do honour to their trusted and undaunted commander. The voyage from the district of the Bangala to the "Pool" had been free from serious contention with the natives, but the expedition had suffered terribly at times from inability to obtain provisions, owing to the distrust of the villagers, who disappeared into the woods immediately the *Lady Alice* and her consorts hove in sight. About the middle of February the prospect had become most depressing. "Where shall we obtain food? What will be the end of all this? What shall we do?" were the questions which each man asked of his neighbour, and the kindly heart of their leader was wrung with pain at the sight of his drooping followers, who without a murmur endured the pangs of semi-starvation with the fortitude of stoics. At Mengo, however, a market was opened with the chiefs after much palaver, and rich stores of cassava, tubers, and bananas and plantains were soon distributed amongst the famished wanderers, who were beginning to fall into a state of deadly callousness, induced by the painful privations they had undergone. A visit of state was paid to the camp by the chiefs of Bwena and Tuguba, who were attended by an immense crowd of armed followers, and whose approach was announced by the sounding of gongs and bells and the usual royal horns of ivory. Stanley felt once more that he was among friends, and that he was for the first time since leaving Urangi secure and at peace with his neighbours. The weapons carried by the native warriors were highly decorated with brass, and their knives and hatchets of fine iron were beautifully fashioned. The people were skilled craftsmen, and some of their brass and iron ornaments were excellent specimens of clever and tasteful native workmanship. Eight canoes were ordered by the chiefs to accompany the flotilla of the expedition for some distance upon its way, and these well-mannered people parted from their white friend and his followers with hearty expressions of good-fellowship and amity. An attack from the Irebu on the south bank was feared, and every precaution taken as the little fleet threaded its way amongst the groups of thickly-wooded islets of the region of this warlike and inhospitable tribe. Strong gales occasionally swept over the face of the river and the canoes were threatened with a new danger. In spite of tempests, cataracts, and the Irebu, however, good progress was made; and on nearing the shores of Bolobo there were signs in the cultivated fields, peaceful villages, and mild demeanour of the natives that the region of pure and unadulterated African savagery was past, and that the expedition had once more reached a territory inhabited by people who were controlled by the primary laws of humanity. The fishermen, who met them in mid-stream, no longer greeted the strangers with opprobious epithets or insulting grimaces; messengers put off from the shore to invite them to land, and to point out to them the most desirable spot for the erection of a camp; and, instead of the frightful " Bo-bo-bo's " and " Woh-hu-hu-hu's " of the frantic savages up the stream, gentle words of friendly import were wafted across the waters to the delighted wanderers. The change from the chequered experiences of the past was most welcome to the little band.

Their terrors had been many. First the rocks and fierce waters of the cataracts. Then the fell visitations of disease. Next the sudden storm raising the waters into huge brown billows, and filling the boats with their angry foam. Then the greatest peril of all, the wild brutal cannibals who had to be fought at every turn of the stream. Then the awful dread of death by famine. Livingstone had described floating down the Lualaba as "a foolhardy feat," and at times Stanley was more than half inclined to agree with him.

Meanwhile the mystery of the terrible river was being silently unfolded as the expedition pressed on its way. Since leaving Stanley Falls, there had been no longer any doubt in the mind of the sagacious and observant commander as to his being on the Congo. To the cautious inquiry on the subject, which he addressed to the kindly old chief of Rubunga, the reply was "*Ikuto ya Kongo*," and these words at once confirmed his own impression. The flotilla was received in the handsomest manner by the King of Chumbiri, who visited Stanley with a royal escort of five canoes crowded with warriors armed with muskets, and who sent the white man on his way rejoicing with replenished stores, and an imposing guard of honour of forty-five soldiers under the command of the heir-apparent, who was charged to see Stanley and his little band in safety as far as the end of the expanse of waters, which was to be for ever after known to the world as "Stanley Pool," and the devout and friendly tribe implored their fetich to protect their white brother from point to point on his perilous journey and to bring him to his friends in peace. The *thirty-second and last fight* of the expedition took place six miles below the junction of the Nkutu river with the Living-stone. The canoes had been drawn up to the bank, and preparations were being made for the morning meal, when the rattle of musketry suddenly startled the commander of the party, who rushed forward to find that the camp had been attacked by a body of treacherous natives, who had approached them unperceived. A desperate conflict at once began, and for an hour the firing was kept up by both sides with spirit; but the enemy was at length beaten off, after having succeeded in wounding fourteen of Stanley's men.

The left bank of the " Pool," a magnificent sheet of water, thirty square miles in area, was found to be thickly populated by the important tribe of the Batcké, who warned Stanley of the perils of the formidable cataracts which they said crossed the western end of the " Pool." These genial people tried to imitate the terrific noise which was made by the falling waters, to the great amusement of the exploring party, who, guided by the chief Mankoneh, sailed on to inspect the rapids. The puzzled natives were most anxious to know how the white man proposed to navigate the boisterous torrents, which by a graphic display of signs they described as appalling in their grandeur. A camp was formed near the first cataract of the series of rapids (which the commander-in-chief of the expedition at once named the LIVINGSTONE FALLS), and preparations were made to receive the great chief Itsi, the Lord of Ntamo, who had sent to say that he would like to shake hands with the white man who had come down from the High Waters. The party was again in a pitiable plight from want of food, the specious Chumbiri having proved "the most plausible rogue of all Africa," and Stanley was most anxious that there should be peace between himself and his black neighbours, especially as at this point of the passage the tedious operation of hauling-up the canoes, and transporting them bodily over land and then re-launching them upon the smooth flood below the broken waters, would have to be repeated.

Itsi arrived at the camp about midday in a splendid canoe, which measured eighty-five feet in length and four feet in width. This noble vessel presented a most imposing appearance, as she drew up to the shore with her rows of paddlers standing in their places and bending their bodies to the measure of a rousing chorus. The canoe, with Itsi enthroned in state "mid-ship," made for the landing-place at the rate of six knots an hour, to the intense admiration of the white men and their followers, who could not restrain their expressions of astonishment at the "style" in which the Lord of Ntamo travelled through his far-reaching dominion. The total number of persons carried by this enormous craft was eighty-six, including the prince. The two canoes which were in attendance upon the royal barge, carried ninety-two persons in all. The young monarch was very anxious to appropriate the last of the "big goats" of Uregga, which Stanley was conveying with great care to the coast, hoping to send it home as a present to an eminent English lady. The animal was not to be parted with, and Itsi was offered one of the asses, but this gift was declined. Itsi sulked and threatened to stop all supplies, unless his wish as to the goat was at once complied with, and with great reluctance

Stanley finally decided to allow his capricious visitor to have his way. The "largest" goat in Africa was therefore transferred to the royal vessel, and provisions were sent into the camp, and the ceremony of blood-brotherhood having been performed with much unction, the Lord of Ntamo retired, having first handed over to Stanley a small gourdful of a curious powder, which he said would secure his white brother against all harm or evil influences throughout his life. Stanley returned the compliment by formally presenting to Itsi the white man's charm against adversity—a half-ounce vial of magnesia.

On the 16th of March the struggle with the great waters was renewed. As the expedition advanced westward, the natives on the shores of the Livingstone had become amiable and even kind. But the terrors of the river had increased. Mile after mile of raging waters, rushing with awful fury down vast steeps of rock, had to be avoided by dragging the flotilla up the hillsides and over the rough boulders along the edge of the noble stream. Some of the rapids were remarkable for their savage beauty; but the work of getting the expedition in safety past the cataracts so occupied the mind and eyes of Stanley, that the natural charms of this strange and awful combination of towering mountains, eddying waters and mighty rocks, had no attractions for him. The whole region seemed to be full of perils to the tiny host that was, day by day, engaged in a stern and terrible strife with the dread stream, which ploughed its way with angry violence through the vast ravine that leads from the highlands of the interior down to the maritime plains and the great sea. Several of the canoes were dashed to pieces upon the sharp rocks, or

P

carried over the eddying floods and swept down into the foaming depths below, with their crews, never to be seen again. The famous craft, the *London Town*, the " Great Eastern " of the fleet, seventy-five feet long by three feet wide, had been torn from the hands of fifty men, in a piece of the river fitly named the " Cauldron," and carried away to instant destruction. On the same day another canoe of great size and value, the *Glasgow*, was drawn into the current, which rushed seaward at the rate of thirty knots per hour; and accidents of all kinds were constantly happening to the men, who were dashed upon the slippery rocks, or hurled into the hissing stream bruised and disabled, in their gallant efforts to secure the boats, or to snatch some member of their party from a watery grave. Painful dislocations and severe injuries were common, from the peculiar nature of the work upon the glazed trap boulders, which were washed by the furious flood, and Kalulu, Mauredi, and Ferajji, the former the favourite attendant of Stanley, were (to the horror and dismay of their leader and their comrades, who stood helplessly watching the catastrophe) carried with lightning speed over the furious falls since known as the " Kalulu," and never seen again. As the men were gazing in awe-stricken silence at the fatal spot over which their friends had for ever disappeared, a cry came over the deafening flood from a second canoe which was being carried on with fearful violence towards the watery precipice. It contained only one man, the brave lad Soudi, who, turning his sorrowful and despairing face to the excited group upon the shore, cried out as he shot with arrow-like speed past his beloved commander, " La il Allah, il Allah ! (There is but one God !) I am lost! Master!" The men watched the tiny craft as it dropped over the falls, till it was out of sight, hidden by the clouds of spray which rose up from the foot of the roaring, crashing torrents. Nine men were lost in that one afternoon! But Soudi had not been drowned after all. He had been swept down over the upper and lower Kalulu Falls and the intervening rapids, and whirled about in the wild river; but he clung to his canoe, and eventually succeeded in springing upon a rock. No sooner had he reached the shore than he was seized by two natives, who bound him with thongs, and carried him off in triumph to their chief. Such terrible stories of the prowess of the white man with large eyes of fire and long hair, who owned a gun that shot all day, had reached these people, however, that they feared to detain Soudi when they understood that he belonged to Stanley's party, and the captive was dismissed and told to go back to his king, and not to tell him what they had done, but to say that they had been kind to him and saved his life.

The safe passage of the *Lady Alice* over the broken waters and treacherous currents of the falls was to Stanley a matter of frequent anxiety, and more than once the gallant little boat was in serious peril from the snapping of her cables, or the irresistible violence of the eddying tide.

Surrounded by the daily horrors and depressing influences of these endless cataracts, deafened by the ceaseless moaning and thunder of their many voices, and confronted on all sides by rugged cliffs and fearful scenes of nature in her wildest and most threatening aspects, the little party of brave men pushed on towards the ocean, as sternly resolved as ever to effect the great purpose of their journey or to die in the attempt. From March 16th to April 21st the dauntless band had progressed only thirty-four miles! Many of the men were suffering from disease and the effects of their terrible toil in the region of the cataracts, food was scarce, and yet fresh canoes had to be built and launched, if the expedition was ever to reach the mouth of the river, and the entire fleet had to be dragged over a steep ascent of 1200 feet before it could pursue its course once more upon the brown waves of the Livingstone.

After a halt of seven days at Mowa, an advance was made to the neighbourhood of the great cataract of the series. Stanley proceeded alone in advance of the expedition to secure a suitable camping-ground, and to prepare the natives of the locality for the appearance of the main body of the force. Strict injunctions to proceed with the greatest care along the dangerous route were given to the men in charge of the boats, and the anxious commander had taken up a position upon the Zuiga Point, about a hundred yards from the great cataract, to watch for the arrival of the fleet, at a fixed point above the foaming cascade. To his horror and amazement he suddenly perceived a capsized canoe, with several men clinging to it, rolling and tumbling about in the angry waves. Help was instantly sent down to the shore, and strenuous efforts were made to succour the drowning men. The wrecked crew at once flung themselves into the surf and struck out for the bank, upon which their terror-stricken comrades awaited them; but the unfortunate craft swept onward with arrow-like speed, and, dashing over the precipice into the great whirlpools below, was seen no more. At the same moment, Kachéché, the faithful police-officer of the expedition, rushed breathlessly up to the spot upon which his leader was standing, with the cry, "Three are lost!—and—*one of them is the little master!*"

"*The little master*, Kachéché?" gasped Stanley. "Surely not the little master?"

"Yes, he is lost, master!"

"But how came he in the canoe?" said the sorrow-stricken leader. "Speak, Uledi, how came he—a cripple—to venture into the canoe?"

The facts of the painful story are as follows. As the canoe was about to push off, poor Pocock had crawled up and asked to be taken in. He had been suffering for weeks from ulcerated feet, and he wished to follow the course along the river, rather than face the toilsome journey over the rough, rocky pathway by land. The men had ventured too near the falls, and the canoe had drifted into the full force of the current before the crew had realized their danger. Uledi had been the first to hear the dread booming of the rapids ahead, and he had said to Pocock,—

"Little master, it is impossible to shoot the falls; no boat or canoe can do it and live."

"Bah!" said Frank, contemptuously; "did I not see, as we came down, a strip of calm water on the left which, by striking across river, we could easily reach?"

"But, master, this fall is not directly across river, it is almost up and down; the lower part on the left being much farther than that which is on the right, and which begins to break close by here. I tell you the truth," added Uledi, as Frank shook his head sceptically. "Little master, I have looked at all the fall, and I can see no way by water; it will be death to make the trial."

The poor fellow spoke the sad truth; but the high-spirited English youth still urged the men to attempt the passage of the falls.

"I don't believe this place is as bad as you say it is. The noise is not like that of the fall which we have passed, and I feel sure if I went to look at it myself, I would soon find a way."

"Well, if you doubt me, send Mpwapwa and Shamari and Mazoutt to see, and if they say there is a road, I will try it if you command me."

Then Frank sent off two of these to examine, and their report was that the place was quite impassable by water.

Laughing at their fears, Frank said, "I knew what you would say. The Wangwana are always cowardly in the water; the least little ripple has, before this, been magnified into a great wave. If I had only four white men with me I would soon show you whether we could pass it or not."

"Little master," said the coxswain sadly, "neither white men nor black men can go down this river alive, and I do not think it right that you should say that we are afraid. As for me, I think you ought to know me better. See! I hold out both hands, and all my fingers will not count the number of lives I have saved on this river. How then can you say, master, I show fear?"

"Well, if you do not, others do," said Frank.

"Neither are they nor am I afraid. We believe the river to be impassable in a canoe. I have only to beckon to my men, and they will follow me to death —and it is death to go down this cataract. We are now ready to hear you command us to go, and we want your promise that, if anything happens, and our master asks, ' Why did you do it?' that you will bear the blame."

"No, I will not order you. I will have nothing to do with it. You are the chief in this canoe. If you like to go—go, and I will say you are men, and not afraid of the water. If not, stay, and I shall know it is because you are afraid. It appears to me easy enough, and I can advise you. I don't see what could happen."

Turning to the crew, Uledi then said: "Boys, our little master is sorry that we are afraid of death. I know there is death in the cataract; but come, let us show him that the black men fear death as little as white men. What do you say?"

"A man can die but once."

"Who can contend with his fate?"

"Our fate is in the hands of God."

"Enough; take your seats," Uledi said.

"You are men!" cried Frank.

"Bismillah (In the name of God)! Let go the rocks, and shove off," cried the coxswain.

"Bismillah!" replied the men, as they pushed off from the rocks.

They were soon amongst the fearful waters, plunging headlong through the billowy foam. The canoe began to fill as the waves leaped over it, and with a desperate cry of, "Hold on to the canoe, my men; seize a rope each one," Pocock rose to battle with the murderous flood. But it was too late. The helpless craft rolled over into the frightful abyss of waters, and the drowning form of the Englishman was seen drifting over the crest of the breakers, and Frank Pocock was seen no more.

The dreadful tidings soon spread over the district: "The brother of the Mundele is lost—lost at Massassa," wailed the natives; and, moved by tenderness and sympathy, crowds of people came down to Zuiga to weep with the white chief.

"Say, Mundele," asked Ndala, the head-man of the place, "where is your white brother gone to?"

"Home."

"Shall you not see him again?"

"I hope to."

"Where?"

"Above, I hope."

"Ah," said the kindly African, "we have heard that the white people by the sea came from above. Should you see him again, tell him that Ndala is sorry, and that he is angry with Massassa for taking him from you. We have heard from Mowa that he was a good, kind man, and all Zinga shall mourn for him. Drink the wine of our palms, Mundele, and forget it. The Zinga wine will comfort you, and you will not be troubled with your sorrow." [1]

The natives spoke in hushed tones of the dread catastrophe, and the members of the expedition were stupefied by despair. To Stanley, the loss of his friend and faithful companion for thirty-four months, was irreparable.

"As I looked upon the empty tent and the dejected, woe-stricken servants," says Stanley, "a choking sensation of unutterable grief filled me. The sorrow-laden mind fondly recalled the lost man's inestimable qualities, his extraordinary gentleness, his patient temper, his industry, cheerfulness, and his tender

[1] "Across the Dark Continent." (H. M. Stanley.)

friendship; it dwelt upon the pleasures of his society, his general usefulness, his piety, and cheerful trust in our success, with which he had renewed our hope and courage; and each new virtue that it remembered only served to intensify my sorrow for his loss, and to suffuse my heart with pity and regret, that after the exhibition of so many admirable qualities, and such long, faithful service he should depart this life so abruptly, and without reward.

"Alas! alas! In vain we hoped that by some miracle he might have escaped, for eight days after a native arrived at Zinga from Kilanga, with the statement that a fisherman, whilst skimming Kilanga basin for whitebait, had been attracted by something gleaming on the water, and, paddling his canoe towards it, had been horrified to find it to be the upturned face of a white man."

A spirit of mutiny once more seized upon the members of the exploring party, and they said they preferred to be slaves to the heathen about them, rather than follow their white commander any longer, for was he not leading them all to death? The dismal legends of the people about the cataracts had infected the superstitious minds of the men, and they looked with horror upon the prospect of once more battling with the dread spirits of the " Falls." The whole band was called together, and each member requested to state his grievance or describe his wrongs. " We are tired," said the panic-stricken wanderers, "and death is in the river; we are not going to work any more, we have no strength."

" I am hungry too, and have no strength left," said Stanley. " I am so tired and sorry that I could

gladly lie down and die. Do what you will; but while
you stay with me, I follow this river until I come to
the point where it is known. If you don't stay with
me, I still will cling to the river, and will die in it."
A large detachment of the men actually left the camp;
but they were, after much parleying, induced to
return and resume their duties. Two large canoes
and one of the most useful men in the expedition
were lost during the difficult operations of hauling
the fleet once more out of the water and overland to
the basin below Zinga, and three lesser falls remained
to be passed before the smooth water could be
expected. Thirty days had been spent in covering
a distance of only three miles, but still the gallant
leader of the rapidly diminishing little band kept up
his heart, and stoutly faced the dangers which lay in
his path. On July 6th the end of the cruel chasm
along which the weary men had fought their way,
since leaving the Kalulu Falls, for 117 days, was
reached, and guides were secured from the Kakongo
people to lead the party to the "Njali Ntombo
Mataka Falls," which had so often been described by
the natives as the last rapids on the river, and which
Stanley fondly hoped would turn out to be the long-
looked-for "Tuckey's Cataract." On the 16th the
canoes, now carried rapidly on towards their destination by the swift current, approached the Ntombo
Mataka, where they were welcomed in the most genial
manner by a vast concourse of natives of the locality,
who next morning conveyed the entire fleet to the
foot of the rapids in splendid style. These people are
described by Stanley as "the politest people in
Africa," and they gladly accompanied the flotilla

down the river for some miles, out of sheer sympathy
and goodwill for the white man who had treated them
so kindly and rewarded them for their willing services
so liberally. The end of these dark years of toil and
suffering was now approaching. The sea was not far
off, and when Stanley cheered on his weakened and
depressed followers with the tidings that away
yonder to the west, at no great distance, lay the
great ocean which they were seeking, Safen, the coxswain of the *Lady Alice*, entirely lost his reason, so
excited had he become with the joyful news.
Throwing himself at the feet of his leader, he cried
out, "Ah, master! El hamnd ul Illah! We have
reached the sea! We are home! We are home!
We are home! We shall no more be tormented by
empty stomachs and accursed savages! I am about
to run all the way to the sea, to tell your brothers
you are coming." The poor fellow at once plunged
into the forest, and although diligent and anxious
search was made for him, he was never found.
Beautiful and impressive scenery surrounded the
party on every side—marvellous and ever-changing
combination of sky and cloud, and river and forest—
but food there was none. Along the deep glens and
wooded ravines, or upon the red banks of the mighty
river the famished wanderers looked in vain for
something to stay the pangs of hunger, which
maddened them at times, and caused them to drift
silently and sullenly over the tawny flood with bowed
heads and sunken eyes, their knees bent with
weakness, and their frames no longer rigid with the
vigour of youth and life and the fire of devotion to
duty. With shrunken limbs, sallow and gaunt

features, and dilapidated garments, this miserable remnant of the noble band of fresh and ardent men who set out years before from the Indian Ocean, trudged on with one thought only possessing it—a longing to look at last upon the great western sea.

The perishing expedition could no longer be restrained by the rules or maxims of civilized life, and the wretched creatures scattered over the country, like ravenous animals, in search of food. The fury of the inhuman natives was aroused, and they resented this summary invasion of their cassava and bean plots, by firing upon the strangers. Uledi returned to the camp, carrying upon his shoulders a poor half-starved comrade, who had with difficulty been rescued from the hands of the people of the district, and he had a doleful story to tell of what had befallen himself and his companions in their raid for the necessaries of life.

"Several men have been captured for stealing cassava and beans," said he, in reply to the questions of his commander.

"Why did you do it?"

"We could not help it," said one. "Master, we are dying of hunger. We left our beads and moneys—all we had—on the ground, and began to eat, and they began shooting." Six men had been wounded during the foray, and three, Ali Kiboga, Matagua, and Saburi Rehanini, had been enslaved by the exasperated villagers. Kiboga afterwards escaped, and made his way, after undergoing extraordinary adventures, to Loanda. He was taken by one of the Donald Currie steamers eventually to Cape Town, where through the kindness of the agent of the Union Company, the poor fellow was given a free passage to Zanzibar on board the *Kaffir*. The steamer was wrecked soon after leaving Table Bay, and in a notice of the disaster the *Cape Times* of February 19th, 1878, says, " On the rocks were some natives of Zanzibar. Among them was the man who had gone through Africa with Stanley. This man was supposed to have been drowned with four others. But early in the morning he was found very snugly lying under a tent made of a blanket, with a roaring fire before him. Of all the wrecked people that night, there was no one who had been more comfortable than Stanley's Arab. The power of resource and the genius of the master had evidently been imparted in some degree to the man."

The cataract of Isangila was safely passed on July 30th, and as provisions were ruinously dear, a handful of ground-nuts costing a necklace of beads, and cowries being of no market value whatever, the order was given to press steadily forward. Boma was now only five days' journey distant. It was decided to leave the river, and make for the settlement of the white men overland. " Allah ! " shouted the delighted men. " God is good ! " Double rations were delivered out to every man, woman, and child in the column ; but the long-suffering people gained little by the liberality of their leader, for there was nothing in this famine-stricken country to buy. Stores of all kinds, which were no longer of use, were distributed to the members of the little band, and their hearts were made glad by rich gifts of iron spears, knives, axes, copper, brass wire, bags of clothing, blankets, waterproofs, and, in fact, the entire impedimenta of the expedition. Still no wholesome food could be obtained. Bitter cassava, a few ground-nuts, or a bunch of bananas, were offered by the greedy natives in return for the valuable articles which the Wangwana of the expedition gladly sacrificed to obtain these miserable supplies. The *Lady Alice* was now abandoned to her fate, and after a journey of 7000 miles up and down the African inland waters, she was left to bleach and rot beside the restless waters of the Isangila cataract. Forty men of the travel-worn and decimated column were sick with dysentery, ulcers, and scurvy, and as the weary band of stricken humanity wended its way over the uplands, or defiled slowly and painfully over the broad prairies of sere scrub and coarse bush, the eyes of its commander were for ever searching the country in front and all around to detect any signs of villages or any promise of food for the tottering and forlorn host which followed him with lagging footsteps and mournful exclamations.

At Ndambi Mbongo the chiefs appeared, superbly attired in smart red military coats, long out of fashion. " Food," said Stanley, " bring us food." Beads were offered. " Cannot." " For wire ?" " We don't want wire." " For cowries ?" " Are we bushmen ?" " For cloth ?" " You must wait three days for a market ! If you have got rum you can have plenty ! " The people were not rude or violent to the strangers, but they were callous and greedy. They conversed freely with the white man, and told him, to his intense joy, that a smart messenger could reach Boma in three days from their village. With stiffened limbs and faltering steps the march was resumed. The old men and the children suffered terribly, but the younger men helped their aged companions, and the fathers shouldered their children and still trudged on through the bleak and desolate land towards the great ocean. A mile from Mwato Wandu, as the file of disconsolate travellers drew near one of the villages, the old chief appeared, followed by fifty followers all armed with guns, and demanded tribute of the wayfarers.

"Know you I am king of this country?" said he, addressing Stanley in excited tones.

"I knew it not, my brother," was the mild reply.

"I am the king, and how can you pass through my country without paying me?"

"Speak, my friend; what is it that the Mundelé can give you?"

"Rum. I want a big bottle of rum, and then you can pass on."

"Rum?"

"Yes, rum; for I am the king of this country!"

"Rum!" replied Stanley wonderingly.

"Rum, rum is good. I love rum," said the old toper with a horrible leer.

Uledi at that moment stepped forward, saying, "What does this old man want, master?"

"He wants rum, Uledi. Think of it."

"There's rum for him," he said, giving his Majesty a sound slap upon his face, of such force that the king fell to the ground from his stool, and having regained his feet made off with his warriors as fast as his legs could carry him back to his village. On August 4th the party encamped at Nsanda, and a letter was

despatched by Stanley by two young natives at once
"to any gentleman who speaks English at Embomma." [2]   The epistle was as follows:—

"DEAR SIR,—I have arrived at this place from
Zanzibar, with 115 souls, men, women, and children.
We are now in a state of imminent starvation. We
can buy nothing from the natives, for they laugh at
our kinds of cloth, and beads, and wire. There are no
provisions in the country that may be purchased,
except on market-days, and starving people cannot
afford to wait for these markets. I, therefore, have
made bold to despatch three of my young men natives
of Zanzibar, with a boy named Robert Feruzi, of the
English mission at Zanzibar, with this letter craving
relief from you. I do not know you; but I am told
that there is an Englishman at Embomma, and as you
are a Christian and a gentleman, I beg you not to disregard my request. The boy Robert will be better
able to describe our lone condition than I can tell you
in this letter. We are in a state of the greatest distress; but if your supplies arrive in time, I may be
able to reach Embomma within four days. I want
300 cloths, each four yards long, of such quality
as you trade with, which is very different from
what we have; but better than all will be ten or
fifteen men-loads of rice or grain, to fill their pinched
bellies immediately, as even with the cloth it will
require time to purchase food, and starving people
cannot wait. The supplies must arrive within two
days, or I may have a fearful time of it among the
dying. Of course I hold myself responsible for any

expense you may incur in this business. What is
wanted is immediate relief; and I pray you to use
your utmost energies to find it at once. For myself,
if you have any such little luxuries as tea, coffee,
sugar, biscuits, by you, such as one man can easily
carry, I beg you on my behalf that you will send a
small supply, and add to the great debt of gratitude
due to you upon the timely arrival of the supplies for
my people. Until that time, I beg you to believe me,

" Yours sincerely,

" H. M. STANLEY,

" Commanding Anglo-American Expedition for
Exploration of Africa

"P.S.—You may not know me by name; I therefore add, I am the person that discovered Livingstone
in 1871.—H. M. S."

The letter was copied in Spanish and French, and
Uledi volunteered to accompany the native bearers.
" Oh, master, don't talk any more," said the generous
fellow, " I am ready now. See, I will only buckle on
my belt, and I shall start at once, and nothing will
stop me. I will follow on the track like a leopard."
" And I am one," said Kachéchi. " Leave us alone,
master, if there are white men at Embomma, we will
find them out. We will walk, and walk, and when
we cannot walk we will crawl." The messengers left
the camp, and foragers were sent out to find food for
the support of the people till supplies could reach
them from Boma. On August 6th the caravan was
suddenly startled by the shrill cry of a lad who said,
" Oh! I see Uledi and Kachéchi coming down the
hill, and there are plenty of men following them ! "

"What—what—what," cried the people, as they rushed out from the tall grass to gaze at the distant hill-side.

"Yes, it is true! it is true! La il il Allah! Yes, it is food! food! food! food at last! Ah, that Uledi! he is a lion, truly! We are saved, thank God!" [3]

The sacks were opened, and soon the famished crowd, with apron, and bowl, and utensil, bore away the rice, sweet potatoes, and fish in triumph to their huts or tents. Water was brought up from the river, fuel was gathered in haste, and hope and joy reigned where a few hours ago all had been bitter despair. A kindly letter of congratulation accompanied the supplies from the warm-hearted traders of Boma, and Stanley turned into his tent with a heart overflowing with gratitude for the mercies of that memorable day.

The long war against famine and the terrible force of nature was over at last! The gracious God be praised for ever! The people were reclad with bright garments and flowing robes of white, and on August 9th, 1877, just 999 days after leaving Zanzibar, the expedition was met by the European traders of Boma, four in all, who had come out to receive the illustrious traveller, and welcome him back once more to civilization and peace. The fame of the commander of the Anglo-American Expedition had preceded him, and the gentlemen of Boma felt proud of the honour of being the first white men to render to the heroic man that homage which they felt was due to the friend of Livingstone, and the explorer of the great river, which flowed past them with majestic volume to the great ocean of the west.

[3] "Across the Dark Continent."

A passage was taken for the whole party from hospitable Boma to Ponta da Lenha, and on to the sea, where Stanley was at once offered a passage for his faithful Zanzibari on board the Portuguese gunboat *Tamega*. On their arrival at Loanda, the brave fellows were transhipped to H.M.S. *Industry*, and safely conveyed to Cape Town. Stanley had resolved to see them back to their island home, and at Cape Town he was most graciously received by Commodore Francis William Sullivan, whose guest he remained at the Admiralty House, while preparations were made by the courteous admiral for the transport of the entire force and its leader to Zanzibar. On the 8th of November the *Industry* sailed out of Simon's Bay amid the cheers of the blue-jackets and the best wishes of the hosts of friends which Stanley had secured during his brief stay at the Cape. Fourteen days after, the palm groves and bright green hill slopes of Zanzibar were sighted, and the people, now robust, bright and happy, looked out with delight upon their pleasant island home.

As soon as the keel of the *Industry* touched the beach, the happy fellows, with their wives and little ones, sprang down the sides of the ship, and threw themselves upon the white sands, and poured out their thanks to Allah! The news rang along the beach, "It is Bwana Stanley's expedition that has returned." Wages were paid, the relatives of the dead martyrs to science whose bones were bleaching upon the banks of the far-off river were consoled and compensated for their losses, and on the 13th December, 1877, Stanley took passage on board the British India steamer *Pachumba* for Aden and home. A magnificent and enthusiastic welcome was accorded to the intrepid discoverer of the Congo on his arrival in England. Addresses of congratulation were forwarded to him from the chief public bodies of Great Britain, and high honours were conferred upon him by the Governments of Europe and America, and by all the great scientific and learned societies of both hemispheres.

CHAPTER XIII.

THE record of the founding of the Congo Free State
has been said to occupy the most romantic page of
modern history. There is nothing exactly like it in
the annals of this or any century. During the time
that Stanley, with heroic fortitude, was pressing westward to the Atlantic, along the course of the Congo,
with only a mere handful of followers, and in the face
of obstacles formidable enough to daunt the bravest
heart, a growing interest in Central African affairs
was manifesting itself both in Europe and America.
The attention of the civilized world had been powerfully drawn to the resources and capacities of the
1,300,000 square miles of well watered and productive
country, with its population of fifty millions, which
the brilliant discoveries of Burton, Speke, Livingstone,
and others had revealed, and brought to the light of
day. In 1876 "The International African Association" was established, under the auspices of the large-
hearted Belgian monarch, Leopold II., who in the
autumn of that year brought together at Brussels a
remarkable gathering of geographical and scientific

notabilities, for the discussion of a plan to secure for Inner Equatorial Africa the solid advantages of civilization, and the benefits of unrestricted and legitimate commerce. It was decided by the conference to open up a safe and direct highway right through the heart of the continent, the security and free passage of which would be maintained by means of a chain of well-furnished "hospitable and scientific stations" established at intervals along the road from the East Coast to Ujiji and the great lake district of the remote interior. The honourable and humane efforts of this association met with speedy success, and before the end of 1880 an excellent route had been secured for the passage of the caravans and the transit of merchandise from Zanzibar to the Belgian settlement of Karema overlooking the blue waters of the Tanganika.

The magnificent results of Stanley's recent discoveries upon the Upper Congo led in 1877 to the formation of a distinct branch of the International African Association, for the purpose of obtaining further information, and devising a scheme for the opening out of the Higher Congo region and the development of its immense and valuable natural resources. This body was known as the "Comité d'Études du Haut Congo," and it declared in an official statement of its objects that it was to devote itself to the special work of investigating in detail the great watershed of the now famous river, and decide upon some method of bringing the newly-found region into closer commercial and political relationship with the other communities of Africa, and with the older nationalities beyond the seas. The scheme of the

Comité met with the cordial and eager approval of the Royal President of the International African Association, its headquarters was fixed at Brussels, and King Leopold not only aided the new organization by his wise counsel and practical co-operation in the discussion of its plans, but he generously assisted it by large subsidies of money from his private purse.

The country about the mouth of the Congo had been known to the Portuguese since 1485, when it was formally annexed to the dominions of Dom Joas II. by Diego Cao, a Portuguese officer, who was trying to find a road to the East Indies by coasting round Africa. Diego completed the ceremony of annexation by setting up a stone obelisk, previously consecrated for the purpose by some prelate of the Church, at the mouth of the tawny stream, to testify to all whom it might concern, that the surrounding territory formed part of the ancient and renowned kingdom of Portugal. Nothing, however, was really done for many centuries to make good the claim of the Portuguese or even to explore the course of the mysterious stream, which now became known as the Rio de Padrao, or Pillar river.

In 1816 an English expedition under Captain James Kingston Tuckey, was sent to the spot, which had begun to derive an unenviable notoriety from the slave-trade which was carried on upon the neighbouring waters. Captain Tuckey was instructed, among other things, to clear up the supposed connection of the Zaire (the ancient native name for the Congo) with the Niger, and to obtain accurate information as to the vast tract of country through which it flowed. It was said at the time that "there never was in this, or in any other country, an expedition of discovery sent out with better prospects or more flattering hope of success than the one in question." Tuckey succeeded in ascending the swift-flowing waters for a distance of 172 miles, when the party was beaten back to the coast by disease, disaster, and death. All the chief members of the expedition, including Tuckey, perished upon the shores of the inhospitable river, but not before valuable information as to its course, soundings, and currents, as well as curious facts about the tribes upon its banks, had been secured and dutifully transmitted to the Home Government. "Tuckey's Farthest" remained the limit of the "long winding Zaire" till, in 1867, Livingstone came upon the sources of the great waterway hidden in the silence of the far-off Uguha Hills. The plan of operations decided upon by the "Comité d'Études du Haut Congo" was to send out an exploring party with directions to enter the river from the Atlantic and proceed eastward, to establish stations for purposes of observation and trade, to arrange treaties between the native chiefs and the Comité, and to carry out a careful scientific survey of the whole country north and south of the stream, as far as practicable. Special attention was to be paid to the character of the stream, to the peculiarities of its flow, currents, soundings, and volume, its capacities for navigation by specially adapted steamers, the disposition of the natives to trade with Europeans, and the quality and amount of native products likely to be available for barter in return for articles of European manufacture.

In January Mr. Stanley was on his way to England for a lengthened period of rest, after the terrible exer-

tion and distressing privations he had undergone in
his journey of 7158 miles through the centre of Africa.
As he stepped out of the train at Marseilles, however,
a fresh and totally unlooked-for call to renewed work
awaited him. Two special Commissioners from the
King of the Belgians received him upon the platform
with a kindly greeting from their august master, and
the request that he would accept the leadership of the
new enterprise which the Comité d'Études du Haut
Congo had decided to inaugurate without delay, for the
ascent of those very waters from the fearful and treacherous perils of which he had only just been delivered.

Utterly wearied in mind and body by the terrible
experiences of the past two years, and oppressed with
a spiritless lassitude begotten of the incessant
worries and anxieties which had pressed upon him
from the moment he left Zanzibar till he beheld the
surging waters of the Atlantic laving the bunda at
Banana Point, he resolutely declined to entertain the
idea of another African journey. He offered in the
most generous and hearty manner, however, to place
all his unique and painfully acquired knowledge of the
river and its tributaries at the disposal of the Comité,
and he agreed to furnish practical hints as to details
for the guidance of that body in organizing its
expedition of exploration, but he shrank altogether
from a return in person to a region which was only
associated in his thoughts, for the time, with pain,
disappointment, and woe. "At present," he said to
the royal emissaries, "I cannot think of anything
more than a long rest and sleep." The public were
eager, however, to read the record, in his own vivid
and felicitous language, of his recent experiences, and

his publishers pressed upon him the necessity of at once setting to work upon the story of his passage " Through the Dark Continent." The book was sent to press in May, and then came blissful months of relaxation, luxury, and liberty, which were spent in roaming over the continent and enjoying once more the pleasures and comforts of civilized life. The existence of the fashionable lounger does not appear to have suited either the taste or the constitution of the man whose creed is one of DOING. The inactivity and the inane pleasures of a man without a purpose, soon disgusted him, and after a few delightful and invigorating weeks spent amongst the Swiss Alps, he welcomed with unfeigned pleasure a message from Brussels, reminding him of the work which the Comité d'Études du Haut Congo had in hand, and of his promise, made in person to the Royal President at his palace in the summer, that he would aid and advance the novel and humane enterprise of the Comité to the best of his ability.

In November, 1878, the formal offer of the honourable post of Commander-in-chief of the expedition was made to Stanley in the royal council-chamber at Brussels, in the presence of a large and influential assemblage of commercial and financial magnates and politicians (English, French, German and Dutch), who had come together to give their most cordial and practical support to the project of the Comité. 20,000l. were at once raised for the initiation of the scheme, and on January 23rd, 1879, Stanley was once more on the wing to Zanzibar, to engage suitable men for escort and carrying purposes for the Expedition du Haut Congo.

Two steamers were secured—the *Albion* of Leith, which was to proceed to the east coast and convey the leader and his band of Zanzibaris round by the Suez Canal and the Atlantic to the estuary of the Congo —and the *Barga*, which was to make direct for Banana Point, with officers for the stations; engineers for the river craft; portable sheds, houses, huts for the native bearers; waggons, boats, and steamers and machinery in sections; and stores and arms and ammunition. Instructions were sent out to Mr. Albert Jung, whom Stanley had previously met in London, and who resided as chief of the largest factory on the Congo at Banana Point, to hire a large body of Kroo boys, to be ready to act as porters and stevedores at the various landing-places up the river, and to receive with all due hospitality and to provide for the various officers and passengers of the *Barga*, and to store her freight pending the arrival of Stanley himself at the base of operations. Meanwhile the *Albion* was pushing on with all speed to Zanzibar, where Stanley had to inquire into the fate of, and send relief and stores to, the first expedition of the International African Association, which had fallen into the toils of the mendacious Mirambo somewhere west of Unyanyembe. Detailed instructions were despatched to Mr. Cambier, the commander of the unfortunate party, in which Stanley advised him as to his future relations with the astute and unscrupulous prince who had detained him, and as to the best course to take for Ujiji, to avoid further complications with the native chiefs.

A second Belgian expedition was on its way from Europe, to follow up the work of the International African Association from Zanzibar westward to Ujiji and the Trans-Tanganikan territory, and Stanley had been requested by King Leopold to assist it with his advice as to hiring pagazis, buying stores, and the best method of meeting and overcoming the difficulties and perils of the road to the interior. He could no longer delay his own departure for the West Coast, however, and he was therefore only able to leave written instructions for the guidance of Captain Popelin, the commander of the undertaking. These papers thoroughly reveal at once the practical spirit and strong common sense of the writer. They are not without touches of quiet humour, and the neat way in which blame is suggested, rather than openly expressed is worthy of attention, whilst the strong self-reliance of the man, and his marvellous grasp of details, that true mark of real genius, are evident in every line even of his most prosaic and commonplace communications and despatches. The gentle, kindly manner, for instance, in which, in his letter to M. Cambier, he reminds him of the real purpose and *pacific character* of the Society which he represented, and of the need there would always be for the greatest care on the part of its agents in forming alliances, offensive and defensive, with slave-trading Arabs, and the habitual caution which he enjoins upon the military chief of the second expedition, thirsting for distinction, and probably somewhat inclined by his professional instincts to prefer martial methods of settling matters, are excellent specimens of his official epistolary style. To the latter he says, " Construct a bush fence round your camp each night after crossing the Kingari River. Rush not into danger by any overweening confidence in your breech-loading rifles, and military knowledge. Be not tempted to *try your mettle* against the native chiefs. Be calm in all your contentions with the natives, and one golden rule which you should remember is, "Do not fire the first shot, whatever may be the provocation."

Having secured a strong band of seventy men for the ascent of the Congo (many of whom had already crossed the continent with him), the *Albion* steamed out of the bustling harbour of Zanzibar, and sped northward on her passage to the West Coast at the end of May, 1879.

Whilst the little steamer was diligently pursuing her onward way over the pellucid waters of the Mediterranean, and along the surf-beaten shores of the Gold Coast, where Stanley had landed a few years before on his way to witness the defeat of King Coffee and the destruction of Coomassie, the leader of the new venture was preparing himself for the undertaking by a thorough and painstaking study of the instructions which he had received from time to time from the Comité, which had now become the "Association Internationale du Congo." He desired to realize for himself, in the quiet of his temporary solitude in the state cabin of the *Albion*, the magnitude, probabilities, and enormous difficulties of the task which he had pledged himself at Brussels to carry out to a successful issue.

At Sierra Leone the presence of a strange craft freighted with a crowd of blacks, and bound upon a voyage upon which no reliable details were forthcoming, soon attracted the attention of the officials of the colony, who probably expected that a tentative revival of the slave traffic, and all the horrors of the

"Middle Passage," was being attempted.   A courteous
and frank note of explanation to Sir Samuel Rowe,
the able and public-spirited Governor of the Colony,
soon set matters straight, and an incident which for
the moment promised to end in an unpleasant exhibition of colonial bullying and ill-humour, was agree-
ably closed by a trip and a lunch in the Governor's
pleasure-steamer, which was thoroughly enjoyed by
all the members of the Congo party.

Twenty days—or if all went well, only eleven days
now—and the keel of the *Albion* would be cleaving
the ruddy waters of the Pillar River of the old
Portuguese navigators ! Stanley was longing to see
the rich brown waves foaming out into the brine of the
great sea, and to find himself once more upon the
broad bosom of the remarkable stream with which his
name will be for ever united—the Zaire of the natives
—the Congo of our geographers.   His mission was
eminently calculated to develop the highest aspirations
and animate the noblest resolutions of the man.   He
was the herald of amity and good-will from the most
civilized powers of the world to the vast and semi-
barbarous tribes of Inner Africa.   He was the pioneer
of a splendid and carefully matured scheme, which
sought to elevate and secure in a condition of honourable independence the population of a land more
extensive in area than India or China, and inhabited
by fifty millions of souls.   He was to build up a Free
Negro State in the heart of Africa, under European
patronage and protection, and to secure for the new
province a future of prosperity and sustained greatness
by opening out well-constructed roads, erecting forts
and trading depôts, building piers and landing-places

at convenient spots along the river banks, locating
stations for observation, defence, and commercial
purposes, by framing just and equitable treaties with
the surrounding people, and above all by creating a
feeling of confidence in and respect for the probity
and good faith of the European merchant and the
Christian missionary.

On August 14th, exactly twelve months after
emerging at the mouth of the river a broken-spirited
and desolate wanderer, Stanley entered once more the
harbour of Banana Point, the chief trading-station and
place of call for ocean steamers on the northern
bank of the estuary of the Congo. As the *Albion*
steamed to her anchorage in the shadow of the busy
factories on the sandy promontory, upon which the
settlement is built, it was at once seen that the
Barga had discharged her mixed cargo of stores,
boats, and building materials, landed the subordinate
officers of the expedition—Englishmen, Belgians,
Danes, a Frenchman, and an American—and had left
the coast on her way back to Europe. There in line
lay the tiny fleet of vessels specially constructed for
the enterprise, awaiting the arrival of its commander,
and everything was being pushed forward for the
advance eastward in good earnest directly Stanley
should appear. Some days were spent by the sagacious chief, however, in thoroughly overhauling and
testing the craft, and seeing that each vessel and boat
was in perfect order for the trying work which they
would have to go through in breasting that mighty
stream of waters which poured down to the sea in a
silent, but almost irresistible volume; in making the
acquaintance of the persons who were to act under

him; and in maturing his plans for the passage up the stream.

Seven days after landing on the coast, Stanley gave the welcome signal for the start, and on August 21st, the *Espérance, Royal, En Avant, La Belgique,* and the *Jeune Africaine,* each having in tow barges or boats laden with material or stores, drew out into the stream and headed eastward, in the face of an opposing current which at once began to test their staying powers. There was nothing attractive about the scenery along the lower reach of waters from Banana Point to Boma. Both banks were covered with dense impenetrable wood, and presented one uniform aspect of dull, dreary monotony. Here and there an island covered with coarse vegetation rose above the heaving flood, but no sound broke the oppressive stillness of the desolate scene, except the hoarse breathing of the engines, as they struggled with the ceaseless tide, or the signals of the various divisions of the party as they pursued their way, now over the full bosom of the mighty torrent which in places spread out to a width of miles, with a depth of 900 feet, and a flow of over four million cubic feet of water per second, now amongst the groups of swampy and repulsive islets of slime and mud, which rose at intervals above the flood. Not the rustle of a wing or the cry of a bird reached the ear, as the long stretches of sullen and uninviting shore were left behind by the advancing flotilla. Even here, however, commerce had already established her outposts, and at Kissanga, on the south bank, some twenty miles from Banana Point, a settlement of white traders was found with three factories in full activity, although as far as the eye

could see there was no sign of a human habitation
or life of any kind a hundred yards from the flagstaff
of the place itself. The outlook gradually brightened
as the little fleet advanced inland, and clumps of wavy
palms began to break the sky-line, and wide, open
savannahs covered with verdure stretched away to the
foot of the hills, which stood out on the distant
horizon. Boma, the first halting-place of the expedition, was reached the day after leaving the sea. This
place is the chief trade-mart upon the river, and the
great commercial centre for the whole Congo region.
Clusters of factories, houses, stores, and official residences, with the crowd of small and large trading
craft at the bunda or pier, and the constant stream of
natives hauling and discharging cargo hour by hour
in the full glare of the sun, give to Boma itself an air
of business, activity, and importance. But apart from
its importance as a trading entrepôt, which is due to
its splendid natural position, and to the capital
anchorage alongside its wharves, it is by no means a
desirable place of residence. The surrounding country
has simply one dull tone of colour, and an air of
barrenness, desolation and emptiness appears for ever
to envelop its grey hills, its silent forests, and its
untraversed streams.

At this point Stanley decided to explore the banks,
to find some suitable point at which a landing could
be easily effected, and a temporary camp or settlement
located, for storing the material and goods of the Expedition (amounting to over 600 tons), and from which
parties could be sent up the stream to search for
a suitable site for the first permanent station and
entrepôt of the Association Internationale du Haut

R

Congo. A place on the south bank, called Mussuko, a few hours above Boma, and easily accessible from the river, was decided upon as a depôt for the time, and here the mass of stores and the various impedimenta of the party were landed and stacked, till the march in force should be resumed, or a location for a permanent settlement secured by formal treaty with the native chiefs who had rights over the soil.

The *Albion* was no longer of service, on account of the rapid shoaling of the stream, and, after discharging her freight, she was sent down to Banana Point on her way back to England.

On September 29th Stanley embarked upon the steam launch *Espérance*, with a company of ten natives and three Europeans, to examine the river ahead, and to select a spot for his first town. The navigation of the tiny craft through the cross currents, sinuous windings, and uncertain depths of the impetuous stream, was by no means an easy task. At times the stubborn torrent threatened to sweep all before it, and to refuse a passage to the struggling, straining *Espérance*. At length, however, a gentler current was reached, and guided by Dé-dé-dé, the singing and gay chief of the Nganda village, who in 1877, had so generously relieved the necessities of the footsore and famished exploring party, Stanley proceeded to inspect the neighbourhood of Vivi, where, upon a small plateaux of rock to be fashioned, blasted, and hewn into a solid and even platform, he decided to establish the first station of the new dominion. But there was much to be done before the foundation-stone of the head-quarters of the expedition could be laid with due ceremony and mutual rejoicing. A conference with the " Lords of the Manor,"—the chiefs and headmen and all who had rights in the soil about Vivi, was at once arranged. The object of the white man in coming into their district was explained to the primitive assembly, and his pacific intentions, and his wish to live amongst them as a friend and brother, were all carefully put before them in the best African style of oratory by Massala, the spokesman of the council.

CHAPTER XIV.

THE Vivi hill, which had been fixed upon by Stanley as the site of the principal settlement of the Association Internationale du Haut Congo, was 250 yards long by 45 yards wide, with an altitude of 343 feet above the level of the river which flowed at its base. Its elevation ensured the presence at all times of a fresh cool breeze, and facilitated an admirable system of sanitation. On two sides it was quite inaccessible, and on the west its summit could only be reached by a road —to be constructed—which might be at once defended or rendered impassable in case of attack. At the same time it was easily reached from the river; the natives of the locality were amicably disposed towards the strangers who wished to dwell amongst them; and the pioneer station of the Comité, if planted at this point of the river, would be sufficiently near the sea to prevent any unnecessary delay in bringing up heavy stores or fresh workers from the coast for the settlements to be established beyond the Falls.

After long and anxious deliberation, the bargain for

the purchase of the huge rocky platform was concluded to the satisfaction of at least one party to
the contract. Beneath the umbrageous shadow of
a friendly tree, according to the usual African custom, the motley gathering conducted its negotiations,
which commenced in due form with an address as
follows:—

"We, the big chiefs of Vivi"—a territory of twenty
square miles in extent—"are glad to see the Mundelé
(trader). If the Mundelé has any wish to settle in our
country, as Massala informs us, we shall welcome him,
and will be great friends with him. Let the Mundelé
speak his mind freely."

To these gracious words of the chiefs, the head of the
Expedition replied, "I am glad to hear you speak so
kindly of the white man. I do not want much to-day.
I want to build my houses, for I am about to build many,
either here or elsewhere. I want ground enough, if I can
get it, to make gardens and fields. Vivi is not good for
that unless I go far up; but what I do get, I want for
myself and people, and the right to say what white man
shall come near me. At Boma the chiefs have cut the
ground up small, there is no room for me. I want
plenty of room, and that is why I have come up here.
I want to go inland, and must have the right to make
roads wherever it is necessary, and all men that pass
by those roads must be allowed to pass without interruption. No chief must lay his hand on them and
say, 'This country is mine, pay me something, give
me gin, or cloth, or so many guns.' You have heard of
me, I know, for Dé-dé-dé, who is here, must have told
you. What I saw on the road to Boma must not be
repeated here. You have no roads in your country.

It is a wilderness of grass, rocks, bush, and then at Banza Vivi is the end of all life. If you and I can agree, I shall change all that. I am going to stop here to-night ; think of what I have told you, and I will listen. To-morrow you can return at the third hour of the day and speak."

Dressed up in their gayest and most grotesque gala attire, chiefly made up of old cast-off military uniforms and showy coloured prints, to mark the importance of the occasion, the great men of Vivi returned at the hour appointed to continue the palaver with the white man as to the disposal of the coveted rock. They had decided, they said, to give the right hand of fellowship to him and his friends. He was to be "their white man," and he only, was to be allowed to settle within their borders. Their people should work for him for wages, he was to have absolute control of his own servants, coloured or white, and if unhappily any of their people should be detected in any crime or misdoing, the culprit was to be handed over to his own chief for trial and punishment. Stanley was to pay 32*l*. for the desired site, and 2*l*. per month rental, and both parties agreeing to these articles of this novel and wisely drawn agreement, the heads of the covenant were written out, and duly signed and attested by the principals in the transaction. "I am glad," Stanley wrote in his journal at the time, "that we have so happily concluded the negotiations. My friend Dé-dé-dé of Nganda pleaded and argued hard, so much so indeed that Vivi Mavunga became suspicious at last, which caused Dé-dé-dé to fall at the feet of each Vivi chief, with finely affected warmth and action, crying out, ' Are not Vivi and Nganda one ? Why should I seek to do hurt or harm to Vivi?' We had the usual scenes of applause and silence in court."[1]

Stanley was far from satisfied with his bargain. He felt that he had paid too dearly for the place, and the 2l. per month was absurdly out of all proportion to the market value of land in that barren and for the most part utterly unproductive district. He consoled himself, however, with the knowledge that little, if any, choice had been left him in the matter. This hill-top was the only available spot, with so many natural advantages, near the extreme limit of the navigation of the Lower Congo; and, making the best of the position, he determined to "rise and build."

The construction of the road along the western slope to the summit of the hill was first taken in hand On October 1st, 1879, a lusty band of over a hundred labourers set to work upon the rocky path, to adapt it for the passage of waggons, laden with bales of cloth, iron goods, and heavy cases of merchandise. The road was to be 1965 feet long, and the ground to be levelled was divided into equal portions, each plot being assigned to a separate gang of men, under the control of a leader, who was held responsible for the due execution of their share of the undertaking.

Old Vivi hill presented a novel spectacle to the bewildered natives, who gazed with open-mouthed wonder at the strange and unaccountable activity of their new friends. The scene was full of excitement and motion, and busy tumult. The air rang with the musical strokes of the iron tools upon the stubborn rocks, and the songs of the squads of earnest workers, as they toiled along with burdens of earth or broken

[1] " Founding of the Congo Free State." (H. M. Stanley.)

stones for the foundation of the highway. Stanley, coatless and bare-armed, with heavy sledge in hand, led the operations, and revealed to the amazed Lords of Vivi —who looked on with exclamations of admiration and surprise—what Anglo-Saxon pluck and muscle can do with the vast boulders of stone and tons of shapeless, impassable rock which had to be thrust bodily out of the line of the projected pathway.

"See, O chiefs," said Bula Matari (the Breaker of Rocks), the distinctive title bestowed upon Stanley by the natives, half in fear and half in delight, as they witnessed his triumphs on the stern and rugged hill-side, "I have begun. My young men are at work. Have you no help to give me? Look at your strong-armed young fellows standing idle, and I have abundance of cloth bound in the bales below, brighter handkerchiefs than any you have yet seen, gay strings of beads and shining brass armlets for the womankind; collect fifty people, and prepare the top of the hill for me to live upon, cut down the grass, clear the ground of stones, and mark your welcome of my coming among you thus, and to-night at sunset the wage due to you shall be paid, and a demijohn of good rum shall celebrate the event!"

Bula Matari had suggested a novel and attractive idea to these black-skinned sons of the soil. They could earn on the Vivi hill cloth, wire, gin, and beads by labour! But the matter was far too serious and too recondite to be dealt with in unseemly haste. It had to be turned over and discussed in all its bearings, and some fear was expressed by the more timid members of the woolly-headed crowd that the words of the Breaker of Rocks, pleasant though they were, only concealed some dark design upon their liberties and lives. Distrust soon gave way, however, to confidence in the good faith of the white man's offer, and parties of the natives, encouraged by their chiefs, were soon swarming over the hill-top, and preparing the ground, with their strong arms and willing hands, for the dwellings and gardens which were to form the delightful settlement of Vivi. The tiny steamers of the Expedition puffed noisily backwards and forwards to Mussuko, bringing up relays of workmen, and fresh supplies of implements, stores, provisions, and tents for the bands of diligent workers on the rough hill-side; and Stanley, with restless energy and watchful eye, went from group to group, directing the efforts of his followers, who were slowly transforming his patch of savage wilderness into a habitable place for civilized men. On the 13th of October, a broad and traversable path was opened out to the crest of the height, and the materials for the erection of the houses and store-rooms, stables and sheds of the new settlement were transported in safety to the levelled platform.

The preparation of the site and the erection of the buildings occupied a period of about four months, from October 1st, 1879, to the end of January, 1880. A large Swiss châlet had been brought out in the *Barga*, and this house was set up at one end of the village as the official headquarters of the Expedition, and the residence of the commander-in-chief of the enterprise. Along each side of the broad central avenue were rows of huts for the labourers, carriers, and soldiers of the Association, and beneath headquarters were commodious vaults and magazines for the storage of reserve supplies of ammunition, grain, cloth, and other valuable property. A stream ran round the base of the rock, yielding at all times an abundant supply of pure water for domestic purposes, and gardens and cultivated plots of prolific soil, in which mango, orange, and avocada pear-trees flourished, and cast their grateful shade over rich patches of cabbage, tomatoes, onions, and beets, added grace and freshness to the scene.

The completion of Vivi station was celebrated with great ceremony and much rejoicing. Handsome presents of beef and cloth were bestowed upon the native chiefs and their people who had assisted in the important work, and the Europeans assembled at headquarters as the guests of the commander, to mark the successful founding of the station by a banquet on a somewhat elaborate scale, provided at the expense of their generous and high-spirited host, who proposed with great enthusiasm the toast of " His Majesty the King of the Belgians," the prime mover and best supporter of the " Expedition d'Études du Haut Congo," and " Her Majesty Queen Victoria," " The President of the United States," and " The Contributors to the support of the Expedition," were honoured in the like manner on this auspicious occasion. The magnificent work to which Stanley had deliberately set his hand was, however, only now commenced. He felt he must not linger at his pleasant " home " on the Vivi Hill, cosy and tempting as it seemed to him, after his rough and comfortless experiences in camp, or aboard the cramped and leaky steamers. A staff of officers was organized for the control and management of affairs at the newly-finished settle-

ment, and a Mr. Sparhawk, of whose ability Stanley
had a high opinion, was placed in charge. Under
him were twelve white men, eighty-one Zanzibaris,
and 120 natives—in all about 215 people.

At times considerable difficulty and annoyance had
been caused by the selfish and indiscreet conduct of some
of the European members of the party, who generally
contrived to be most useless when their services were
most needed, and who failed sadly to realize the dignity
and responsibility of the undertaking to which they
had attached themselves. Disease, disgust at the
duty required of them, and dismissals soon thinned
the ranks of these half-hearted and unreliable employés
of the Association, to whom, in spite of their egregious
follies, and most provoking conduct, Stanley showed
the greatest forbearance, good temper and sympathy.
The tact which he displayed in dealing with some of the
vexatious episodes in which he found himself involved
through the utter incapacity of certain of his co-workers,
would have done credit to a diplomatist of the first
rank. He had, however, no patience with indolence or
silly self-importance. " I have no preference for any
nationality here," he writes home to the President of the
Association from Vivi in January, 1880, " *Duty is our
law, rule and guide.* Be he Dutchman, Greek, Turk,
Portuguese, Dane, Belgian, Englishman, or American,
it is perfectly immaterial so long as he works according to his agreement. We are here charged to perform
a task which I believe is a sacred one. While the
task is unfulfilled there is no place here for the trifler,
or for the laggard, indolent, peevish, undisciplined man
hostile to his work."

At this point of the river it was no longer possible

to proceed eastward along the course of the stream. The waterway was effectually closed by the mighty and impassable barrier of the Livingstone Falls, which extended in a broken series of minor cataracts and shoals and sunken rocks for a distance of fifty-two miles, and it became necessary to construct a permanent waggon-road, which would enable the Expedition to avoid the Falls, and strike the river again at Isangila. Attended by a small company of natives, Stanley set out on February 21st to explore the district up to this point, and find out what facilities it offered for the construction of the first public highway in Equatorial Africa. Chiefs would have to be interviewed, measurements of heights and depressions taken, observations as to the nature of the soil made and carefully noted down, and the questions of hired labour and voluntary help thought out and discussed with the heads of the various clans and tribes in the localities to be traversed by the new thoroughfare. A great palaver of the chiefs of Usanda was summoned by the invaluable Dé-dé-dé, to hear from Stanley an outline of his plans with reference to the road and its construction, and the purposes for which it was to be made. He told the great men of Usanda that he wished to make a way, broad and smooth, through their land, along which he hoped to convey his steamers upon specially constructed carriages, to the highest waters of the Congo. They might approve or not approve of his scheme. It was for them to say. He was willing to pay for the land which he should need from them and their dependents in carrying out the formidable enterprise. Hill-sides would have to be blasted, ravines bridged or filled in, and rocks overthrown or broken up. All this would need many stout hearts and ready hands for its accomplishment, but he did not despair if they, his friends of Usanda and their neighbours of Chiouzo and Nsekélélo, would help. The road would be good for all, and all could use it, the trade of the region would be increased, markets would be opened along the route, and produce and food of all kinds from the villages would be eagerly bought up and liberally paid for by the white men and their followers. But care must be taken that the road was not "killed" in any sudden outbreak of hostilities between the tribes who occupied the territory traversed by the pathway. The proposal of the white chief of Vivi Hill was duly discussed and finally accepted by acclamation, and no difficulties were raised as to keeping open the way as well in times of war as in peace for a "consideration" in the shape of liberal gifts of old livery suits, knives, and finery for the women. A painful and exhausting journey through the wild and desolate region onward to Isangila resulted in the conclusion that the construction of a road all the way from Vivi to the navigable waters above the Livingstone Falls was a possible feat. The task would be a difficult and gigantic one, entailing incessant toil and exhausting effort upon those who would be called upon to control and execute the stupendous project. But the thing could be done, and Stanley was the man to do it. He hurried back to Vivi in June for men, tools, stores, and ample supplies of tribute for the native chiefs, whose help he was anxious to secure on the road which he was intent upon carrying up the steep hill-sides, through the spreading forests, and down into the dark ravines, and across the grassy plains of their wild and rugged land. Once on the smooth waters above Isangila, the flotilla of the Association could steam on its peaceful way over the broad bosom of the majestic river for a distance of ninety miles. On February 21st, 1880, Stanley entered upon the second important undertaking of the Expedition—the road from Vivi to Isangila—with a force of 106 men. The attack upon the great barriers, with which nature appeared to have closed the entrance to Central Equatorial Africa, was begun in the Loa Valley, and day by day the narrow, sinuous track of newly cleared and rudely levelled soil lengthened and stretched itself, like a ribbon of dull red over hill and valley, plain and river bottom, till about the end of February, 1880, to the intense satisfaction of everybody concerned in the operations, the final stage was finished, and Vivi and Isangila were united by a well-made thoroughfare fifteen feet wide and 274,472 feet or fifty-two English miles, less eighty-eight feet, in length. Stanley had surveyed the ground in advance of the workers, mile by mile, assisted by a small band of native helpers whom he had trained for this special work. He was a staunch believer in the truth of the old saying that there is nothing like "a stout heart for a stae brae," and at length, after a year of patient and unremitting toil, he saw the little fleet of boats and steamers once more afloat upon the main stream of the Congo, and the Expedition preparing for the ascent of the river to Manyanga, which he had fixed upon as the site of the next station. Steaming off from the shore in high spirits, the flotilla, headed by the fussy little *Royal*, and laden with stores, a company of native labourers and other passengers, turned east-

ward, and the dreaded region of treacherous rapids
and foaming cataracts was soon left far behind. A
dreary tameness pervaded the scenery along the banks.
No signs of human life were visible for leagues as the
heavily-freighted craft pressed onward, battling with
the sweeping current of the deep brown flood. At
times the hills rose up to formidable and impressive
heights, and the broad, verdure-clad plains were
broken at rare intervals by clumps of palms or patches
of jungle, which sheltered enormous herds of buffalo
and elephants. In the swampy ground by the river
side hippopotami and crocodiles abounded. But the
land seemed for the greater part of the way to be
altogether deserted by the natives, and given over to
solitude and desolation. Cold winds swept over the
face of the waters, and virulent sickness attacked the
party, so that one officer after another had to be
relieved from duty. On May 1st, after a passage of
seventy days, the camp of the Expedition was pitched
at Manyanga, and Stanley set about the tedious
labour of bargaining for a permanent site for the
central depôt which he was anxious to erect at this
most eligible and convenient spot. The headmen of
the locality duly presented themselves for their accustomed tribute, and the proposal was made to them
that they should apportion a space of ground for the
white man's town. The great men of Manyanga,
however, by no means accepted the proposition with
alacrity. Permission was given for the Expedition to
remain where it was for the time, but nothing definite
could be elicited from them as to the permanent concession of a site for a regular settlement. A total
journey of 2464 English miles had been now com-

pleted by ascending and descending the various reaches from camp to camp in fourteen voyages, over the entire distance of eighty-eight miles of navigable water that extended between the cataract of Isangila and the cataract of Ptombo Mataka, abreast of the district of Manyanga. The Expedition was now exactly 140 miles above the Vivi Hill. 436 days had been occupied in road-making, and in hauling up fifty tons of stores, with a force of sixty-eight Zanzibaris and an equal number of West Coast and inland natives. During this period 4816 miles had been traversed, which, divided by the number of days occupied in the heavy transport work, shows a progress of above eleven miles per day !

The sustained exertions and anxieties of the past year now began to tell seriously upon the worn frame and debilitated constitution of Stanley. Four days after the tents had been set up, and the property of the Association Internationale du Haut Congo stored at Manyanga, the fever demon of the tropics laid his scorching finger upon him, and day after day he lay prostrate and unable to move, or think, or even to speak coherently. The palaver about the purchase of a site from the native magnates had to be indefinitely postponed. The work of the Expedition was at a standstill, and an indescribable gloom lay over the whole party, natives as well as Europeans, who gazed with helpless dismay upon the forlorn and perilous condition of their popular leader. All the usual remedies, hitherto so effectual in mitigating the attack of the insidious and relentless enemy of the white man in these regions, were tried in vain. The fell disease would run its pitiless course. The chill blasts sweeping down upon the heads of the road-makers in the narrow gorges of the Congo, and the constant exposure to the heat of the fierce sun thrown back from the stony hill-sides and iron faces of the rocks which overhung and enclosed the workers, had done their work upon the enervated system of Bula Matari, and he felt that at last he was dying. Six weeks of illness and hourly paroxysms of pain had reduced him to a condition of mind and body from which he could not hope to recover. The completion of his great plan must be entrusted to other heads and hands. As for himself he had only, while consciousness remained, to lay down his high commission and say " Farewell " to the men who had, with few exceptions, so nobly aided him in his endeavours to open up the heart of that great continent to light and peace. The curtains of his tent were rolled back, and one by one the gallant fellows who had followed him thus far, stepped forward to the almost lifeless sufferer, and received a kindly word and a brief " Good-bye." Meanwhile his native attendant, Dualla, had prepared a potion of alarming strength—sixty grains of quinine, mixed with a few drops of hydrobromic acid and an ounce of Madeira wine—and handed it to him as a last expedient. The effect of the dose was marvellous. The mixture was poured between the lips of the patient, as he was too feeble to lift it himself. The powerful remedy at once began to operate upon the malady, and check its ravages. Stanley fell into a deep slumber, which lasted for twenty-four hours. At the end of this time he awoke a new man. To the astonishment of his servants he cried out for food. His appetite was insatiable. On the 30th of May a

striking procession made the tour of the camp.
Stanley, who was terribly emaciated and feeble, was
carried past the tents of his men, to cheer them with a
proof of his gradual convalescence. On the morning of
June 4th an unusual commotion was noticeable in the
temporary settlement, and the glad news was brought
to the commander that a strong body of fresh
labourers and European officers had come up from
the coast. The new arrivals appeared to bring with
them the atmosphere of home. Letters, papers, and
scraps of the latest intelligence poured in upon the
grateful leader of the Expedition. He recovered
strength daily. The Manyanga palaver was opened,
and the business of the site arranged without further
delay. Wooden huts and the heavy materials for the
various buildings of the station were at once ordered
up from below the falls, the ground was speedily
prepared for the settlement, and in a few weeks, with
the ready help of the newly arrived auxiliaries, the
town was ready for occupation. The Association
had now two fully-equipped and well-established
colonies on the river—Vivi and Manyanga; and a
minor station had been founded at Isangila, in accordance with instructions from Stanley, by an energetic
young Belgian officer, Lieutenant Janssen, who had
recently come out from Europe. On the 12th of
June arrangements were made for an advance upon
Stanley Pool. The " spirit of movement " was once
more upon the undaunted leader and his host of eager
companions. Stanley began to find himself among
old friends. The white man who had passed down
the river some years before, and who was known to
the natives as " Tanley," was welcomed by his dusky

admirers with loud cries of pleasure and satisfaction
as soon as he was recognized; and Ngalyema, the
Chief of Ntamo, with whom he had made blood-
brotherhood in 1877, at once sent a party of his
people to bring Stanley to his presence. This royal
reception of the travellers by the warm-hearted and
generous African prince at once secured for them
attention and respect throughout the district. The
journey from Manyanga had not been altogether free
from distress or anxiety. The disposition of some
of the great men towards the party of exploration had
been by no means friendly. On more than one
occasion the firm boldness and personal courage of
its commander had alone saved the whole column from
disaster, and it was with the greatest difficulty at
times that the suspicious and rapacious dwellers on
the north bank of the river could be induced to allow
the Expedition an unmolested passage through their
borders. At Malima, a straggling village of about
fifty huts, the Expedition made a halt to pay due
respect to its chief, Gamankono, an old acquaintance
of Stanley. He was, however, so gorgeously arrayed
on this occasion that he was scarcely recognizable as
the toiling fisherman who had palavered with the
white chief four years before on the river bank.
Gamankono was so delighted at seeing his friend of
former days that he proceeded to execute a most
extravagant triumphal dance, to the music of a rude
chorus raised by 400 of his stalwart liegemen. The
song was at once taken up by the followers of Stanley,
whose feelings, in the midst of this uproar and babel
of languages and chords, may be more easily
imagined than described. The hospitable prince

was a fine specimen of his race. A well-made figure, frank, honest features, genial but dignified manners, and a regal costume of red and yellow, and blue and white, with armlets of finely twisted brass wire, interlaced with hair from the elephant's tail, combined to make Gamankono a person of mark in this out-of-the-way corner of the world. He gladly acceded to the request that permission should be given for his white visitor to establish a town in his territory, and to reside, build, plant, and sow as it pleased him. But matters were not destined to be so amicably and speedily arranged, after all. Malameen, a lieutenant of the French agent, M. de Brazza, had followed Stanley into Malima, and had contrived to whisper evil counsel into the ear of Gamankono, so that during the dark hours of the night the tom-tom sounded through the streets of the native village, and it was officially announced that no dealings whatever were to be allowed with the Expedition or its leader. Stanley rose to the occasion. Gamankono was sent for, to come and explain his duplicity. This he declined to do, and in order to avoid strife it was decided to march on at once for Ntamo, the kingdom of the amicable Ngalyema, whose emissaries were met on the road, bearing a hearty invitation to his country and words of kindly greeting from their lord to his old intimate " Tanley," whose approach had been announced to him long before. Since their last meeting Ngalyema had risen in social rank. He had enriched himself by successful trade, and had become a chief of the first rank. His record was not a spotless one, however, and his cruelty, superstition, and avarice caused him to be mistrusted and disliked by his peers. He was, according to his own words, a man not to be lightly regarded by his white brother. He could open or close, at his own will and pleasure, the whole territory of the Higher Congo to the Association. The country of Ngalyema was situated on the southern bank of the river, and it was decided to accept his friendly overtures, with a view to a treaty for a concession of land in his district for the erection of the station of Stanley Pool. Stanley felt that the presence and support of the powerful chief were advantageous. Expressions of mutual affection and kindly remembrances of their past intercourse were exchanged, and presents were brought forward for the visitors. The lord of Ntamo (known as Kintamo, on the southern bank) at once displayed his characteristic and innate vice of greediness, and requested for himself the two asses, then a large mirror, which was succeeded by a splendid gold-embroidered coat, jewellery, glass clasps, long brass chains, a figured table-cloth, fifteen other pieces of fine cloth, and a japanned tin box with a "Chubb" lock. In return he bestowed upon Stanley his batôn, or emblem of sovereignty, a staff decorated with brass hoops and rings of wire, to be exhibited as a proof that he was a kinsman of the great Ngalyema of Kintamo. Still the lust of the African for the white man's treasures was not abated. It soon became clear that the favours of the Prince of Kintamo were valued by himself at a very high rate. It was impossible to satisfy his repeated demands. Whereupon he threatened to make war upon his blood-brother, and drive him from the neighbourhood. But it presently appeared that the position and influence of the insolent rogue had

been over-estimated. He had deceived the strangers
altogether as to his power and rank, and it was found
after a time that the would-be lord of Kintamo was a
runaway slave, who had been allowed to settle and
trade in the territory by favour of the actual owners
of the soil. By industry and cunning he had secured
great wealth, and a large band of hired retainers and
slaves, and had assumed the outward state of a high-
born chief. On November 7th, after the exploring
party had crossed the river, the news reached the
camp that the actual lord of the country, the premier
chief of the surrounding region, was on his way to visit
the leader of the Expedition in state, accompanied by
a large retinue of head-men and persons of rank.
Advancing with quiet dignity, the old man announced
himself as Makoko, lord of the region between
Kimtompé and Stanley Pool, and offered the right
hand of fellowship to the white stranger. Seating
himself upon his leopard skin, the emblem of his
exalted dignity, he waited for the address of Stanley
to be interpreted to him. " People call me Bula
Matari (Rock-breaker)," he said. " In old times I
was known to Kintamo as Stanley. I am the first
Mundele seen by the natives of this country. I am
the man who went down the great river with many
men and many canoes years ago. I lost many men in
that river, but I promised my friends at Kintamo that
I would come back some day. I reached the white
man's land, but remembering my promise, I have come
back. I have been to Mfwa already. The people of
Mfya have forgotten me, but the people of Kintamo
have remained true. I saw them again, and Ngalyema
asked me to return to my people, and lead them along

the south bank to his village. Here is his staff as a
sign that I speak the truth. I am going to live with
him and, to build a town alongside of his village; and
when this is done, I will put the boats you see on the
waggons here into the water, and I will go up the
great river, and see if I can build more. That is my
story. Let Makoko speak to his friend, and say it is
good." [2] The reference to the importance of the
turbulent Ngalyema was by no means relished by
Makoko and his followers, and the old chieftain in
warm language denounced his pretensions as entirely
baseless, and declared that neither " Ngalyema nor
any of his clan, who were mere ivory-traders and
nothing else, had any country on the south side of the
river." " I am glad," continued the aged orator, " to
see Bula Matari and his sons. Rest in peace. Land
shall be given you. I want to see plenty of white
men here. Be easy in your mind. You shall build at
Kintamo, and I should like to see the man who says
' No' to Makoko's ' Yes.' " Another heavy tribute
had to be paid to seal the compact of good-will with
Makoko, who completed the transaction by saying to
Stanley, " Ngalyema gave you his staff to show the
people he was your friend. Take this sword from
Makoko as a sign that Bula Matari is Makoko's
brother." This new alliance at once aroused the
rancour and ill-blood of the mendacious ivory-dealer,
who prepared to attack the camp with as many
followers as he could collect for his audacious purpose.
The place was at once put in a condition of defence.
The men were armed, but carefully hidden out of sight
for the moment, and when the braggart chief appeared

[2] " Founding of the Congo Free State." (H. M. Stanley.)

he found Stanley quietly reading at his tent door. The latter was profuse in his exclamations of welcome, wuen Ngalyema approached with his men of war all armed and ready for the fray. The dealer in ivory was not in a mood for friendly intercourse, and furtively looked about him, and took careful note of the defenceless state of the camp, and inwardly gloated over the thought of the vast stores of rich cloth, silks, and other costly merchandise which it was now in his power to seize and carry off in triumph. Quietly, but not without attracting the attention of Ngalyema, a body of natives suddenly appeared upon the scene and betook themselves to a corner of the enclosure, where they watched the course of events with great interest. These were a party of old Makoko's people. It was evident from his bearing that the visit of Ngalyema was not one of ceremony, but of war. In imperious tones he demanded to know why Stanley had come to Kintamo. The brass-bound staff was produced with the reply, " This is what brought me. I have done exactly what you asked me." The chief then hinted that he would like to inspect the last additions to the stores of the Expedition. Willing, if possible, to avoid a conflict, Stanley led the way into the tents, and allowed his unwelcome visitor to select some articles for himself. But the Expedition was not to advance nearer Kintamo. If it did so after this warning, there would be war, and he would no longer be the protector of Bula Matari. So said Ngalyema.

" What is this ? " said the sullen chief as he stood before a huge gong hanging in the doorway.

" It is a fetish," replied Stanley.

" Strike it ; let me hear it."

" I dare not; it is a war fetish!"

" Beat it, Bula Matari, that I may hear it sound," said the obstinate visitor.

" I dare not, Ngalyema. It is the signal of war; it is a bad fetish that calls up armed men, it would be too bad."

" I tell you to strike. Strike it!" said the African, as he stamped angrily upon the ground.

" Well, then," said Stanley, grasping the stick, "remember I told you it was a bad fetish—a fetish for war; shall I strike now?"

" Strike—strike it, I tell you!"

In a moment the gong rang out with a fearful crash, and the Zanzibaris, bearers, and native labourers, who had been carefully concealed from the eyes of Ngalyema and his party, rushed out with hideous cries, and terrible gesticulations, and surrounded the astonished chief. From behind tents and boats, and other hiding-places, they swarmed forth, leaping over the ground like men bereft of their senses. The earth appeared to tremble beneath their tread. Tents fell crashing down and added to the din, and the stampede of the warriors of Ngalyema in a frenzy of fear struck terror into the heart of their chief.

" Be not afraid, Ngalyema; remember Bula Matari is your brother. Stand behind me, I will protect you," said Stanley.

" Save me!" said the affrighted Ngalyema; " I did not mean anything."

" Hold hard, Ngalyema!" cried Stanley, " keep fast hold of me; I will defend you, never fear. Come one, come all! Aha!"[3]

---

[3] See Stanley's "Founding of the Congo Free State."

Peace was gradually restored, and the Zanzibaris and their friends marched off the ground, to the no small satisfaction of the still trembling Ngalyema, who gladly renewed his treaty of eternal friendship with his white blood-brother, and promised that for the future he would be the close ally and defender of Bula Matari. The day after this useful exhibition of Stanley's powers as a practical joker, a prospecting party under the direction of Susi, the foreman of the Zanzibaris, was sent off to secure a suitable position for the new town. An elevation near Kintamo was selected, and approved of by Stanley, and a road was cut through to the spot, which was a savage-looking strip of wilderness, covered with rank herbage, but admirably suited, as regards situation and contour, for the site of the projected settlement. The ground sloped from a height of eighty feet down to the banks of the river, in the midst of magnificent views of the broad expanse of the Pool, the opposite shore, and the surrounding country. Ngalyema continued to give trouble, and his threatening attitude caused considerable anxiety to the Expedition at times, but nothing occurred to hinder the steady progress of the work of erecting the town, to which the name of Leopoldville was given, in honour of the Royal President of the Association Internationale du Haut Congo.

By the 19th April, 1882, Leopoldville was in perfect order, and had already established a reputation as a centre of commerce, and meeting-place for native traders from all parts of the surrounding region on both banks of the river. Upon the broad and airy terrace which had been cut out of the slope, the residences of the Europeans were erected. Below

stood the native village and the huts of the coloured
residents in the settlement, and the entire colony was
protected by a substantial house, built of solid blocks
of timber of vast size, and loop-holed for musketry in
case of attack. The walls of this timber citadel were
solid enough to resist any attack from the natives, and
it was large enough to shelter the entire garrison
within its gates if obliged to seek a place of refuge in
any time of serious danger. The view from the summit
of the rising ground upon which the station had been
erected, was one of striking grandeur. To the eastward lay the broad gleaming surface of the Pool, with
its framework of rugged hills and steep cliffs, and its
islands carpeted with verdure; on the other hand the
enormous cascade of the Kintamo Falls sparkled and
foamed in savage wrath as it flung itself over the lofty
precipice, and rushed on towards the great ocean far
away; and all about the terraced hill, as far as the
horizon, lay broad fields and plains of rich alluvial soil,
intersected by flowing streams, and covered with every
variety of vegetation in rich profusion, and capable of
producing grain, cotton, coffee, wheat, maize, or sugar,
sufficient to nourish and sustain in comfort half a
million of people.

CHAPTER XV.

A magnificent watery expanse—The Kwa—An African princess—Royal commands—Lake Leopold II.—"No fuel, no steam"—Worn to death—A complication of ills—Vivi—Home to England—Interview with the Comité at Brussels—Reporting progress—Three years of toil—Back to Vivi—Desolation—Ruin and decay—Deserters—New stations founded—Leopoldville a ruin—In peril at Bolobo.

EARLY on the morning of April 19th, 1882, the first Upper Congo Expedition set forth from the landing-place at Kintamo Inlet. The *En Avant*, the first vessel whose keel had furrowed the magnificent watery expanse of Stanley Pool, led the way with a full cargo of stores, and a company of forty-nine natives and four Europeans. A whaleboat and some canoes completed the flotilla with which the commander of the Expedition was about to navigate the Pool which bore his name, and carefully explore the great Central Equatorial watershed of the noble stream for which he had already sacrificed health and comfort and friends. The long, swampy inlet of Bamu lies in the centre of the broad expanse of the Pool, and is the favourite resort of the buffalo, elephant, and river-horse. It divides the volume of the river into two branches, which reunite at the point of Inga eastward and the point of Kallina to the west. The extent of water between these points is estimated at 200 square miles.

The passage was by no means a rapid one, as the current of the Congo was running furiously in places at the rate of seven knots an hour, and the upper reaches of the river with its affluents were pouring a mass of three millions of cubic feet of water into the Pool per second!

On April 26th, the people of Mswata were visited, and after a palaver lasting near a fortnight, a most desirable plot of land near the stream was given up to the Association for building purposes. Taking the young officer who was to be placed in charge of this village to the summit of a mound overlooking the whole district, the chiefs (who had expressed in the warmest terms their desire for intercourse with Bula Matari) told him to select for himself the place which pleased him most. The whole land was his, and he had only to make a choice of a site, and the spot would at once be handed over to his detachment. A commencement was made by setting up a house for Lieut. Janssen; a road was opened out down to the waterside, the bush and scrub and rank undergrowth for some distance round the settlement was cleared, and the Mswata settlement, owing to the energy and capacity of its youthful but sagacious head, soon assumed, with its flourishing gardens, well-planted terraces, and nicely ordered rows of dwellings and magazines, all the appearance of a prosperous and well-established trading town.

Again the spirit of movement was upon Stanley, and he longed to penetrate, if possible, to the sources of the Kwa, a mighty but only partially-explored tributary of the Congo, running into the main waters from the south. Weird and melancholy fables were

repeated to the white man about the swift and dangerous torrent, and his love of adventure revived as he
listened to the strange stories of the natives who had
visited the uplands of the Kwa, concerning the wonders
to be met with in its waters and on its banks. Entering the broad estuary of the affluent, the little *En
Avant*, provisioned for a voyage of 200 miles, and
carrying a crew of fourteen men and three guides, was
soon battling with the chafing current, as she ploughed
her way over the tawny flood between steep, evenly-
shaped banks of dull red clay. For miles no object of
interest disturbed the calm of the pensive group of
idlers upon the deck of the steamer. But soon the
landscape began to wear an aspect of rich fertility,
and the abundant vegetation covering the wide-stretch-
ing valleys and fruitful lowlands on all sides, and
fields of banana, sugar-cane, and cassava, testified
everywhere to the rank prodigality of the soil.

"What could not be done with these fat pastures
and loamy meadows, these oases of promise in the
midst of the sterile wilderness?" Stanley often asked
himself, as hour after hour he viewed with careful eye
the bosky hill-sides, the dense groves of finely developed trees, and the verdant plains reaching away to
the far horizon. Birds swept across the bosom of the
waters, or flecked its teeming surface with their snowy
wings as they dived for fish in its lucid depths.
Families of ungainly hippos floundered in the muddy
shallows, populous villages were seen at intervals all
along the banks of the great tributary stream. The
En Avant was an object of great curiosity and some
dread to the prying natives, who stared in stupid
wonder at the huge monster propelling itself through

the water by means of its paddle-wheels, which to
them suggested the idea of enormous fins.

"Where are you going? and what is all this for?
What kind of thing is this that goes up by itself on
our waters?" asked the unsophisticated sons of the
Mabula.

"Oh," replied the guide, Ankoki, in a superior sort
of way (forgetting that he had been terribly scared
himself by the boat only a few days before), "we are
going to visit Gankabi, the great queen of the Wabuma. This is Bula Matari, you know, brother of
great Gobila, and this is the white man's boat. Ah!
it takes the likes of white men to do things like this,
you know." [1]

The course of the boat lay directly under the groves
and spreading palms of Kemeh Island, the sacred place
of sepulture for the royal rulers of the Wabuma.
Flocks of birds—gay parrots, doves, and fierce hawks
—filled the air with their cries as they flew overhead
or hovered over the surface of the water in search of
the flies and insects which infested the sedgy banks of
this final resting-place of kings, and the *En Avant* was
found to be steaming through waters of distinctly
opposite hues, yet both flowing in the same river-bed.
On the right the Kwa was black as could be, and the
left half of the stream was pale grey. The reason of
this singular phenomenon was that just ahead of the
party the two branches, the Mfini and the Mbihé,
combined to form the main body of the Kwa. Crowds
rushed to the river bank to see the smoking craft pass
along its foamy path, heedless of the rushing current,
and forcing a way for itself, unaided by any human

[1] "Founding of the Congo Free State." (H. M. Stanley.)

arm, into the heart of their country. At Musyé, a
well-placed native trading-station and village of some
importance, situate at the point where the Mfini and
the Mbihé combine, Stanley landed with his party to
pay the usual visit of homage to the illustrious chieftainess, Gankabi, who had, however, gone a journey of
some days up the sable stream of Mfini. In her
absence the white men were refused hospitality, and it
was decided to continue the advance up stream, in the
hope of meeting with a more cordial welcome elsewhere.

On the passage the party suddenly came upon the
canoes of the Queen of Musyé, who was returning
homewards with a number of attendants, from her
tour up the Mfini. Her Majesty was seated in the
bow of the boat, and she was at once recognized by
the native guides of the Expedition, who exclaimed,
in tones of veneration and surprise, "There is Gankabi."

The *En Avant* was at once brought to, and the
boat of the dusky chieftainess was rowed to the
side of the steamer. Gankabi was, in person and
bearing, the perfect ideal of an African princess. Her
fine stature, firm, determined face, and calm self-
possession, at once proclaimed her to be a woman of
character and power. She was simply arrayed in a
robe of ordinary grass-cloth, and the only outward
sign of her dignity which she displayed was a solitary
but heavy armlet of copper.

"So you are Bula Matari!" she said with some
imperiousness.

"Yes."

"Then come with me."

" No, I am going to see the end of this river, and when I return, if you are at Musyé, I will see you — that is, if you wish ; if not, I will go down, as I came up, past you."

" Well, what next, I wonder ! How will you get past Ngeté ? The people are bad. No one is allowed to pass Ngeté. The people will fight you ; they will kill you all."

" Ah, well, I shall be very sorry to get killed, of course ; but I must go all the same."

" What for ?"

" To see the river."

" And what will you do with it, when you do see it ?"

" Nothing, when I have seen the end I will return." [2]

Stanley informed the Queen of the fact that he had been scurvily treated by her subjects at Musyé the day before, and he preferred now to go on his way without troubling her people further. The interview ended by a present of food and a goat to the white men, and Gankabi passed on her way, after again warning Bula Matari of the danger into which he was so obstinately thrusting himself, in continuing his course through the country of the barbarous Ngeté.

Considerable difficulty was now experienced in procuring sufficient fuel for the boilers, and no wood or brush of any kind could be discovered near the banks. Bits of dried wood were easily secured at first for the fires, but at length it became absolutely necessary to purchase the precious commodity from the native chiefs at any price. A heavy payment in brass rods was

[2] See Stanley's " Founding the Congo Free State."

T

demanded, and upon these terms the furnaces were plentifully and speedily supplied. The upper region of the Kwa appeared to be thickly populated, well-watered, and abundantly productive of all the necessaries of life. The streams were stocked with fish, and every village had its well-cultivated plot of ground covered over with fine crops of millet, bananas, grain, and cassava. The long spear-grass which rose to a height of seven or eight feet and covered the district for miles, was burnt when dry by the natives, and from the ashes, which they boiled, they managed to extract a dirty-grey saline substance which served them as salt.

Three days were spent in exploring Lake Leopold II., a magnificent sheet of shallow water in the district of the dark Mfini, with an area of 800 square miles, and an average depth of sixteen feet. The rude villagers on the shores were terrified at the sudden appearance of the *En Avant* steaming across the calm waters with her motley company of white and coloured men, and churning the lake into seething foam with her ever-revolving arms. The incessant worry about fuel, and the insufficient supplies of food at times, together with the exertion of circumnavigating this vast inland sea, induced a return of Stanley's old enemy the fever of the country, and he was obliged to hasten back with all speed to Lieutenant Janssen's thriving settlement at Mswata, where he arrived on June 7th in a terribly prostrate condition, and utterly unable to shake off the feeling of " deathly languor" which had settled upon him. In a condition of painful weakness, and unable to take any interest in what was passing around him, the exhausted leader was conveyed from station to station down the river as fast as his anxious and sorrowing followers could effect the mournful passage. At Leopoldville he had only an indistinct idea of the locality and of the events which attended his arrival there. He was ill, terribly ill, that he knew, and when consciousness returned for a brief space, between the paroxysms of the disease, he tried to make those about him understand that he wished to be carried down to Vivi. His faithful Zanzibaris were to escort him on the road and see to his comfort, as far as they could, and on the 23rd of June the melancholy procession filed down from the terrace of Leopoldville, bearing to the steamer their brave Bula Matari, who to all outward seeming was stricken for death. The symptoms of an alarming complication of ailments, incipient gastritis, and dropsical enlargement of the lower limbs, added to an almost chronic physical debility, induced by successive attacks of fever and dysentery, created something approaching to despair amongst the officers and members of the Expedition, who, in bidding him " Farewell," scarcely dared to hope that he would ever return to lead them on to further and greater triumphs. With trembling fingers he wrote a few lines on the road to his officers in charge of Leopoldville, in favour of Mr. T. I. Comber of the Baptist Mission, whom he wished to see settled on the southern shore of the Pool, and at noon on July 8th, 1882, he was carried up the broad pathway to his headquarters on the crest of the old Vivi Hill. The faithful Zanzibaris, whose contract for a three years' period of service had expired, were returned, under the charge of a competent officer, to their home on the East Coast. Doctor Peschuel Loeche, a German

vast territory which he had added to the map of Africa.

On Nov. 23rd, with restored health and freshened hopes, the steamship *Harkaway* left Cadiz for Banana Point with Stanley and a number of fresh recruits for the service of the Association on board. About 600 tons of merchandise of all sorts were taken out for the purposes of the Expedition, and on Dec. 14th the party landed at the mouth of the Congo. By the 20th of the same month Stanley had reached the Vivi Hill, only to find that one station after another had been deserted by the officials who had been placed in charge of them before his departure for Europe. In five short months the work of years had been ruthlessly upset or ruined. The German doctor, a man of large African experience who had been appointed to take the direction of the entire enterprise in the absence of Stanley, had left for Europe some weeks before. Vivi was chiefless. The head of the Leopoldville settlement was down at Banana Point, and his second officer had vanished altogether. *La Belgique* was captainless, and the machinery of the little *En Avant* had been hopelessly disabled. Quarrels had arisen with the natives, and the condition of affairs generally was as bad as it could well be in so short a time. Happily the arrival of the founder of the work upon the scene prevented further disorganization and disaster. A detachment was at once sent off to open a new route to the Upper River with an outlet to the coast between the French Colony of the Gaboon and the Congo estuary. The malingerers were sent back to their duties, and formal treaties were entered

into with all the chiefs who had any rights of owner-
ship in the regions bordering upon the river, securing
to the Association the supreme control of the territory
for some distance inland on either bank. A new line
of stations was established, and favourable treaties
arranged with the native owners of the ground,
greatly to the satisfaction of the commander of the
Expedition, by Lieut. Van de Velde, an officer of
whom his chief speaks in the highest terms of commendation. A road was opened up on the south bank
from Manyanga to Leopoldville, a medical superin-
tendent was located at Stanley Pool and, all the
stations were re-provisioned and set in order once
more. The *Royal* was hurried up to Leopoldville by
waggon overland, and a new steam launch, the A.I.A.
(Association Internationale Africaine) was built upon
the upper waters of the river for special service
eastward of the Pool.

On arriving at the Inkissi River on Feb. 27th, the
alarming intelligence was brought to Stanley that the
colony on the Pool was absolutely without food.
" Bread was at famine prices," and no supplies could
be obtained from the natives of the district. Truly
the post of head of the Congo Expedition was one
which required a clear brain, and firm nerves, and a
stout heart. What was wrong and who was wrong ?
were points which Stanley with his natural shrewd-
ness and experience of the devious ways of men, soon
settled in his own mind. He found no scarcity of
provisions on the way as he hurried forward to see for
himself the actual condition of the famishing settlement. The natives, who crossed his path, or with
whom he had dealings, were as kindly and as well

disposed to the white man as they had been in his former visits to the territory. At last Leopoldville came in view. The picture was a sad one, and it would be impossible to describe the feelings of the Pioneer of the Congo as he looked down upon the neglected terrace, the grass-grown streets, the forsaken huts, the overgrown gardens, foul with rank vegetation and fast returning into their primitive wilderness condition, the broken fences, and the forlorn aspect of all things connected with his once bright and flourishing and busy town on the Kintamo slope. At the dilapidated landing-stage the *En .lvant* was discovered cracked and seamed by the sun. Hostilities had arisen with the neighbouring chiefs, and the trade between the white man and themselves had been "killed." This was the explanation of the startling condition of the station, in the midst of a land overflowing with the necessaries and even some of the luxuries of life. Amicable relations had to be re-established with the native lords of the Kintamo region, and a grand palaver was called to discuss the strained position of affairs and to find a remedy. The results of this conference were most gratifying. An alliance, offensive and defensive, was formed between the Association and the various tribes inhabiting the Wambundu and Kintamo district, for the purpose of securing the entire territory west and south of the Pool from disturbance or outrage. The chiefs were to acknowledge the authority of the Association, and as a sign of this the dark blue flag of the Association with its gold star in the centre was to be displayed on public occasions at the native towns of the confederacy.

Leopoldville soon assumed much of its old brightness and activity. The roads were cleared of grass, the terrace was restored to something of its former dignity, and the *En Avant* was docked, repaired, and re-painted. But, best of all, confidence was again restored between the white man and his dusky neighbours, and soon the market of the settlement was crowded with women and children, bringing in the produce of the district for barter as of old, without fear or reserve.

The advance along the Higher Waters was continued on May 9th, 1883. The new steamer *A.I.A.*, the *En Avant*, and the *Royal*, which had been hauled up from Vivi, forming the fleet of exploration and observation. Eighty men and six tons of goods for the stations to be established up the river, were taken, and food for the support of the Expedition for at least six months was stowed away in the holds of the crowded vessels. Every kind of article useful or ornamental had to be thought of and packed for the voyage—axes, shovels, picks, scythes, saws, cloth, fancy ornaments, medicine, ammunition, oil, flour and salt, seeds, and every conceivable thing which could tempt the natives to barter or attract their attention with a view to stimulate trade between the white man and themselves, had to be laid out and kept ready to hand in the cabin of the *A.I.A.* for the benefit of any visitors from the tribes on shore, or at the various landing-places where the Expedition halted to get fresh supplies of fuel and provisions.

At "Good View Station" matters were found to be progressing satisfactorily. The buildings were advancing towards completion, and the officer in charge seemed to have his work well in hand. A grand stretch of river was visible from the rising settlement, reaching to a distance of five miles, where it was merged in the fleecy mist which hung over the far-off horizon. The day after leaving Kimpoko, the native name for the "Good View Station," the steam launches and whale-boats passed the portals of the Higher Congo, at the extreme limit of the Pool. Mswata Station looked pleasant and attractive, with its well-built homestead and cultivated surroundings, and its thriving condition amply justified Stanley's high opinion of the industry and ability of the young lieutenant whom he had placed over the colony thirteen months before. The native population round the station had considerably increased since the last visit of the head of the Expedition, and fresh villages had sprung up in the district for the purpose of carrying on a regular trade with the agents of the Association upon the banks of the river. Between Gobila, the kindly-disposed and benevolent chief of the Mswata, and the youthful but astute head of the station, the kindliest feelings existed, and the old man day by day visited the colony for a gossip with his son " Nausi Mpembé " or the " White Chicken," a name which he had himself bestowed upon young Janssen. Sailing and steaming on their course over the great Congo waters, the flotilla was now approaching the real heart of the African Equatorial region, the vast watershed and catchment of the wonderful stream which has an onward flow of 2500 miles from the Lake Region of the interior to the Atlantic Ocean. The primary object of the Expedition had been to pierce through the sterile and profitless borders of the Lower Congo, extending over a distance of 235 miles right up into this almost limitless expanse of fertile and densely peopled country, where Stanley " believed that under European control there could be formed a great African Empire, open to the commerce of the world, to become the centre of future civilization over a large portion of the Dark Continent." The old mythical description of Central Africa as a vast and silent tract of arid wilderness, without a sign of vegetable or animal life, and given over to solitude and desolation, had been altogether disproved by the splendid achievements of modern explorers. What had been for ages regarded as a Southern Sahara, was found to be a magnificent area of wide-swelling and fruitful plains and levels of productive pasture-land, sustaining " myriads of dusky nations," numbering, in the aggregate, according to Stanley, over thirty millions of people.

A station had been established in the thickly-inhabited locality of the Bolobo, who were, however, not well disposed to the strangers, and presently gave serious trouble. Stanley arrived just in time to save the settlement from a great danger, if not from positive ruin. A quarrel had arisen between the officers in charge and a native magnate of considerable influence, and open hostilities were threatened. Some of the great men of the district were at once consulted by Stanley as to the right method, according to native custom, of conducting such matters, and happily the unfortunate affair ended by the payment of a fine of £42 by Gatula, the chief who had in retaliation for an alleged insult to a member of his family, slain in cold blood two of the employés of the settlement. The position for a time was painfully critical, as an open fight must have resulted in the defeat and probable massacre of Stanley and his men. He knew this, but put, as was his wont, a bold front on the matter. Conscious of his weakness, he yet spoke thus to the friends of Gatula : "We are strangers in Ibaka's country. Ibaka gave us ground, for which he took much money. Our people were put into his hands. Two of these people are not to be found. I want them. I cannot do without them. They were freemen. They had families. Those families will ask me for them. Shall I show them empty hands? Blood must be shed for blood, or money must pay for it. *Gatula must pay or fight.* Ibaka says he has heard of Bula Matari before. Ibaka and the other chiefs must advise Gatula which is best. I will wait two suns for the money. If it is not paid, I will go to Gatula's village and bring him out."

Both parties to the quarrel were secretly in dread of each other, as it afterwards turned out, and it was intimated to Stanley that Gatula had been so scared by the message of Bula Matari, that he would rather sacrifice a dozen slaves than go through such an experience again.

At a state council of the Bolobo lords later on, a definite and stringent agreement was formulated and signed between themselves and Stanley by which they agreed to ally themselves with the Association and to hand over their territorial rights to that body, as represented by the Commander of the Expedition, their friend and intimate Bula Matari, and for the time peace and good-will once more prevailed.

CHAPTER XVI.

IT was necessary for the complete success of the
plan of the Association, that at least two important
stations should be at once established on the Upper
Congo waters, and on the 28th of May, 1883, the
tiny fleet, flying the flag of dark blue with the gold
star, was once more ascending the river. The
troubles at Bolobo had caused considerable delay, and
Stanley feared that he might not be able, after all
to keep his promise to the Comité, that he would
reach Stanley Falls by the end of the year. Twenty
miles per day was the average speed of the flotilla.
The constant need of fresh supplies of fuel and food
for the eighty men of the Expedition, for whom a
meal had to be provided twice a day, was a frequent
cause of stoppage, but after a wearisome voyage of
some days through most uninteresting scenery along

the silent but ever-flowing stream, signs of life began
to appear upon the banks, and the country opened
out and revealed everywhere rich groves of tropical
fruits, pleasant villages embedded in palms, and
sheltered by forests of enormous and valuable timber,
and towering hills on the distant horizon, whose
pointed crests were wrapped about with a beautiful
mantle of purple haze. Considerable difficulty was
experienced in opening up communications with some
of the villages on the banks. In vain were rich cottons, rolls of crimson cloth, and sparkling beads or
sheaves of brass rods held up as signs of the pacific
intent of the white man. The smoke-boats terrified
the people, and they fled in terror from the belching,
hissing, and powerful monsters, which beat the waters
with strange hands on either side, and groaned and
sighed like human beings. At times hostilities were
threatened if Stanley or his party attempted to land
for purposes of barter, or to get wood for the furnaces,
and at one spot a novel but ineffectual expedient was
adopted to get rid of the white-faced strangers and
their mammoth fire-canoes. As the steamers neared
the shore the usual display of goods was made upon
the deck, but the only response which came from a
miserable group of abject natives on the shore was
that small-pox, that most fearful of all African
scourges, had swept over the spot, and every chief
and person of consideration had fallen victims to
the frightful virulence of the plague, and that the
few unhappy wretches who had survived the fell
disease, were perishing from hunger, owing to the
want of able-bodied men to till the land or gather
in the perishing crops. The crews of Stanley's

vessels were aghast at this recital of irremediable
woe, "but," said they, "those men on the banks
look too fat to be suffering from famine." There
was nothing for it, however, but to turn away from
the village and press onward to more hospitable
scenes. It was decided to camp higher up the stream
at no great distance from the famine-stricken tribe,
in the "hope that they would make some effort to
relieve our need and enrich themselves by bartering
any provisions they might be able to get together
for our merchandise." No sooner was the camp *in
situ* than the arrant rogues put in an appearance,
laden with fowls, goats, bananas, green plantains,
cassava roots, yams, eggs, and palm oil; in fact, all
the luxuries and dainties of the continent, and a brisk
trade was done, and the fleet was provisioned for
some days on the spot. Inexhaustible stores of
fowls, goats, and "good things" were obtained and
stored away against a time of need, and then the
question was asked why the story of famine and
small-pox had been invented when the Expedition
first hove in sight. The reply was, "O! why do you
remember what we said in fear of you? Neither our
oldest people nor their fathers before them ever saw
or heard of such things as these," pointing to the
En Avant and her consorts.

Vast teak forests lined the banks for days at certain
portions of the route, and wide park-like expanses,
covered with a fine growth of majestic trees, were
frequently visible beyond the low, reedy marsh-lands
by the river sides. The contrast between the cold
sterility of the Lower Congo district, and the luxuriant verdure and rich productiveness of the Upper

Congo basin was most striking. Day by day the surroundings of the river increased in interest, and fresh evidence was constantly afforded to the eye and ear of the leader of the flotilla, which was patiently steaming onwards over the brown waters, that he had by no means over-estimated the material wealth and productive power of the finest and least known of African watersheds. The reception of the vessels at Usindi was overpoweringly kind. A party of natives dashed over the foaming waters in a canoe to the side of the *En Avant*, and shouting out words of welcome, sprang upon the deck to guide the fleet to the safest anchorage off their town. News had reached the place from the Pool of the achievements of Stanley in opening markets, planting settlements, and creating trade all along the banks of the great river. No weapon of war was seen about the place during the stay of the party, and Stanley verily believes that the chief of the tribe would gladly have given him the half of his kingdom had he agreed to settle down and build a station there.

Passing on to the great Irebu tribe, which they visited by invitation of Mangombo, the great chief of this well-known mercantile tribe, whose members formed the most accomplished of the native traders on the upper waters, Stanley had to go through the by no means agreeable ceremony of blood-brotherhood with Mangombo. The right arm of each was punctured by the fetish-man, and the oozing blood mixed with gunpowder, salt, and scrapings from the gunstock of the white man and the spear of the chief, and sprinkled over the bleeding arms, which for the moment were rubbed together. The fetish-man then with much ceremony touched the head, arms, necks, and legs of the two men with some kind of dust in a large pot, and the mystic rites were completed, and the white man was admitted to all the honours and privileges of a prince or member of the royal house to which his blood-brother belonged. The Irebu were at the time engaged in a war with a neighbouring tribe, and Stanley was asked to intervene, and, if possible, prevent further hostilities. An armistice was arranged between the combatants for fifteen days, and on June the 6th the expedition was once more under weigh in mid-stream. The banks were now occupied at frequent intervals more or less all along the way by villages or considerable towns, having enormous native populations, and carrying on a brisk trade up and down the stream and far away into the interior in ivory, grain, palm-oil, and other marketable produce of the region. From Irebu to Ikengo, a distance of fifty miles, the stream was bordered by a continuous and extensive growth of stately wood—mahogany, teak, plane, and fine gum—and the islets, which in places broke the current of the river, were surrounded with rich forests of timber, of extraordinary altitude and massive bulk. The dislike or distrust with which some of the people on shore regarded the strangers was exhibited in a variety of ways; and on one occasion the *En Avant*, followed by the rest of the vessels, passed up stream between banks lined with masses of people, who kept up a frantic motion of their bodies, and, armed with bows, rushed forward in serried ranks to the edge of the river as if about to overwhelm the tiny craft with an attack in force. The display was only intended as

U

a hint to the travellers to keep on their way, and not venture to molest those who had no wish to injure them.

On June 13th, 1883, a site was selected at this point of the river for a fixed settlement, and Equator Station was founded in 0° 1' 0" N. Lat. in the district of Wangata, and placed under the charge of Lieutenant Vangele and a garrison of twenty-six men. The position of this advanced and isolated outpost of the Association was one of the first importance. It was surrounded on all sides by vast multitudes of people, the natural wealth of the region was incalculable, and under judicious management there was every prospect that it would become the centre of a flourishing and influential trading community. With a light heart the patient Pioneer of the Congo returned once more to Irebu, after seeing the little detachment thoroughly settled down to their task of erecting the buildings of the new colony, which was exactly 770 miles distant from the Atlantic. On the return of Stanley to the district of Mangombo, his blood-brother, and chief of the wide-spreading Irebu, it was found that war had again broken out, and that the truce which the white man had arranged had been broken only two hours before the fleet came in sight. Stanley once more proceeded to act as peace-maker, and his efforts were crowned with success. To his friend Mangombo, who showed a disposition to renew the quarrel, Stanley thus delivered himself in his character of chosen arbitrator. "Magwala and Mpika have both agreed that they will leave the case in my hands: you, Mangombo, must do the same. The war lies in the obstinacy of Mangombo alone. It is enough, Mpika and Magwala

offer their hands in friendship to Mangombo. Give
the pledge of peace, and bury the war. Bula Matari
has spoken!" The speech was electrical in its effects.
Mangombo was "nowhere," so to speak, after the de-
livery of these stern but wholesome words of his white
brother, and peace was at once proclaimed, for "had
not Bula Matari spoken?"

The stations of Mswata and Kimpoko were visited in
turn, and although the former was found in excellent
order, the latter was still suffering from some inex-
plicable lethargy and tendency to decay. Leopoldville was rapidly rising to a position of dignity as a
central market for the entire Stanley Pool region, and
it had every mark about it of the assiduous care with
which its chief officer continued to discharge the oner-
ous duties of his responsible post. Valeke was Stanley's model officer. But alas! of Vivi, unhappy Vivi,
what shall be said? Confusion reigned supreme in
the pretty village which Stanley had left upon the
Vivi Hill. "Divided counsels, strife, and mutual re-
criminations, all declared themselves in the bundle of
correspondence which reached the Expedition at the
Pool station." Valeke was sent down the stream with
authority to settle the unfortunate difficulties which
had arisen at Manyanga and Vivi, and then came fresh
troubles to distract the weary, but hopeful man, who
had determined to devote his whole powers to opening
out the Equatorial regions to the beneficent influences of Christianity, civilization and commerce. His
mind was ever dwelling upon "that vast domain which
lay around him, and far away beyond, with its 80,000
square miles of lake water, the second largest river
and river basin in the world, and a fertility that no

tropical or equatorial region elsewhere could match, with its great independent native empires, kingdoms, and republics like Uganda, Kuanda, Ungoro, and the pastoral plains of a country like the Masai Land ; gold and silver deposits, abundant copper and iron mines ; valuable forests providing priceless timber, inexhaustible quantities of rubber, precious gums and spices, pepper and coffee, cattle in countless herds, and peoples who are amenable to the courtesies of life, provided they are protected from the attacks of the lawless freebooter and the murderous wiles of the slave-trader."

Kimpoko station, after repeated disasters, had to be abandoned for the time.   Janssen was drowned whilst generously conveying a French priest to a location up one of the affluents of the river, and Bolobo was suddenly destroyed by fire, with a large reserve store of merchandise amounting to something like 150 tons. Proceeding to relieve the houseless contingent at Bolobo, the flotilla was attacked by the Itimba and Btangala people, and matters assumed so grave an aspect that the *Royal* was sent down with all speed to Leopoldville to bring up the Krupp cannon and fifty charges of ammunition.   Before the gun reached the spot, however, a peace was arranged, the unfriendly tribes paying an indemnity of 600 matako.   The performances of the cannon produced a profound effect upon the native hordes, who were asked to see it fired " just for fun," and they did not hesitate to accept the suggestion of Bula Matari that it was worse than foolish of them to attempt to fight with their white friends.   In the centre of a forest of unusual magnitude and beauty, a young Englishman named Glave was commissioned by Stanley to establish the station of Lukolela. The task was by no means an easy one, but after assisting him by clearing an open space of some fifty square yards for his buildings, the Expedition left him to push on the work, with a small company of labourers, to the best of his ability. At the end of September, after an absence of one hundred days, the fleet was once more off Equator Station. The progress which had been made on all sides was most marked. What, three months before, was a bare strip of African wilderness, had become a highly cultivated and well-constructed European village. A strong serviceable bungalow, surrounded by gardens, well-stocked with vegetables and fruits, gay with coloured blinds and painted jalousies, and furnished with taste and an eye to ornament as well as use— had been erected by the young lieutenants Vangele and Coquilhat, who shared the responsibility of the management of the place. In the native quarter also, the clay huts, in the midst of nicely laid-out garden plots, and surrounded by sugar-cane, cucumbers, and other products, betrayed at once the presence in the settlement of the spirit of order and industry, and the heart of Stanley was made glad by the smiling welcome with which even nature apeared to greet him at his " ideal station." The Expedition had penetrated inland 757 English miles from the sea, and 412 above the western outlet of Stanley Pool.

The Flotilla now steamed away direct for Stanley Falls, some 600 miles further up the river, for the purpose of establishing a station in the region of the great cataracts. On October 21st the town of the dreaded Bangala, the tribe which had attacked the exploring party with such implacable ferocity in 1877, came in sight. If the Ibanza ever returns, they had said, we will fight him " over every inch of the way." Stanley, however, determined, if possible, to come to terms with his old enemies, and he awaited the turn of events at a camp which he pitched within sight of the chief village of the Bangala, which was of such enormous extent, that the vessels were seven hours in passing it from end to end. An interview with the senior chief, Mata Buryki (Lord of many guns), was sought and granted, and Stanley crossed the river for a palaver, with some anxiety as to the result of the meeting. A crowd of native warriors 1700 strong lined the shore, and Yumbila, the eloquent guide and linguist of the Expedition, explained to Mata Bwyki, a stalwart old grey-haired man, with the frame of a giant and the voice of a stentor, the mission of the white man, and the work he had done in building towns, and entering into friendly treaties along the waters of the Congo.

" Is this Tandelay ? " asked the old warrior, as he gazed steadily and sternly upon the stranger before him.

" Yes."

A low murmur ran through the vast assembly of savage men. The moment was a critical one for all present, and Stanley perfectly realized the gravity of his position, as he sat powerless in the midst of the excitable and war-loving Bangala. Howbeit, as Yumbila proceeded with his narrative, a visible change passed over the attitude of the vast assembly, and at the mention of the irresistible powers of the Krupp gun, the hearts of the bellicose warriors of Mata Bwyki sank within them. It was to be peace between themselves and Bula Matari; and the son of Mata

Bwyki, taking one end of a forked branch of palm in his hand, offered the other end to Stanley, and then cut the branch in two with his sword, saying, " Thus I declare my wish to be your brother." Again the indispensable ceremony of blood-brotherhood was performed, and the friendly alliance was sealed by the due observance of this sanguinary rite. At once the mighty voice of old Mata Bwyki was heard thundering above the heads of the curious multitude, as he proclaimed the fact that the enmity between himself and " Tandelay " was now buried. " People of Iboko, you by the river-side, and you inland. Men of the Bengala, listen to the words of Mata Bwyki," said the energetic Lord of many guns. " You see Tandelay before you. His other name is Bula Matari. He is the man with the many canoes, and he has brought back strange smoke-boats. He has come to see Mata Bwyki. He has asked Mata Bwyki to be his friend. Mata Bwyki has taken him by the hand, and has become his blood-brother. Tandelay belongs to Iboko now. He has become this day one of the Bangala. O! Iboko, listen to the voice of Mata Bwyki. Bring food to sell to Bula Matari at a fair price, gently, kindly, and in peace, for he is my brother. Hear ye, ye people of Iboko! You by the river-side, and you in the interior." " We hear Mata Bwyki!" was the universal response. An offer of a site for a station was made, and Stanley promised to complete the arrangements for taking over the concession on his way back from the falls.

Leaving the Bangala in the happiest of moods, the course of the steamers now lay for days through walls of leafy beauty, sometimes reaching a height of 150 feet and scenes adorned by a wealth of gorgeous tropical vegetation in all its native and unrestrained luxuriance. The ficus, the gum, the calamus, the orchilla weed, the oil palm, and all the priceless treasures of African forest life, are present in the Congo basin. Forests of gum copal and rubber bush overshadow the fruitful soil, and the fleet sailed at times for days through one unbroken growth of copal trees, covered with the precious dye-weed, the market value of which could scarcely be estimated. On approaching Basongo, where a terrible conflict had taken place in the memorable passage of 1877 over these waters, the whole of the tribe were discovered drawn up on the banks for a distance of three miles in full war-paint, and ready once more to try conclusions with Stanley. Making for the centre of the town, the *En Avant*, with Yumbila perched upon her cabin-roof, was allowed to drift gently past the armed legions upon the shore. The voice and accents of the speaker, as he turned to the ranks of scowling imperturbable warriors of Mokulu, were full of energy and pathos, and the effect was at once seen in the stillness which reigned amongst the brown multitudes on the bank. In "tones which melt and words which burn," the powerful orator portrayed the blessings which would result to the land if peace and good-will were established between the Mokulu chiefs and the renowned Bula Matari. Weapons were silently conveyed away or hidden out of sight, as the oration proceeded, till at last, when Yumbila descended from his perch, words of amity and friendship came from the crowded bank, and the wild Basoko were added to the now lengthened roll of the allies of the Association

Internationale du Haut Congo. A digression was made from the main course to investigate the condition of the Biyerré River, an affluent of considerable magnitude, which was clearly shown to be identical with the Werré or Miani of Barth, Junker, and other travellers.

On the return to the Congo proper, tidings began to reach the fleet of the presence on the waters of a gang of Arab slavers, who had been carrying desolation, destruction, and death in all directions, and who had left behind them ghastly reminiscences of their detestable trade in the ruined, scorched, and depopulated towns, which were seen at intervals of a few miles all along the water's edge. The whole region was up in arms, and on the alert in defence of home and life. The shores were strewn with barbed hooks of dried reed to wound the feet of any raiders who might land in the darkness, and villages were fortified, scouts were posted up and down the stream, and in one spot a fleet of canoes filled with exasperated warriors covered the waters for a distance of over three miles in close fighting order and carrying something like 5000 men. Eight villages which had been burnt to the ground were passed, whole towns had vanished altogether, and a panic had seized numbers of the people, who had fled for security into the jungle, or to the interior of the country. The Arabs were overtaken at Yavunga, a town on the north bank, at a bend of the river, which afforded them a convenient base of operations for the godless traffic in which they were engaged. The band was composed of 300 men who had come up from the Trans-Tanganika country to raid for ivory and slaves. They had secured 2500

captives, chiefly women and children, and about 2000
tusks of ivory. To obtain these, however, they had
destroyed 118 villages, and probably shot in cold
blood 3000 people. The district they had traversed
so far was equal to an area of 34,510 square miles,
with a population of perhaps 1,000,000 people. The
condition of the captives was simply horrible. The
Arab camp was strewn over with groups of wretched,
half-starved victims of Arab greed. Chained in gangs,
and languishing in a condition of indescribable filth,
these waifs of humanity presented a spectacle from
which Stanley turned with feelings of suppressed
indignation and disgust. Had he caught these
emissaries of Abed-ben-Salim red-handed at their
bloody work, the chances are that the Krupp gun
would have been brought into action, with a view to
protect or deliver the helpless children of the soil
from the clutches of their diabolical adversaries.

The district in the neighbourhood of the Arab camp
was one of striking beauty, and offered everywhere
splendid opportunities for the profitable growth of
cotton, sugar· wheat and maize, but it had been ruthlessly swept of its entire population by the raiders,
and given up to silent desolation.

On December 1st the Falls were reached. They
extend for a distance of fifty-six miles, and consist of
seven cataracts, and a series of smaller rapids. The
limit of the enterprise had now been attained, and the
chiefs of the region were called together to discuss the
terms upon which the last station of the the Comité
should be established within the confines of their
territory. The meeting was by no means conducted
with the reserve and decorum usually observed at

an African palaver. The proposal of the white man to
settle and build at the foot of the sounding waters was
warmly debated in loud tones and with excited gestures.
At length, however, the decision was given in favour
of the leader of the Expedition, who lost no time in seal-
ing the important compact by handing over the price of
the desirable and extensive site which he had secured.
Entire control and possession of a number of islands
on the left mainland was granted to the Association
with all rights to ground not already appropriated or
built upon by the natives themselves. The price of
the concession was 160l., which was distributed in bales
of cloth and other merchandise to the various owners
of the soil. The great chief of the locality, Siwa-Siwa,
assented most graciously to the transaction, and
assured Stanley that he would protect the settlement
during the explorer's absence. "Your people shall be
my children," said he, "in your absence. Go in safety.
It will be my task to feed them, and until you return
I shall dream every night of you." A space to the
extent of four acres was at once prepared for the
erection of the houses and magazines, and an officer
chosen to take charge of the settlement. The heart
of the gentleman who had been chosen for the task of
erecting and developing the station failed him at
the last moment, and he begged to be allowed to go
back to the coast. The difficulty of finding a white
substitute threatened to be a formidable one, but the
matter was settled by the plucky conduct of little
Binnie, the engineer of the *Royal*, a canny Scot, who
offered to stay at the Falls and assume the direction of
the work. He was furnished with an abundant store
of supplies and ammunition and a detachment of

thirty-one armed labourers, and on the 10th of December the Expedition was on its way back to Vivi, and the coast. The labour of extension was for the time to cease, whilst every effort was to be made to secure the ground already taken up, by further treaties with the natives who held the lands along the line of stations already planted. The return voyage was rapidly made upon the full flow of the now friendly current. At Iboko, the home of the fighting Bangala, a halt was made on Christmas Day, and the homeward-bound wanderers received a most hospitable welcome from their former foes. The name of Bula Matari and the fame of his great achievements had travelled from bank to bank of the great stream. So strong was the affection of the valiant Iboko for their pale-faced brother that they did not hesitate to secure, without leave or licence, any portion of his property which they could conveniently appropriate, probably to preserve as precious souvenirs of their illustrious relative. So serious had these pilferings become, that strong measures had at last to be taken to check this curious mode of showing their respect for Bula Matari. But the peace was kept, and Stanley parted from his kinsmen-by-blood with every good wish on their part for his safe arrival in his own land across the sea. Friendly greetings reached the fleet, as it steamed down towards the west, from the tribes along the shores, who had learned to regard the smoke-boats as harbingers of peace and prosperity to their country. Equator Station was found still prosperous and progressing. Glave, the Yorkshireman, was making headway with the difficult work of erecting and developing his settlement upon the rocky soil of Lukolela. The

natives spoke of him in the kindest way, and his
subordinates trusted him to a man. But what of
Bolobo the unlucky? Once more it had been reduced
to ashes. Houses, goods, ammunition, and, sad to
tell, the very carriage of the Krupp gun, had perished
in the flames. The thatch of the station had been
fired in the dead of night by a dying madman, who
wished to expire in the glare of the conflagration.
Murder, fire, and rapine had dimmed the fair fame of
Bolobo. Truly some malignant spirit hovered over the
unhappy place. The settlements of Kwamouth and
Kinshassa were steadily developing into active and
profitable colonies, and Leopoldville, which was
reached on January 20th, 1884, was found still in a
most satisfactory condition. So much had the outward
aspect of the spot improved during the absence of the
steamers, that when the returning Expedition beheld it,
after a lapse of 146 days, the men gave vent to their
feelings of admiration in warm expression of surprise
and delight. All had gone well with the neighbouring
tribes. Ngalyema had become a reformed character,
and a trusted friend of the white officer, the trusted
Valeke; and an air of peace, prosperity and security
surrounded Leopoldville, which abundantly testified
to the wisdom, energy and sterling good sense of the
young official who had been charged with the direction of its affairs. The condition of things upon the
Lower Congo was still one of chaos. Vivi, was, as of
old, the source of anxiety. The second-in-command
promised so long ago by the Comité had never
arrived, and one officer after another had visited the
unhappy place, stayed a few months, and then retired
ingloriously from the scene. At Manyanga, an

expenditure of 10,000*l.* in three years had only resulted in the erection of a few ill-built and almost useless tenements, and the whole place presented the look of a colony of about a month old! Isingila was in a bad way. Its houses were still unfinished, and valuable stores were rapidly decaying for want of proper care and shelter.

By April, 1884, Stanley had taken Vivi and its affairs once more in hand, and it was decided to move the whole settlement bodily across the ravine to the Castle Hill. The old settlement had become a miserable desolation. Nothing had been done to keep the buildings (erected by Stanley with so much pride at the outset of his mission) in order, and the road to the crest of the hill whereon he had gained for himself the immortal cognomen of "The Breaker of Rocks," had never been touched or mended. A new road was constructed in the direction of the fresh sites, and the Nkusu river was bridged before the commander-in-chief embarked for home. In May, 1884, Colonel Sir Francis De Winton reached the Congo, and at once took over the control of the work of the Association from Stanley, who left Banana Point by the African steamer *Kinsembo.* On his way up to the West Coast, the Pioneer of the Congo was interested to see the practical results of legitimate trade with the natives, who, in return for their casks of palm oil, were receiving and erecting cosy iron houses, well furnished with every accessory to comfort—such as carpets, mirrors, chairs, and curtains!

On July 29th the *Kinsembo* landed the late commander-in-chief of the Expédition du Haut Congo at Plymouth, and a few days after he reported himself at Ostend to his Majesty the President of the Association, and rendered to his august patron an account of his labours and the work he had been privileged to accomplish during the past six laborious and "bitter" years. The mission entrusted to Stanley in the Royal Council-Chamber at Brussels in December, 1878, had been accomplished. The Congo State had been founded. So far the arduous enterprise had been attended by success. But at what cost of suffering, anxiety, and personal sacrifice to the dauntless man by whose intrepid skill, extraordinary fortitude, and singular good sense and well-balanced judgment, these sublime results had been brought about, the amplest records of the undertaking can but faintly suggest.

THE high commission which had been entrusted to
Mr. Stanley by the Association Internationale du Haut
Congo had been faithfully and loyally discharged.
The flag of the Society had been carried in triumph to
the foot of the Stanley Falls, in the face of colossal
difficulties, and through many vicissitudes and changes
of fortunes. A line of permanent stations had been
planted from Banana Point to the inner Equatorial
regions, practicable roads had been constructed, 450
treaties had been made with independent chiefs, vast
tracts of eligible country had been secured for the
Association on both sides of the Congoese Water, and
an open way had been established through Central
Africa, from the Atlantic Ocean to the Indian Seas.
But something more remained to be done for the con-
solidation and future development of this unparalleled
enterprise.

The province of the Congo State had been created;
it was now necessary that its freedom should be secured,

its boundaries fixed, and its position as a sovereign power defined, by a formal acknowledgment of its independence on the part of the Great Powers.

There could be no doubt as to the abstract right of the Association to acquire the privileges of sovereignty over the riverain territory of the Congo by treaties with the native authorities and original holders of the soil. The chiefs who had transferred to Mr. Stanley, as the Commissioner of the Association Internationale du Haut Congo, their sovereign powers over the country, were without doubt in possession of their lands by the best of titles, long ages of successive inheritance. Other companies had, under similar circumstances, taken over tracts of territory from native owners, e.g. the Puritans under Penn in 1620, the colonists of New Hampshire in 1639, and in later days the East India, Sarawak, Liberia, Hudson's Bay, and Borneo companies. "It can scarcely be denied," says the Report of the Committee on Foreign Relations with the United States, "that the native chiefs have the right to make these treaties. The able and exhaustive statements of Sir Travers Twiss, the eminent English jurist, and of Professor Arutz, the no less distinguished Belgian publicist, leave no doubt upon the question of the right of the African International Association in view of the law of nations to accept any powers belonging to these native chiefs and governments which they may choose to delegate or cede to them."

The prospects of a speedy and complete recognition of the Independence of the Congo State were clouded for the time by the action of the Governments of Great Britain and Portugal. In 1884 these powers entered into a treaty, by which the West African Coast

between S. Latitude 5° 12′ and S. Latitude 5° 18′ was
declared to be Portuguese territory. This action was
merely the practical assertion, however, of the old
claim of the Portuguese to the whole of the south-
west African coast, from the Equator to the Cape of
Good Hope. From the time that Diego Cao had set
up his pillar of possession at the mouth of the Congo,
the Portuguese had exercised a merely nominal control
over the maritime regions between the Gaboon and
Loanda. This treaty with the British Government
threatened effectually to close the estuary of the river
and the adjacent lands on both banks to the Association, and thus deprive it of its natural outlet to the
sea. It was formally decided by Earl Granville, on
behalf of England, that the assent of the Great
Powers would be necessary before the treaty could
be regarded as valid, and, happily for the infant state,
this assent was never given to the distasteful document.

The most serious blow to the pretensions of Portugal was dealt, however, by the American Government. A deep interest in the affairs of Central
Equatorial Africa had been created in the United
States, and on the 10th of April, 1884, the independence
and sovereign authority of the Congo Free State within its own territory was formally recognized by an
Act of the Senate. This friendly and timely support
from the great Republic across the Atlantic at once
gave new help and courage to the authorities of the
new province.

The Anglo-Portuguese Treaty had been firmly
opposed by the most influential Chambers of Commerce in Great Britain, and the great manufacturing

centres of Manchester, Liverpool and Glasgow had
passed resolutions strenuously objecting to its formal
ratification. The objections of Prince Bismarck to the
treaty were unanswerable. "I do not think," said
the illustrious Chancellor, "that the treaty has any
chance of being universally recognized, even with the
modifications which are therein proposed by her
Majesty's Government. We are not prepared to
admit the previous rights of any of the Powers
who are interested in the Congo trade as a basis for
the negotiations. Trade and commerce have hitherto
been free to all alike, without restriction. We cannot
take part in any measure for handing over the
administration, or even the direction of their arrangement to Portuguese officials. In the interests of
German commerce, therefore, I cannot consent that a
coast of such importance, which has hitherto been free
land, should be subjected to the Portuguese Colonial
system." With a view to secure the support of France,
an agreement was come to between the Association
Internationale and the Government of the Republic,
by which the entire possessions of the Association were
to be placed under the French flag, in the event of the
failure of the Comité to carry through the negotiations
for the recognition of the independence of the Congo
State by the Great Powers. The following is the text
of the agreement signed by Colonel Strauch on behalf
of the Association:—"The International Association
of the Congo in the name of the free stations and
territories which it has established on the Congo and
in the valley of the Niadi-Kwilu, formally declares
that it will not cede them to any power under reserve
of the special Conventions which might be concluded

between France and the Association, with a view to settling the limits and conditions of their respective action. But the Association, wishing to afford a new proof of its friendly feeling towards France, pledges itself to give her the right of preference, if through any unforeseen circumstances the Association were one day led to realize its possessions." The reply of M. Jules Ferry, on behalf of the French Government, was a formal recognition of the territorial rights of the Association. After an interchange of notes between the cabinets of Paris and Berlin upon the various points of the proposed international understanding with reference to the entire West African Coast, including the basins of the Niger, the districts of the Gaboon, the Senegal, and Guinea, it was decided to hold a conference at Berlin of representatives of all the powers who had interests, commercial or political, in the West African regions.

Plenipotentiaries were sent by France, Austria, Great Britain, Belgium, Holland, Denmark, Spain, Portugal, America, Russia, Sweden and Turkey to meet those of Germany under the Presidency of Prince Bismarck. The Conference met on the 15th of November, when Mr. Stanley was appointed to take part in the deliberations of the august body, as technical adviser on behalf of the United States Government. The meetings were held in the Palace of the German Chancellor in Wilhelmstrasse, in the apartment which had been distinguished as the place of assembly of the famous Berlin Congress in 1878. Count H. Bismarck, M. Raindre, and Vice-Consul Dr. Schmidt were chosen as secretaries of the Conference, which was formally opened by Prince Bismarck in a brief address in which he announced that the objects of the gathering were :—

1. To discuss the questions of free navigation, with freedom of trade on the River Congo.

2. The free navigation of the Niger.

3. The formalities to be observed for valid annexation of territory in future on the African continent.

The meetings were held, with scarcely any interruptions, from November 15th, 1884, to February 26th, 1885, when the final Act was duly signed by all the Powers represented. A special commission was nominated to deal with the important question of the area and limits of the regions of Western Africa, which were to be open at all times to subjects of any nation for free and unrestricted commercial enterprise, and another committee of the Conference was chosen to define the extent of the Congo basin. An interesting discussion took place before this committee as to the exact amount of territory to be included in the new province. Various questions bearing upon the internal administration of the Congo state were earnestly and carefully considered. The slave trade, the traffic in spirits, the free navigation of the river, the formalities to be observed in any future acquisition of territory, and the necessity for some guarantee on the part of the Powers that Central Africa should be open to the trader and the missionary from sea to sea, were points which occupied the closest attention of the Conference, and in all these matters the opinions of Mr. Stanley, founded upon his unique experiences of African life, were frequently asked for, and eagerly listened to by the illustrious men who surrounded the council-board. " I argued for a broad commercial delta," says Mr. Stanley, " 380 miles wide to a free commercial basin, that is from the mouth of the Logo river to 2° 30′ S. Lat., and also suggested, quite unexpectedly to the members, that it would be wise to extend the same liberty for trade across Africa to within one degree from the sea coast, from N. Lat. 5° to and inclusive of the lower Zambesi." This bold suggestion was strongly approved of by the able and astute representative of the English Foreign Office, Mr. Anderson, and it was warmly supported by M. de Bloeme, the Dutch delegate, and ultimately adopted by the Conference, to the intense satisfaction of its author.

But the primary question of the exact limits of the frontiers of the Congo State had now to be definitely settled. After considerable delay, an agreement was come to with Portugal, and the boundaries of the new territory were laid down as follows :—The dividing-line was to proceed from Banana Point along the sea-board to Cabo Lombo, a distance of twenty-two miles, then to follow the north bank of the Congo as far as the cataracts, and beyond Likona above Stanley Pool, embracing also the south bank as far as Nokki. It was to take in the geographical basin of the Congo, from the sources of the Chambezi to 4° N. Lat., and from Tanganiza to the Kwa river, and its entire superficial area was estimated at 1,065,200 square miles, with a population of 42,000,000. Having thus defined its limits, the Congo State was formally recognized by the Conference as a sovereign power. The Powers, through their delegates, proceeded to negotiate private conventions with Colonel Strauch, the President of the Association, and the official head of the newly constituted dominion, who was introduced to the Council by Prince Bismarck, and the signature of the Acts of the Conference by the members of that high diplomatic body, crowned the anxious work of many years, by securing for ever the inviolability of the constitution and government of the new African state. By the decisions of this historical assembly, the trader is protected from outrage or spoliation in the exercise of his lawful calling, and is amenable for his conduct and probity to a consul of his own nationality, who is vested with ample authority to deal with any case regarding which he may be required to exercise his jurisdiction. The wholesale degradation of the native races by an unrestricted liquor traffic is guarded against, and the slave-trader peremptorily warned off the protected territory; the teacher of truth and righteousness is specially cared for, and the pioneers of science are entitled to many privileges. The reception accorded to Mr. Stanley at Berlin was most complimentary and ceremonious. On the evening of the day upon which the Conference had decided to accept his proposal as to the delta of the Congo, he was invited to dine with the Chancellor at his palace, and he was much impressed by the honesty, resolution, and clear-eyed common sense of the great Prussian minister.

On November 30th the attention of the delegates of the Conference was directed to the important question of the openings for religious and missionary work in Congo-land, and on January 7th, 1885, a splendid banquet in honour of the distinguished traveller was given by a deputation from the Rhine Provinces and Westphalia, who were delighted with a speech from him upon the many openings for commercial venture which existed upon the banks of the Congo. On January 8th Mr. Stanley proceeded to Frankfort, where he lectured before a vast and most sympathetic audience upon Central Africa, and the good results which were likely to follow the labours of the delegates lately assembled at Berlin.

The diploma of the senior Geographical Society of Germany was bestowed upon the great Explorer, and another was handed to him by Prince Hohanlohe Langenburg, from the German Colonial Association. At Wiesbaden also he was honoured by a banquet, and his extraordinary efforts for the amelioration of the condition of the people of the Central Equatorial regions were frequently referred to in terms of the warmest admiration.

France and Portugal had every reason to be gratified with the results of the Conference. To both these powers a considerable and valuable accession of African territory had been awarded. The former power had long been ably represented in the equatorial regions by M. de Brazza, who had spent some years in exploring the continent north of the Congo, and in extending the influence of his government amongst the tribes east and south of the Gaboon, and in the districts watered by the Ogowai River. M. de Brazza had been the guest of Mr. Stanley for some days at one of the stations on the Congo, and the latter speaks highly of the indefatigable energy and diplomatic skill of his foreign guest. Count Pietro Savorgnan de Brazza, who had succeeded in reaching Stanley Pool a few weeks before the arrival there of the expedition of the Association Internationale du

Haut Congo in 1881, was born on the banks of the
Tiber, of a noble and ancient Italian family, in 1852.
In his school-boy days he evinced a taste for adventure,
and showed by several daring exploits that he possessed the true courage necessary to succeed as an
explorer of savage lands. In 1868 his relations removed to France, and he entered the naval academy
at Brest as a cadet, leaving it with the rank of mid-
shipman after about two years. In 1872 he was
appointed to the *Venus*, a French ship of war
then lying off the Gaboon. The French colony " here
seated astride of the equator" was founded in 1842,
and its area extended in 1862, so as to embrace
a sea-front of eighty miles about the delta of the
Ogowe a river which had never been explored beyond
a few miles from its mouth. The idea of tracing this
river to its sources, so completely took possession of
the mind of the young naval officer, that he asked for,
and readily obtained, leave to investigate the mystery
surrounding its course and rise. Could the Ogowe be
one of the great highways of nature, as the Nile, the
Zambesi, or the Niger, and was it after all the
embouchure of the Lualaba? were questions De Brazza
asked himself, and which he determined to solve. An
expedition was fitted out at Gaboon to assist him in
carrying out his purpose, and he started full of hope
upon his self-imposed task; but in three years he
returned to the coast disappointed and dismayed.
The river which he had examined had proved to
be only a " mere littoral stream," of no importance,
geographical or commercial. In his wanderings,
however, the resolute Frenchman had come across
two splendid streams flowing due east, which he

endeavoured to ascend. Driven back by the savage hostility of the natives, when only five days from the trunk-waters of the Congo, of which these streams, the Ahina and the Licona, were affluents, he returned to Europe in 1879, and was re-commissioned in the same year, by the Government of the Republic, to establish a French State and enter into treaties of amity and friendship with the tribes of Inner Equatorial Africa. He at once returned to the region of Stanley Pool, where he succeeded in securing an important alliance with the Makoko or King of the Batekes, by a treaty which was ratified by the French Chamber November 21st, 1882. The result of the action of M. de Brazza was to give the French precedence and priority of possession and influence in the district of the great inland sea, and Brazzaville, the French station, was founded in October, 1880, on the right bank of the Pool, the native chiefs in the surrounding region acknowledging formally the protectorate of the French flag. In 1882 the French Commissioner, who had succeeded in extending the nominal influence of his government throughout the entire region north of the river, returned to Europe to report progress. De Brazza and Stanley have many characteristics in common. Both have shown celerity, endurance, resolution, and undaunted courage; both have shown power to look into the face of difficulties which would have dismayed most men, and skill to overcome them. To neither of these remarkable men would the word " adventurer " apply in any sense. Both are inspired by the highest motives which can give an impulse to human effort. Both men are working for the good of Africa and the interests of humanity, and never even in their personal rivalry have they forgotten that they are brothers united in a common cause.

The new territory assigned to France by the Berlin assembly is of vast extent, and consists of rich, productive lands, well endowed with mineral deposits, and destined to become the field of important commercial undertakings. The superficial area of this newly acquired country is estimated at 257,000 square miles. It will be seen that this addition to the possessions of the French in Western Africa is equal in size to England and France united. On its eastern side it has 5200 miles of available water-way, and on the west it has a sea-board of 800 miles in length. Within the borders of this enormous province there are no less than eight extensive river-basins, and the entire land is without a single square mile of barren or absolutely worthless soil.

Portugal was fortunate enough to secure 103 miles of the south bank of the Congo, and a strip of sea-board 995 English miles in extent, with a wide stretch of territory inland amounting altogether to 351,500 square miles of area, a region larger than the united areas of France, Belgium, Holland and Great Britain. The country thus placed under the dominion of the Portuguese crown is fertile, and embraces fine pastoral districts, extensive forests, and large mineral fields, as well as valuable tracts of land well adapted for agriculture, bordering the inner region of the lakes. By another important act of the Conference a zone of Free Trade was created right across the continent, and the benefits of unrestricted commerce were secured for all the countries (including the new possessions of Portugal and France), within the limits of this belt,

and it was decreed that the provisions of the various
Acts were to be upheld, if necessary, by the combined
forces of the signatory powers.

The chief points of the convention between Great
Britain and the Association of the Congo Free State,
which was signed at Berlin on December 16th, 1884,
by Sir Edward Malet, H.M.B.'s Ambassador Extraordinary and Minister Plenipotentiary, and Colonel
Strauch, the President of the Association Internationale
of the Congo and the Free States, are as follows:—
The flag of the States, a gold star upon a blue ground,
is to be recognized as the flag of a friendly government.
No import duties are to be levied upon the merchandise
of British subjects, nor are any charges to be put
upon any goods in transit upon the roads, canals, or
waters of the State. British subjects are to exercise
the right of settling in the territories under the
government of the Association without let or hindrance,
and they are to enjoy all the privileges and protection
in regard to their lives and property which is afforded
to the subjects of the most favoured nation, and they
shall have the right to buy, sell, lease and let lands,
buildings, mines, and forests within the said territories; to found houses of business, and to engage in
commerce and coasting-trade therein under the British
flag. No advantages are to be accorded to the subjects of another nation which are not immediately extended to British subjects. An undertaking is to be
given by the Association that the consuls or consular
agents of the Queen should be received and protected
in the ports and stations on its territories. Freedom
of action is to be allowed to consuls and consular
agents to establish tribunals for the exercise of sole

and exclusive jurisdiction, civil as well as criminal,
with regard to the persons and property of British
subjects within the said district, in accordance with
the British laws. No British subject is to be absolved
from obedience to the laws of the States applicable to
foreigners, but all infractions of the laws on the part of
a British subject are to be referred to the British consular tribunal. Any person doing injury to a subject
of her Majesty is to be arrested and punished by the
authorities of the Association conformably to the laws
of the Free States, and justice is to be administered
without respect to person, or race, or nationality. Any
British subject having cause of complaint against the
inhabitants of the territories of the Free States, must
lodge a statement of his grievances with the British
Consul. Inquiry is then to be made, and, if possible,
an amicable settlement arranged. Any inhabitant of
the said territories failing to pay any debt contracted
with a British subject, is to be brought to justice and
compelled to discharge his liability, and in like manner
if any British subject fails to pay any debt contracted
with one of the inhabitants, the British authorities
are to proceed to bring the defaulter to account and
recover the money. The British Consul, however, or
the authority of the Association are not to be held
responsible for any debt contracted by a British subject, nor by any inhabitant of the Free States. In the
case of any future cession of territory, the obligations
contracted by the Association in this convention are
to apply to the grantee, and the engagements and
rights accorded to British subjects are to remain in
force after any cession with regard to any new occupant of every part of the said territory.

Similar agreements, in almost identical terms, were signed by Colonel Strauch and the delegates of the powers represented at Berlin, and it will be seen that nothing was neglected which was at all possible to open up into the interior of the African Continent a broad road for the moral and material progress of its native races, and for the development of the general welfare of commerce and navigation. The domain of public international law had been enlarged, and the cause of religion, of peace, and humanity simultaneously advanced. Article VI. of the General Act of the Conference is as follows :—" All the Powers exercising sovereign rights, or having influence in the said territories, undertake to watch over the preservation of the native races, and the amelioration of the moral and material conditions of their existence, and to cooperate in the suppression of slavery, and, above all, of the slave trade : they will protect and encourage, without distinction of nationality or creed, all institutions and enterprises, religious, scientific, or charitable, established and organized for these objects, or tending to educate the natives and lead them to understand and appreciate the advantages of civilization.

" Christian missionaries, men of science, explorers and their escorts and collections, to be equally the objects of special protection.

" Liberty of conscience and religious toleration are expressly guaranteed to the natives as well as to the inhabitants and foreigners. The free and public exercise of every creed, the right to erect buildings, and to organize missions belonging to any creed, shall be subject to no restriction or impediment whatever."

The Congo State was at length not only established but Free, and acknowledged by the great nations of the Old and New Worlds as an independent and sovereign power. Who will be bold enough to predict the results, to the great African continent, of this brilliant and beneficent enterprise, or to estimate the blessings which will flow from it to fifty millions of Central Africans, those countless myriads of dark-skinned children of the soil, who will learn, as time goes on, to welcome the star of gold upon the dark blue as the harbinger of peace, and the token to them of a higher and a happier life ?

The great obstacle to the immediate development of the unlimited natural resources of the Free States is the break in the line of water transport at the Livingstone Falls and the cataracts of Stanley Pool; but Mr. Stanley has devised a practical method of overcoming this serious hindrance to commercial operations, and to the transit of goods and produce from the inner basin to the sea. He has advocated most strenuously, the construction of a surface railway from Vivi to Leopoldsville, a distance of 343 miles, with a break of 88 miles of available water-way. In 1885 the Government of the Free States granted a concession to the Congo Railway Syndicate, represented by Mr. Stanley and Mr. J. F. Hutton, M.P., President of the Manchester Chamber of Commerce, to construct a line from the Upper to the Lower Congo. Considerable interest has been taken in the scheme, and it has been supported by several distinguished men, and subscription lists have been opened to obtain the requisite capital—2,000,000l.—which will be needed for the completion of the road. Such a railway would, according to the reliable estimates of Mr. Stanley, be one of the most remunerative speculations of the day. If it were possible to send steamers or sailing-ships direct to the upper basin of the Congo river, it is calculated that they would obtain three times the amount of produce which they carry away from the west coast of Africa at the present time. It is believed by those who are competent to give an opinion upon the matter, that the total value of the export trade thus opened out would reach something like 50,000,000*l*. As the region cannot be reached by ships or steamers of heavy tonnage, the alternative is by no means a hopeless one. " Build a railway," says Mr. Stanley, " in two sections, respectively fifty-two and ninety-five miles in length, connected by steamboat navigation, or a connected railway 238 miles long, and you will obtain as much produce as such a railway can convey, from the trading agents on the Upper Congo, who will collect it from over 1,000,000 native Africans, who are waiting to be told what further produce is needed beyond ivory, palm-oil, gum-copal, palm-kernels, gourd-nuts, orchilla-weed, corn wood, furs, hides, feathers, copper, india-rubber, grass fibre, bees'-wax, ginger, castor-oil nuts, nutmeg, bark-cloth, &c." The tonnage upon such a railway would be equal to $427\frac{1}{2}$ tons per day, an amount of traffic which would fairly task its resources. At a charge for transport of one penny per ton per mile, the total receipts of the line would equal 152,000*l*., and the revenue from imports going up-country would probably reach a like sum, bringing up the grand total of receipts to 300,000*l*. per year, without calculating for passengers. The cost of constructing the road is estimated at 4000*l*. per mile.

Fuel could be readily obtained from the inexhaustible forests of Bondi and Ngoma, which border upon the proposed track; and with the enormous facilities for transport which such a line would possess, it has truly been said that every square mile of the Equatorial Congoese territory is reclaimable.

The results of the Berlin Conference were most pleasing to Mr. Stanley. They secured, in a great measure the end for which he had so long and so arduously toiled—a Free African State. He left the German capital with many expressions of respect and regard for the illustrious men whom he had been privileged to meet in council there. His admiration for Prince Bismarck grew as his knowledge of the real powers of that remarkable man increased, and he shows us the great Chancellor in quite a new light, when he describes him as a statesman who is glad to be advised and ready to act upon the advice which he receives. On his return to England, at the conclusion of his labours at Berlin, Mr. Stanley was received by men of all ranks and parties as a man who was worthy of all honour, not only for his estimable personal qualities, but for his latest and most splendid and heroic achievement—the founding of the Congo Free State in the heart of the African Continent.

Mr. Stanley's dream had at length become a reality, and he was permitted to see (as few men have seen) completion crown his work.

CHAPTER XVIII.

THE various races which inhabit the Congo basin from
the Chambezi sources to the Atlantic are branches of
one family—the Bantus,—which occupies the entire
area of Central Africa from the Soudan to the borders
of the regions occupied by the Hottentots and the
Bushmen of the South. The tribes of the great
central lake district and the Upper Congo differ both
in physique and language altogether from the negroes
of the north-west, or the Hamitic populations of the
north-east, and they have nothing in common with
the degraded populations in the southern portion of
the continent. The Bantus occupy the widest range
of any people in Africa, but at the same time they
themselves have no racial bond or special type of
feature or figure which could be distinctly called
Bantusian. "They are essentially Negroid rather
than Negro people, presenting every shade of transi-
tion from the pure Negro of Guinea and the Soudan
to the pure Hamite and Semite of the Middle Nile and

north-east coast. Between these two extremes they
oscillate in endless variety, showing nowhere any fixed
physical features, and bound together only by their
common Bantu speech. The definition " Bantu" is to
be taken therefore in a linguistic rather than an ethnological meaning. In the region of the upper waters
and about the Lualaba, there are certain dwarf races,
described by Mr. Stanley and Lieut. Weismann;
and two specimens of dwarfs were seen in slavery by
Mr. Johnston in the Ba-yansi country, who differed in
every way from their masters in physique and manners.
Towards the west, the people along the basin of the
great river begin to lose their distinctly Bantu
characteristics as they become mixed with the inferior
negro population of the coast. The Bantu is a fine,
tall, well-proportioned, and erect type of manhood,
with well-shaped hands and feet, striking features, a
beard and moustaches, and a good covering of hair,
and the type improves as you advance into the region
of the Upper Congo. In colour the Bantu is not
black, but a warm bronze, and some of the men about
Bélibó have been described as "perfect Greek statues,"
in the splendid development, and easy poise of their
forms. All throughout the lake country, and probably
as far as the broad waters of Stanley Pool, the best
specimens of the pure Bantu are to be found. From
the Pool to the coast the race rapidly degenerates,
both in physique and in character. On the north
bank, in the region of Stanley Pool, and reaching far
away into the interior, is the famous tribe of the
Batéké, with whom M. de Brazza has been so successful in making treaties and obtaining concessions on
behalf of the French Government. The energetic

traveller visited Makoko in 1880, "the ruler of thirteen kingdoms," and managing to forestall Stanley, he made good a footing on the north bank of the Pool some time before the illustrious commander of the Expedition du Haut Congo reached the spot.

There is no mixture of negro-blood in the pure Bantu (= meri) race, which occupies that portion of the continent, roughly speaking, which lies between the Sahara and the Orange River.

The Bantu is as distinct in physical features, language and intelligence from the negro, as the Englishman is distinct from the Bantu. The characteristic of the race is an abundance of hair on the face and body. Stanley describes the beard of one of the friendly chiefs near the Pool as measuring six feet long when unrolled for his admiration, and bushy whiskers and flowing beards are common. The natives paint their bodies in streaks of white, brown, yellow, or red, when about to proceed to war, with pigments composed of lime, or ochre, or common charcoal, and then each bears a distinguishing tribal mark upon the forehead or temples. These signs are short slashes in the skin, and they vary in number and size. Their entire bodies are in some cases covered with these weals, which amongst the Bantu are very much admired as adding considerably to the personal attractions of the wearer. The tribes on the upper waters are fond of music, colour, and motion. They dance well, and are graceful and intelligent in their movements. They are domesticated in their habits, fond of their children, and appear at ordinary times to be happy and contented with their lot. In time of war, however, they are fierce and sanguinary, and are suspected of consuming the bodies of their enemies in a kind of sacrificial feast. The boys are carefully trained from childhood to the sports of the field and the practice of the peaceful arts of a pastoral life. They are all taught to swim directly they can be trusted alone in the water, and soon become quite at home amongst the torrents and currents of the mighty river, in which the crocodiles, which lie in ambush under the shadow of the sedgy banks, or in the dark cool depths of the stream, are the only objects of fear. The girls are instructed in household duties, preparing food, weaving cloth, and planting grain or roots for the consumption of the family. The men of the Upper Congo regions are great traders. They have a peculiar gift for bartering, and have a marvellous faculty for keeping the most intricate accounts, simply by memory, without the aid of books or paper. The boys are encouraged to begin to speculate in small business adventures very early in life, and Stanley records his astonishment on more than one occasion at witnessing the unnatural precocity of the youths in the region of the upper waters in the matter of securing a bargain.

It appears that from the coast to the Pool the currency is beads, but in the neighbourhood of the Pool and inland, brass rods and Sami-Sami (long white beads resembling bits of broken pipe stem) are the only recognized mediums of exchange or traffic. The Bantus are far behind the plucky and cosmopolitan Wangwana or Wanzamwesi people of the East Coast, from whom the great explorers always took care to select the *personnel* of their expeditions. As porters, or escort, these men are unequalled upon the continent of Africa, and without them it would have been impossible to have " Found Livingstone," or to have travelled " Through the Dark Continent."

The Kroomen of the West Coast and the debased race about the estuary of the Congo are spiritless, cowardly, and entirely unfitted for any enterprise requiring courage, or discipline. They are also indolent, and given over to the fatal fascination of the gin or rum bottle, and consequently utterly unreliable in any time of emergency or in any special and responsible service.

The natives of the lower or Bakongo region from Stanley Pool to the coast are altogether of a lower type of humanity. In the upper region the arts of life are more or less cultivated with success. The houses of the higher riverine tribes are large and well constructed, with lofty rooms and stout walls, and in some instances are nicely decorated with carved work or native hangings of dyed grass-cloth, and an air of domestic peace pervades the palm-shaded villages. In the lower maritime region there is too often that offensive squalor and barbarous rudeness about the native towns which has always been associated in the popular mind with African village life. These people have no morality, they lie, cheat, steal and quarrel from infancy, their remembrance of kindnesses received is fleeting, their sloth incurable. In the fifteenth century, the Kingdom of Kongo was one of the most formidable empires upon the continent. In the height of its prosperity it included all the countries to the south of the stream, from the Atlantic to the head of the Pool, and reached down to Ngola (Angola), but to-day the King of Congo is only a petty chief, with no power beyond his own town. The day of native rule on the West African Coast is past and gone. At the cost of a few bottles of spirits or a dozen coloured handkerchiefs it can be superseded or entirely overturned by treaty, and it is with great satisfaction, therefore, that the important future of this vast territory has been safeguarded by the work of the Association Internationale du Haut Congo.

Many of the villages upon the fearful journey from Nyangwe to the Stanley Falls were found to be decorated with hideous rows of bleached skulls, fixed in the ground on each side of the pathway, about ten feet apart, and reaching the entire length of the town. In one place 185 " cerebral hemispheres " were counted, ghastly and gleaming from long exposure to the weather. In reply to the inquiry of Stanley, who was anxious to come at the truth of the man-eating propensities of the tribes of this region, his Arab companions told him that the skulls were those of the " Soko " (Chimpanzee or Gorilla) of the forest, which were, the villagers themselves explained, animals about the size of the boy Mabruki (4 ft. 10 in.). He walks like a man, and goes about with a stick, with which he beats the trees in the forest, and makes hideous noises. " The Nyama ' Soko ' eat our bananas and we eat them.

" Are they good eating ? " asked Stanley.

" Very good."

" Would you eat one, if you had one now ? "

" Indeed we would. Shall a man refuse meat ? " [1]

From the observations of Professor Huxley, who examined some skulls of supposed " Soko " which

" Across the Dark Continent." (H. M. Stanley.)

Stanley brought home, and handed to the famous
expert for his inspection, it appears, however, that
the skulls were the remains of people of the ordinary
African negro type, and that from some disinclination
to tell the ghastly truth to the white man, they, as
well as the rows of skulls which adorned the streets, had
been passed off to him as the bones of the " Soko."
All these people had the top row of teeth filed
to a point, and they were known by the title of the
Wasongoro Meno (" the people of the filed teeth.")
A dwarf was captured outside the camp at Ikonda,
above the Stanley Falls, and taken to the leader of
the Expedition. He was a vicious little fellow, armed
with a tiny bow and sheaf of poisoned arrows. The
creature was only about four and a half feet high. He
had a large head, a ragged fringe of whiskers, and a
complexion of light chocolate. He was altogether
a miserable specimen of humanity, with his bow legs
thin shanks, and forlorn aspect. He said he belonged
to the tribe of the " Watwa," who were known to
Stanley's men as a vindictive people of diminutive
stature, nearer Nyangwe. No European traveller has
actually seen the tribe or traversed the country inhabited by it, but there is little doubt as to the actual
existence of the " Watwa " dwarfs, with their long
beards and bushy whiskers, somewhere in the region
west of the Lualaba.

It has been already said that the only tie which binds
together the various tribes of Congo Land is that of
Language. Taking speech as the basis of the division,
the whole continent of Africa may be said to be peopled
by six distinct races, of which the Semitic, Hamitic,
and Bantu are the chief. Of the Bantu, till quite

recently the Zulu Kaffirs were the best known representatives, and their language is pure Bantu, although
much disguised by the clicks, which they have
acquired from their Hottentot neighbours. Dialects
of the Bantu are spoken by the various tribes of the
Congo basin, all of which display a remarkable affinity
to each other, while differing in almost every particular
from the speech of the other races of Africa. For
instance, there is nothing in common between the
speech of the Congoese people and that of the West-
Coast negroes, the Abyssinians, or the Soudanese
tribes. A striking characteristic of the Bantu
tongue as it is spoken upon the Congo is the use of
the " euphonic concord," which is described by the
Rev. W. Holman Bentley, an old resident in the
territory of the Free States, as " a principle by which
the characteristic prefix of the noun is attached to
the pronouns and adjectives qualifying it, and to the
verb of which it is the subject. Thus *matadi mama
manipwena mampembe mejitanga beni* = these great
stones are very heavy." Mr. R. N. Cust, the learned
Secretary of the Royal Asiatic Society, in his recently
published and most valuable book upon the languages
of Africa, says, " The Bantu languages are soft, pliant,
and flexible, to an almost unlimited extent. Their
grammatical principles are founded on the most
systematic and philosophical basis, and the number
of words may be multiplied to an almost indefinite
extent. They are capable of expressing all the
nicer shades of thought and feeling; and perhaps no
*other languages of the world are capable of more defi-
niteness and precision of expression.* Livingstone justly
remarks that a complaint of the poverty of a language

is often only a sure proof of the scanty attainments of the complainant ; as a fact the Bantu languages are exceedingly rich." The fact that the degraded tribes of this wonderful region possess to-day a language of such completeness and richness and superiority would seem to point to a decline in the race, and to the possibility that in remote ages it occupied a nobler and a loftier position amongst the "dusky nations" of the dark continent than it holds in our own times. The Bantus have no memorials of past greatness, no books, no monuments, no ancient buildings, and no crumbling cities still bearing the marks of past grandeur upon their broken walls or shattered towers. But that they are the descendants of a once mighty and far-reaching power, which probably dominated Africa, there can be no doubt ; and, under the fostering care of the Association Internationale, there are promises of an ultimate return to their former pre-eminence, at least in the Inner Equatorial regions. There are four distinct dialects spoken upon the Western Congo, from the Equator to the sea, viz. The Kongo or Shi-Kongo, 2. The Kitéké, 3. The Ki-Buma, 4. The Ki-Yansi.

The rules of pronunciation are as follows :—

(a) The *consonants* are sounded as in English, except " gh," which is pronounced as " zh," the z taking the sound of the French " j," or of our " z " in " azure."

(b) The *vowels* are sounded fully, and exactly as in the Italian language.

In *diphthongs* each vowel is distinctly sounded.

The *accent* is upon the penultimate syllable, but there are a few words which have the accent upon the last syllable, owing to mutilation of the word or loss of a syllable.

(c) The consonant M used as a prefix, as in Mtu, has a shortened sound of Um. The prefix Ki- denotes language, U represents country, Wa a plural denoting people, M signifies a person, thus :—

U-Sagara—Country of Sagara.

Wa-Sagara—People of Sagara.

M-Sagara—A person of Sagara.

Ki-Sagara—Language, manner, custom, or style of Sagara, as "English" stands for anybody relating to England, &c.

The Ki-Swahili is the French of the East Coast, and is the language of diplomacy and the only means of intercourse between many of the communities which border the Indian Ocean. Far up into the interior Swahili is spoken or understood, and it was found by Stanley to be the court language of his royal friend Mtesa of Uganda.

It was always the strong desire of Mr. Stanley that the way which he had opened to the long-forgotten heart of Africa should be used as a channel for the introduction of the beneficent influences of Christianity to the swarming populations of the interior. The records of his great journey across the continent aroused the sympathies of the English and Continental religious and philanthropic societies, and arrangements were at once made, and money subscribed by them to occupy the new territory in the name of their Divine Master.

There are at the present time upon and about the Congo something like seventy-five missionaries, who are settled amongst the various tribes to instruct them

in the higher morality and holier aspirations of the
Christian life.   There are twenty stations scattered
over the region from the sea to the district of Stanley
Falls, and there are several mission steamers afloat
upon the Congo's tawny flood at various points up the
river.   Roman Catholics, Baptists, American Episco-
palians, a Swedish Society, the London Missionary
Society, the Scotch Free Church, and the Church
Missionary Society are all busily engaged in the educational and evangelical work in the Central Equatorial region, and, in fact, the Free-trade belt from
ocean to ocean may be said to be covered by a
net-work of mission stations, from which the most
humanizing influence will be exercised over the whole
length and breadth of the continent.

The Congo tribes have nothing which can be called
a Religious system.   They have no temples, priest-
hood, or ritual of worship.   They possess no idol
shrines or sacred groves, and have only a vague idea
of a supreme being whom they designate Nzambi, or
Molongo, the word being changed to Mulungu or
Muungu on the east coast.   The great spirit is to
them by no means an object of dread, and there are
no signs of any feeling on their part of a need to
propitiate or even to invoke, the being of whose
immensity and majesty they appear to have a deep
impression.   To these poor untaught heathen, Nzambi
is too far above them in his nature to be approached
or moved by earthly supplications; and though they
regard him as the Creator and Protector of man, yet
the gulf between themselves and their Divinity is too
great to be bridged by prayer or lessened by the
most devoted service.   They have a strong belief in a

future life after death, and all their funeral rites are conducted with the idea that their dear friends are only passing on to some new state of existence, in which they will still be mindful of the conduct of those who are left behind. Great reverence is shown to the spirits of the departed, and the living are careful not to anger the dead by any neglect to pay them every respect by attending their honoured burial, and preserving their tombs in a proper condition of repair. Human sacrifices are offered at the interment of chiefs of great dignity, and a terrible story is told by Stanley of a massacre of slaves at the burial of an old potentate of Iboko in 1884. As soon as the old man died his relatives and friends began to collect as many slaves as could be bought, and so anxious were they to obtain a large supply, that they even applied to Lieut. Vangele, the chief of Equator Station, to sell them some of his men, whom the natives thought to be the chattels of the white man. The proposal was rejected with indignation, and the astonished would-be purchasers of Stanley's loyal Zanzibaris were driven out of the station with sticks and other weapons by the enraged garrison. The lieutenant, however, was curious to witness the funeral rites of these people, and he proceeded with some of his followers to view the horrible spectacle. Fourteen miserable wretches had been secured for immolation at the grave-side, and a crowd of men had assembled to witness the massacre. The captives were kneeling, with their wrists lashed behind them near a tall tree, to the top of which a strong rope had been attached. A band of men seized the rope and dragged down the tree till it was bent into the shape of a bow. One of the captives was chosen and the cord placed round his neck : the tree started up several inches, straining the neck of the doomed man, and nearly lifting his body from the ground. The executioner, bearing a short broad-bladed weapon, now approached, and marking the distance by touching the nape of the man's neck with the tip of his sword twice, at the third stroke severed the head from the body. It flew up into the air, and was thrown yards off by the rebound of the sapling, and the operation was repeated till the whole of the victims had been despatched. The bodies were dragged away and flung into the Congo, but the skulls, after being denuded of the flesh by boiling, were carefully collected for exhibition at the grave of the deceased prince. The blood-stained soil was taken up and buried in the grave with the body of the chief. The spirits of the dead slaves are supposed to accompany the departed potentate and to escort him into the great unseen land. Plates, food, knives, cloth, beads, wire, are cast into the tomb after being bent and broken or in some way " killed," in order that they may pass into the unseen country with their lord. A widow on the death of her husband mourns for him in solitude for fifty days, during which she is made a hideous object by applications of charcoal powder to the face and body.

The people of the Upper Congo do not practise witchcraft, or put much faith in the pretended powers of the medicine-man. They have a dread of death, but no fear of meeting Nzambi, or of being punished for wrong-doing, which they are taught to avoid simply on account of the unpleasant results if found out.

The poison ordeal is practised for the detection of crime. The ceremony is a very simple but awful one, and clearly points out the need of light and knowledge in these " dark places of the earth." The market-day of the district in which the crime has been committed is chosen for the trial of the suspected evil-doers, and vast multitudes of excited and exasperated people assemble to witness the condemnation of the criminals. The Nganga-a-ngombo, or witch-doctor, who is entrusted with the task of finding out the authors of the wrong which is to be avenged, then pounces upon a few people, whose antecedents or connection with the person bewitched or injured give some slight ground for suspicion, and each in turn is obliged to drink the terrible potion which is to decide his innocence or guilt in the face of the jeering mob. Unhesitatingly, but with a despairing horror, he grasps the judicial cup. If he has in any way become conscious of the fact that he was a suspect, he will have taken due precautions to avoid the fatal effects of the poison by drinking copious draughts of water, which will cause his stomach to reject the deadly draught of the witch-doctor with little trouble. If no evil results follow the absorption of the poison the person is declared free of blame, but if the unfortunate creature has had no hint of his position, and is suddenly seized and made to drink of the terrible cup, he falls instantly, overcome by its effects, and in a few moments his battered and outraged corpse is floating upon the brown waters of the Congo.

The inhabitants below the Pool, the Bakongo, are simply, to use the expressive words of a recent writer, " embedded in the mud of gross and cruel superstitions,

by which the vague aspirations towards the unknown
implanted in every human breast are turned into the
fatal instruments of further degradation. The ignoble
parody of religion which they profess is fetichism in
its vilest form ; sorcery gives the only admitted
rationale of disastrous occurrences, and reaps a
plentiful harvest of victims ; each death is investigated
or revenged by the witch-detecting draught of
' caxa,' the Bakongo philosophy of life including no
idea of its natural limitation. The *nganda* or fetish man
raised to that ' bad eminence ' by superior intelligence
or villainy, represents justice, exorcises the demons of
sickness, guides the fury, or imposes the tyranny of
superstition and reaps the wages of power." These
people have no idea of the use of medicines in healing or
mitigating the ravages of disease. Directly a person
falls ill his friends declare that " some one has done it,"
and they are not content till this " some one " is
hunted out, found, and either killed or fined.

The life of the Bakongo is described as the most
dissipated and worthless existence that can possibly
be conceived. Dwellers upon a prolific soil, which
yields an abundance of good things without any effort
on the part of the occupiers, they give themselves up
to feasting, drinking, and aimless idling. Their one
desire is to possess rum and muskets.

The women till the fields, gather in the crops of
ground-nuts, bananas, manioc, and sweet potatoes,
whilst the men smoke or loiter about, or exert
themselves sufficiently to hunt such small game as
rats, lemurs, field-mice, frogs, and grasshoppers;
occasionally they fish in the river, or snare birds, but
a spirit of inertia possesses them at all times, pro-

crastination is their favourite ally, and their slothful leisure, devoted to sensual gratifications, soon brings upon them disease and death. The week of the Bakongo consists of four days, but they have no calendar, and take little note of the progress of time.

Children are considered as belonging to the relatives of the mother, and they are almost entirely free from the control of the father. The right to inherit property does not pass from father to son, as with us, but from uncle to nephew, and real property goes to the eldest son of the eldest sister. This peculiar and unique arrangement works very badly, and entirely destroys all ideas of family life as accepted amongst civilized nations. The Bakongo sacrifice to the moon, which they recognize as a potentiality of the first importance, and they also propitiate the malignant spirits, to which they attribute the power to afflict them with small-pox, fever, and other ills, mental and physical. The early hours are chosen for any work requiring bodily effort, as they are the coolest and the most pleasant for travelling or exertion of any kind. As soon as the sun begins to make itself felt, and its ardent beams penetrate the clouds and cast their scorching glare upon the land, the people return from the fields and seek the shelter of their verandas, or the shade of their plantain groves, where they pass the fervent noon-tide in gossip, smoking, and hair-dressing. As the heat becomes less oppressive, they go forth once more to their various occupations, till the sun falls into the western waters, when they return home to spend the night in song, feasting, and sleep. But with the opening up of the Congo route to Inner Africa, this state of things is already showing signs of a change for the better. The men are employed as porters or labourers at the trading or mission stations, they have begun to see the value of labour, they have found that the sale of the products of the gardens and fields will bring increased comfort to their homes, cloth for their families, and independence for themselves ; and the future of these people is by no means without hope.

The principle of native government is, as stated in a previous chapter, tribal or patriarchal rather than imperial. There are no potentates of the first rank to be found on the west of the Tanganika equal in dignity and importance to Mtesa of Uganda. Each tribe enjoys a practical independence, and is controlled by its own chief, who is chosen for his natural gifts and prowess, and by no means on account of his birth or rank. Occasionally a chieftainship is found which descends from father to son, but more often the strong arm and the cool head secure for their possessor the first position in the councils of the tribe which mere family or rank would be powerless to confer. But the power of the chiefs is on the wane. With increased intercourse with the ways and thoughts and doings of the white man, there is a gradual relaxation of the tyrannical rule of these native potentates ; fetishism and witchcraft are losing their terror over large masses of the population slowly but surely ; and a more just and equitable and enlightened policy is already adopted towards their own people and their neighbours by the headmen of the Congoese races, which proves that the leaven of truth and righteousness is already permeating the vast myriads of people who a few years ago were buried in the darkest ignorance, and were dwelling unknown and unsought in the most habitable and most public region in the world. The novel and absorbing spectacle of the working out of an anthropological experiment of unparalleled proportions, and pregnant with results of the first importance to countless millions of human beings, is presented to us in the great watershed of the Congo to-day, and the enormous central table-land of tropical Africa. Girdled and closed against the outer world by thirsty deserts, fever, cataracts, and rapids, the region seemed to have been destined by nature to remain a perpetual mystery to the outer world. But an assault has been made upon the citadel of desert and rocks and water, by which nature has so long guarded the secrets of Inner Equatorial Africa, by science, religion, and commerce combined, and a territory twice the size of Europe has been brought to light and added to the ever-increasing area of the known world. As the result of a letter, already referred to, which appeared in the *Daily Telegraph* of November 15th, 1875, from Mr. Stanley, in which he described his marvellous intercourse with Mtesa, the Emperor of Uganda, and the desire of that monarch for Christian teachers, the Church Missionary Society immediately decided to establish a Mission on Lake Victoria. An offer was made in response to Mr. Stanley's appeal, of 5000*l.*, by a friend for this special work, and a few days after the latter appeal, another 5000*l.* were added to the former donation. In less than a year the first division of the mission party had reached Zanzibar, and a line of stations was established in course of time from the east coast to the capital of Uganda. But beside all this, a staggering blow has been dealt at the power of the Arab traders by the labours of Mr. Stanley in Central Africa. To these men the appearance of such Pioneers of human liberty as Livingstone, Speke, Burton, Cameron, and Stanley meant the destruction of their fiendish traffic. Slavery in Inner Africa will die hard. It is the outcome of ages of degradation, lust, and crime. It cannot be uprooted in a day. But with the arrival of the Expedition of the Association International at Stanley Falls, a new era dawned upon the entire central Lake region, the fruitful hunting-ground of the slavers in past times. The devastation wrought by these inhuman monsters upon the population of the Upper Congo and Lake regions has been often described by Livingstone as well as Stanley in sad and bitter words. The great lesson which it was hoped the natives would learn from their contact with the officers and chiefs of the various stations of the Association is gradually being acquired. The people already see that the white man is not merely seeking to use them and their land for his own selfish profit: they have sense enough to see that the pale-face stranger is a peace-maker and a protector. "Father of slaves," was the proud title M. de Brazza earned by his tender regard for his brethren in bondage. The natives have begun to feel wants which the European alone can supply, and to see the manifold advantages of industry and honest toil over indolence and rapacity. "A lair of human beasts," having its headquarters at Nyangwe, on the head-waters of the Lualaba, has threatened and still threatens the peace of the country for some time to come. But the end is near, and sooner or later the people themselves will rise as one man, under the combined influence of true commercial instincts and a higher knowledge of the philosophy and ends of life, and put an end for ever to the Arab man-stealer and the horrors of these slave raids. At the end of 1884 the blue flag with the golden star was floating over nearly forty stations; 2000 persons were actively employed upon and about the great highway of the Congo; the territory of the Association Internationale, the New Congo Free State, was measured by degrees of latitude, and a flotilla of thirteen vessels navigated the brown flood and breasted the swift currents of the mighty stream throughout 2000 miles of its course. The Aruwimi, for ever associated in the mind of Stanley with terrible scenes of conflict and death, had been explored, and a way opened to the innermost recesses of Gahazal-land. Settlements had been founded at the base of the Stanley Falls, in the very heart of the slave-hunting country, and a fresh line of communication had been opened with the new Belgian station of Karema on the eastern shores of the Tanganika Lake. The humane and courageous design of the Comité du Haut Congo for opening out a road to Equatorial Africa which had been formulated in the council-chamber at Brussels in 1876, and entrusted to Stanley for execution in 1879, had been magnificently accomplished, and a door has at length been opened to Africa by which, we have every reason to hope, the continent so long oppressed and forsaken will eventually escape from the degradation which has for ages blighted its fairest regions, and destroyed generation after generation of the noblest races within its borders.

CHAPTER XIX.

THE *African Climate* is a subject about which travellers and others have written much, and expressed various opinions. Generally speaking, however, the continent has had the unenviable reputation of being the most unhealthy region in the world. The name of Africa in the past, has always carried with it unhappy suggestions of fevers, debility, and premature death. The climate of the Inner Congo Basin—"Yes," says the critic of these pages, "now tell us all about the climate of Equatorial Africa. You have introduced to us a veritable Land of Promise, flowing over with good things, productive to prodigality, splendidly endowed with inexhaustible stores of natural wealth, and offering an open and unlimited field of action to the trader and the lover of his fellow-men; but is not this Equatorial Africa after all only a mere charnel-house for Europeans, a place where no one can exist who has not been born upon the soil; is it not in serious fact 'the white man's grave'?" To such a pointed query Mr. Stanley, with an experience of seventeen years of tropical life, during which he has safely passed through 120 fevers, severe and slight, would reply most emphatically, " No ! Africa is not impossible for the white man, its climate has been maligned, and, with due attention to *habits* and *conduct*, there is positively no more danger to be apprehended from the atmospheric conditions of the Dark Continent than from the sudden climatic changes in countries which have a high reputation amongst us for salubrity and general healthiness." " Fatal," " Abominable," " Deadly," " Treacherous," are some of the epithets which are in common use in describing the atmospheric conditions of tropical lands. Wrong impressions are created by the constant re-iteration of the cry that white men cannot live in Africa. The Duke of Wellington's receipt for the promotion of health in India, Mr. Stanley thinks is thoroughly applicable to life in Congo-land. " ' I know of but one receipt for good health in this country, and that is to *live moderately,* to drink little or no wine, to use exercise, to keep the mind employed, and, if possible, to keep in good-humour with the world. The last is the most difficult, for, as you have often observed, there is scarcely a good-tempered man in India.' Doubtless in Africa, as in India, the waste of life has been considerable. Men of fine intellectual powers, great capacity, and with the physique of giants, have fallen and drooped and withered after a few months' experience of tropical life. Promising careers have been cut short and high hopes blasted by a fatal attack of malaria or dysentery, and the ' fearful ' climate has been arraigned as responsible for the dis-aster. But after a residence of several years upon what was described to me as ' the worst coast for malarious fever on the whole East African sea-board,' I have deliberately come to the conclusion that with care and stern self-control the European can live as safely, if not quite as comfortably, in Africa as in England."

During three months of the year in the Congo region it is cold, and all the year round there is an abundance of shade from the phenomenal amount of cloud which hangs over the territory. A delicious breeze from the South Atlantic cools the heated atmosphere, and residents in the district seldom feel any bad effects from the excessive temperature. The nights are decidedly chilly, and sleep is almost impossible without blankets or warm woollen coverings. The heat of the Congo corresponds with the definition of Bruce, the celebrated African traveller, who says that a man is warm when in ordinary dress, he does not sweat whilst perfectly at rest, but upon moderate motion perspires and cools again, a degree of temperature which may be represented as 75°. The mean of the highest observations of Congo heat is only 90° Fahrenheit, whilst the lowest mean is 67°. Careful attention must be paid to the *variableness* of the temperature of Congo-land, and the constant changes in travelling from the dense moist air of the ravines to the sharp cutting blasts which howl through the rocky cañons of the mighty stream, or sweep with piercing violence over the hill-tops or elevated plains of the upper Equatorial region.

That the atmosphere is saturated with miasma there can be no doubt. The rank vegetation, falling into decay by the process of nature, and shedding its leaves and withered branches into the stagnant pools and fetid morasses which cover vast areas of country in the neighbourhood of the river and its many affluents, is continually throwing off the fatal fever-germs which are carried up by the wind-currents, and wafted far and wide over the land. But care, and attention to such seemingly trifling details as the preparation of food, the position of the sleeping-room, head-gear, and clothing will do much to render the most heavily charged atmosphere comparatively innoxious.

Care should be taken, in choosing a site for a town or a dwelling-house, to avoid draughts or strong currents of cold air, and at the same time to secure a thoroughly well-ventilated position well out in the open and not too much overshadowed by forest or hill. There is nothing really to fear in the broad, full sunlight of the tropics. It is not the sunshine which kills, but the neglect of simple precautions against its effects. A healthy man, provided the head is well covered, the nape of the neck carefully shaded, and the head and shoulders protected by a good durable umbrella, may cross Africa in the full glare of a vertical sun without dread of the consequences. To the man debilitated by self-indulgence or weakened by evil habits such exposure would on the other hand be fatal. Congoland is no place for the man who is predisposed to moodiness. Good spirits and a readiness to make the best of things are essential to a pleasant or useful existence in the tropics. Active habits are also indispensable for the life of a successful pioneer of civilization or religion in the region of the Equator. Slothfulness begets depression, depression induces an unhealthy habit, and the unhealthy habit brings on disease, and disease entails discomfort or death. In the watershed of the Congo the thermometer ranges in the sun from 100° to 115°, and it is absolutely necessary that all active labour requiring physical exertion should be got over in the early part of the day. In the matter of diet there can be no doubt that a generous supply of good food is necessary to sustain the system under the constant strain to which it is exposed by a continuous residence in Equatorial regions. Good bread, rice, milk, and the native fruits, if well-ripened, are all that are needed, with fresh meat, fowls, and fish, to provide a Congo banquet " fit for a king," and all potted meats and preserved delicacies should be most carefully banished from the table of the white man who wishes to live long and comfortably on the banks of the great brown river. Care should always be taken not to go for too long a period without food. The system, when depressed by a protracted fast, voluntary or otherwise, is more readily open to the insidious assaults of disease, and on journeys of uncertain length old campaigners always provide themselves with some refreshment for the way. Damp shoes, and sitting about in wet or moist clothing after completing the day's travel or duty, are prolific sources of fever attacks ; and the bath slightly heated, with a complete change of attire before the evening meal and the hours of recreation and relaxation which close the day, are strongly recommended by one who has thoroughly tested all that he here commends for making a sojourn in the dreaded tropics not only possible but most enjoyable.

On no account should the dwelling-house of the European settler be built upon the ground. An elevated platform, with a free space between the floor and the surface of the soil of some eight or fifteen feet, should be erected, and the house placed upon it. with a deep veranda all round the building. The poisonous exhalations of the soil which rise at night are thus avoided, and the winds have free passage below as well as above and around the hammock or tent-bed of the sleeper. As to the use of stimulants I can add nothing to the forcible words of Mr. Stanley himself, who gives some painful instances of the terrible effects of spirit-drinking by Europeans.

The *Flora* of the Congoese territory and the Great Lake Region of Inner Africa is rich and diversified. Along the lower course of the river from Banana Point to Leopoldville, which embraces a narrow tract of maritime land and a section of the hill region. the surface of the surrounding country is covered with patches of dark green vegetation, in long wavy bars, which mark the line of the belts of fertile alluvial deposit, which have been formed in passages, by the scour of the higher lands during the season of the heavy rains. Clumps of palms and dense masses of umbrageous forest-growth clothe the valleys and lowlands in a refreshing garment of perpetual verdure, whilst the hill district produces the beautiful India-rubber creeper, the bright green orchilla moss, and the gum-copal tree. But the region between Leopold-ville and the Stanley Falls is the great depository of the natural wealth of Equatorial Africa. The Congo, with its innumerable tributaries, here flows through a tract of country with a superficial area of over one million square miles, supporting upon its fruitful surface a population of something like four millions of people, who are sunk in degradation and indigence, simply because they have no channel of communication open to them for free intercourse with the outer world, and with those benign influences which alone can assist in permanently raising and enriching them. Dr. Pogge and Lieut. Wissman say of this region :—

"The country is densely peopled, and some of the villages are miles in length. They are clean, with commodious houses, shaded by oil-palms and bananas, and surrounded by carefully divided fields, in which, quite contrary to the usual African practice, man is seen to till the soil, whilst the woman attends to household duties.

" From the Lubilash to the Lumani there stretches almost uninterruptedly a prairie region of great fertility, the future pasture-grounds of the world. The reddish loam overlying the granite bears luxuriant grass and clumps of trees, and only the banks are densely wooded.

"The rains fall during eight months of the year, from September to April, but they are not excessive. The temperature varies from 63° Fahr. to 81° Fahr.; but in the dry season it occasionally falls as low as 45° Fahr."

Tippo Tibb, the great Arab chief of the Inner Basin, declared to Mr. Stanley that he was amazed at the vast population which he found throughout the north-eastern portion of the country. He has seen many towns which had occupied two hours in passing through, and the abundant fertility of the magnificently wooded plains and mountain slopes was almost beyond description. Of the north-east portion of the same area Dr. Schweinfürth says, " From the Wellé to the residence of the Monbutta king, Munza, the way leads through a country of marvellous beauty, an almost unbroken line of the primitively simple dwellings extending on either side of the caravan route, with a population of 370 persons per square mile." The unique position and superior elevation of the Upper Congo basin, which is divided by the Equator, and has a rainy season of ten months' duration, have contributed to render it the most prolific province upon the African continent. Foremost amongst its valuable natural productions are its palms of every variety. From one species of these, the oil-palm, the dull red palm-oil of commerce, is produced. The tree grows everywhere, and whole forests of it are met with in the country lying between the Lower Lumani and the main riverland. The islands are clothed with it to the water's edge. The India-rubber plant is also found in great abundance, and on the islands of the Congo, Mr. Stanley saw sufficient rubber to pay, if collected, in one year for the entire construction of a Congo railway!

The beautiful white and red gum-copal in its fossil state is common in the district, and in the country of the Wenya huge blocks of the precious product were seen, each block being over eighteen inches in diameter.

Copious supplies of oil were extracted by the natives from the ground-nut, oil-berry, and castor-oil, and large tracts of forest were traversed which were simply draped with the deep green moss of the orchilla plant. Redwood powder was found in process of manufacture all through the district, and a large trade in this saleable commodity always exists on the Upper Congo. Fibrous substances suitable for making paper, rope,

basket-work, fine and coarse matting and grass cloths
were everywhere noticed in rich abundance, and at
Lukolela, an important mart for the exchange of
tobacco, fine timber, and coffee, for European wares
and fabrics, was in full operation at the time of Mr.
Stanley's visit to the locality. The value of the vegetable produce of the Upper Congoese watershed is
estimated by the Founder of the Free State at not less
than 5,000,000l. Every native village has its rice-
fields and plantations of maize, sugar-cane, bananas,
plantains, cassava, manioc and black field-bean, and
its plots of yams, brinjalls, melons and tomatoes, and
in recent years the potato, onion, and other English
vegetables, have been acclimatized, and promise to
flourish as well in African as in their native soil. The
Arabs from the east are gradually and successfully
advancing the cultivation of the large-grained upland
rice, and on the west the agents of the Association du
Haut Congo are busily employed in planting and rear-
ing and distributing broadcast over the land the
mango, lime, papaw, orange, pineapple, and guava.
The whole land abounds with plants which would be
invaluable to the physician as well as the merchant,
and wild cotton is found flourishing in certain favourable localities, where a considerable profit could easily
be made by its careful and systematic cultivation.
The Chambezi region embraces the whole of the extensive central area of 46,000 square miles which forms
the watershed of the Chambezi river and its tributary
streams, and in whose deep recesses the primary
" sources and fountains " of the mighty Congo have
their origin. It was in this hitherto unknown land of
water that Livingstone commenced his great enter-

prise, which Stanley so bravely carried out to a successful issue. The lamented and honoured traveller says that the district consisted of immense swampy plains everywhere except in the neighbourhood of Kapendé. "The water of the country is exceedingly large; plains extending farther than the eye can reach have four or five feet of clear water, and the adjacent lands for twenty or thirty miles are level. We went through papyrus, tall rushes, arums, and grass till tired out. We were lost in still grassy prairies from three to four feet in water for five hours. The country is all so very flat that the rivers down here are of necessity tortuous. Fish and other food abundant, and the people civil and reasonable. One sees interminable grassy prairies with lines of trees occupying quarters of miles in breadth, and these give way to plain again. The plain is flooded annually; but its vegetation consists of grasses. The country is undulating, and well covered with rich succulent herbage, which supports vast droves of cattle. On the western borders of Tanganika the Wajiji and the Wanyamwezi are pastoral tribes, and large crops of maize, millet and cereals are raised by the native population, who also possess fine herds of cattle which find pasture upon the broad prairies and meadow-lands between the watercourses and rivers which intersect the district in every direction. Tobacco of excellent quality is grown in Usanzeland, Ukawendi contributes to the market of Ujiji copious supplies of honey and wax, and the wide provinces of Urundi and Ubba are famed through Inner Africa for the cattle which are reared in ever-increasing numbers upon their breezy uplands and grassy fields."

The ivory harvest of the Congo basin is described
by Mr. Stanley as one of vast promise, and only
waiting to be gathered in.   There are also other rich
sources of commercial wealth which are ready to be
developed in this remarkable country.   A new native
industry might be inaugurated, which would, if judiciously directed, soon render abundant returns, by the
collection and preparation for the European market
of monkey, goat, antelope, buffalo, lion and leopard
skins; the resplendent plumage of the birds of the
region, hippopotamus teeth, bees'-wax, frankincense,
myrrh and tortoiseshell, all of which are at present
to a great extent lost to the white trader through want
of an open road to the sea-coast.

The mineral deposits of the upper region are
by no means unworthy of the consideration of the
magnates of commerce.   Iron is found in large
quantities.   The smiths of Iboko and Basoko have
already a high reputation for their finely-tempered
swords, and the spear-heads (some of them six feet
long) of the Yakusu and Basoko are marvellous
specimens of metal-work, welded and wrought by
means of one or two clumsy native tools.

There are large supplies of copper ore in the district
of Philippéville, which are worked in a rude fashion by
the natives, and which supply the vast area of Western
Africa with blocks of the valuable metal.   At Manyanga alone, the quantity of copper which is brought
into the market for purposes of barter amounts to several
hundredweight annually.   In the south-east also this
metal is found in great abundance, and is purchased
by the trading caravans, who convey it to the coast.
Plumbago is common, and gold in nuggets, as well as

dust, has been picked up by the lynx-eyed Arabs in their wanderings over the land, in the sand of the swift-flowing streams.

From these facts, some idea of the value of the country which has been opened out to the civilized world by the courage and perseverance of Mr. Stanley, can be formed. We have seen, thanks to the efforts of this remarkable man, that a region which for ages had been regarded as a mere extension of the silent and barren Sahara, is a fruitful and pleasant land, watered by the largest of African rivers, and gathering to itself the united waters of thousands of tributary streams. Its forests are composed of valuable and marketable timber—redwood, lignum-vitæ, mahogany and odorous gum-trees, the graceful rubber plant, the oil palm, and the wild coffee-tree. Over its vast plains roam herds of elephants, which furnish the precious ivory; and its population of fifty millions of industrious and intelligent people are nourished by crops of rice, and maize, and fruits, and other products which a generous soil yields with marvellous prodigality, and with scarcely any outlay of capital or labour. The temperature of the new province has been shown to be such that the European may venture to make his home in it without fear of death by disease or violence from the native tribes, and it has been clearly demonstrated that the pressing needs of the Congo Free State are the presence of the legitimate trader, and the softening and refining influence of the Christian teacher, to whom Mr. Stanley, with all the powers of persuasion which he can command, cries aloud, " Go ye up and possess the land."

The *Animal Life* of the region is purely African in

type. The elephant, buffalo, zebra, giraffe, and the antelope range over its wide savannahs, and browse upon its verdant mountain slopes, the hippo in troops are found basking in the mud of the shoaly streams, or seeking shelter in the reeds and sedge of the marshy jungle, the lion and the leopard have their lairs in the bushy recesses of its wooded depths, and the monkey and the lemur make their homes in the wide-spreading branches of its magnificent forest-trees. Birds of rich plumage, and in vast flocks, are seen in the neighbourhood of Stanley Pool, and at some distance from the main stream in the district of the Kwa, while for a considerable distance along the waters of that river, an abundant supply of game, sufficient at times for the needs of the entire expedition, could be obtained in a few hours by a smart shot.

The lordly crocodile of the Congo is always attended by his faithful little wading-bird,—a species of plover, which never forsakes the locality—favoured by the presence of the unwieldy monster. At the approach of danger the bird sets up a shrill cry of alarm, which arouses the hideous beast from his slumber upon the bare and heated rocks, and sends him plunging headlong into the flood to escape pursuit. Snakes are almost unknown upon the waters of the Congo. Swarms of butterflies of every variety and hue flit over the face of the dark-brown stream, or dart through the green foliage; and the banks of the river afford a splendid field of action for the collector of the magnificent crimson, black, and apple-green, and dead gold-spotted moths which are common to both the lower and higher reaches of the Congoese waters. Honey-bees and wasps of every

size and colour are found, some, building habitations
for themselves of paper, and others, of more ambitious tastes, erecting dwellings and store-rooms of
clay. The structures of the mason-wasp are very
clever contrivances. They are fixed upon any pro-
jecting ledge or spot which appears to offer immunity
from disturbance, and in them the miserly creature
carefully stows away the caterpillars and spiders and
other prey which he has secured in his raids upon the
territory of the feebler insects; but his greediness is
generally punished, as soon as his hoard is discovered,
by a wholesale confiscation of the contents of his
larder, for the purpose of supplying the pet birds of
the family with a dainty meal ready gathered to hand.

Scorpions are unknown; but poisonous centipedes
are common in the dead branches and dry brushwood
of the forests. The crocodile, according to the
natives, will follow the canoes for long distances when
a storm is beating down upon the waters, as if the
creature felt that there was a chance of an accident,
and that some plump negro or choice European might
fall into his cavernous jaws. If attacked by these
monsters, which swarm in the upper waters, the
natives, it is said, force them to lose their grip of their
victim, by thrusting their fingers into the eyes of the
brute, or by sticking a knife into the tender skin
beneath its shoulder.

Amongst the birds in and about the Congo region,
may be mentioned the *Podica*, a dark, mottled-brown
web-footed specimen of feathered life, found on the
shores of Stanley Pool. Its throat and lower part of
the body are of a dirty white hue, and above its eyes
it has a streak of light colour, with another and

broader line of dark brown running beneath it. The breast is spotted with dark brown, and the tail is four inches long, and faintly lined with white. The feet and bill are bright orange, and the whole appearance of the bird suggests an odd combination of the darter, the heron, the duck, and the grebe. When swimming, it lies low down in the water, and moves its long and crooked neck slowly backwards and forwards in search of the fish, upon which it pounces with a sudden forward jerk. The peaceful frigate-bird, the tropic-bird, the garnet, the cormorant, and the pelican are located near the estuary of the river, and high up the stream. Mr. H. H. Johnston tells us that he saw, on an unapproachable island above the Falls of Yellálá, a colony of pelicans, which had established itself there, and made the island, which could not be approached owing to the rapids, except by balloon, its permanent home. The waters of the Pool are much frequented by cranes, storks, giant herons, Egyptian geese, bitterns, and large terns with beaks of deep scarlet. There are, however, curious to relate, no vultures, although almost every species of this family of birds is represented in other parts of the continent. The Congo basin only possesses one specimen of the vulture, which is also found in the lands between the Kunéné and the Senegal. . Mr. Johnston speaks in terms of high admiration of the great blue plantain-eater, which has a feathery covering of rich verdite-blue, a yellow-green breast, light brown legs, and a violet top-knot ! This gaily adorned and attractive bird is timorous, and difficult to shoot. It lives chiefly upon figs, and the scarlet date of a kind of Calamus palm.

The grey parrots pervade, so to speak, the waters of the Upper Congo. They are seen in flights of thousands. The forest swarms with them, and the air at times rings with the melodious cries of these red-tailed denizens of the woods.

The absence of animal life in the maritime section of the Congo territory has already been noticed. You may travel from Banana Point to Stanley Pool and not see a snake or a monkey. The gorilla and chimpanzee are both found on the upper waters, and also upon the Lualaba, where they are spoken of by the natives as " Soko."

Lemurs are common in the neighbourhood of Leopoldsville, and the soft rich skins are made up into " Karosses," or cloaks with fringes of tails, by the natives. The leopard, or " the great lord," is the most dreaded of the larger animals upon the Congo. The lion, the hyæna, and the side-striped jackal and civet-cat are all known to dwell in the region of the Stanley Falls and the Inner Equatorial Basin, and the elephant has already been frequently referred to in the course of the narrative of Mr. Stanley's journeys and explorations. The rhinoceros is entirely absent from Congoese waters, but the river-horse is found everywhere in vast herds, and hippo-shooting is a recreation which is in high favour with the European settlers at the stations by the river-side.

The section of the river between Iboko and Matembo is by far the most attractive portion of the stream. The islands in mid-Congo at this point are enveloped in one dense mass of beautifully variegated and rare vegetation, the green of which shimmers in the bright rays of the vertical sun like some cunningly-woven texture of the finest satin. Some of the smaller islets appear to be on fire, with their deep crimson hues, and the purple fronds or the gold and white blooms of the flowering plants add a delightful variety to the whole scene. "Untainted by the marring hand of man," says Stanley, " or by his rude and sacrilegious presence, these isles, blooming thus in their beautiful native innocence and grace, approached in aspect as near Eden's loveliness as anything I shall ever see on this side of Paradise. They are blessed with a celestial bounty of florid and leafy beauty, a fulness of vegetable life that cannot possibly be matched elsewhere, save where soil with warm and abundant moisture and gracious sunshine are equally to be found in the same perfection."

Till the problem of the flow of the Chambezi and its affluents, the head-waters of the Congo, was satisfactorily and for ever solved by the patient researches of David Livingstone, in the Central Lake Region, that river had always been looked upon by our geographers as the parent stream of the Zambesi. Gathering up the rivulets and the smaller contributory rivers from the southern heights of Tanganika, and from the Muslinga range to the south, the Chambezi enters Lake Bangweolo or Bema (discovered in 1868), a vast oval-shaped expanse of water, 150 miles long by 75 miles wide, at an elevation of 3690 feet above the sea-level. Here the country is unattractive, and destitute of vegetation; but in the great Moevo lake, about 100 miles west of Bangweolo, it is covered by a dense growth of tropical wood, which affords shelter to the buffalo, zebra, and elephant. There are thirty-nine varieties of the first in Moevo, and an active and profitable trade in salt is carried on by the population of the district, who supply the tribes far inland with this useful and valuable commodity. West of this lake, in the country of the Katanga, there are vast deposits of copper ore, from which the steady and warlike Babunbu manufacture large supplies of copper wire, bracelets and anklets. The Ulungu people, also in the district of the Chambezi of Livingstone, adorn themselves with pearls, with which they bind up the hair or encircle the brows ; and every man carries an axe, as if to testify to the daily warfare which these industrious people have to wage with the milky fruits by which they are environed. The men and women weave mats, baskets, and cloth ; and the delightful slopes of the Tanganika heights are overshadowed by the dense vegetation, which completely covers them. These verdant terraces are the grazing-grounds of antelopes, elephants, and buffaloes, and the waters below sustain herds of hippos, and crocodiles, and fish in abundance. " It is," says Livingstone, " as perfect a paradise as Xenophon could have desired." Katanga, the celebrated copper country of the South Central Equatorial Region, is so far only known very imperfectly to Europeans. No traveller has yet penetrated its borders, to describe for us its wonders or the marvellous wealth of its unexplored mineral-fields. It lies somewhat west of the country of the Cazembe (visited more than once by Livingstone), and west of Rua, or it has been more accurately described perhaps as lying between the waters of the Lualaba of the veteran explorer, and the Lufiva stream. The mineral obtained from this territory finds its way to every market in South Africa. In the region of the Manquema it is the ordinary medium of exchange and barter, being made up in the form of "handa" or pieces of two and a half or three pounds in weight, melted up in the form of a rough St. Andrew's cross. A regular traffic in copper has been organized by the Portuguese of Loanda, whose trade caravans are constantly passing between their own territory and Katanga-land with European goods to exchange for the salt and ivory and copper of the locality. Arabs from the east coast, and native traders from the upper waters of the Zambesi flock to the great mart of this comparatively unknown land, to secure supplies of copper, and there is, without doubt, a considerable gold deposit in the country, but, so far, it has not been in any way exploited by the natives. It was reported to Livingstone that the people were afraid to dig the gold because Ngolu (the Arab name for Satan), to whom it belonged, had placed it there for his future use. Cameron states that when at Benguela he was informed that gold had been found in the copper brought from Katanga in such quantities that a company had been formed to buy up the latter mineral for the purpose of getting out the gold from it.

The whole land west of Tanganika and Nyana, opened out by Livingstone and Stanley, is proved to be one of extraordinary natural productiveness, with an entirely new set of zoological, botanical and ethnological facts. In Ubiza and Uvinza the mountain ranges attain a height of 3000 to 4000 feet above the sea. Their slopes are inaccessible, except by climbing up them hand over hand, by means of the creepers or tough fibrous plants which cover their flanks, and the northern sides are riven and scored by immense ravines and fissures, which are never lighted by the sun, and which are shrouded in an impenetrable gloom on the brightest day, by the dense mass of overhanging foliage which closes them in. Of this country Livingstone says, " Between each district large belts of the primeval forest still stand. Into these the sun, though vertical, cannot penetrate except as sending down their pencils of rays into the gloom. The rain-water stands for months in stagnant pools made by elephants' feet, and the dead leaves decay on the damp soil, making the water of the numerous rills and rivulets of the colour of strong tea. One feels himself the veriest pigmy before these gigantic trees ; many of their roots high out of the soil, in the path, keep you constantly looking down, and a good gunshot does no harm to parrots or guinea-fowls on their tops; the climbing plants, from the size of a whip-cord to that of a man-of-war's hawser, make the ancient paths the only passage. I have heard gorillas—here called sokos—growl at me within fifty yards without my being able to get a glimpse of them; their call to each other is like that of a tom-cat, and not so loud and far-reaching as that of the peacock. His nest is a poor contrivance, not unlike that of our wood-pigeon. Here he sits, even in pelting rain, with his hands and arms over his head. The natives call it his house, and laugh at him for being such a fool, as after building a hut not to go beneath it for shelter." A great deal of good iron-work is obtained in Manyuema-land. The people who, it must be confessed, are cannibals, are expert musicians, as well as smiths, and their towns are well built, their fields thoroughly cultivated, and their habits (apart from their terrible partiality for human flesh) are superior to those of the tribes by whom they are surrounded. In the kingdom of Nua, directly north of Nyangwé, large plains of forest land or broad areas of park-like open meadow country, intersected by streams, afford abundant sustenance for herds of wild cattle, elephants, and antelopes. Iron ore is found in rich profusion, and is worked by the natives in every part of the territory. Each village has its smelting-furnace and foundry, and with careful management a splendid African iron industry might be developed here. The region is devastated, however, by the Arab slavers, who have in some districts cleared off the entire population. The lake villages of Mohrya, north of Kilemba, visited by Cameron, were found to occupy a series of variously-shaped platforms placed about the lake without any attempt at order. The platforms were constructed upon piles, and the huts were built upon these platforms. The inhabitants occupy the huts, and only visit the shore to cultivate their gardens, or to secure food for their domestic pets —fowls, goats, &c. The floating rafts of Kassal are more remarkable even than the lake houses of the people of Mohrya. Their rafts are made up of " masses of vegetation cut from that which lines the shore, overlaid with logs and brushwood, and covered with earth. On these rafts huts are built, bananas are planted, and goats and poultry reared." The people of Lo-valé are described by Cameron as very savage, and much dreaded by caravans for their rapacious demands in the matter of tribute. They are in fact the Ugogians of the Trans-Tanganika Land ; but they are clever workers in iron, and have a great reputation for their arrow-heads and ornamental hatchets. Bee-culture is carried on to a large extent by the Kibokivé, another tribe in the region of the head-waters of the Congo. These people, who are peaceful and disposed to a domestic life, collect large quantities of wax, which they exchange with the caravans for European goods. Iron ore is also found in the beds of the streams of this locality, and it is industriously worked by the natives, who are expert smiths. The town of Kagnombe, in Bihe, one of the adjacent independent sovereignties of the Central Lake region, is described by Cameron as the largest town ever seen by him in Africa. It was more than three miles in circumference, and combined a number of separate enclosures, belonging to the different chiefs, and large spaces were occupied by pens of cattle and pigs, and patches of tobacco gardens. The place is situated exactly 250 miles in a direct line from the West Coast. The homely beauty of the adjoining territory is thus painted in words by Cameron :—" Neither poet with all the wealth of word-imagery, nor painter with almost supernatural genius, could by pen or pencil do full justice to the country of Bailada. In the foreground were glades in the woodland, varied with knolls crowded by groves of large English-looking trees, sheltering villages with yellow-thatched roofs; shambas or plantations with the fresh green of the young crops, and bright red of new and old grow in vivid contrast, and running streams flashing in the sunlight, whilst in the far distance were mountains of endless and pleasing variety of form, gradually fading away till they blended in the blue of the sky. Overhead there drifted fleecy white clouds, and the hum of bees, the bleating of goats, and crowing of cocks filled the air.

As I lay beneath a tree in indolent contemplation of the beauties of nature in this most favoured spot, all thought of the work still before me vanished from my mind ; but I was rudely awakened from my pleasant reverie by the approach of the loaded caravan, with the men panting, yelling, and labouring under their burdens."

Such is the territory of the great Congo basin for which Stanley has endeavoured to secure the benefits of civilization and the benign influences of Christianity. Is it too much to hope that before the end of this century this mighty region will have taken its place in the orbit of the world's civilization; and that the historians of future times will be able to declare, that when the august founders of the Association Internationale du Haut Congo planted their neutral flag in the heart of Africa, they quite understood the spirit of their age?

CHAPTER XX.

EARLY in January, 1884, General C. Gordon, C.B., the illustrious White Pasha and former Governor of the Provinces of Upper Egypt, and the famous commander of the " Ever Victorious Army," was commissioned at Brussels, by the King of the Belgians, to proceed to the Congo, as successor to Mr. Stanley, in the post of Chief Administrator of the Free States. The gallant officer announced his appointment in a letter which reached Stanley on his way down the river from Vivi, and frankly declared that he had simply accepted the position in order effectually and finally to grapple to the death with the hated slave-hunters, in the very heart of the Equatorial Region.

Gordon at once proceeded to the Belgian capital to receive his final instructions from Leopold II., for the formidable anti-slavery crusade which he hoped to lead into the innermost recesses and rocky fastnesses of the Soudan, along the northern tributaries of the Congo Lualaba, and to take a formal pledge of fealty

to the central authority of the Free States (January
5th, 1884). He expected to reach Boma before the
great Founder of the new territory, whom he was to
succeed, left the coast for Europe.

But Gordon and Stanley were never destined to
meet and take counsel together upon the brown waters
of the mighty African stream.

After sixty years of misrule, the Egyptian power
south of Wady Halfa had suddenly and completely
collapsed. Goaded beyond endurance by the harsh
and heartless treatment to which they had been
subjected for half a century by the Turco-Circassian
officials, who had been placed over them, the subject-
races had broken out into open revolt, and under
the banner of the Mahdi—Muhammed Ahmed—the
Ethiopian tribes between the Nile and the Red Sea,
the riverain population of the Nile Valley, the Negroes
of the southern districts, and the nomad Arabs of the
western desert, united for the first time in their
history by a religious fanaticism, banded themselves
together to drive the Egyptians from the Soudan, to
restore the old system of administering justice
according to the precepts of the Koran, to abolish all
taxes except the time-honoured tithe, to pay this tax
and all spoil seized from infidel hands into a common
treasury (Beit ul mal), whence it was afterwards to
be disbursed for the good of the community, to reform
Islam, to bring all Moslem countries to a better
observance of the true faith by force of arms if
necessary, and finally to conquer the lands and
completely crush the power of the Giaour.

The Khedive and his Council were in despair. The
rude levies of the Mahdi were sweeping everything

before them, for the Egyptian troops, seized with panic, fled at the first onset of the fanatical hordes of the soldier prophet.

It was felt that the responsibility for the relief of the unhappy garrisons and European officials, who were environed by the rebels in the midst of leagues of waterless desert and arid, limitless wastes of rock and sand, rested with the English Government, and the gravity of the situation throughout the whole of Upper Egypt was attracting universal attention.

A few hours after Gordon's return from Brussels, bearing his high commission as Head of the Congo Free States, he was requested by the cabinet of Mr. Gladstone to accept the perilous but honourable mission of British Plenipotentiary to the tribes of the Soudan, for the purpose of securing the safe retreat of the Egyptian garrisons from those countries, and to arrange for the final evacuation of the entire region south of Dongola. Gordon had himself suggested this solution of the Soudanese problem, in an interview with a correspondent of the *Pall Mall Gazette*, at Southampton, three days after his appointment to the Congo, and he lost no time in obtaining the sanction of the King of the Belgians to the new arrangement by which he was to go to Khartoum instead of to Boma. Gordon was to be sent out to Egypt with *carte-blanche* to do the best he could to effect the purposes for which he was entrusted with the special and extraordinary powers of a British Plenipotentiary. The press, irrespective of party, and the public demanded that the hands of the liberator of the garrisons should be left quite free, and to this the Government finally assented. On the

evening of Friday, January 18th, 1884, Gordon left
Charing Cross. The news that he had consented to
go to the Equatorial Provinces, on his sublime errand
of justice and mercy, had excited the warmest
gratitude and deepest enthusiasm, throughout the
whole civilized world. " I go," said this intrepid and
marvellous man, "to cut the dog's tail off. I've got
my orders, and I'll do it, *coûte que coûte.*" At eight
o'clock he started. He was calm and cheerful, and
even hopeful. "The scene at the station," says an
eye-witness, "was very interesting. Lord Wolseley
carried the General's portmanteau, Lord Granville
took his ticket for him, and the Duke of Cambridge
held open the carriage door."

It is only necessary here to follow in outline that
chapter of the history of the Soudanese provinces,
which opened some seventy years ago, when, in
September, 1820, Mohammed Ali, the founder of the
tributary kingdom of Egypt, sent forth an expedition
of 4000 men to subjugate the then unknown countries
of the Upper Nile, and the entire region south of
Wady Halfa. The command of this force, which was
made up of Osmanli and Arab cavalry, Bedawin and
Osmanli infantry, 400 Ababdehs, and 300 artillery-
men, was given by Ali to his younger son Ismail, who
was already distinguished by his courage, his indifference to the comforts and luxuries of life, and his
utter disregard of danger in any form, as well as by
his unquenchable ardour and his anxiety to cover
himself with martial glory by some great deed of
daring and heroism in the face of the enemy. On
setting forth for Assouan, Ismail declared that he
was proceeding to allay certain disorders which had

arisen in the districts beyond the Wady, and to renew
those amicable and profitable relations which once
existed between the tribes of the Soudan and the
government at Cairo, but which had been disturbed,
to the great loss of Egypt, by the frequent internecine
quarrels which had arisen too frequently between the
Meliks, or petty kings, of the region. There can be no
doubt, however, that the chief results which Ali
proposed to secure for himself by means of the
formidable host which Ismail led southward along the
left bank of the Nile were—the conquest of Upper
Egypt, slaves, gold, and glory. The gold-mines on
the Abyssinian frontier had aroused the cupidity of
Ali, he wished to obtain efficient reinforcements for
his army from the physically perfect negro slaves of
the interior, and he was at the same time anxious to
procure congenial employment for the half-savage
Circassians, Albanians, and Anatolians, who had been
his faithful and constant allies all through the eventful
period, during which he was patiently yet boldly
establishing himself as the supreme power and
authority in Lower Egypt and the provinces of the
Nile Delta. This ambitious scheme for the wholesale
enlargement of his frontier was pushed forward exactly
at the moment most opportune for its success. The
ancient kingdom of Funj, long established at
Senaar, was *in extremis* owing to civil strife; the
important state of Kordofan had succumbed to the
superior military power of the Sultan of Darfur;
Berber, Shendy, and Halfaya had each asserted their
perfect independence, and had risen to the dignity of
separate and distinct principalities, the resolute and

B b

clannish Shagiyeh had thrown off the hateful yoke to a neighbouring state, to which they had impatiently submitted for many years, and were fast rising to the condition of a free and powerful people; and Dongola was held by a small band of Mamelukes, led by the dauntless Ibraim Bey, who had escaped a terrible death, by leaping his horse boldly from the parapet of the Cairo citadel, when the brutal order was given for the massacre in cold blood of his brave comrades whenever they were found within the walls of the citadel of Cairo. Ibraim amply avenged the death of many of his own relatives in this massacre, by the wholesale slaughter of the Shagiyeh governors and chiefs of Argo, and by the sanguinary measures which he took in union with his companion in arms and in fortune, Abd er Rahman Bey, to hold the province, which he had thus boldly secured with the aid alone of his own strong arm at the point of the sword. The march of Ismail's expeditionary force partook very much from the outset of the nature of a triumphal progress. One *Melik* (kinglet) after another submitted quietly to the invader's terms directly his banners were seen above the horizon, and the boom of his cannon fell upon the startled ears of the desert tribes, and even the haughty Mamelukes were forced to retire to the remote fortresses of Shendy after sending the following reply to the summons of Ismail to surrender themselves into his hands, "Tell Mohammed Ali that we will be on no terms with our servant." 2000 followers, chiefly native Egyptians and Ababdehs, and a train of 3000 camels for land service, and boats for water transport, were attached to the expedition, and learned Ulemas were taken to act as interpreters, conduct diplomatic relations, and frame treaties with the various strange and hitherto unvisited tribes about the waters of the Blue and White Niles.

In the face of terrible struggles day by day, with the terrors of the desert, the hungry and deadly rapids, the treacherous floods of the great Nile, and indescribable hardships and dangers, the Soudanese beheld the weary and battered but undaunted warriors emerge from the perils of the cataracts and the almost insurmountable difficulties of their march by land, and press forward, mounting the current in their boats—"water-mares," as the natives called them—without the aid of oars. Terrible outrages and horrible violations of all laws, human and divine, everywhere marked the track of the advancing host, which swept off the entire population and property of the region along its front with the force and completeness of an insatiable conflagration or a consuming pestilence. Ismail offered a reward of fifty piastres a piece for human ears, which he forwarded from time to time to his father at Cairo as evidences of his triumphs. An eye-witness, an Englishman who accompanied the troops of Ali, says, "Our servants in their expedition into the village found only an old woman alive, with her ears off. The Pasha buys human ears, which leads to a thousand unnecessary cruelties, and barbarizes the system of warfare, but enables his highness to collect a large stock of ears, which he sends down to his father as proof of his successes. The shore is putrid, and the air tainted, by the carcases of oxen, sheep, goats, camels, and men. The latter, in particular, are found every fifty yards, scattered along the road and among the corn; some, in an attempt to cross the Nile and escape by swimming, have been overtaken on the bank and there killed; others are found with their oxen in the sakies, where they had been labouring together; some near the houses they probably inhabited." ("Journal of a Visit to some Parts of Ethiopia." By George Waddington and Rev. Barnard Hanbury. London, 1822. Page 118.) After the battle, boxes of human ears were sent northward to the capital, and the brutalities practised in order to secure this novel poll-tax from the wretched Shagiyeh were too terrible to dwell upon here. The records of this horrible war are lightened, however, by the touching stories of the careful tending of the wounded son of a brave foe by the surgeons of Ismail, and the capture and chivalrous restoration of Zebehr's beautiful daughter Safi, who, when a prisoner in the power of the youthful commander of the Egyptian army, was clothed by his orders in costly and lovely garments, suited to her rank, and sent back unharmed with a large escort to her father's tent on the Soudanese plain. It is worthy of record that the delighted parent was so touched by this unlooked-for magnanimity on the part of the victorious invader, that he at once submitted himself and his people to the authority of Ismail. A force was sent across the desert to invest Berber, and at the same time the boats conveying the main body of the force were wearily forcing a way round the great bend of the Nile. The difficulty of forcing the cataracts at this

point was so great that Ismail ordered the flotilla
to be abandoned, and the guns, ammunition, and baggage to be landed and sent overland to Berber. The
march across the hot sands and desolate wastes was
a weary and painful one to officers as well as men.
Many camels fell dead on the road. The heavy guns
were drawn by camels, but were taken into action by
horses, which were usually led on the line of march,
ready harnessed beside their respective guns. The
charms and amulets of the Shagiyeh (like those of the
Arabs at Abu Klea in our own day), failed in the hour
of peril to save them from the bullets of their enemies,
or to render their bodies invisible upon the field of
battle; and even the Mamelukes at length were glad to
sue for peace and forgiveness of the past at the feet
of "the son of their servant." Scorched by the heat,
and weakened by famine, the victorious army passed
on from province to province, and Omdurman,
Metemmeh, and Halfaya submitted to the authority
of the head of the dynasty of which Tewfik, the reign-
ing Prince of Egypt, is the sixth ruler in order of
descent. The nomadic and warlike Shagiyeh soon
became close allies of the Egyptian power, and they
were rewarded for their adhesion and fidelity by
liberal grants of the lands which Ismail had wrested
from the ancient inheritors and holders on the right
bank of the Nile between Khartoum and Atbara. Of
these people the received opinion is that of all the
Soudanese tribes they are the most unreliable, and
General Gordon's last Journal contains many allusions
to the extreme difficulty he experienced at times in
dealing with these impulsive and excitable sons of the

desert. He describes them pathetically as "the worry of my heart," and declares that he "will back them to try a man's patience more sorely than any other people in the wide world, yea, and in the universe."

Three days were taken up in the passage of the White Nile by the troops of Ismail. The expedition was carried over in nine small boats, which had, with difficulty, been brought round the great bend of the river. The horses and camels were ferried over upon rafts and boards laid upon inflated skins by the skilful Ababdeh and Shagiyeh, who were thoroughly at home upon the swift and turbulent rapids and drifty currents of the ancient river. On May 30th, 1822, the Egyptian army was drawn up upon the low spit of white sand, RAS EL KHARTOUM, which will for ever be known in history as the scene of the heroic self-devotion and final martyrdom of Gordon. Ismail at once entered the capital of the Nile Provinces in triumph. Disappointed in not finding the gold-mines and inexhaustible deposits of the precious metal which had been described to him as existing in this region, Ismail turned his attention to the collection of slaves, but the blacks, knowing their own country well, and being thus able to select the strongest natural positions, were able to defeat the Egyptian troops in more than one sharp encounter. It was now that those slave wars and raids and quarrels commenced, which have continued in the Equatorial Regions to our own day, and for the suppression of which Gordon and many others have freely yielded up their lives. To Ismail may be attributed the foundation of the Soudanese

slave-trade, " the open sore of Africa," to the healing
of which Livingstone dedicated his life, and for the
removal of which Stanley has once more ventured, with
his life in his hands, into the hidden heart of the
Dark Continent.

The Egyptian army was at this point attacked by
grievous sickness, and Ismail determined to fall back
upon Senaar. On reaching Shendy, his insolent
conduct exasperated the people to such an extent, that
in the dead hour of the night they collected heaps of
dry brush-wood about the house in which he was
sleeping, and in the morning all that remained of the
conqueror of the Soudan was a charred corpse. Kordofan had already been annexed to Egypt by Ismail's
brother-in-law the Defterdar, who conquered the army
of the native prince under the walls of Bara, after a
terrific struggle, in which the cavalry of the Darfur
force, clad in helmets of metal and coats of mail, and
riding horses clothed in linked plates of native copper,
proved at times too strong even for the splendid
horsemen of the Egyptian expeditionary force. The
death of the commander of the local forces, however,
turned the tide of battle in favour of the Defterdar,
and soon Obeid was taken and sacked, and the whole
of Kordofan, which had attained, under its own ruler,
to a high state of prosperity, passed under the dominion
of the Government of Cairo. The people of the
conquered province were by no means to be congratulated upon this change of masters. Before the arrival
of the invaders, the district known generally as Kordofan, had been a rich, contented and busy commercial
state, maintaining relations with Central Africa and

Abyssinia by means of frequent caravans which kept up a constant exchange of commodities and products between the different countries. Trade was free; a light tribute was the system; the people were happy and contented; and everywhere gold and silver ornaments attested the general wealth. The Defter-dar soon changed all this. His troops robbed and plundered everybody and everything; his greed was insatiable; taxes were imposed on every description of goods and produce; the rights of property were set aside altogether; every one who possessed goods, cattle, or money was first charged with some crime, and then condemned to death, in order that his pos-sessions might pass into the hands of the Egyptian commander. It fell to the lot of the Defterdar to avenge the murder of Ismail, and he at once marched on Shendy, as soon as the news of the tragedy reached Kordofan. Shendy was razed to the ground, and the offending tribe was well-nigh exterminated.

But enough has been said to show the nature of the conquest of the Soudan. The history of the territory has been, from the days of Ismail and the Defterdar, one continued record of revolts ruthlessly suppressed, of rule by force, exaction, chicanery, and double-dealing, unequalled probably in the annals of any other region in the whole world. The Egyptian system of government was quite unsuited to the needs and habits of the people, and the rough Turkish soldiers of fortune who had to administer it, thought only of enriching themselves by any and every means, at the expense of the people over whom they were placed. The main result of the Egyptian occupation of the Soudan appears to have been the proving how utterly unable Turks and Circassians are to govern subject-races anywhere, even under the most favourable circumstances. From the governors of provinces downwards, every one plundered; pillage was reduced to a system; the exaction of specie from the wretched populace was the one absorbing study of the officials, and for every pound the soldiers collected from the taxpayers they squeezed out for themselves another from the peasants; impossible requisitions of grain, cattle, camels, butter, leather, &c., were made for the troops, and the people were reduced to a state of abject and hopeless poverty. During the reigns of later Pashas these disorders increased, and in 1857 Said Pasha, who visited the Upper Nile Provinces in person to see for himself the condition of the people, was horrified at the extortion and oppression practised by the officials, and the widespread misery which was the result of years of this treatment. Reforms were at once ordered, and Said Pasha even contemplated giving up the Soudan altogether, so much was he impressed with the suffering which he witnessed during his tour through the unhappy district, but other counsels unfortunately prevailed.

The reforms of Said were short-lived, and Sir Samuel Baker says of the condition of things in 1862-64:— " During the administration of Musa Pasha, who is described as a rather exaggerated specimen of Turkish authorities in general, combining the worst of Oriental failings with the brutality of a wild animal, the Soudan became utterly ruined; governed by military force, the revenue was unequal to the expenditure, and fresh taxes were levied upon the inhabitants to an extent that paralyzed the entire country. . . . From the highest to the lowest official, dishonesty and deceit was the rule; and each robs in proportion to his grade in the Government employ." ("Albert Nyanza," i. 13, 14.) To Col. Stewart, one of the officers of the Khedive, Jafa Pasha, openly declared that " he was quite aware the tax was excessive, but he fixed it at that rate to see how much the peasant could really pay."—" In consequence of this excessive taxation " (says an official report) "many were reduced to destitution, others had to emigrate, and so much land went out of cultivation, that in 1881 in the province of Berber there were 1442 abandoned sakies, and in Dongola 613." Sir Samuel Baker thus describes the condition to which the rule of Jafa Pasha had brought the country. " Khartoum was not changed externally ; but I had observed with dismay a frightful change in the features of the country between Berber and the capital since my former visit. The rich soil on the banks of the river, which a few years ago had been highly cultivated, had been abandoned. Now and then a tuft of neglected date-palms might be seen, but the river's banks, formerly verdant with heavy crops, had become a wilderness. Villages once crowded had entirely disappeared; the population was gone. Irrigation had ceased. The night, formerly discordant with the creaking of waterwheels, was now silent as death. There was not a dog to howl for a lost master. Industry had vanished, oppression had driven the inhabitants from the soil." The whole population was ripe for revolt against the plunder, extortion, and oppression of the Egyptians, and gladly accepted the leadership of the Mahdi, who announced his fixed determination not to rest day or night as long as one official of the Khedive remained in the Soudan. Sir Samuel Baker, as Governor of the Equatorial Provinces, and General Gordon who succeeded him in 1874, strove earnestly to ameliorate the condition of the people placed under their charge, but they found the Egyptian officials busily engaged in thwarting them at every turn, and ready to connive at the slave trade, slave-wars, oppression, illegal trading or any rascality or dark dealing, so long as they could enrich themselves at the expense of the unhappy Soudanese. Meanwhile, notwithstanding all the efforts, expostulations and menaces of Gordon, who was appointed in 1877 Governor-General of the Soudan, for the avowed purpose of suppressing the slave-trade, the miserable traffic evinced on all sides unmistakable evidence of increased vitality. Slave-hunting is without doubt the great disturbing influence of the entire Upper Nile Territory. The "merchants" of Khartoum who deal in human beings keep large armed forces of from 10,000 to 15,000 troops for the purpose of hunting down the blacks of the adjacent districts. and Sir Samuel Baker found one man who assumed the sole right of running down and enslaving all his fellow-men over an area of 90,000 square miles of territory. 50,000 slaves are said to be annually taken in the Soudan, and the horrors perpetrated by the "dapper-looking fellows, like antelopes, fierce, unsparing," who are the sleuth-hounds of the traders in this detestable work, would be incredible if they had not been described to us by such reliable authorities as Speke, Grant, Baker, Schweinfurth, Gordon, Stanley, and Gessi. Amassing large fortunes out of the large profits of their abominable calling, the slave-hunters live in princely magnificence, and are able to exercise considerable influence even at Cairo, as Gordon found to his cost when he attempted to destroy their power, and clear them altogether out of his province. Evidence has lately come to light which proves that the Egyptian Government itself actually shielded the slave-dealers of whom Gordon complained, and even made a profit out of their trade, which publicly it denounced. The protest of civilization against this monstrous condition of things moved the late Khedive from time to time to feign a serious earnestness of intention to put down slave-wars and slave-hunting in the Upper Nile Basin, but Gordon soon saw through the hollow decrees of Ismail, and he ultimately resigned the position of Governor-General of the Soudan with the full conviction that no good could be really done, so strong were the influences used against him by the corrupt officials whom he rebuked or removed from their posts, and so powerful was the "loathsome lust for human flesh" which seemed to possess the great men of the entire dominion of the Khedive, north as well as south of the Wady Halfa.

During his administration of the Equatorial Provinces, Gordon travelled many times to the extreme southern limits of his satrapy, and everywhere peace and prosperity resulted from his policy of justice to all, protection to the weak, and government by affection rather than by force of arms. He mapped out the White Nile from Khartoum down to the Victoria Nyanza. He had dealt a fatal blow at the slave-trade on the White Nile and its affluents. He had restored confidence and peace to the industrious people of the Nile Valley, so that they freely entered into commercial relations with him, and attended his markets. He had opened up a water-way between Gondokoro and the Lakes. He had established pacific relations and made satisfactory treaties of friendship with Mtesa, the great Uganda king. He had divided the province into districts, with responsible and capable chiefs over them, and open roads between them. He had astonished the authorities at Cairo by forwarding a substantial contribution to the revenue of the Khedival exchequer, and he had secured this without any attempt at coercion or oppression. It may be said truly, that "the Taiping rebellion established Gordon's genius as a military commander; the Equatorial Provinces when he left them testified not less to his genius as a philanthropic and practical administrator."

On February 17th, 1877, the Khedive Ismail, writing to Gordon, who had just arrived from England, said, "Setting a just value upon your honourable character, on your zeal, and on the great services you have already done me, I have resolved to bring the Soudan, Darfur, and the provinces of the Equator into one vast province, and place it under you as Governor-General." He was to be assisted by three under-governors, and the two chief points to which he was to direct his attention, by the instruction of Ismail, were the total suppression of slave-wars and the opening up of new and rapid means of communication between the various military and commercial centres of the united provinces. In July, 1879, after more than two years of weariness and scheming and counter-scheming to circumvent the machinations of his old foes at Cario and at the head-waters of the Nile, during which time Gordon's energy had caused him to be feared and respected, but not loved over-much, by the populations of the territory under his rule, he received the news of the abdication of the Khedive Ismail and the succession of Tewfik. Feeling that his mission was over, and that his work in the Soudan was done, he at once placed his resignation in the hands of the authorities at Cairo only to anticipate his dismissal. The Pashas hated him to a man, and intrigued against him, for the success of his policy meant the ruin of themselves and their families, by the loss of revenue from the slave-trade and the oppression of the unfortunate people in the far-off provinces of the Upper Nile waters. So Gordon turned his back upon the Soudanese land; but he had not seen the last of that fatal region.

On leaving London on January 18th, 1884, as British Plenipotentiary, with powers to secure the retreat of the Egyptian garrisons, and evacuate the territory, Gordon proceeded at once to Cairo and thence to Khartoum, where he arrived on February 18th, to the intense delight of the garrison and inhabitants, who pressed about him as he rode in state into the city in his "gold coat," and in all the pomp beseeming a British representative. With his arrival a change came over the people once more. The stick, the lash, and the prison of the Bashi Bashoukery *régime* were instantly swept away. As he passed to the palace from the Mudisieh, where he had been granting audiences to which the most beggarly Arab was admitted, the excited populace thronged him, kissing his hands and feet, and hailing him as "Sultan," "Father," and "Saviour." A fire was made in front of the palace, and the records of the out-standing debts of the people to the Government at Cairo, the bastinado rods which took the place of collector's notices, and the kerbashes, whips, and all the devilish instruments of torture, were thrown by Gordon's own hand upon this funeral pyre of Egyptian tyranny. "From the council-chamber," we are told, "he hurried to the hospital; thence to inspect the arsenal. Then he darted to the heart of the misery of the prison. In that loathsome den two hundred wretched beings were rotting in their chains. Young and old, condemned and untried, the proven innocent and the arrested on suspicion,—he found all clotted together in one union of common suffering. With wrathful disgust Gordon set about the summary work of liberation. Before night fell the chains had fallen from off scores of the miserables, and the beneficent labour was being steadily pursued." The defence of Khartoum and the final overthrow of the city and the death of the heroic man of whom it has been said that "there was no figure during our generation to which the popular feeling and sympathy were so much attached," are now matters of never-to-be-forgotten history. The news of the failure of Gordon, and of his tragic fate, created a widespread feeling of the deepest sorrow throughout Europe and America, and it was at once felt that the condition of the isolated Egyptian garrisons far away over the desert, without any possibility of succour reaching them, and severed by implacable foes, was altogether hopeless. To all human seeming they were left to perish.

CHAPTER XXI.

UPON his appointment, in 1877, by the Khedive Ismail to the post of Governor-General of the Soudan, Gordon proceeded to carry out his favourite policy of reforming the administration of the vast territory under his jurisdiction with characteristic vigour. " With terrific exertions," he wrote, " I may in two or three years' time, with God's administration, make a good province, with a good army, and a fair revenue, and peace and increased trade, and also have suppressed slave-raids ; and then I will come home and go to bed, and never get up again till noon every day, and never walk more than a mile." In his speech at his installation in his capital of Khartoum, where the firman announcing his elevation was read by the Cadi, amid the thunder of a royal salute, and the tumultuous applause of the populace, he made a formal declaration of his policy. It was brief and to the point. Justice to all was to be the distinct aim of his official life amongst these warm-hearted but wayward and irresolute sons of the desert.

c c

"With the help of God, I will hold the balance level," he said, solemnly addressing the polyglot multitude which swayed and surged about the steps of his vice-regal throne. And then "he directed gratuities to be distributed, in Eastern fashion, to the deserving poor, and in three days he gave away upwards of three thousand pounds of his own money."

The control of the Equatorial Region, "the very pearl and heart of the Soudan," he at once handed over to one of the most tried and trusted of his lieutenants, EMIN PASHA, whom he formally appointed chief executive officer, and Governor of Equatorial Egypt and the countries about the White Nile (1878), and for whom he ever afterwards entertained the highest regard, not only for his work's sake, but also for the high character, great administrative ability, and varied accomplishments, of the man himself. Till early in 1887, however, Emin Pasha, " the last white chief of the dread Soudan," was altogether unknown to fame. A few scientists and personal friends only, in England and Germany, were acquainted with the stirring details of that desperate struggle for civilization and liberty, which he has carried on single-handed, as " Gordon's heir," in the immense province entrusted to his charge, since the Fall of Khartoum, and the tragic death of his illustrious friend and patron. Emin Pasha is a European and a German by birth and education, notwithstanding his Egyptian cognomen, which signifies *The faithful one.* His name is Eduard Schnitzer, and he was born on March 28th, 1840, at Oppeln, a prettily situated little town, upon the banks of the Oder, in the Prussian province of

Silesia. His father, Ludwig Schnitzer, was a merchant of repute, and a Protestant. In 1842, for commercial reasons probably, the family removed to Neisse, a smaller town, situated in the same province, upon the banks of a southern tributary of the Oder, where the relatives of the distinguished Pasha still reside.

Eduard was educated at the Gymnasium, or public school, of Neisse, and in due course he proceeded to the University of Breslau (1858). He completed his medical studies by attending a course of lectures by eminent specialists at the University of Berlin, where he graduated, and received his diploma of M.D., in 1864. Free now to indulge the dreams and fancies of his youth, the young surgeon, who had from boyhood evinced a taste for travel and the study of natural history, set off upon a tour of adventure through Turkey and Syria. As he was the bearer of high credentials, and was also well recommended by eminent German physicians and others, he soon obtained employment, and he was posted to the staff of Ismail Hakki Pasha, Governor of the Turkish provinces of Antivari and Scutaria. On the death of Hakki Pasha in 1873, Schnitzer decided to return to Neisse, and devote himself for a term to the closer and more direct study of the phenomena of natural history and biology. In 1876 the "Spirit of movement" again possessed him, and he set out for Cairo, determined to seek employment under the Government of the Khedive. His offer of service was at once accepted, and he was ordered to join the staff of the Governor-General of the Soudan at Khartoum. From Khartoum he was sent down south to act as chief medical officer in the

Equatorial Province of Egypt, of which territory Gordon Pasha was then Governor. Gordon was the very man to value an officer of parts and resources, as Emin soon proved himself to be, and to afford him abundant opportunity for the employment of all those gifts and powers, in the face of difficulties and impossibilities, which he soon began to display.

For medicine alone by no means engrossed the attention of Schnitzer. He soon showed that he had a special power for dealing with the native mind. He was able to secure the confidence of the " black-skinned children of the soil," and to carry out to ultimate success difficult diplomatic missions which other officials had given up in despair. We soon find, therefore, that Gordon frequently selected Emin to undertake negotiations of considerable importance with neighbouring tribes and kinglets, which required peculiar gifts, and called for the exercise in a more than ordinary degree of the " Suaviter in modo, fortiter in re " method of discussion and settlement.

Two of these missions were to the great Central African Emperor of Uganda, and one to the Unyoro monarch, a formidable rival and frequent foe of the Lord of Uganda.

The Governor and his zealous lieutenant, in 1876, made a journey of exploration up the White Nile, with a view to becoming acquainted in detail with the head-men, officials, and circumstances of the populations along the banks of the stream; and in company these two intrepid men circumnavigated the Albert Nyanza, noting many fresh features of interest to the naturalist and the geographer, and entering into amicable relations with all the various tribes and island communities on the route. In the same year, Gordon Pasha and Emin passed northward to Khartoum, to prosecute some notorious slave-hunters, who had been caught "red-handed" in the traffic, and who had been cleverly "checkmated" by Gordon.

In describing the appearance of the Albert Nyanza region, seventy miles of which, stretching eastward from the *débouchement* of the Victoria Nile into Lake Albert, Gordon and Emin carefully surveyed, the former says,—"A dead, mournful place it is" (near Murchison Falls), "with a heavy, damp dew penetrating everywhere; it is as if the Angel Azrael had spread his wings over this land; you can have little idea of the silence and solitude." The river was found to be quite open to the foot of the cataracts, and then there was nothing for it but a weary tramp through the almost impenetrable jungle in a flood of tropical rain. The road was broken by frightful ravines of extraordinary depth, opening out laterally from the terrace-land into the deep gorge through which the river rushed onward to the Nyanza. Five days more were occupied in forcing a way through a perfect network of creepers, and clinging rope-like vegetation, which had all the holding power of a ship's cable. Eighteen miles per day was the longest march possible under these circumstances, and it was with a weary heart that the dauntless Pasha and his companion plodded on towards Foweira, the station which marked the limit of the survey. Arriving within easy distance of Speke's Nyamyango, the expedition turned back, and arrived at Mapuyo on September

29th, having succeeded in actually occupying, as well as annexing in the name of his Highness the Khedive, a magnificent and important tract of fertile territory in the extreme Equatorial lacustrine region.

Emin's special mission to Uganda was not accomplished without some difficulty, and at times the party were exposed to considerable peril. One of Gordon's officers had invaded the Empire of Uganda with a body of 300 troops, and, acting entirely upon his own responsibility, had proceeded to annex the kingdom of the famous Mtesa to the Khedivate of Egypt. The effect of this rash and fanatical act upon the trained levies and vast population of the threatened country, was at once seen in the demeanour of the outraged people; and the outcome of this piece of sheer folly might have been the total destruction of the Egyptian outposts and garrisons, as far north as Khartoum, by Mtesa and his exasperated followers. Happily, other counsels prevailed, and Emin was sent to bring back the offending troops, and to make peace with the haughty Lord of Uganda. The sagacious German eventually accomplished his difficult task without losing a life or firing a shot, and was warmly congratulated by his chief for the able manner in which he had conducted and carried out a most hazardous enterprise.

In 1877, Emin was again ordered southward, to negotiate with Kabarega, the monarch of Unyoro, who was frequently engaged in raiding the Soudan portion of the Egyptian frontier. It was important that Gordon should secure the good services of this potentate, if possible, as in the event of trouble with

Uganda, he would be an invaluable ally; and again the
young German surgeon was successful, and succeeded
in the task of making a treaty with the Unyoro people,
which in Gordon's own opinion probably saved himself
and his garrison from massacre. "This mission,
although carried out so far back as 1877, has recently
borne fresh fruit," says Dr. Felkin; "for the friendly
relations then brought about have enabled Dr. Emin
to obtain scanty supplies from Kabarega, and to send
through him letters to the Church Missionary Society's
representatives in Uganda, and have also assisted the
intrepid German traveller, Dr. Junker, to escape, viâ
Unyoro and Uganda, to Zanzibar." A second journey
to Uganda was undertaken by Emin, under orders
from Gordon Pasha, in 1877, and Lake Albert was
also re-visited, for scientific and administrative purposes, in 1879.

In 1878, on his appointment to the Governorship of
Equatorial Egypt, Emin was raised to the rank of
Bey, and he entered upon the duties of his responsible
office with the determination of developing his province,
and protecting his frontier. At the close of Gordon's
administration, the affairs of the territory were in an
orderly and fairly prosperous condition. Taxes had
been paid with regularity, slavery had been virtually
suppressed, commerce had been developed, and the
condition of the people had been altogether changed
for the better. But the rule of the English Pasha had
been succeeded by an interval of Turkish and native
administration, by which the old evils had been revived
with tenfold power, the tide of civilization had been
rolled back, and oppression, poverty, and misery once

more brooded over "the pearl of the Soudan," one of
the fairest and most fertile, and most populous, of the
Central African States. Emin had now entered upon
the serious work of his life. When he assumed the
reins of government, and cast his eye over the country
which his great predecessor had ruled with so much
success for a brief period of something like eighteen
months, he found that the only portions of his
dominion in peace and security were the narrow strips
of territory on either side of the White Nile, reaching
on one side from Lado, his capital, to the Albert
Nyanza, and extending on the other side for some
distance into the land of the Shalis, between the east
bank of the river and the Galla country. At the end
of 1880, however, a change was manifest throughout
the length and breadth of the entire province.
Stations long since fallen into decay, through neglect
and indifference, were rebuilt, and re-provisioned, and
re-manned ; peace, order, and respect for constitutional
authority were established amongst the tribes within
the borders of the state ; and all the principal towns
and fortified villages were connected together by good
roads and regular weekly posts. Crime was reduced,
slavery once more received a crushing blow, slave-
raids and slave-wars were sternly put down, markets
were thrown open and protected, agriculture was
encouraged, strangers were invited to enter the
territory for the interchange of commodities and the
opening up of new trade-routes, and the slave-traders
were swept clean out of the region altogether.
The Government officials, chiefly pardoned criminals,
convicts and felons gathered out of the prisons of

Cairo and Khartoum, whom Emin found established throughout the province, were replaced by trustworthy men, selected by the Governor himself from the ranks of his own assistants and subordinates. The Egyptian soldiers, the scum of the regiments of Lower Egypt, were disbanded, and new forces recruited from the Negro population of the subject territory ; and although the remote, isolated region was cut off for years from all communication with Khartoum, and no supplies could be forwarded, in consequence of a block on the Nile, the Equatorial Provinces, which in 1878 were maintained at a deficit of 38,000*l.* per annum, had, three years later, a surplus of 8000*l.*, a financial improvement which was effected entirely by the efforts of Emin Bey, without having recourse to any measure of oppression or excessive taxation, and simply by the exercise of rigid economy, and the suppression of long-standing abuses. A spirit of loyal obedience had everywhere been developed, discontent had disappeared, and an era of sustained prosperity and peace was incorporated. The organization of this vast dependency was not effected without an immense amount of patient and wisely directed labour, and it was made possible only by a careful, and even painful, attention to the minutest details, and to the peculiar and ever-varying characteristics of the numerous tribes and populations inhabiting the region, which is divided into districts, each having a military station for its official centre, to which the taxes of grain and cattle are brought by the natives at stated periods. At Lado, the central stronghold of the province and the seat of government, on the White Nile, Emin was constantly employed in discharging the varied and responsible duties of his office, and in ministering to the sick in the large hospital which he had established for the reception of his distressed and afflicted subjects. " Lado is a well-built town, the divan, offices, mosque, and government buildings being built of burnt bricks, and roofed with corrugated iron ; all the other buildings being of wood or grass. The streets are wide and straight, and surrounding the station there is a broad promenade, a clear space of thirty yards being kept between the houses and the earthwork fortifications. Beyond there are large gardens. The station has three gates, at which sentries are mounted night and day, the gates being open from 6 a.m. till 8 p.m. No gun is allowed to be fired near the station from sunset to sunrise, unless as a signal of an attack. At 5.30 a.m., the bugle sounds the *réveille;* and shortly after 'Light your fires.' At 6 a.m., the muster-roll is called, and the gates are opened. The soldiers then drill, and the women begin to sweep the streets, for in Emin's stations, sanitary precautions are adopted, and the people are taught that cleanliness is next to godliness. At 8.30 a.m. all, excepting the sentries, turn out to draw water, and to fetch wood ; and, the dew being by that time dried up, the cattle are sent out to graze. Work lasts till 11.30 a.m. ; when there is an interval of rest till 2.30 p.m. : the people then set to work again till 5 p.m., when all return inside the fort. At 8.30 p.m. the roll is called, and the gates are shut ; and at 9 p.m. all fires are extinguished, an officer going the rounds to see that this regulation is carried out. Curfew in those parts is a very important precaution, for should a hut once catch fire, the whole station is threatened with destruction. In the spring of 1878, before Emin's rule began, Lado itself was burnt down, and the immense stores which Baker Pasha had taken to the province were all destroyed. Near each of the principal stations are groups of native villages. The soldiers are nearly all Makraka men, and, physically, a finer body of troops it would be difficult to find. They are brave (one might almost say recklessly brave), civil, and high-spirited; they obey orders with alacrity, and are at the same time intelligent in the performance of their duties. They are armed with the Remington rifle, which they pride themselves upon keeping bright and clean. Their uniform, when on duty in the station, is a white tunic and trousers, boots, fez, and a cartridge belt made of leopard-skin, which is bound round the waist, and holds a sword, bayonet and knife. On the march they are dressed in brown clothes, with knicker-bockers, and they seldom wear boots. I should have said they *were* clothed in this fashion, poor fellows, for now they are scantily provided with kit." (Dr. Felkin.) Every large village of the province is bound to supply a fixed number, according to population, of armed drago-men, who act as a kind of native police, and these are held responsible to the central authority for the peace of the place, and the prompt payment of the taxes. Some twenty or thirty of these officers live near each fort, and are expected to provide porters and messengers for government service when required.

There was a marked contrast between the region

ruled by Emin and the surrounding country. In the latter, slave-dealers still ravaged the land, and their inhuman traffic went on unheeded and unrestrained. Brutal acts of cruelty were daily perpetrated, villages were burnt to the ground, the aged killed, the women and children carried off for sale, and the strong men who resisted were subjected to tortures, which were applied with fiendish ingenuity. Emin succeeded in introducing the steady cultivation of indigo, cotton, rice, and coffee, and the revenue from these industries alone, he hoped would enable him eventually to contribute a substantial sum to the treasury of the Khedive. When Khartoum fell before the attacks of the Mahdi, and the northern portion of the Egyptian Soudan was given over to anarchy, it was feared that the whole of the territories of Egypt, south of Dongola, was lost. Such, however, was not the case. After the death of Gordon, the forces of the Mahdi spread southward, and threatened Emin, who had entrenched himself in his citadel at Wadelai, on the banks of the White Nile, just north of the Albert Nyanza. To the summons of the Mahdi that he would surrender and adopt the faith of Islam, Emin replied by a bold message of defiance, and a promise that if the followers of the false prophet attacked him, they would meet with a most determined resistance. Hemmed in on every side, and cut off from all communication with the outer world, the brave German surgeon held his own, although sadly in want at times even of the necessaries of life, and it was not till 1886 that news reached Europe of the terrible condition to which the little garrison of Wadelai and

its brave chief were reduced by famine, sickness, and
the constant assaults of the Mahdi's infatuated hordes.
Unsupported by a single word of sympathy from the
civilized world, and alone with his handful of black
troops, Emin bravely held his own, bidding defiance
to the raiding slave-hunters, and to the disaffected
natives, who harassed him night and day for four
bitter years without being able to force an entry into
his fortlet, to break down his indomitable, splendid spirit, or to destroy his hopes that all would yet
be well with him and the people over whom he had
been placed as ruler and father. Emin, who was
raised to the rank of Pasha on the arrival of the news
at Cairo that he was thus bravely holding his own in
the face of implacable foes, and a combination of
difficulties calculated to try the boldest heart, was
described as a tall, thin man of military bearing.
" The lower part of his face," says Dr. Felkin, who saw
him in the Soudan in 1870, " was hidden by a well-
trimmed beard, and a moustache of the same colour
partially veiled his determined mouth. His eyes,
though to some extent hidden by spectacles, were
black, piercing, and intelligent ; his smile was pleasing
and gracious ; his actions graceful and dignified ; and
his whole being that of a man keenly alive to everything passing around him. Courteous, but somewhat
reserved, he is distinguishable as a thorough gentleman. He addressed us in English ; but subse-
quently finding I spoke German, we conversed and
corresponded in that language." The last of the
White Pashas is an accomplished linguist. He has a
knowledge of most European languages, of several

spoken in Asia, and of nine of the native dialects
spoken by the tribes of his region. The word-por-
trait of him, drawn by one of his intimate friends, is
delightfully true and distinct. It describes a man
who prefers at all times duty before pleasure. Much of
the drudgery of his daily life would naturally have been
repulsive to a more scientific expert, but Emin Pasha
was ready at any moment to relinquish the pursuit of his
favourite studies and researches in natural history, and
put aside his specimens, of which he is a passionate and
indefatigable collector, to visit the hospital or listen to
the complaint or appeal of the poorest of his subjects.
Although a born naturalist, Emin has also shown all
the qualities of an efficient military commander and
strategist, and his defence of Wadelai is rendered the
more remarkable by the remembrance of the fact that
his education and training had been essentially peaceful and rather that of the student than the soldier.
" I am," he wrote to his sister, " a general as well as an
M.D., a surgeon qualifying as a general in strategy."
From sunrise to sunset, his time was employed during
the first year of his command in hearing cases and
administering justice. At Lado his hospital duties
always occupied certain hours of the early morning, and he never failed to visit all the wards, and to
prescribe for the inmates with the greatest tenderness and care, no matter how pressing his official
duties as supreme executive officer might be. His
attitude towards the natives was one of genuine
sympathy and gentleness. He heartily adopted the
policy of Gordon, and in all ways identified himself
with the people he loved to help and protect. He

sought to forget his Frankish origin as far as possible, and to lose all identity as a German ; he adopted an Egyptian name and the Egyptian official dress. Writing to his sister from Trebizond, in 1871, he says, —" Here I have already gained a reputation as a doctor. This is due to the fact that I know Turkish and Arabic as few Europeans know them, and that I have so carefully adopted the habits and customs of the people that no one believes that an honest German is disguised behind the Turkish name." But Emin Pasha is no renegade, or half-hearted Christian, or one of those who think even favourably of the superiority of Mohammedanism as a civilizing agency in Central Africa. He is in thorough sympathy with Christian effort on the Dark Continent, and, like Stanley in his strange interview with Mtesa of Uganda, Emin has ever held that for the African the faith of Christ is infinitely superior to the legends of Mohammed. Commenting upon the inability of Islam to influence the African, he says, that to his certain knowledge, in his own district Mohammedanism has not made a single convert for twenty years. This he considers indisputable evidence of the effete and feeble character of Mohammedan traditions. The intercourse between Gordon and Emin was unbroken till the fatal 26th January, 1885, when the great and heroic soldier met that death in the streets of his own capital which was the crowning and adequate finish to his devoted life. The news of the catastrophe at Khartoum reached Emin, on the banks of the Nile, as he was preparing an expedition to march northward to Khartoum. It was told him by the exultant followers of the Mahdi, and

for the moment the blow was overwhelming. But the
heart of faithful Gordon's lieutenant never quailed:
"I feel now that I am Gordon's heir, and that I must
continue, at all risks, the work for which Gordon paid
with his life's blood."

The hope of Central Africa, says the eloquent and
apostolic Archbishop Lavigerie, who has lately called
upon the nations of Europe, "in tones which melt and
words that burn," to deal a final blow at the slave-
trade, lies in the armed resistance of the natives themselves, assisted by Europeans, to the attacks of the
man-stealers. Maritime barriers formed by cruisers
and gun-boats can do little to kill the traffic effectually.
It must be dealt with at the source and fountain of
supply. The Cardinal, who has spent over twenty
years as a missionary in North Central Africa, is no
advocate of half-measures. He sees, as other friends
of Africa have seen, the possibility of a temporary
revival, at least, of the Mohammedan superstition, and
he fears that unless the Christian nations of Europe
unite to stem the flood, a wave of fanaticism may
sweep over the entire Central Zone of the continent,
and, for the time, obliterate the very footprints of
Livingstone, Gordon, and others who have patiently
laboured and gladly died that Africa might be free.
The number of slaves still annually sold on the shores
of the Red Sea, the Cardinal estimates at 400,000, and
when we remember that for every slave taken at least
ten lives are sacrificed, and when we consider the
massacres caused by resistance, the deaths by exposure
of the old and feeble, the ruin created by the incur-
sions of the slave-hunting parties, we may safely

calculate that *over two millions of persons* become victims of the slave-dealer every year, and that more than 1500 negroes are daily forced from their homes in the Central Equatorial Provinces and carried down to the coasts for sale. That slavery is contrary to reason, to the laws of religion natural and revealed, and hateful in the sight of that God who is a Providence to all His creatures, there can be no doubt. Commercially, the sale of human beings as chattels in the public market is fatal. Legitimate trade is hindered, and there is no inducement given to cultivate the fruits of the earth, or to develop the natural resources of the region, while men and women and children are the chief objects of purchase and barter. And it is abundantly proved that slave-labour is the most expensive kind of labour. With no incentive to exert himself, the bondsman does as little as he can, and wastes as much of his master's time as he can. The waste of power, time, and wealth in slave countries is enormous, and the magnificent capacities of the great African Equatorial Zone can only be properly developed by a free people wisely directed by Europeans like Stanley, Emin Pasha, Cardinal Lavigerie, or David Livingstone. It has lately come to the knowledge of the English Government that on the East Coast of Africa, numbers of slave caravans are constantly wending their way with long lines of captives to be exported secretly, but still to be exported from the coast, and the Arab slave-dealers of the district have an impression that English interest in the suppression of their traffic has died out; or that we have not the far-reaching arm and

the strong hand to deal with this curse of the race.
There can be no doubt that till quite recently the
feeling of England was stagnant upon this question.
But the labours of Emin Pasha upon the White Nile,
and in the region which is *par excellence* the "happy
hunting-ground" of the Arab, have already drawn
public attention once more to this matter, and it is
felt that the time has come when, for the honour of
our national name as well as for the honour of our
Christianity, slavery must cease, and cease for ever,
on the African Continent. There is no longer any
obstacle to united action on the part of all Christian
nations, in the direction of adopting some judicious
method for putting a speedy end to, or greatly
diminishing, the horrors which far exceed those of
former days, when the traffic was mainly from the
West Coast or trans-oceanic. The remedy is to
declare the trade in slaves by land or sea to be piracy,
and to treat it accordingly, and the arrangement by
which the English and German influence is divided
behind the strip of coast-line governed by the Sultan
of Zanzibar is the very best that could have been
devised for civilization and humanity at large.

In 1885, Mohammed Ahmed, who had driven the
troops of the Khedive out of the Soudan, and had
established himself at Khartoum, succumbed to an
attack of virulent small-pox, and before the close of
the year a successor was appointed, who gave himself
out to be the heaven-sent prophet of God, and none
other than the rightful and lawful successor to all the
titles, dignities, and privileges of the Mahdi Mohammed
Ahmed. The new leader of the rebel army lost no

time in reorganizing his rude battalions, and in
reviving in them that spirit of fanatical valour which
had inspired them and carried them on to victory in
past days beneath the banner of the hermit of Aba.
Several of the forsaken garrisons in the far-off desert
stations, and many European officials, fell into the
hands of the new Mahdi, and the lot of the captives
was by no means a pleasant one if they refused, as
many of them did, to embrace the tenets of Islam and
swear upon the Koran to devote their lives to the
propagation of the creed of the Prophet of Mecca.
The population of Khartoum, who were suspected of
entertaining a secret sympathy with Gordon, were
reduced to great misery, and clothes, money, and even
food were denied them by the exultant conquerors
after the fall of the city. For months, hanging, and
murder, and massacre were the order of the day in
the dishonoured capital of the Soudan; whoever
smoked or sold tobacco, traded, or refused to give up
his cash, or stored food or corn, was instantly
executed. It was useless to send ransom-money to
Khartoum to secure the release or more humane
treatment of the European captives, as any one
attempting to journey to that city with money or
wares, whether Christian or Moslem, friend or foe,
was robbed before he reached his destination by the
tribes who had been beggared by the Mahdi's reign
of terror. It was equally vain to enter into any
negotiations for the release of the prisoners, as in the
event even of the Mahdi's consenting to such a course,
his councillors were sure to oppose it. Attempts
have been made from time to time to bring about the

release of the captives still held by the Mahdi, but
with no good results. The intervention of the Sultan
of Turkey and the Grand Shereef of Mecca have been
invoked, but the Mahdi declares himself to be the
true Prophet, and consequently standing high above
the Sultan and the Shereef, and declines to take
any notice of either of these authorities. It has
been feared that more active interference on behalf of
the prisoners might result in additional cruelties being
inflicted upon them, as it is felt that an expedition
would be fatal to them, for they would doubtless be
murdered directly it was known at Khartoum that
troops were on the way to effect their release. Owing
to the blind fanaticism of the followers of the present
Mahdi, they would never consent to release the
prisoners even to save themselves. If it is declared
of importance to the Egyptian, or rather the English
Government, that Statin Bey, Lupton Bey, and other
innocent victims, should be freed by some means from
their sad position, it will be easy (when the time
arrives) to come to an understanding with those
who know the Soudan well, as to ways and means.
Lupton Bey is an Englishman, and an old friend and
former companion of Emin Pasha at Wadelai;
Neufeld is a German; Statin Bey is an Austrian.
There are also three missionaries and four nuns, all
Austrians or Italians. Seven Greeks are also at
Khartoum; and thus four of the principal states of
Europe are curiously enough represented among the
little band of prisoners held by the false prophet in
durance upon the Upper Nile waters. As late as July
last, a messenger arrived from Khartoum, bearing some

slips of paper from Lupton Bey and the missionary
Urwedder. The latter asked for a receipt for dyeing
grey cottons, by using which the missionaries and
sisters hoped to earn a living. According to the
statements of this messenger, the condition of the
prisoners is even worse than was represented in the
former report. Statin Bey sits the whole day at the
Mahdi's door, where he is exposed to all sorts of ill-
treatment and insults. He is not allowed to speak at
all to the other Europeans, nor to visit the bazaar.
Lupton Bey has to work like a slave in the arsenal;
and Neufeld is in chains. The missionaries and the
Greek dealers may freely walk about in the town, but
are not allowed to leave it. They are not permitted
to trade openly; but they do this secretly, as it is the
only means they have of procuring food. There does
not appear to be any chance of ransom or rescue for
these unhappy people. Some time since it was proposed
to the Mahdi to exchange his prisoners for several
important dervishes who had been captured by the
Kababish tribes. The Mahdi took the proposal with
every sign of extreme vexation and anger, and sending for the European prisoners, he placed a soldier
behind each, and then called, "Who wishes to be
exchanged?" Of course no one replied.

Such, doubtless, would have been the fate of Emin
Pasha had he not been able to beat off the levies of
the Mahdi, and to preserve his little fortress of Wadelai
intact. In October, 1886, nearly two years after the
fall of Khartoum, letters were received in England, by
Dr. Felkin, from Wadelai, describing the condition of
affairs, and begging for help and food to be sent to

relieve the handful of men who were holding out against overwhelming odds for life and liberty on the head-waters of the Nile. The letters were forwarded by the missionaries of the Church Missionary Society in Uganda to Zanzibar, and were about five months on the way from the Albert Nyanza to Edinburgh. The critical position of the Pasha and his garrison was at once made known in the public press, and considerable interest was at once manifested everywhere in the gallant defence which Emin was making at Wadelai, and admiration was expressed at the noble self-abnegation which had marked his Egyptian career from the outset. The public interest in him and his work soon took a practical form, and it was decided to send out an armed party to convey supplies of men, ammunition, food and clothing to the beleaguered Pasha and his companions in peril, and to offer them the means of escape from the Soudan, if they finally decided to leave the territory to the Mahdi and the slave-hunters. The proposal to send relief to Wadelai, was laid before the British Government, and the plan was sanctioned, although it could not, from its nature, receive the official support of the authorities. A committee of gentlemen interested in the welfare of the African races, and in the development of legitimate commerce upon the great continent, was formed (1887) to carry out the novel and hazardous enterprise, and funds were freely contributed for the humane and laudable purpose of the organization. Encouraged by a splendid donation of 10,000l. from Mr. W. Mackinnon, application was made to the Khedive for help, and a grant of 10,0 00l. was imme-

diately made from the Egyptian exchequer in aid of the
enterprise. Sir Francis De Winton, who for two years,
after the retirement of Mr. Stanley, had administered
the Government of the Congo Free State, and who
has been identified with every effort which has been
made of recent years for the highest good of the numberless communities and peoples of Central Equatorial
Africa, undertook the position of Secretary to the
Relief Committee; and to his indefatigable exertions,
and unique personal influence, we may mainly attribute
the success of the scheme in its initial stages. But
after all, Who was to lead the Relief Party? was the
great question to be settled. And a thrill of gladness
and gratitude passed over both hemispheres, when it
was at last definitely announced that the man who
Found Livingstone, Discovered the Congo, and Founded
the Free State, was once more ready to face the unknown terrors, risk the deadly perils of a journey
through the cannibal belt and the trackless forests of
Equatorial Africa, for the cause of humanity and
liberty in the heart of Africa. At the call of duty,
Mr. H. M. Stanley turned back from a lucrative and
pleasant lecturing-tour in America, and hastened to
confer with the Emin Pasha Relief Committee as to
how Wadelai was to be reached in the shortest time
and with the least possible risk to health and life.
This task of daring heroism, so fearlessly undertaken
by Mr. Stanley, has been appropriately regarded as the
boldest, as well as the most interesting and beneficent,
African enterprise of this or any age. From the first,
it was clearly seen by geographers and explorers and
others familiar with the peculiar difficulties and vicis-

situdes of African travel, even under the most favourable circumstances, that the relief of Gordon's faithful
lieutenant, on the northern shores of the Albert
Nyanza, would be an undertaking full of dread uncer-
tainties and manifold dangers. Stanley thoroughly
understood that he was not leading his armed force
into the heart of Africa upon anything which could par-
take of the nature of a holiday review or dress parade.
In a public reference to the expedition, just before leaving England, its brave leader thus defined his duty : " I
am taking an expedition into the heart of Central Africa,
for the relief of an Egyptian officer, who is in straitened
circumstances, and environed by breadths of unknown
territory populated by savage tribes. I intend to
proceed at once to Zanzibar, to recruit a force of
followers and bearers from among any of my old friends
and former companions who may be once more disposed to cast in their lot with me and share the
labours and dangers of the expedition to Wadelai. I
shall leave for the Congo, if I find a steamer ready
to take us, and I shall not return till I reach Emin,
unless I perish in the attempt."

CHAPTER XXII.

THE chosen leader of the *Emin Pasha Relief Expedition*
had long ceased to be regarded merely as a "smart
newspaper correspondent." As the discoverer of the
second largest river in the world, as a pioneer of
civilization in remote and savage regions, and as a
persistent worker in the sacred cause of humanity,
his fame had spread over both hemispheres, and he
was a man whom potentates and statesmen, as well as
savants and philanthropists, delighted to honour.
By his distinguished services to science and humanity,
he had fairly won the first place in the first rank of
that illustrious band of brave men—the Explorers of
Central Africa—who have not only lifted up for ever
the thick veil of mystery which once enveloped the inner heart of the Dark Continent, but have revealed to
us the existence of "myriads of dusky natives," hidden
for long ages altogether out of sight, in the fertile
plains and teeming basins of the Zambesi, the Congo,
and the Nile. Mr. Stanley, by his own discoveries
alone, had added a population of 50,000 to the sum-

total of the known people of the world, and his departure for the Southern Soudan, at the head of the Emin
Pasha Relief Expedition, was made the occasion for
the bestowal upon him of several public honours. On
January 13th, 1887, a few days before he left England
for the region of the White Nile, he was presented with
the freedom of the City of London, and a farewell banquet was given in his honour at the Mansion House.
A large and distinguished company of men of letters,
statesmen, scientists, and " lovers of their fellow-men,"
had assembled at the invitation of the Lord Mayor,
Sir John Staples, K.C.M.G., to do honour to the
famous explorer, and to wish him " God-speed " upon
his fresh errand of mercy and peril to Equatorial
Africa. Eloquent references were made, in the course
of the proceedings, to Mr. Stanley's career as a Press-
man, and his great enterprise—boldly initiated and
nobly sustained by the *Daily Telegraph* and the *New
York Herald*, which resulted in the grandest geographical achievement of the Victorian era, the discovery
of the mighty Congo Lualaba, and placed the name of
Stanley in the forefront of African discoverers—was
appropriately dwelt upon in the laudatory *résumé* of
Mr. Stanley's services to humanity and science, which
preceded his admission to the privileges of a freeman of
the first city of the world. In an earnest and thoughtful address, the guest of the day briefly sketched out
the course which he had decided to follow in order to
reach and succour Emin and his faithful garrison
environed by savage enemies on the White Nile banks.
In calm and measured tones Stanley expressed his
firm conviction that success would once more crown
his efforts, and that the purpose for which he was giving

up, for the time, the society of friends and the comforts
of civilization, would eventually be accomplished. In
the course of his remarks the illustrious speaker more
than once hinted at the fact that the relief of the
discovered Pasha was not the only object which he
had in view in going out to the Equatorial Provinces.
It was hoped that he would clear up the still unsolved
problem of the outflow of the Tanganika Lake and the
Lukuga River, and its real relationship to the Lualaba
and Lake Tanganika. Stanley was of opinion, after
careful examination of the stream (in 1874-75),
that it was an influent of the Lake, but in a most
interesting and circumstantial account of his in-
vestigation of the phenomena of the river in 1880, Mr.
Thomson seeks to establish the curious theory that the
Lukuga is an effluent of the Nyanza, and that it is the
channel through which the great lake pours out its generous contribution to the floods which unite to swell the
dark-brown stream of the Congo Lualaba. Thomson
also declares of the waters of Tanganika, that though
potable they never quench thirst, and that they are
impregnated by a strong saline deposit, which corrodes
metal or leather with all the power and virulence of
a fiery acid. The physical conformation of the unknown area between the Congo and the Albert Nyanza, and the condition of its population of mixed and
savage tribes; the true course of the Kabrilla, a stream
flowing out of the Victoria Nyanza, and the chief
southern fountain and source of the great Nile; and the
actual area and special physical features of the Alexandra Lake and the surrounding district—were all to
receive attention, and Stanley looked forward with
confidence to carrying out a complete and exact sur-

vey of the wide expanse of fruitful and densely peopled country between the Albert and Victoria Lakes.

Mr. Stanley referred at the Mansion House to the happy and practical results which had attended his former travels in Eastern and Western as well as Central Africa, and spoke, with some excusable pride, of the irresistible proof thus afforded of the truth of Livingstone's memorable statement as to the priceless value of the work of the explorer, and the valuable stimulus which every journey undertaken by a traveller in foreign parts, however obscure, has given to political, commercial, and religious enterprise.

Four roads to Emin Pasha's Province were open to Mr. Stanley, and for some time these alternative routes formed the subject of keen debate and close discussion in scientific circles and in the public press. The first route, proposed by the young but already distinguished explorer of Masai Land, Mr. Joseph Thomson, struck into the interior from the port of Mombasa, on the east coast. It would lead through Masai Land, along the base of Mount Kenia, and over the waters of Lake Baringo, somewhat north of the Victoria Nyanza, and enter the Equatorial Province at Foweira, Koro, or Fadjulli. Mr. Thomson proposed, as amply sufficient for all purposes, a small caravan of four hundred porters and fifty or sixty camels or donkeys, and he claimed the following advantages for his route :—It would be the shortest and most healthy, the country presents no topographical difficulties, camels and donkeys agree admirably with the climate, " and," said Mr. Thomson, " taking everything into consideration, I myself pronounce emphatically in favour of the Masai route."

It was estimated that the beleaguered garrison at Wadelai could be reached from Mombasa in less than four months. The proposal of Mr. Thomson was warmly supported by the late celebrated traveller, Dr. Fischer, but it was less keenly advocated by, perhaps, the most trustworthy authority of these days, and a recent visitor to Wadelai, Dr. Robert W. Felkin, F.R.S.E., F.R.G.S., &c., who said, " I do not say that this route is an impracticable one, but I think that its difficulties and dangers are too great to be risked. The greatest objection I see to it is, that the King of Uganda, the son and successor of Mtesa, would inevitably hear of the expedition, and would most certainly try to prevent it reaching its destination. Since the murder of Bishop Hannington, he has been kept in constant alarm by rumours from the east, partly coming from Dr. Fischer's journey that way, and partly from the German annexations on the East Coast. It must be remarked that Mr. Mackay, of the Church Missionary Society, who has nobly held his post for seven years, and who is now virtually a prisoner in the king's hands, is still in Uganda, and I think that an expedition for the relief of Emin Pasha should avoid any route which would in any way render his position more precarious. It should not be forgotten that Mr. Mackay, at great personal risk, has done all he could to help Emin, and indeed he has formed the channel of communication between him and Zanzibar, thus generously repaying the services which Emin rendered to the Church Missionary Society's missionaries in previous years. The district too, to the north-east of Uganda, which would have to be passed by a caravan following this route, has been the slave-hunting ground of the Waganda for many years, and its inhabitants fear them, so that the expedition would have to rely upon its own resources in withstanding any attacks the brutal boy-king chose to make upon it. Any one who remembers Mr. Stanley's account of the military organization of the Waganda, the prowess and the hundreds of thousands of men they can put into the field, must be convinced that it would require a strong party indeed to cope with this, the strongest Central African power."

A second proposed route for the expedition was one which would lead directly through the heart of Uganda. This was at once voted to be quite impracticable. The chances were that once in the power of the tyrant emperor of the great Central African state, the expedition would be detained upon one pretence or other, and prevented from ever proceeding northward to the Victoria Nile and the Albert Nyanza. The policy of the Waganda is still unchanged. Duplicity, greed, and heartless lust for blood are still the characteristics of these powerful people. No European would ever be permitted to leave their borders till they had spoiled him of everything he possessed, and this policy they will continue "till they have learnt a lesson which it would be beyond the power and the province of a relief expedition to teach them."

A third route was suggested to Wadelai *viâ* Bagamoyo to Lake Alexandra, and then north to Muta Nzige and the southern shore of the Albert Nyanza. By pursuing this road the territory of Uganda would be entirely avoided, as well as the unsettled country of Kabrega, and the relief party would be able to lighten the weariness of the way by boat passages over the Alexandra Lake, the gleaming waters of the Muta Nzige, and the Albert Nyanza.

On the shores of the Albert Nyanza the expedition could be met by the two steamers of Emin and his life-boats, and safely conveyed to the fortress. All possibility of contact with the bellicose Waganda would by this route be rendered impossible, and these people in fact, might never even hear of the passage of the white man's forces through the Equatorial Region. The only drawback to this road was the fact that it traversed an entirely unknown region of country for something like 300 miles, but the same objection could be raised to the Masai route, as well as to the Congo road, which Mr. Stanley decided to follow, and which traverses far wider tracts of unexplored wilderness, and crosses territories inhabited by tribes far more warlike and barbarous than any to be met with in an advance upon the White Nile from Bagamoyo.

The finest possible road to Wadelai was by the Congo, and this was the route fixed upon by Mr. Stanley as the one most suitable for his purpose. He determined to proceed to the east coast once more to enlist a strong party of his favourite Zanzibaris, and then to go round to Banana Point and again breast the turbulent waters with which he had sternly battled in bygone days. Ascending the main stream of the Congo to about 23° E., he decided to leave the trunk river at the point of its juncture with the Aruwimi or Biyerré, which flows from about 5 N. in an almost direct southerly direction through the heart of the Niam Niam country, and follow the course of the tributary waters as far up as the navigation was practicable.

At this point he decided to form a reserve camp, and then to press on overland, through the unexplored cannibal belt, for Emin's stronghold in an almost easterly direction. The only objections to this course were:—the time it would occupy, the long delay which would inevitably attend the uncertain progress of the party through the terrible district of the Niam Niam, and the disturbed condition of the entire region north and east of the Stanley Falls. The distances of the various routes were as follows:— Mombasa to Wadelai, 1200 miles (Thomson's route); Bagamayo to Wadelai, 1600 miles (Felkin's route); Bagamoyo to Wadelai, 1350 miles (Uganda route); Congo route: water journey (Congo route to Biyerré), 1500 miles; land journey (Biyerré to Wadelai), 900 miles.

It was at a farewell dinner given to him by the President of the Relief Expedition, Mr. William Mackinnon, of Balinakill, that Mr. Stanley first announced his decision as to the Congo route. The King of the Belgians had generously placed the whole naval resources of the Congo Free State at the disposal of the leader and heads of the expedition for the purposes of this enterprise for a period of ninety days, and Mr. Stanley determined to leave Zanzibar with his force on the 25th February, expecting to reach the estuary of the Congo in twenty days after that date. He calculated on taking up five days in steaming up to the point above Vivi, where it would be necessary to avail himself of his road (or "staircase," as Brazza

playfully called the African highway). After a march
of seventeen days to Stanley Pool, he expected to
embark on the Congo for a voyage of thirty or thirty-
two days, which would bring him to the highest point
of possible navigation on the Biyerré. At this point
he hoped to establish, as has been named above, a
strong military fort and entrenched camp, under an
efficient officer, with a reserve of stores, ammunition,
and recruits. His plan was then to march on Lake
Albert, through an unknown land of nearly 900 miles.
It was at once seen that Mr. Stanley had a very distinct idea as to the serious nature of the work he had
in hand. He had a pretty clear understanding as to
the country he was about to traverse, and of the kind
of people he would have to encounter, and with
the wisdom and prudence which are characteristic
of the man, he took every precaution, which human
experience and foresight could suggest, to secure
the safety of himself and his followers in their
risky journey from the Aruwimi to the shores of the
Albert Nyanza. He knew that his way to Emin
Pasha lay through "a zone of the fiercest and most
relentless cannibalism in the world," and across a
tract of country never trodden by the foot of a
white man. He was fully alive to the possibility of
hindrances arising at every step of the way to arrest
the progress of the party, and to try its resolution.
The task of leading a caravan into the heart of Central
Africa is at all times a difficult one, but the march
which Stanley contemplated from the shores of the
Congo tributary to the banks of the White Nile, was
an undertaking bristling with difficulties, and altogether an enterprise of daring heroism worthy of the

man who had found Livingstone and traced the dread waters of the Congo Lualaba from Nyangwe to the Atlantic. If, as has been supposed by eminent scientists and geographers, the dense forest growth, which extends upwards from the Zambesi, is continued to the borders of the Soudan, we can well understand the serious nature of the obstacles which the relief expedition would have to be prepared to face, not only from the anthropophagi on all sides of it, but from the endless and gigantic vegetation which proved so terrible a barrier to the progress of the Congo exploration party in 1876, when a passage had to be ploughed through the wall-like bush by means of the sharp sections of the *Lady Alice*, which had often to be forced through the forest ahead of the men, to clear a path on the road from Nyangwe to Stanley Falls. Of the Equatorial belt, through which the relief party would have to force its way, the chief feature is its prolific vegetation. From about 10° north and south dense tropical forests were known to prevail, consisting of giant trees, with foliage so closely spread as almost to shut out the light. The heat is thus rendered less extreme, although Stanley, in his "Through the Dark Continent," speaks in burning words of the painful trials he and his party underwent, in the journey of 1876, from the close, moist atmosphere, as they pressed on northward from Nyangwe; but the dense undergrowth, composed of tenacious creepers and roots and fibrous plants, is so mixed and woven together, that it makes the country in places altogether impenetrable. In the beautiful Manyuema country, west of Lake Tanganika, Livingstone found forests so dense, he tells us, that the vertical midday sun could only send down thin pencils into the interior. A rank and prodigal luxuriance of creeping plants of every degree of thickness, from small cords to a man-of-war's hawser, interlaced the stems and branches of the trees, so that only when a path was recently used could a passage be obtained. When one of the giant trees falls across the path it blocks it breast high ; the fallen trunk soon becomes fenced with creepers, and it is no one's business to cut a path across it. Animal life, of course, abounds in these luxuriant regions, from herds of elephants to innumerable swarms of insects. To the north and south of the equatorial belt, as the rainfall gradually diminishes, the forest region is succeeded by an open pastoral and strictly agricultural country. This pastoral belt extends north across the Soudan, and south to the Zambesi. The population with which the expedition would have to deal, is probably the most savage of all the peoples of Africa. Stanley had a taste of their quality in his famous passage from Stanley Falls to the Port in 1874-77, and he therefore determined to secure a strong and well-trained band of Zanzibaris, to be officered by Europeans, upon whom he could rely in the hour of peril, when face to face with the dreaded man-eaters in the forests of the Niam Niam and Mombuttu countries. He also decided to take into his counsel and service the Arab chief Tippo Tibb, whose name has already appeared in these pages as the man who deserted Stanley in the forest north of Nyangwe, upon his exploratory journey ten years before.

Almost the last hours which Stanley spent in this country before proceeding to Zanzibar, were passed at Sandringham, the delightful country home of H.R.H.

the Prince of Wales, who has always been a hearty admirer and warm friend of the Pioneer of the Congo Free State. The Prince and his family were much interested in Stanley's projects and plans for the relief of Emin; and the traveller, by means of maps and sketches, was able to lay before his illustrious entertainers a detailed description of his intended journey. The last " Farewell " had however now to be said, for the date fixed by Stanley for starting upon his eventful and adventuresome journey had arrived, and on June 21st, 1887, the most intrepid and foremost traveller of this present age of universal exploration, was once more upon the " war-path." From the moment of his departure from Europe for Africa, it need scarcely be said, that his noble mission " held the field " in the public mind, as far as popular interest in Africa was concerned, and if good wishes could insure success, the triumph of the leader of the Emin Pasha Relief Expedition, would have been speedy and complete. Making his way to Zanzibar, he recruited the members of his force, and with his usual punctuality, at the date fixed upon, reached the mouth of the Congo, and proceeded up its course to the fortified station of Yambunga, on the Aruwimi or Biyerré River, where he encamped, and at once proceeded to make arrangements for the land-journey of 900 miles to the beleaguered Egyptian stronghold, which was to be the goal of the expedition.

Another way of reaching Emin, by way of the Nile Valley, had been suggested by experts, and it was thought at one time that the Relief Expedition would finally select that route, as it would give them the advantage of water-carriage for the entire distance

from Dongola to the Albert Nyanza. Stanley, however, clung to his great swift-flowing river, as he saw at
once that he would not only secure water transport for
his men and stores by the Congo, for a considerable
portion of his journey, but he would also have a line of
stations at intervals in his rear, governed by Europeans, and therefore capable of sending on intelligence
and affording active and speedy help to him and his
people, in any case of difficulty or disaster. Tracking
the length of the enormous stream, which sweeps in
a huge curve half-across Africa, in a north-easterly
direction, till he reached the apex of the curve, he, as
we have said, deserted the Congo, and followed the
course of the Aruwimi northward to Yambunga.
There can be no doubt as to the splendid facilities
afforded by the Congo water-system for opening out a
direct road to the great Central Lake Region, and notwithstanding the increased distance involved, this road,
when the Congo railway is once completed, will be the
great trade-route and main highway into Central Africa
for European commerce and civilization, and the chief
means of communication with the Central Soudan, and
the numerous tribes upon the shores of lakes Albert,
Muta Nzige and Tanganika, Nyangwe, and the Ulyga
Range.

On April 3rd, 1887, the Relief Expedition had
passed Matade Station, on its way up the river from
Boma, where it was joined by Mr. Herbert Ward,
who thus describes the appearance of the column on
the march for Yambunga :—" I was on my way down
country to embark for Old England. About two days
from here, however, I met two armed Abyssinians
(Soudanese). Immediately behind them, and mounted

on a fine mule, whose new-plated trappings glistened in the sun, was Stanley himself. Behind him came a Soudanese giant about 6 ft. 6 in. high, bearing a large American flag. I saluted the 'Congo King.' He smiled, and indicating the bare ground, said, 'Take a seat.' We squatted accordingly. He handed me a cigar. We talked about half an hour. He was very nice and kind. He accepted me as a volunteer, and it was at once arranged that I should see to the transport of some of his remaining loads. Of the eight whites he has with him, two have contributed to the expenses of the expedition for the privilege of accompanying him—'The Congo King'—through the heart of Africa, and the others are English (how refreshing!) officers on full army pay as volunteers.

" I never in my life was so struck with any sight as with Stanley's caravan on the march. Egyptians, Soudanese, Somalis, Zanzibaris, and others, nine hundred strong. It took me two hours to pass them, and then I met the second in command, Major Barttelot, a young fellow, burnt very dark, with a masher collar fixed on a flannel shirt, top-boots, &c. He was carrying a large bucket that some fellow had abandoned.

" ' I say, are you Ward?' he shouted.

" ' I am Ward,' I said, ' and I now belong to your expedition.'

" ' I am very glad to hear it,' he replied; ' Stanley has spoken of you; and so you are coming along; that's right!—very good business! '

" He seemed to be full of tremendous spirits, and looked very fit, and I admired him immensely. Tippo Tibb, the notorious slave-trader of Stanley Falls, has come round from Zanzibar with Stanley, and in

his silken robes, jewelled turban, and kriss, looks a
very ideal oriental potentate. It is thorough 'good
business,' as Major Barttelot would say, getting him
for an ally. He has forty-two of his wives along with
him, and some of them are handsome women. Stanley is about 5 ft. 7 in. in height, broad shouldered and
muscular. His thick hair is streaked with grey. He
wears a long military moustache, and has a piercing,
steely-grey eye, which is a factor in the marvellous
command which he wields over the natives.

"An early riser, he had finished his correspondence,
had breakfasted, and was smoking over a book when I
entered his apartment at 10.30. Edwin Arnold's
'Light of Asia' was in his hand, and all around him
on the floor were a number of English and American
newspapers. He greeted me with a fresh and cordial,
'How do you do?' and a genial grip of the hand. It
is some years ago since I met him first. on a memorable and exciting night at the Savage Club, when he
had returned from his splendidly successful search for
Livingstone. There is but little alteration in his sturdy
appearance, but his manners have more repose than
formerly; the expression of his face is less eager;
there is more of retrospection and less of perspective
in it than in those early days. He has a quieter and
less aggressive look in his grey eyes than of yore, and
there is a deeper suggestion of power and less consciousness of it, giving one the idea of a man who is
content to leave his deeds and his work to speak for
themselves. In those days of his first great triumph,
he had to fight his African battles over again in
London; for there were men, American and English,
who had doubts (and expressed them) of the truth of

his simple, circumstantial, and most remarkable story. You gather this from the appendix of his book, ' How I Found Livingstone,' in the letters of the Queen's Ministers, and in the gracious recognition of his powers, his courage, and his success by the Queen herself. A large room plainly furnished, it contained no evidence of luxury. Stanley, like most travellers, is somewhat of a Spartan in his mode of life. ' Do you write on so small a table?' I asked him; for one is interested in the way men work, and the table in question was a small round one such as a lady might use for a work-table.

" ' Yes, always,' he said, ' and for this reason, I can sit right in the midst of any notes and papers and move about easily. I wrote " Through the Dark Continent " on this table, and in this very wicker chair;—wrote it in three months.'

" ' Did you indeed—at a white heat, they say?'

" ' Yes, my notes here on my right, my writing-paper here,' he said, indicating the positions, ' and if you read the book with this explanation, you will, I think, realize the method. I wrote it straight off, throwing the manuscript sheets aside as I went on.'

" Then we talked of the Congo jungle fever, of accidents by flood and field, of the great broad view of universal usefulness that overlies the operations of the African International Association. ' Most of the deaths by so-called fever on the Congo might fairly be called accidents,' said the Founder of the Free State. ' I had a fine, strong, hearty officer engaged with a gang of men road-making; he met another officer from a neighbouring district whom he had known as a boy. For such a possible occasion as that

he had saved up a bottle of Burgundy. His friend
had a bottle of brandy. Men do these things away
from home. They retired to the shade of a tree and
pledged each other. On the Hudson or the Thames
they might have drunk their liquor and been well.
The brandy sending the blood rushing to his head—
when my first-named officer came from the shade of
the tree into the broad day the sun struck him, and
within twenty-eight hours he was dead and buried ; his
death set down to fever—it was an accident. I lost
another fine fellow, who got wet and neglected himself ; and many, very many deaths are caused through
this kind of thoughtlessness. As regards the Congo,
we want all the world, not one country only ; all the
world as clients of the association, and we want them
all to come and trade freely.

"Stanley is full of humanity. As a traveller his
heart goes out to the people of the new countries
he visits. It is not the entomology of a district, its
ornithology, or its climate or natural history, that
is his first concern ; but its people,—what they are,
how they live, what they think, and how they regard
him and the countries he has come from ; what is their
mental condition, shut out as they are from the world's
civilization. The glory of a traveller, says Burton, in
' To the Gold Coast for Gold,' results not so much
from the extent or the number of his explorations, as
from the consequences to which they lead ; and judged
by this test it may be said that Stanley's glory rests
upon a most sure foundation."

On the arrival of the caravan at the point of debarkation on the Higher Aruwimi, a strong camp was
established, consisting of 163 Zanzibaris, 40 Soudanese

soldiers, and Messrs. Jamieson, Troup, Bonny, and
Ward, as a reserve in case the main body should be
obliged to fall back on account of famine or loss of
men in forcing an advance in the face of openly hostile
natives. Major Barttelot, who had already proved himself a zealous and able officer, was placed in command
of this station, with instructions to keep open the line
of communication with the outer world down the entire
course of the Congo to the ocean; and to keep up the
strength of the garrison and maintain undiminished the
bulk of the supplies, stores, and ammunition, so that
he might at any moment be able to send on reliefs of
men and rations to the front. The point chosen upon
the banks of the Aruwimi as a rallying-point for the
party of relief was admirably suited for the purpose,
and everything being in order, on the eventful June
28th, 1887, Stanley plunged boldly into the unknown
region of swamp and forest and mountain, which
constitutes the great watershed between the Congo and
the Nile, and took the eastward road to Wadelai.
The news that the expedition had entered upon the last
and most formidable stage of its journey through
Tropical Africa created considerable interest and some
anxiety in Europe, although it was felt that there was no
reason to doubt the ability of Stanley to deal successfully with any difficulty which might confront him on
his perilous and trying march. The departure from
the higher Congo waters of the party recalled to the
minds of his many friends in England and elsewhere
his conduct in that great crisis of his life at Nyangwe,
in 1876, when he boldly severed his connection, and
broke the last link of his slender chain of communication
with Europe and civilization, and pushed undauntedly

on over the dangerous, inhospitable waters of the swift-flowing river, fighting for his life with cannibal tribes on either hand day after day, and still pushing onward, hauling his boats overland at times to avoid death in the rapids, and losing his English companions and native followers one after another in the hungry rapids of the cruel stream, till at length, after three terrible years of agony and prolonged misery he emerged once more into the light of day at Boma, footsore and hungry, and heartsick, and grey-headed, but bringing with him the solution of some of the profoundest geographical problems which have exercised the minds and intellects of thoughtful men from the days of Ptolemy (300 B.C.) down to the present era.

CHAPTER XXIII.

TOWARDS the close of 1886 the tidings reached Emin
that an expedition, under the command of Mr.
Stanley, was being organized in England to penetrate
the heart of Africa, and open a door of escape for
himself and his loyal band of native followers.

The isolated but invincible Pasha had long given up
all hope of succour from Egypt or Europe. He had,
however, determined at all hazards to hold on to his
post as best he could with the feeble forces at his
command, to go steadily on in the path of duty, and
patiently to abide the issue of events till the end
should come. But the marvellous devotion of this
heroic man was not destined to go unrewarded.

As the weary months of watchfulness and suspense
dragged slowly and painfully along, the din of conflict
died out, and the dark war-cloud, which for years
had hung over Wadelai and its gallant defenders,

drifted away to the north-west, beyond the frontier
of the Equatorial State, and the tide of fortune appeared to set once more in Emin's favour. The siege
of his stronghold, from which the flag of the Khedival
Government had never been lowered, was gradually
relaxed, and the wild levies of the second Mahdi with-
drew to other districts at the call of their fanatic
warrior-chief, or wandered northward in the direction
of the Bahr el Ghazel, and the starved and tattered
" faithfuls " enjoyed a period of welcome respite from
the daily and nightly attacks by which they had been
harassed, well-nigh to despair, since the disastrous
failure of Gordon's defence, and the triumphant entry
of the rebel troops into the Soudanese capital.
Emin had even succeeded in regaining his hold over
a wide area of the outlying country, his authority had
been partially re-established over a considerable portion of his province, and, although still sorely ham-
pered by the want of ammunition, rations, and clothing
for his troops, he began to cherish a hope that the
worst was past, and that a brighter day was dawning
for the limitless region over which he still considered
himself to be the legally constituted and responsible
ruler. For four years he had preserved " the pearl of
the Soudan " from fiendish anarchy and total spoliation, by his own unaided exertions and his wonderful
strategic skill, and when, after a long silence of three
years, the letter from Wadelai, dated October 28th,
1886, reached his friends in this country, conveying
the intelligence that Emin was well and fairly holding
his own, the news was welcomed with inexpressible
pleasure and thankfulness.

The Pasha was cheered and encouraged by the

prospect of greeting Mr. Stanley and his relief party on the banks of the White Nile, and he was anxiously looking forward to the arrival of the fresh stores and supplies which his friends were sending out to him. Another long period of absolute silence then intervened, and for a year, at least, no message of any kind reached Europe from Wadelai. In the spring of 1888, however, Emin was again able to communicate with his friends at home, and it was satisfactory to find, from his graphic and always hopeful despatches, that he had been able to continue his beneficial sway, without serious interruption, over the province which he had governed so wisely and so well for so many eventful years. Writing to Mr. Charles Allen, F.R.G.S., the Secretary of the British and Foreign Anti-Slavery Society, on August 16th, 1887, from Wadelai, Emin said :—

"DEAR MR. ALLEN,—"Your most welcome letter of the 19th November, 1886, reached here at the end of June, 1887, and I should have answered it at once, had I not been detained by a month's work on the western shores of Lake Albert. A new station which I formed towards the south needed inspection, and a little caravan with goods from Uganda had to be brought home. Forgive, therefore, the delay, and accept my thanks for your considerate and cordial words.

" Convey, also, please, my and my people's heartiest thanks to the ANTI-SLAVERY SOCIETY. Their ready sympathies with our position, their unselfish advocacy of help to be sent, their generous exertion in our behalf—have greatly rejoiced and obliged us, and our warmest thanks will never equal our obligation. As to myself, if ever I wanted an encouragement to pursue my work, the acknowledgment of what, by God's permission, I was allowed to do until now, will spur me to go on and to do my duty cheerfully.

"I am sorry to disappoint your kind wish that your letter may find me safely arrived at Zanzibar, and I may as well tell you that I have been greatly amused by the doubts expressed in some papers if I would stay or leave when Mr. Stanley arrives. I think there can be no doubt that I stay, and I wonder how one could suppose the contrary. I need not dwell on the reasons of my decision; would you desert your own work just at the dawn of better times?

"Since my last letter to you I have been able to resume the regular turn of affairs, relaxed somewhat by the events you know. I have inspected our stations, and erected two new ones. I have put order everywhere, and our native chiefs have been consulted. The crops for this year are luckily abundant, the cotton plantations yield very fairly, and altogether things look more brightly than before. By Mr. Mackay's kind help I have procured a considerable lot of sheeting and prints from Uganda; if not sufficient to cover our wishes, they are enough for giving to every one some little gift. But as our self-made 'damoor,' or cotton stuff, is more appropriate for wear and tear, we reserve these for holy-days. The value of what they receive, I make my men pay from their wages.

"I cannot speak too highly of the untiring exertions and valuable assistance afforded me by Mr. Mackay, the Church Missionary Society's missionary, in Uganda. At great personal inconvenience, he has not only provided for the despatch of our posts from and to Zanzibar, and done his utmost to facilitate our transactions in Uganda, but he has actually deprived himself of many valuable things to assist myself. He has done splendid work in Uganda, but lately his labours have been somewhat interfered with *by the Arabs trying to have him turned out of Uganda*. His position, therefore, has become dangerous, but I hope he may be able to hold his own. In the interest of the Uganda Mission, I am very glad that Mr. Stanley chose the Congo road for his expedition. He will there encounter numberless difficulties, arising mostly out of the soil to go across, yet he will, without doubt, succeed in vanquishing them ; whilst, coming by Uganda, he would never have obtained permission to come here, except by sheer force, besides imperilling the life and work of the missionaries.

" Once provided with the necessaries, I deem it not at all difficult to open a direct road to the sea-coast by way of the Lango and Masai countries. A chain of stations in suitable places and distances is more than sufficient for holding the road open, and the country itself is so rich in camels and donkeys, and so eminently fit for breeding them, that means of transport will never want. The only obstacle to conquer is the fierceness of the Lango people. I think, nevertheless, that by cautious and energetic proceedings they may become more manageable. I should like respecting this, to hear the opinion of Mr. Thomson, whose book I have not yet been able to procure. At all events, you see, I have a good lot of work before me, and if, by God's help, I succeed in carrying out only a part of it, I shall feel more than rewarded for whatever I have had to undergo. Privations do not

terrify me, twelve years' stay in Central Africa are a
good steel.

"The death of Gordon has been, as you truly say, a
great blow to civilization in Africa. Certainly, he
would have done better to make his way here, where
friends awaited him. Through prisoners, we had
heard of his arrival in the Soudan, but we never could
make out what he was doing, and the news of the fall
of Khartoum, and of Gordon's death there, on the 21st
of January, given me by the Mahdi's Commander,
Kerem Allah, seemed too incredible for acceptance.
Gordon lies in rest; he died, as he wished, the death
of a soldier. Now it is our duty to carry on his work,
and upon myself, his last surviving officer in the
Soudan, devolves the honour to develop his intentions.
Be sure that, by God's will, I shall succeed.

"The King of Uganda is again at war with Kabrega,
who would not listen to my warnings, incited as he
was by an Arab trader.

"The whole western part of Unyoro has been laid
waste. Kabrega had to escape, and is now somewhere
near Kisuga, on the road to Mrooli. The Waganda
established themselves in Mayangesi, and seem unwilling to quit the district again. All communications
are closed. I do not, therefore, know when I may be
able to forward this letter, but I trust it will reach
you safely, some day or other. Do not forget your
promise to write to me sometimes, and believe me to be,

"Yours very faithfully,

"DR. EMIN PASHA."

The lofty and kindly spirit of the man comes out in
every line of this brief, but delightfully frank and

F F

touching communication. It tells little of the trials of
the past. It dwells much upon the work in hand, and
the prospects of success in the future. Emin, in his
isolation, had by no means fallen a victim to helpless
lassitude or nerveless despair. He had enlarged his
southern frontier; he had managed to carry out a
hasty survey of his more distant stations; he had got
up a caravan of goods in safety from Uganda; he had
found time to indulge in pleasant memories of old
friends far away, and he had grateful words of
acknowledgment for their sympathy and "generous
exertion" on his behalf.

In June, 1888, Dr. Felkin received a fresh batch of
important letters from Emin, the last of which was
dated November 2nd, 1887. The first of these letters
was as follows:—

"DEAR FRIEND,—In my last letter I told you how
Mahomet Biri arrived with the second caravan of
goods.

"I have been prevented sending him back to
Uganda owing to the amount of war which still exists
between Uganda and Unyoro. The Arabs will only
make use of the situation in obtaining a higher price
for the gunpowder they manage to smuggle into
Unyoro. Will the introduction of gunpowder from
Zanzibar never be stopped? The one who really
suffers most from these everlasting quarrels is myself.
The route to Uganda is rendered almost impracticable.
Sometimes, it is true, M'Wanga permits the Arabs to
send people to me; at other times he forbids them to
do so. Kabrega addresses all the people who come as
spies, has their goods examined, and confiscates all

correspondence which he sees. It is due to this fact
that since May 3rd, 1887, I have never had a single
letter from Mr. Mackay, and I do not even know
whether he is still in Uganda or not. On the
22nd of September, I was able to send letters to
Mr. Mackay, and I am in hopes he has received
them. In a few days it is my intention to go myself
as far as Kibiro, taking Mahomet Biri with me to the
station. Kabrega is sending some of his officials to
confer with me. There is little enough to be gained
by these conferences. To be sure, when all is said
and done, Kabrega does as he likes, or as his advisers
for the time being suggest. I expect that I shall gain
permission for Biri to pass on through Unyoro. If I
had only sufficient soldiers at my disposal, they would
enable me to obtain concessions to my requests and
wishes. If Mr. Stanley arrives, as I hope he may do,
in November, many of my difficulties will be done
away with. Not that I intend to undertake another
warlike enterprise; that is very far from my desire;
but the mere fact that I have received them will,
I confidently expect, soon bring to an end all the
quarrels among my foolish neighbours. If I cannot
report that our relations with Unyoro and Uganda are
satisfactory, I can say that the chiefs nearer me are
more friendly. Chief Befo, of Mount Belinian, near
Gondokoro, who played such a great rôle in the last
Bari and Ormka revolt, has just sent me some broken
rifles as a present, and has also requested a conference.
He is, undoubtedly, the most important of the Bari
chiefs, and he is also the most cunning, and I greatly
wish it was in my power to accede to his request. I
should do so were it possible for me to visit him, but

in the meantime I felt it my duty to remain here. My sphere of action has been greatly confined to Lake Albert, but I have made some days' journey to the west towards Alanda, and I intend, as soon as I come back to Kibiro, to pay a short visit to some of the friendly chiefs in that district.

"All goes well personally. I have to thank Mr. Mackay for many little luxuries. By last caravan he sent me some of Wills's best bird's-eye, and you may imagine what an unexpected present this was for one like myself, who for years has been cut off from such articles.

"With regard to my personal state, I may tell you, you need not have any anxiety about me. As soon as I have become aware of the possibility of now and again corresponding with you and with one or two others, I have tried to throw care to the winds, and look with a certain amount of confidence to better times in the future."

In a postscript, dated the Island of Anuguru, October 31st, 1887. Emin further writes:—

"At last I arrived here, the day before yesterday. To-morrow I take Mahomet Biri by steamer to Kibiro. From there he goes to Bjuaia, where he will remain with Captain Cassati until Kabrega sends him the necessary powers. This will probably occupy three weeks, although I will use every endeavour to expedite matters. Biri has promised that directly on his arrival at Cassati's, he will send one of his people on with my post to Uganda, so that it is just possible they may return with letters before he leaves Cassati's. I calculate with some certainty upon his doing so, because up to the present he has proved himself pretty

reliable. If he is delayed in Unyoro, I shall probably
return from my visit to Alanda before he leaves. I
have sent on this occasion, several boxes full of collections of birds, &c., to the British Museum, addressed
to Professor Flower, and I hope he will find not a few
interesting specimens among them. I have not been
able to send a quantity of very valuable objects, as the
cases and boxes have come to an end. I have been
compelled, therefore, to write to the Professor asking
him to send me supplies, which I hope he will do, and
not object to these requests, which I only make on
account of my isolation."

In a second postscript, dated November 2nd, 1887,
from Kibrio, the Pasha continues :—

"Everything has now been arranged, so that
Mahomet Biri started to-day. We have had very bad
weather. Storms and rain have prevailed, so that the
steamer has had very bad work. Kibrio lies exposed
on all sides to the winds, therefore I cross over the
lake to-morrow to Ni'Soa, where I shall establish my
camp and send the steamer back to Wadelai. Biri's
people take this letter. Excuse its length. Write as
often as you find time, for the only holidays I get are
those days on which letters come from you.

" (Signed) Dr. Emin Pasha."

It was evident from this despatch that the courage
and ability with which the White Chief of the
Equatorial Soudan had confronted his enemies, and
the skill and energy which he had displayed in the
partial re-organization of the province, had produced
a wholesome impression, for the time at least, upon
the semi-barbarous tribes upon the borders of the

state, and the anxiety of the powerful prince of Belinian to come to terms with Emin was a substantial proof of the growing power of the Pasha. These letters, at the same time, revealed the fact that the situation was surrounded by complications which might at any moment place Emin in a position of difficulty, if not of danger.

Owing to the guilty fears and persistent intrigues of the Arabs, the entire region of Tropical Africa was in a state of excitement and unrest, and a covert hostility was everywhere manifesting itself, from the banks of the Zambesi to the head-waters of the Nile, against the scattered settlements of the white men. It was, therefore, possible that the lurid flame of war— war for the suppression of all European influence in the Equatorial Region—might leap forth without any warning, and sweep through the entire length and breadth of Mid-Central Africa, overwhelming and effectually destroying the work to which Emin had devoted his life, before the friendly aid could reach him, which he hoped would enable him successfully to resist any attack which might be made upon him.

In August, 1888, an alarming report reached England, *viâ* Zanzibar, to the effect that the Mahdi was marching upon Wadelai, with a powerful force, and his purpose was to destroy the fortress and capture Emin and his garrison.

Some prisoners who had succeeded in escaping from Uganda, stated that on April 4th, Emin received from the Mahdi a summons to surrender himself into his hands and disband his troops. This imperious mandate of the Nubian prophet was accompanied by a letter purporting to be from Lupton Bey, requesting an instant compliance with the request of the rebel commander, and stating that by such a course alone would he be able to preserve the lives of the European prisoners at Khartoum, and adding details of the expedition which was being organized against Wadelai. Emin doubted the authenticity of the letters said to be from Lupton Bey, who has since died of consumption at Khartoum, and in response to the further demands of the Mahdi, that he would adopt the faith of the Arabian prophet and join his standard, Emin declared his resolution to maintain his independence, and to fight on to the end, rather than hand over the Khedival flag or yield for a moment to the pretensions of the rebels. Hearing from his scouts that the vanguard of the Mahdi's forces was advancing southward, and that a flotilla of armed vessels upon the White Nile was supporting the troops of the enemy, Emin saw that no time was to be lost; and as he could gather no news of Mr. Stanley and the Relief Expedition, he decided to quit Wadelai, to move rapidly on the left bank of the river, and to attack the levies of the Mahdi, before they could even have notice of his approach.

CHAPTER XXIV.

WHEN the relief column turned away from the Congo for the Albert Nyanza no serious difficulty hindered its progress for a few days. The party, consisting of 389 officers and men, followed the course of the Aruwimi, till it struck an inland forest road which trended due east. Opposition now began to manifest itself. The natives surrounded the compact little army, and sought by every means to delay and prevent its advance. Day after day the struggle was renewed between the caravan of the white stranger and a succession of barbarous tribes whose villages were burnt as soon as the Expedition was known to be in the neighbourhood, in order to prevent Stanley's party from receiving supplies or obtaining shelter. Every device of savagery was resorted to for the purpose of defeating or disheartening the relieving force, but the advance was pushed on for some time successfully without the loss of a single member of the column. From the 5th of July till October 18th, the waters of the ever-friendly Congo Luabala were never out of reach. On August 1st dysentery broke out among the Europeans, and soon the rank and file also began to succumb to the terrible privations of the march;

men falling out by scores. Nine days were occupied
in crossing a waste wilderness, where famine rapidly
thinned the already weakened ranks, and numbers of
Zanzibaris perished of sheer starvation upon the road-
side.

Profiting by the proximity of the Congo, Stanley,
with his usual fertility of resource, at once had his
sick conveyed to the friendly river and placed upon
rafts. On August the 13th the news was passed
round that a vast concourse of hostile natives was
assembled at some distance up the stream. Careful
preparations were at once made against surprise. The
Expedition was divided into two parts, and the men
were carefully instructed in the use of their new
magazine rifles. Stanley soon found that he had by
no means overrated the fierce opposition or rude
strategic skill of his foes, and in the conflict which
ensued, Lieutenant Stairs was seriously wounded by a
poisoned arrow near the heart, and for some time the
whole party was in serious peril from the resolute and
persistent onslaught of their enemies. On the 25th of
August the column reached the point of junction of the
Nepoko with the Aruwimi, and its leader at once began
to realize the extent of the baneful influence of the Arab
slavers. The great traveller had taken this very route,
he tells us, on purpose to avoid these human vampires,
who would, he knew, seduce his men from their
allegiance, and so probably wreck the entire Expedition. Twenty-three men, indeed, did desert within
three days of the meeting between the relief column
and a party of Arab marauders, led by the infamous
Ungarrowwa, or Uledi Balzaz, who eventually proved
to be none other than a trusted tent-boy of Captain

Speke's. The whole region had been turned into a desert by this Arab and his cannibal band of followers. Provisions could not be obtained in anything like sufficient quantities to feed the advancing party, and at this point Stanley had to report sixty-six men as lost by death or desertion, fifty-six men, including all the Somalis, broken down and useless, and the rest of the column sadly demoralized by the want of food and hardships of the journey. Fifty-five men deserted as soon as the station of Kilonga-Congo was sighted on October the 18th, and the clothing, rifles, and ammunition of many of the party were soon surreptitiously bartered with the Arabs, who never left the flanks of the column, for the necessaries of life. The consequence was that when the rapidly decreasing party left this place, to struggle on towards the yet far-distant Nyanza, Stanley, to his horror, discovered that scores of his soldiers were unarmed, and many of them positively naked.

But the White Nile, which was the goal of the enterprise, was still many weary miles away, and the word was given to press onward. The men, however, were so reduced by famine and fatigue, that the steel boat which they had conveyed so far on the way, had, with a large quantity of useful stores, to be left in charge of Surgeon Parke and Captain Nelson, at one of the native villages. Fungi, ground nuts, and wild berries formed the staple food of the party, who were now traversing a land described as "one horrible wilderness." When Ibwiri was passed, however, the travellers to their delight found themselves in a veritable land of plenty. The country abounded with corn, fruits, and wholesome food, and the famine

period which had begun on the ever-memorable 31st
of August, was ended. But of the 389 men who had
started from the Aruwimi, only 174 were left to
Stanley, and these were in a most pitiable condition.
A temporary camp was formed to enable the wanderers
to gain strength and refresh themselves after their
terrible wilderness journey. The poor fellows had
almost despaired of ever being able to cross the unknown land which still separated them from the
pleasant plains, the teeming pastures and the green
corn-fields of the Nyanza region. They had begun
also to doubt the word of their intrepid leader as
to the object of his mission, and the actual existence
of the famous White Pasha whom Stanley professed
to be anxious to succour. Desertions, pillaging, and
the wholesale disposal of the arms and equipments
of the men had to be punished by death, and it was
with extreme reluctance that in several cases, those
who had been tried and found guilty of mutinous
or dishonest conduct were ordered by Stanley to be
hanged in the presence of their comrades. The
excellent food supply at once brought about a happy
change in the condition of the force. The effect of
the new diet in a few days was remarkable upon the
173 men still available for the advance. "I set out,"
says Stanley, "for the Albert Nyanza on November
the 24th, with a body of followers who were positively stout and robust men." In a letter to the Royal
Geographical Society on April 9th, 1889, giving the
details of this journey through a belt of cannibalism
and savagery, probably unequalled on the face of the
globe, the leader of the relief column sets forth the
horrors of the Congo forest in most graphic language.

After touching upon the obstacles to his advance which the nature of the country everywhere presented—the foul, fetid atmosphere of the forests, the barren plains, and the almost impenetrable jungle, which covered the land—the famous traveller went on to reveal something of the tactics of the hitherto unknown peoples of the Central Congo region. With diabolical skill the roads were planted with sharpened skewers and crows-feet made of hard wood, and frightful thorns three inches long. Pits were dug and then covered over with a thin layer of branches, in order to entrap the advancing company, and " one of the approaches to every village was a straight road, perhaps, a hundred yards long and twelve feet wide, cleared of jungle, but bristling with these skewers carefully and cunningly hidden at every place likely to be trodden by an incautious foot. The real path was crooked, and took a wide detour, the cut road appeared so tempting, so straight and so short. At the village end was the watchman, to beat his drum and sound the alarm, when every native would take his weapons and proceed to the appointed place to ply his bow at every opportunity. Yet despite a formidable list of hostile measures and attempts, no life was lost, though our wounded increased in numbers."

" The river," continues Mr. Stanley " retained a noble width—from 500 to 900 yards, with an island here and there, sometimes a group of islets, the resort of oyster-fishermen. Such piles of oyster-shells ! on one island I measured a heap thirty paces long, twelve feet wide at the base, and four feet high. At almost every bend of the river, generally in the middle of the bend—because a view of the river

approach up and down stream may be had—there is
a village of cone huts—of the candle-extinguisher
type. Some bends have a large series of these villages
populated by thousands of natives. The villages of
the Banalya, Bakubana, and Bungangeta tribes run
close to each other along a single long bend. The
first has become famous through the tragedy ending
in the death of Major Barttelot. An island opposite
the site of the Bungangeta villages I occupied, to re-
organize the expedition, which had almost become a
wreck through the misfortunes of the rear column.
The abundance found by us will never be found again,
for the Arabs have followed my track by hundreds,
and destroyed villages and plantations, and what the
Arabs spare the elephant herds complete ”

“ One of the most serious features in the opposition
of the natives was the fact that they were armed with
poisoned arrows. At Avissibba, about half-way between
Panga Falls and the Nepoko, the natives attacked our
camp in quite a resolute and determined fashion.
Their stores of poisoned arrows they thought gave
them every advantage; and indeed when the poison
is fresh it is most deadly. Lieutenant Stairs and
five men were wounded by these. Lieutenant Stairs’
wound was from an arrow the poison of which was
dry—it must have been put on some days before.
After three weeks or so he recovered strength,
though the wound was not closed for months. One
man received a slight puncture near the wrist;
another received a puncture near the shoulder in the
muscles of the arm ; one was wounded in the gullet ;
tetanus ended the sufferings of all. We were much
exercised as to what this poison might be that was so

deadly. On returning from the Nyanza to relieve the rear column, we halted at Avisibba, and, rummaging among the huts, found several packets of dried red ants, or pismires. It was then we knew that the dried bodies of these ground into powder, cooked in palm oil, and smeared over the wooden points of the arrows, was the deadly irritant by which we lost so many fine men with such terrible suffering. The large black ant, whose bite causes a great blister, would be still more venomous prepared in the same way; the bloated spiders, an inch in length, which are covered with prickles most painful to the touch, would form another terrible compound, the effects of which makes one shudder to think of."

Stanley resumed his journey on the 24th November, and on the 5th of December, the head of the column approached the village of the mighty Mazamboni, "a lord of many villages," whose vast territory was studded with fruitful fields covered with corn and fruit and yams. The natives were on the alert, and at once took steps to drive back the white man's caravan. Stanley was, however equal to the occasion; with his usual promptitude and courage, he at once seized upon an elevation, which he strengthened by erecting a zareba, within which he placed his men and stores, and then awaited the next move of Mazamboni. The position was an anxious one. Was it to be war or peace? The relief party were a mere handful of men compared with the masses of brown-skinned warriors who were clustered about the standards of the fierce Congo king. There was nothing for it but to strengthen the zareba by a deep trench and piles of brushwood, and to watch the course

of events with patient vigilance. Time after time the
war-cry of the natives rang up the hill side, and the
beleagured garrison prepared to meet an attack. The
native levies were observed to gather in dense crowds
away below in the valley in response to the summons
of Mazamboni. Village after village sent forth its
contingent of men, fully armed, and Stanley, anxious
to prevent a catastrophe, sent off an embassy of
peace, in the course of the day, to the "lord of many
villages," with a present of brass rods and valuable
cloth, proposing to make a treaty of amity and friendship with the black monarch.

The night wore on and no response came to this
appeal. With the dawn of day the shout of
"Kurwana," war, was heard rising up from the
valley, and Stanley knew that he must fight. There
was no time to lose. With splendid tactical skill a
picked party of the garrison was sent down into the
valley to the east to attack the enemy on the flank,
another small detachment under Lieutenant Stairs
was sent out to fall upon the levies of Mazamboni in
the rear. This plan of Stanley's, boldly conceived
and splendidly carried out, was altogether successful,
and before evening the way to the White Nile was
once more clear. On the 13th the last stage of this
terrible journey was reached, and the excellent leader
cried, as he turned to his men, " Prepare yourselves for
a sight of the Nyanza ! "

Next day, to the delight and astonishment of the
rank and file of the column, about 1.30 p.m., the
glorious expanse of the Albert Lake lay shimmering
at their feet, like a vast plain of molten gold. At an
altitude of 5000 feet above the sea, the weary travellers

feasted their eyes upon one of the fairest scenes in Central Africa. With streaming eyes and quivering lips the members of the little band threw themselves upon the ground, kissed the feet of their leader, and then the difficult descent to the shore began. Still another fight! The natives poured down upon the Expedition, as it was slowly making its way along the rocky defile to the great watery expanse below. After a brief but sharp and desperate struggle the enemy were beaten off and the shores of the lake were reached. At the village of Kakengo, on the south-west corner of the Nyanza, Stanley had hoped to find some tidings of Emin Pasha, but it appeared that all communication between Wadelai and this point had been cut off. The relief Expedition had no large boats or indeed any means of navigating the vast inland sea in force northward towards the White Nile. Stanley therefore decided to send on a native messenger in search of the famous Pasha, and to return himself, meanwhile, to Ibwiri, build a zareba, garrison it, and then collect as much grain as possible for his men, as the one great peril of the position appeared to be *famine*. A council of war was held at once, and this course was formally determined upon. On January 7th, 1888, the Expedition was back at Ibwiri, where a stay was made of some weeks. Lieutenant Stairs was ordered to return to Kilonga-Conga, to bring up the steel boat and stores left there under the charge of Captain Nelson and Surgeon Parkes. Eleven only of the party left behind in October accompanied the Lieutenant with the boat, all the rest had become too feeble to proceed any further on active service.

April 2nd saw the re-united column once more on the march eastward, under Stanley's command.

As the Nyanza was approached all fears as to the attitude of the natives were soon dispelled. Mazamboni entered into friendly relations with the dreaded white chief. Food was sent into the camp in abundance, and the famine had soon ceased any longer to distress the travellers.

As the party neared the shores of the lake for the second time, a messenger placed a packet in the hands of Stanley, which he said had been given to him by another white man, " Malezza," to give to " his son," the " leader of the strangers."

" If your words are true," said Stanley, " I will make you rich."

The messenger was carefully interrogated as to the appearance and surroundings of the " Malezza," who had sent him with the packet, and he spoke of " big ships, as large as islands, filled with men,' and other things which at once convinced the relief party that the great "Malezza" was Emin Pasha.

A note, wrapped in a strip of American cloth, was handed to Stanley. It proved to be from the Pasha, who stated " that as there had been a native rumour to the effect that a white man had been seen at the south end of the lake, he had gone in his steamer to make inquiries, but had been unable to obtain reliable information, as the natives were terribly afraid of Kalrega, king of Unyoro, and connected every stranger with him. However, the wife of the Nyamsassie chief had told a native ally of his named Mogo, that she had seen Stanley in Immisuma (Mazamboni's country). He therefore begged Stanley to remain where he was,

G G

till he (Emin) could communicate directly with him." The communication bore the signature " (Dr.) Emin," and was dated March 26th, 1888.

Jephson at once set out in the boat to get some tidings of the Pasha. Emin was found at Mswa, his most southern post on the Nyanza, and he at once decided to proceed with Jephson southward to meet Stanley.

Towards evening, on April 29th, the smoke of the *Khedive* steamer attracted the notice of the illustrious explorer from his camp at the south end of the lake, and was seen about seven miles off, steaming for the zareba. At seven o'clock, the Pasha, with Signor Casati and Mr. Jephson, reached the spot where Stanley and his officers were awaiting them, and the Governor of the Equatorial Provinces met with a joyous welcome from the entire relief Expedition.

Emin and his deliverer remained together discussing their plans for the future, till the 25th of May. It was agreed that Mr. Jephson should return with the Pasha to the Equatorial Province to bring out the garrisons that still remained faithful to the Khedival flag. Meanwhile, Stanley proposed to return along the route to the Congo, in order, if possible, to effect a junction with his rear column under the command of Major Barttelot, and bring on the whole party with the reserve stores to the rendezvous at Kavillas, on the south-east side of the Albert Nyanza, where the Pasha and the leader of the relieving force decided to meet again and join their companies for a united march to the east coast.

Unfortunately the great German was unable to per-form his promise. A series of events quite put it out of his power to carry out his scheme, and entirely falsified the impression he had conveyed to the illustrious traveller of his resources and freedom of action. The power of the Pasha had been shattered. His troops were practically in revolt, and on his return to his own territory, he, with Mr. Jephson, fell prisoners into the hands of the rebels, who at one time had conceived a plan of entrapping and despoiling the Emin Relief Expedition itself.

Turning westward, by a more northerly route than the one he had hitherto followed, Mr. Stanley reached the Aruwimi once more with 111 Zanzibaris and 101 of Emin's people to act as porters, after a march of eighty-two days. On the road the messengers who had been sent out months before to glean some tidings of the rear column, were overtaken. On August 17th, Mr. Stanley arrived before the stockade of Banalya, on the Aruwimi, without having heard any tidings of the lost party on the entire route between the Nyanza and the Congo.

A white man, who turned out to be Mr. Bonny, presented himself as the leader of the expedition drew up to the fort.

" Well, my dear Bonny," said his commander, somewhat anxiously, " where is the Major ? "

" He is dead, sir ; shot by the Manynema, about a month ago," replied Mr. Bonny.

" Good God ! And Mr. Jamieson ? "

" He is gone to Stanley Falls, to try and get some men from Tippoo Tibb." (Mr. Jamieson died some time after this of fever, on his way down the river).

" And Mr. Troup ? "

" Mr. Troup has gone home sir, invalided."

" Hem!   Where, where is Ward ? "

" Mr. Ward is at Bangala, sir."

" Heavens alive!   Then you are the only one here."

" Yes, sir."

Trouble after trouble had fallen upon the unfortunate rear column, only seventy-one men were left out of 257 placed under the command of the Major when the main body of the force left the river in June, 1887.   Out of these seventy-one, only fifty-two were fit for duty.

The terrible but happily false report of the massacre of the great explorer and all his followers had reached the camp at Yambaya early in 1888.   The news was carried to the Major by a deserter from Stanley's camp, and a party of Arabs also declared that they had heard the same rumour from some Soudanese who had originally formed part of Stanley's personal escort, but who were met on the hills making their way homeward to the north.   The Major, a young officer of great promise, at once left the camp with his force to press on and find out the truth of these dread tidings.   The rear column consisted of forty porters and 100 soldiers.   The Major decided to follow up the traces of the advance column step by step.   His bearers were well laden with supplies, and his relations with the natives were most friendly.   The chief object of the rear-guard was to keep open direct communications with Europe by the Congo route. Instructions had also been left for the forwarding of stores, if needed, to Stanley and for the protection of the road, so as to facilitate his return to the Congo, should he decide to use that route on the completion of his mission to the White Nile.

No letters, however, passed between the two leaders from the day that the commander left the shores of the Aruwimi. The Major resolved, therefore, to set out and succour his leader, if yet alive, at all hazards, and he chose the river course as the one which he knew had been always favoured by his illustrious chief. In a few weeks, alas! the Major was murdered by his own carriers, and, as has been truly said, "another name was added to the already long list of notable men who have given up their lives, almost with joy, as a sacrifice on the altar of humanity."

On the 5th of September the return to the Albert Nyanza was resolved upon. The stores Stanley had come so far to secure were dispersed, or had been sent back down the Congo, and nothing remained but to go back to Emin, and do the best for him and the Expedition that could be done under the circumstances.

On January 18th, 1889, the relief Expedition was once more encamped on the Albert Nyanza, awaiting the arrival of Emin and those of his officers and followers who had decided finally to leave the Equatorial Territory for the east coast and Zanzibar. Many difficulties arose, and a delay of several months arose before a start could be really made. On May 8th the whole party, including the Pasha and his people, set out for the south-east. Emin appears to have been unwilling to the last to leave his life's work. He perceived, at length, however, that his influence had been permanently shaken, and he decided to accept Stanley's offer of an escort for himself and his party to the coast.

On the 10th of November the column reached
Mpwapwa, *en route* for the east coast and Zanzibar,
after a journey of 188 days from the Albert Nyanza.
The returning party consisted of 750 souls, Emin's
people numbering 294, of whom fifty-nine were
children, mostly the orphans of Egyptian officers.
The whites were Stairs, Nelson, Jephson, Parkes,
Bonny, M. Hottman, Emin Pasha and his daughter;
Casati, Marco and others.

The homeward journey lay through a vast unexplored region between the Nyanzas, and along the
base of the snow-clad mountain range of Ruwenzori.
The Southern Nyanza discovered by Stanley in his
first journey to the Congo, was revisited and named
Lake Albert Edward. It is smaller than either the
Victoria or Tanganika Lakes, but its importance
consists in the fact that it is the reservoir all the
streams of the south-west Nile basin, and discharges
these waters by a river—the Semliki—into the Albert
Nyanza, the Victoria Nile and the Semliki amal-
gamating in the Albert Lake, and leaving it under
the name of White Nile.

With the arrival of Stanley and his tiny army at
Mpwapwa with Emin Pasha and his people the task of
the Expedition was virtually completed. The district
which remained to be crossed between Mpwapwa and
Bagamoyo, the point of embarkation on the east
coast, presenting no exceptional difficulties. The
leader of the gallant host of brave men was once more
on familiar ground. Supplies of food and personal
necessaries had been forwarded to this place by
generous friends of the Expedition and by the agents
of the Emin Relief Committee at Zanzibar. The rest

of the progress of the party was therefore rendered comparatively easy and pleasant.

On April 20th, 1887, Mr. Stanley took command of the Expedition at Leopoldville, and started up the Congo ten days later. On June 28th he left Yambuya on the Aruwimi, and plunged into the dense forest which divided him from the Albert Nyanza. On April 29th, 1888, he first met Emin Pasha. The fall of Wadelai occurred on August 18th, and on January 18th, 1889, Mr. Stanley reached the Albert Nyanza for the third time, and began to prepare for the journey to the east coast. On May 8th the whole party set out for the sea, and in the last weeks of the year the whole of the party—relievers and relieved were safe in Zanzibar, thus bringing to a triumphant conclusion the most remarkable and adventurous enterprise of modern times.

The relief of Emin Pasha was an accomplished fact. But the outlook for Central Africa in the near future is not a cheering one, for Mr. Stanley brought with him to Zanzibar all, alas! that was left of civilization between Wady Halfa and the Nyassa region. To recover this lost ground is the work of time and of system. This, the next stage in the great African problem, is unfortunately likely to be a long one.

The principal facts of this extraordinary undertaking, with its singular and dramatic episodes, and the full account of the homeward march, with the striking details of capture and ultimate relief of Emin, all contribute to add fresh lustre to the name of Henry Morton Stanley, who in this his last heroic exploit has completely changed the map of Equatorial Africa, and added much that is valuable to our scanty store of geographical knowledge of the hidden heart of the Dark Continent. The universal belief in the power of resources of the man has been abundantly justified ; and the wisest and the best of men in both hemispheres will unite to offer a tribute of unqualified admiration for the fine combination of patience, resolution, and undaunted courage which has carried this remarkable mission of humanity to a brilliant and successful termination.

THE END.

PRINTED BY GILBERT AND RIVINGTON, LIMITED, ST. JOHN'S HOUSE, CLERKENWELL RD.